INVADER ZIM

VOLUME 4

Created by
JHONEN VASQUEZ

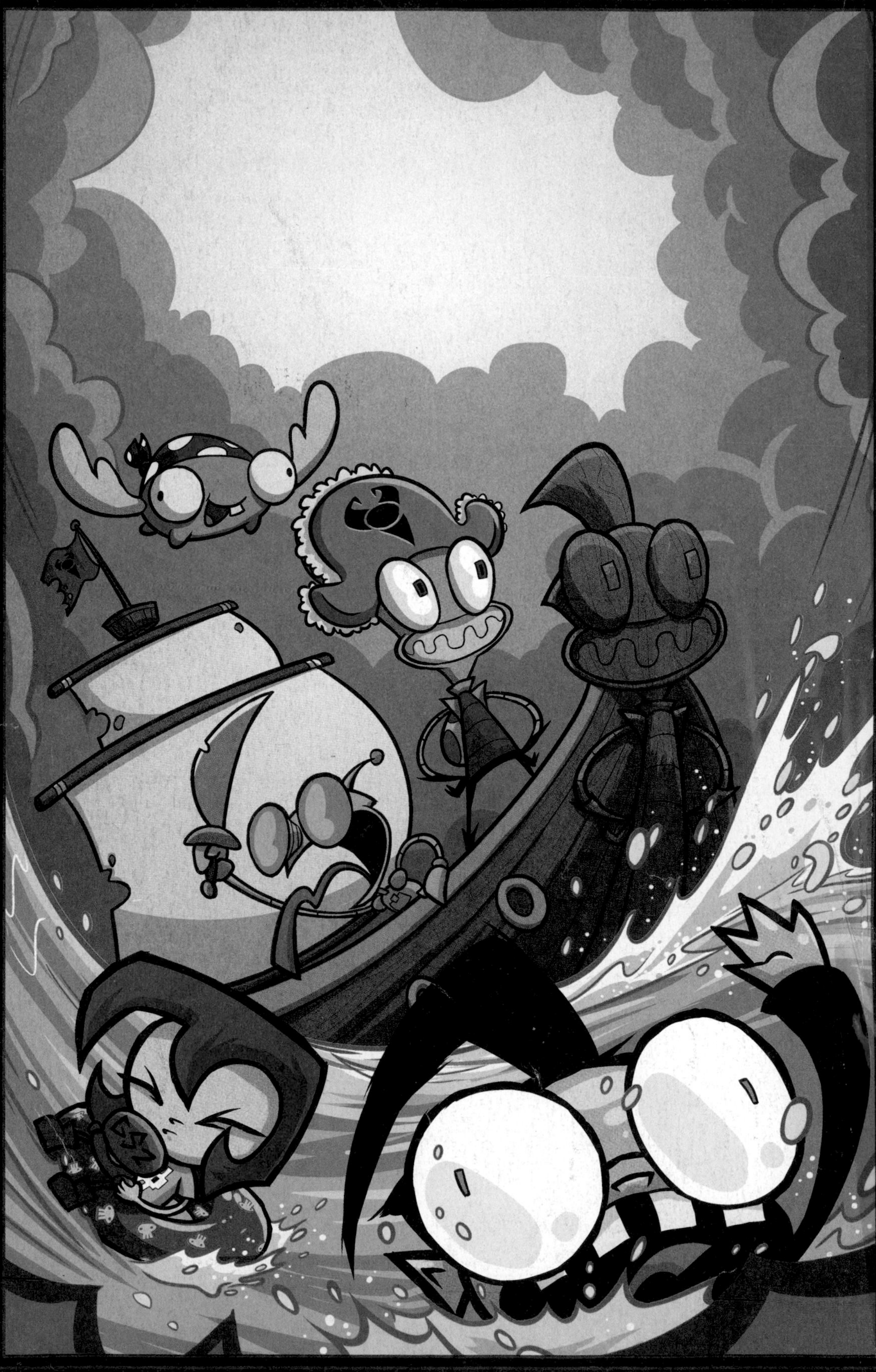

INVADER ZIM

VOLUME 4

Control Brain, Chapters 1-5 and Writer, Chapter 5
JHONEN VASQUEZ

Writer, Chapters 1 and 4 & Illustrator, Chapter 1
AARON ALEXOVICH

Writer, Chapter 2
DANIELLE KOENIG

Writer, Chapter 3
ERIC TRUEHEART

Illustrator, Chapters 2-5 & Letterer, Chapters 1-5
WARREN WUCINICH

Colorist, Chapter 1
CASSIE KELLY

Colorist, Chapters 2-5
FRED C. STRESING

Retail cover illustrated by
WARREN WUCINICH

Oni Press variant cover illustrated by
PAUL ROBERTSON

ONI PRESS

AN ONI PRESS PUBLICATION

Special thanks to JOAN HILTY and LINDA LEE

Designed by KEITH WOOD

Edited by ROBIN HERRERA

Published by Oni Press, Inc.

publisher JOE NOZEMACK editor in chief JAMES LUCAS JONES

director of operations BRAD ROOKS director of sales DAVID DISSANAYAKE

publicity manager RACHEL REED marketing assistant MELISSA MESZAROS MACFADYEN

director of design & production TROY LOOK graphic designer HILARY THOMPSON

junior graphic designer KATE Z. STONE digital prepress technician ANGIE KNOWLES

managing editor ARI YARWOOD senior editor CHARLIE CHU

editor ROBIN HERRERA administrative assistant ALISSA SALLAH

logistics associate JUNG LEE

This volume collects issues #16-20 of the
Oni Press series *Invader Zim*.

Oni Press, Inc.
1319 SE Martin Luther King Jr. Blvd.
Suite 240
Portland, OR 97214
USA

onipress.com • facebook.com/onipress • twitter.com/onipress
onipress.tumblr.com • instagram.com/onipress

First edition: August 2017

ISBN: 978-1-62010-428-6 • eISBN: 978-1-62010-430-9
Oni Press Exclusive ISBN: 978-1-62010-429-3

nickelodeon

Library of Congress Control Number: 2015950610

1 3 5 7 9 10 8 6 4 2

PRINTED IN USA.

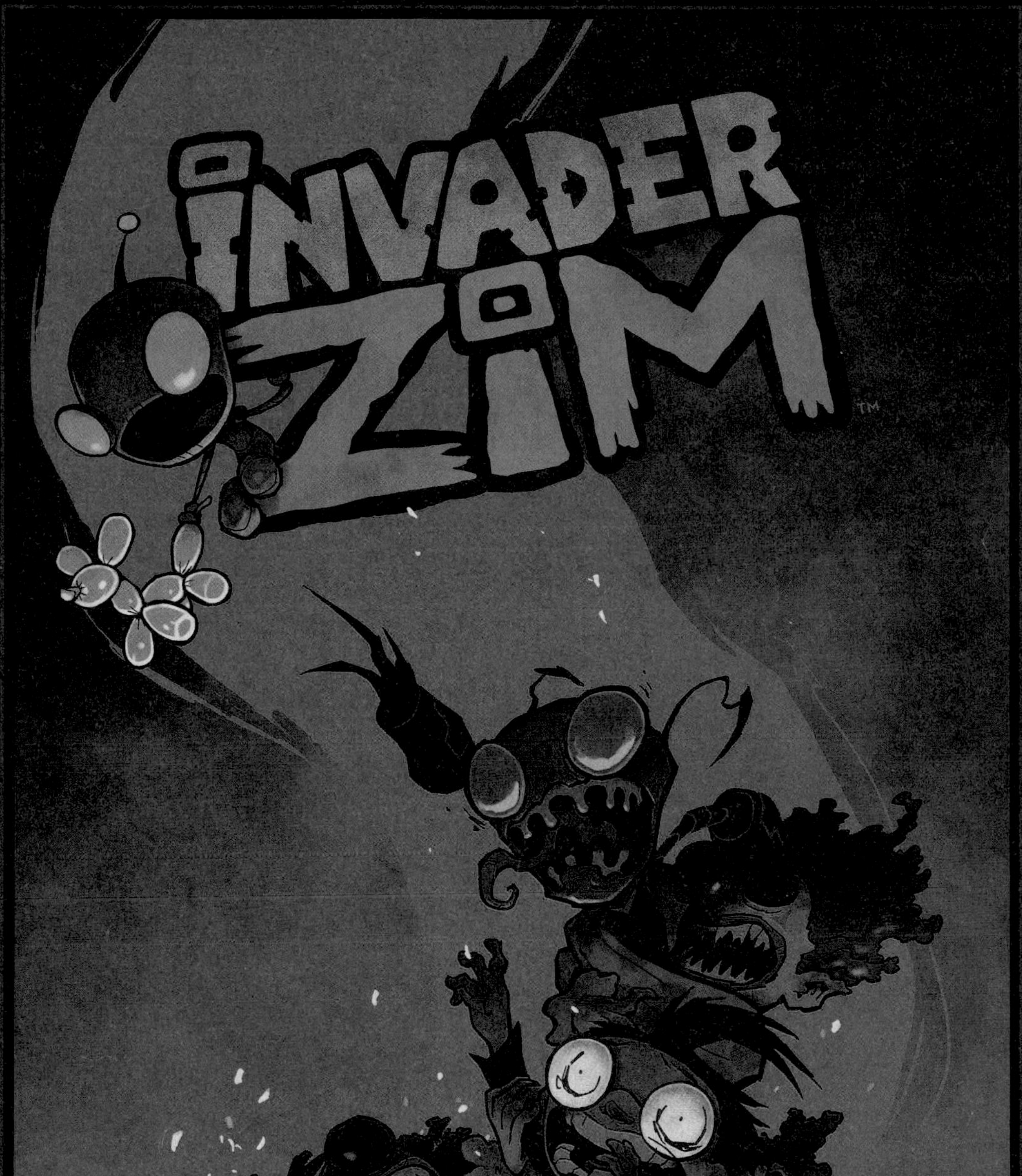
INVADER ZIM™

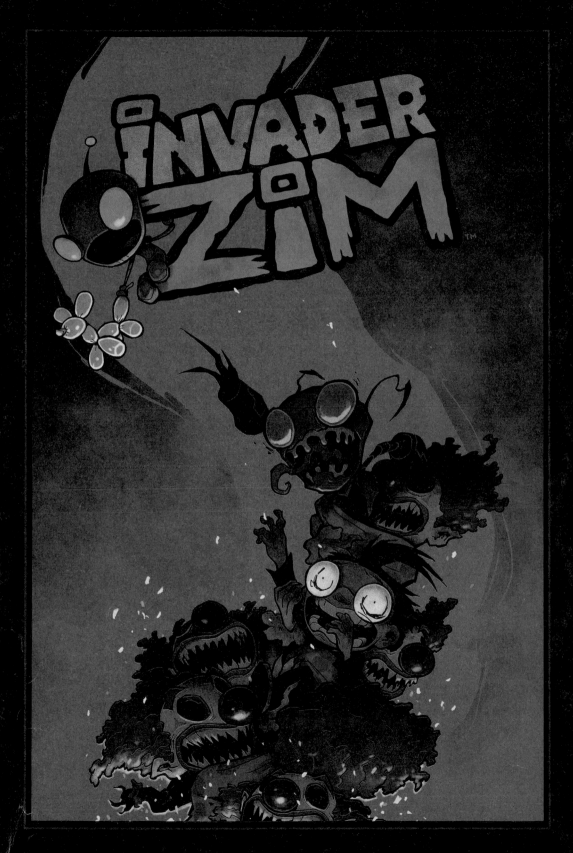

CHAPTER: 1

illustration by **AARON ALEXOVICH**

Happy Holidays from me, your best pal Recap Kid! Things have gotten REALLY WEIRD in the ZIM universe! Last issue was all those creepy stories about Ms. Bitters, and this issue's just got a BUNCHA CLOWNS?!!! DON'T WORRY, THOUGH! I'm not scared of clowns! I'm scared of heights, weights, gyms, yoga mats, dogs, dogs on leashes, dogs on roller skates, dogs on roller blades, dogfights, hotdogs, flesh-eating hot dog viruses, and that thing where they change they style of the ZIM comic too much! SO AWFUL! Hope that doesn't happen this time! GOODBYE!!!

Recap Kid by **AARON ALEXOVICH**
with **WARREN WUCINICH**

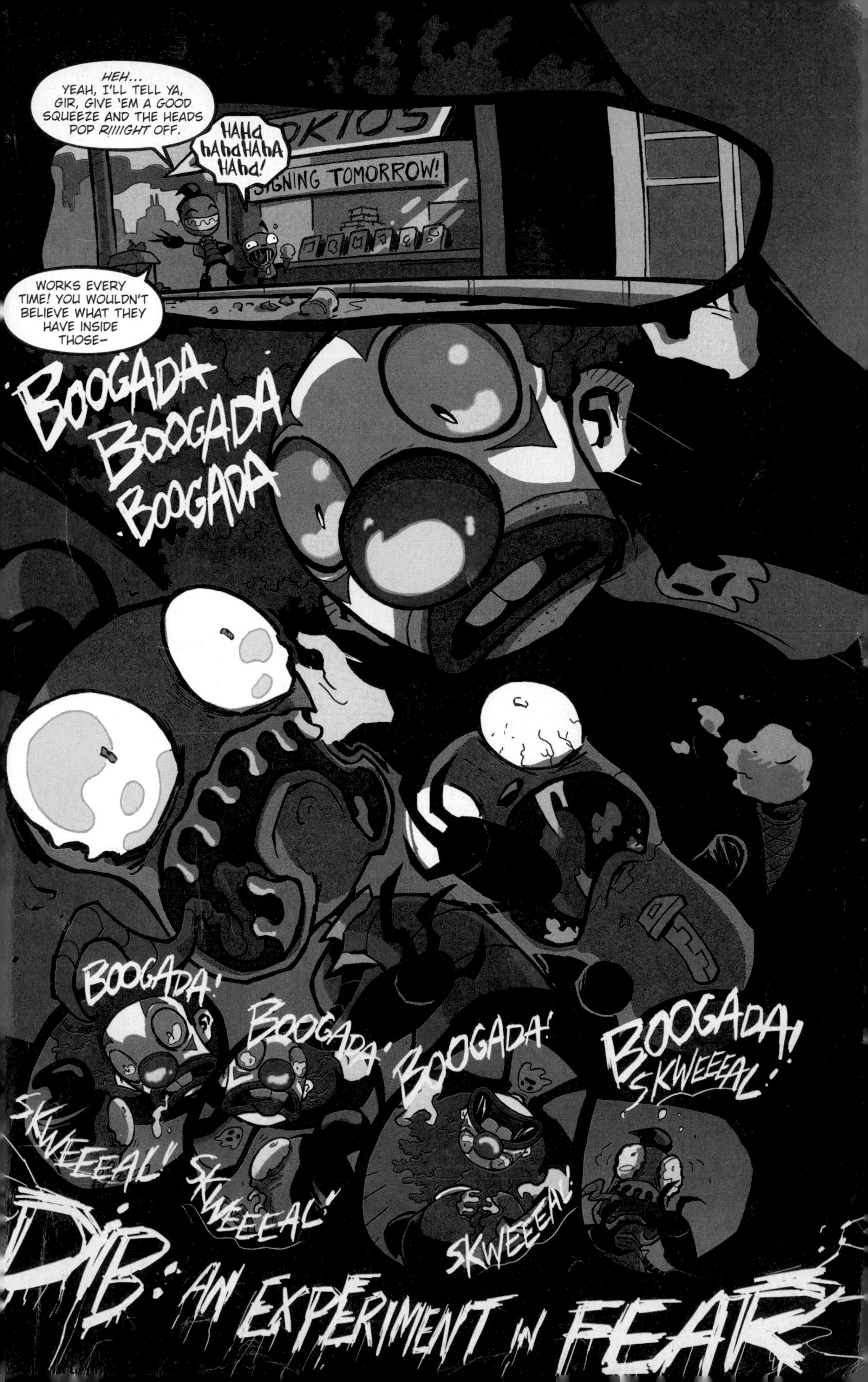
HEH... YEAH, I'LL TELL YA, GIR, GIVE 'EM A GOOD SQUEEZE AND THE HEADS POP RIIIIGHT OFF.
HAHA HAHAHAHA HAHA!
SIGNING TOMORROW!
WORKS EVERY TIME! YOU WOULDN'T BELIEVE WHAT THEY HAVE INSIDE THOSE-
BOOGADA BOOGADA BOOGADA
BOOGADA!
BOOGADA!
BOOGADA!
BOOGADA!
SKWEEEAL!
SKWEEEEAL!
SKWEEEEAL!
SKWEEEEAL!
SKWEEEAL!
DIB: AN EXPERIMENT IN FEAR

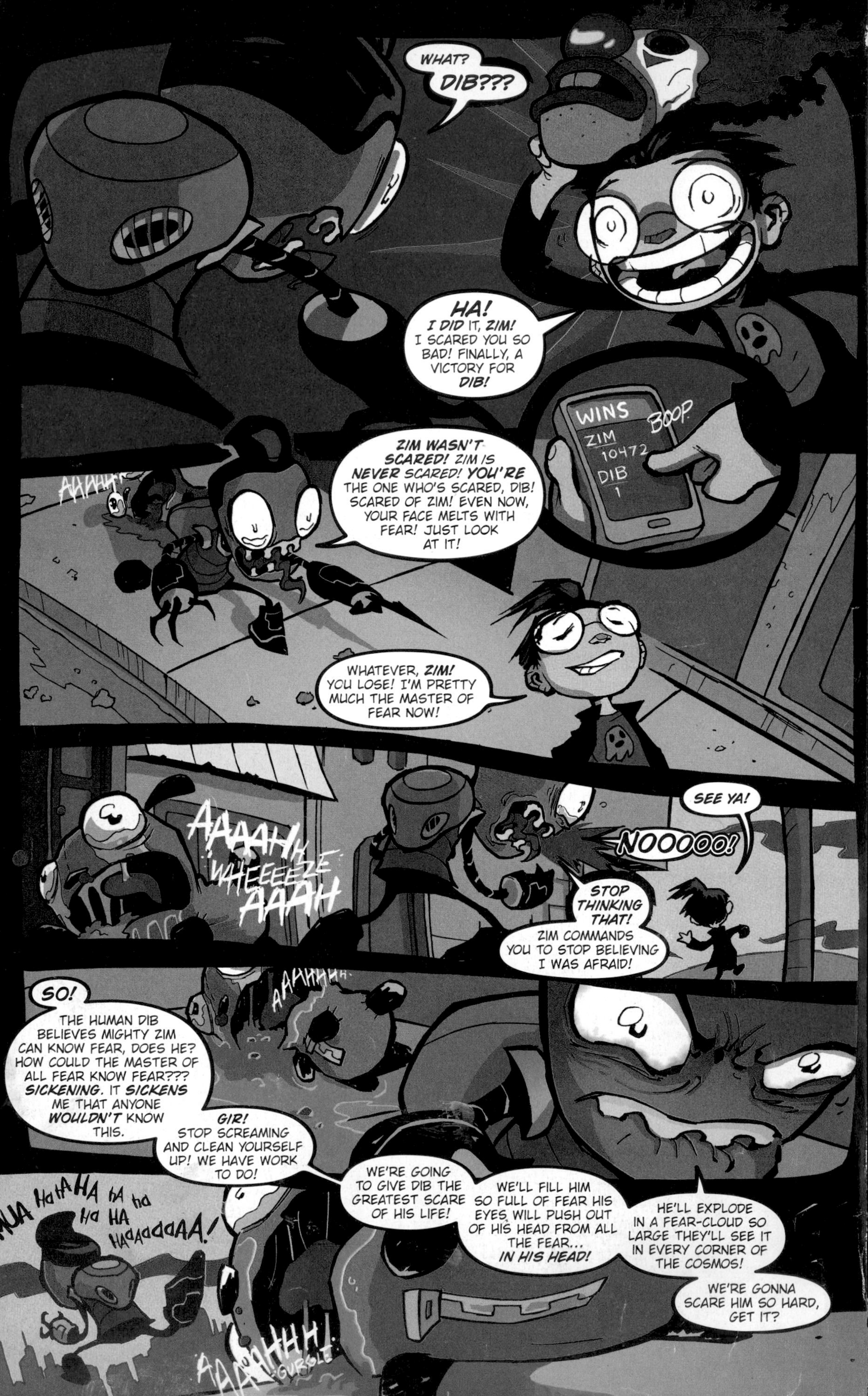
WHAT? DIB???
HA! I DID IT, ZIM! I SCARED YOU SO BAD! FINALLY, A VICTORY FOR DIB!
WINS
ZIM 10472
DIB 1
BOOP.
ZIM WASN'T SCARED! ZIM IS NEVER SCARED! YOU'RE THE ONE WHO'S SCARED, DIB! SCARED OF ZIM! EVEN NOW, YOUR FACE MELTS WITH FEAR! JUST LOOK AT IT!
WHATEVER, ZIM! YOU LOSE! I'M PRETTY MUCH THE MASTER OF FEAR NOW!
AAAAHH WHEEEEZE AAAH
SEE YA!
NOOOOO!
STOP THINKING THAT! ZIM COMMANDS YOU TO STOP BELIEVING I WAS AFRAID!
SO! THE HUMAN DIB BELIEVES MIGHTY ZIM CAN KNOW FEAR, DOES HE? HOW COULD THE MASTER OF ALL FEAR KNOW FEAR??? SICKENING. IT SICKENS ME THAT ANYONE WOULDN'T KNOW THIS.
GIR! STOP SCREAMING AND CLEAN YOURSELF UP! WE HAVE WORK TO DO!
MUA HA HA HA HA HA HA HA HAaaaaAA!
WE'RE GOING TO GIVE DIB THE GREATEST SCARE OF HIS LIFE!
WE'LL FILL HIM SO FULL OF FEAR HIS EYES WILL PUSH OUT OF HIS HEAD FROM ALL THE FEAR... IN HIS HEAD!
HE'LL EXPLODE IN A FEAR-CLOUD SO LARGE THEY'LL SEE IT IN EVERY CORNER OF THE COSMOS!
WE'RE GONNA SCARE HIM SO HARD, GET IT?
AAAAHHH! GURGLE

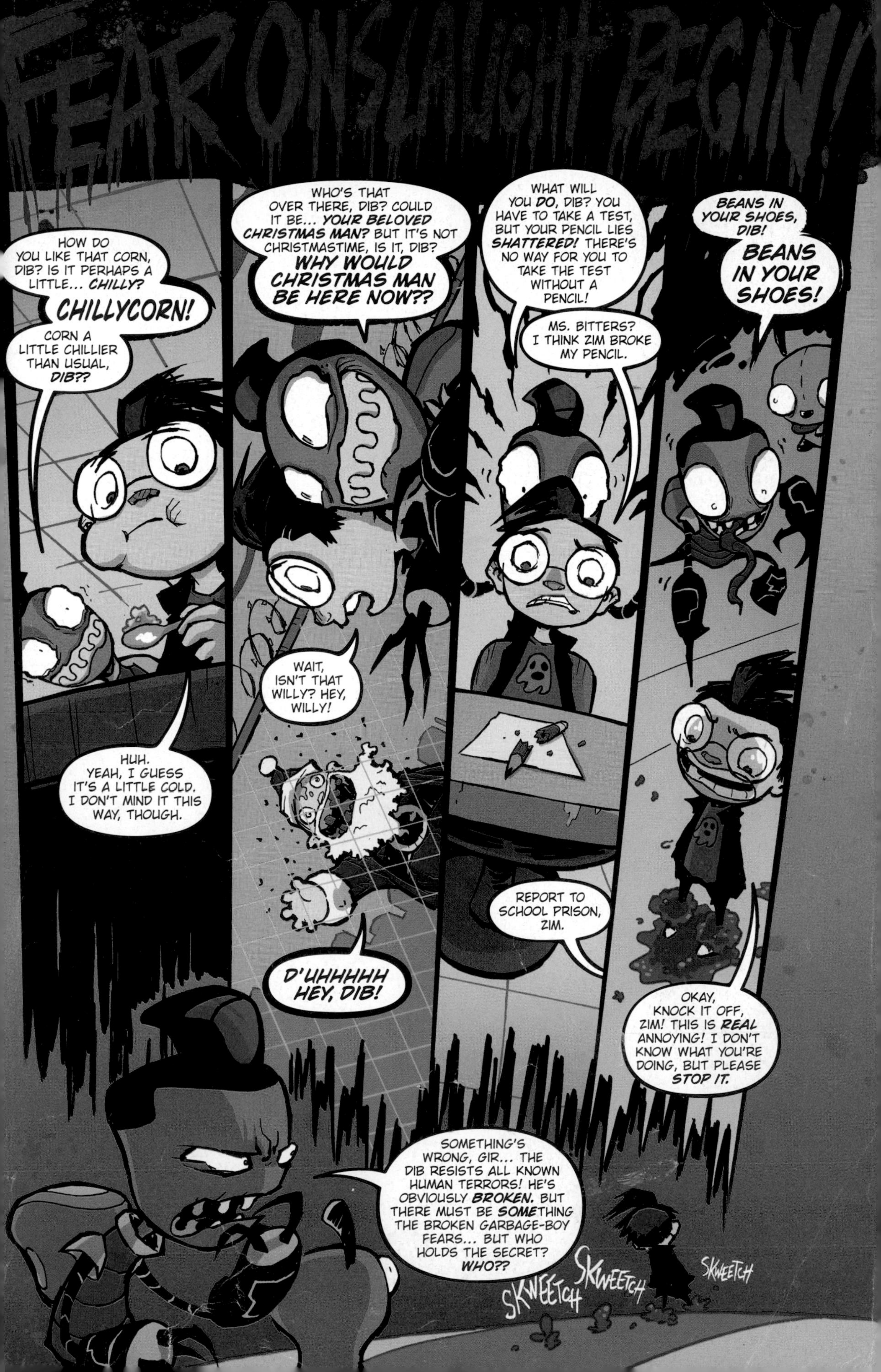
FEAR ONSLAUGHT BEGIN!
HOW DO YOU LIKE THAT CORN, DIB? IS IT PERHAPS A LITTLE... CHILLY?
CHILLYCORN!
CORN A LITTLE CHILLIER THAN USUAL, DIB??
HUH. YEAH, I GUESS IT'S A LITTLE COLD. I DON'T MIND IT THIS WAY, THOUGH.
WHO'S THAT OVER THERE, DIB? COULD IT BE... YOUR BELOVED CHRISTMAS MAN? BUT IT'S NOT CHRISTMASTIME, IS IT, DIB?
WHY WOULD CHRISTMAS MAN BE HERE NOW??
WAIT, ISN'T THAT WILLY? HEY, WILLY!
D'UHHHHH HEY, DIB!
WHAT WILL YOU DO, DIB? YOU HAVE TO TAKE A TEST, BUT YOUR PENCIL LIES SHATTERED! THERE'S NO WAY FOR YOU TO TAKE THE TEST WITHOUT A PENCIL!
MS. BITTERS? I THINK ZIM BROKE MY PENCIL.
REPORT TO SCHOOL PRISON, ZIM.
BEANS IN YOUR SHOES, DIB!
BEANS IN YOUR SHOES!
OKAY, KNOCK IT OFF, ZIM! THIS IS REAL ANNOYING! I DON'T KNOW WHAT YOU'RE DOING, BUT PLEASE STOP IT.
SOMETHING'S WRONG, GIR... THE DIB RESISTS ALL KNOWN HUMAN TERRORS! HE'S OBVIOUSLY BROKEN. BUT THERE MUST BE SOMETHING THE BROKEN GARBAGE-BOY FEARS... BUT WHO HOLDS THE SECRET? WHO??
SKWEETCH
SKWEETCH
SKWEETCH

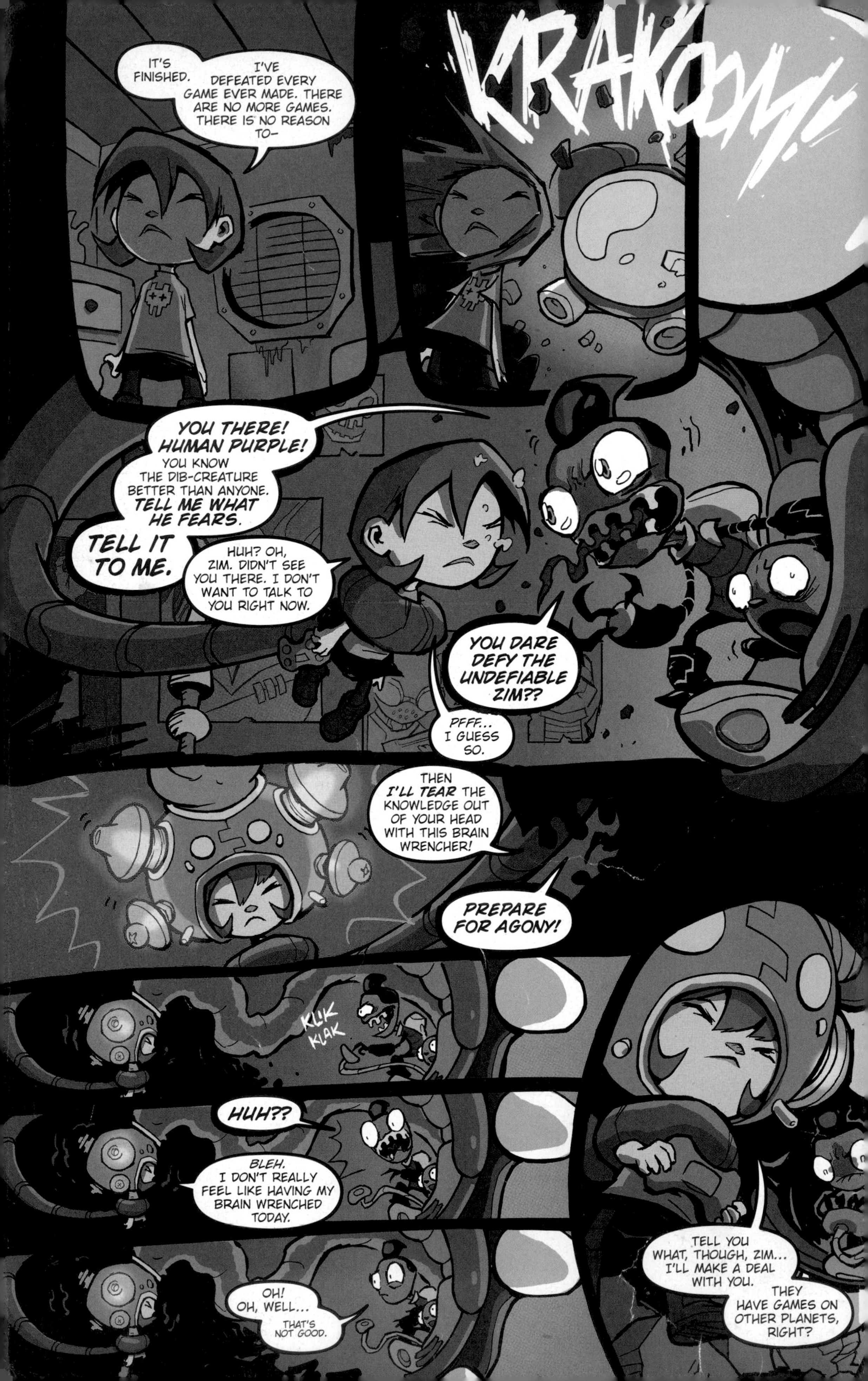
IT'S FINISHED.
I'VE DEFEATED EVERY GAME EVER MADE. THERE ARE NO MORE GAMES. THERE IS NO REASON TO–
KRAKOOM!
YOU THERE! HUMAN PURPLE! YOU KNOW THE DIB-CREATURE BETTER THAN ANYONE. TELL ME WHAT HE FEARS.
TELL IT TO ME.
HUH? OH, ZIM. DIDN'T SEE YOU THERE. I DON'T WANT TO TALK TO YOU RIGHT NOW.
YOU DARE DEFY THE UNDEFIABLE ZIM??
PFFF... I GUESS SO.
THEN I'LL TEAR THE KNOWLEDGE OUT OF YOUR HEAD WITH THIS BRAIN WRENCHER!
PREPARE FOR AGONY!
KLIK KLAK
HUH??
BLEH. I DON'T REALLY FEEL LIKE HAVING MY BRAIN WRENCHED TODAY.
OH! OH, WELL...
THAT'S NOT GOOD.
TELL YOU WHAT, THOUGH, ZIM... I'LL MAKE A DEAL WITH YOU.
THEY HAVE GAMES ON OTHER PLANETS, RIGHT?

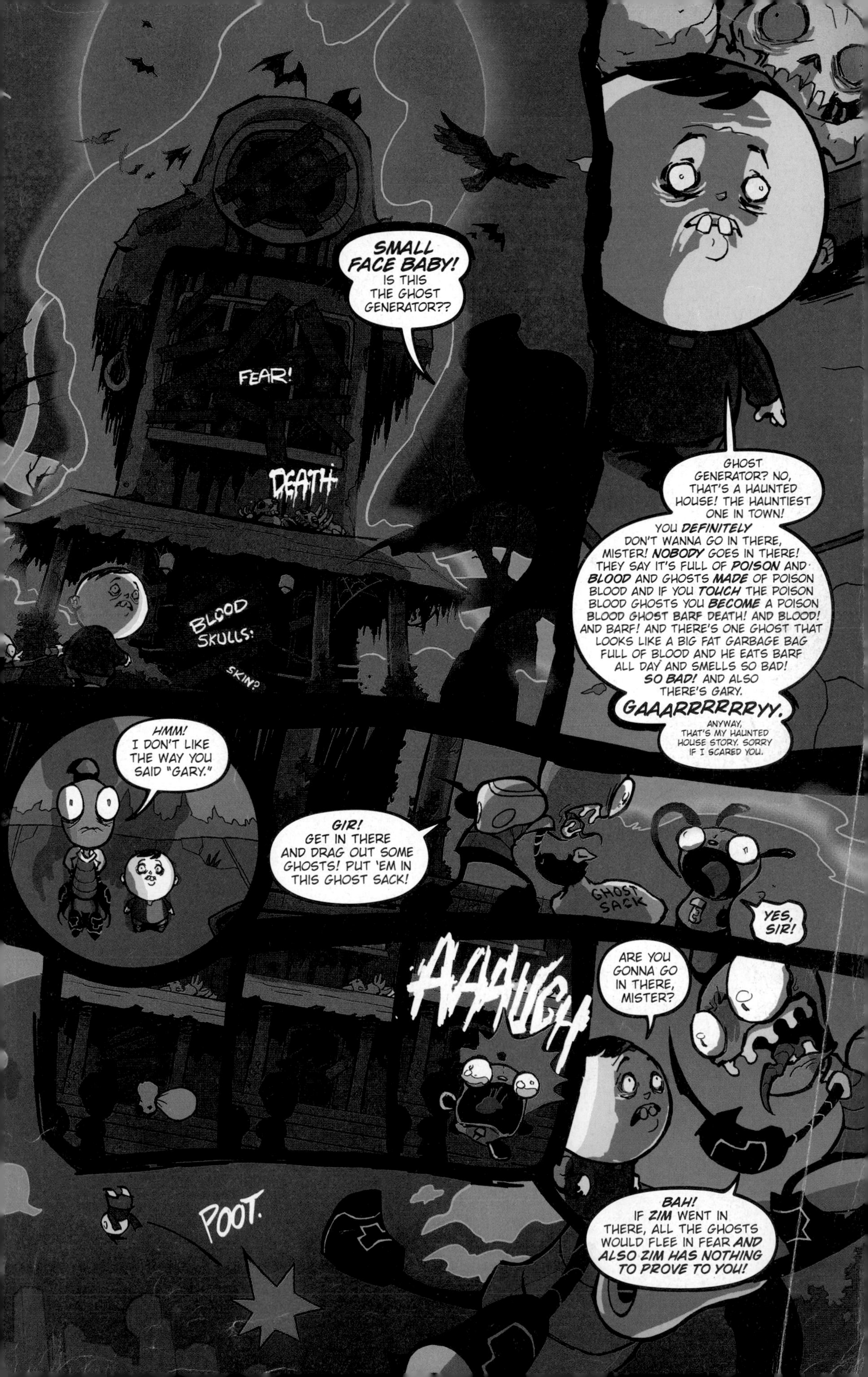
SMALL FACE BABY! IS THIS THE GHOST GENERATOR??
FEAR!
DEATH
BLOOD SKULLS:
SKIN?
GHOST GENERATOR? NO, THAT'S A HAUNTED HOUSE! THE HAUNTIEST ONE IN TOWN!
YOU DEFINITELY DON'T WANNA GO IN THERE, MISTER! NOBODY GOES IN THERE! THEY SAY IT'S FULL OF POISON AND BLOOD AND GHOSTS MADE OF POISON BLOOD AND IF YOU TOUCH THE POISON BLOOD GHOSTS YOU BECOME A POISON BLOOD GHOST BARF DEATH! AND BLOOD! AND BARF! AND THERE'S ONE GHOST THAT LOOKS LIKE A BIG FAT GARBAGE BAG FULL OF BLOOD AND HE EATS BARF ALL DAY AND SMELLS SO BAD! SO BAD! AND ALSO THERE'S GARY.
GAAARRRRRRYY.
ANYWAY, THAT'S MY HAUNTED HOUSE STORY. SORRY IF I SCARED YOU.
HMM! I DON'T LIKE THE WAY YOU SAID "GARY."
GIR! GET IN THERE AND DRAG OUT SOME GHOSTS! PUT 'EM IN THIS GHOST SACK!
GHOST SACK
YES, SIR!
AAAUGH
ARE YOU GONNA GO IN THERE, MISTER?
POOT.
BAH! IF ZIM WENT IN THERE, ALL THE GHOSTS WOULD FLEE IN FEAR AND ALSO ZIM HAS NOTHING TO PROVE TO YOU!

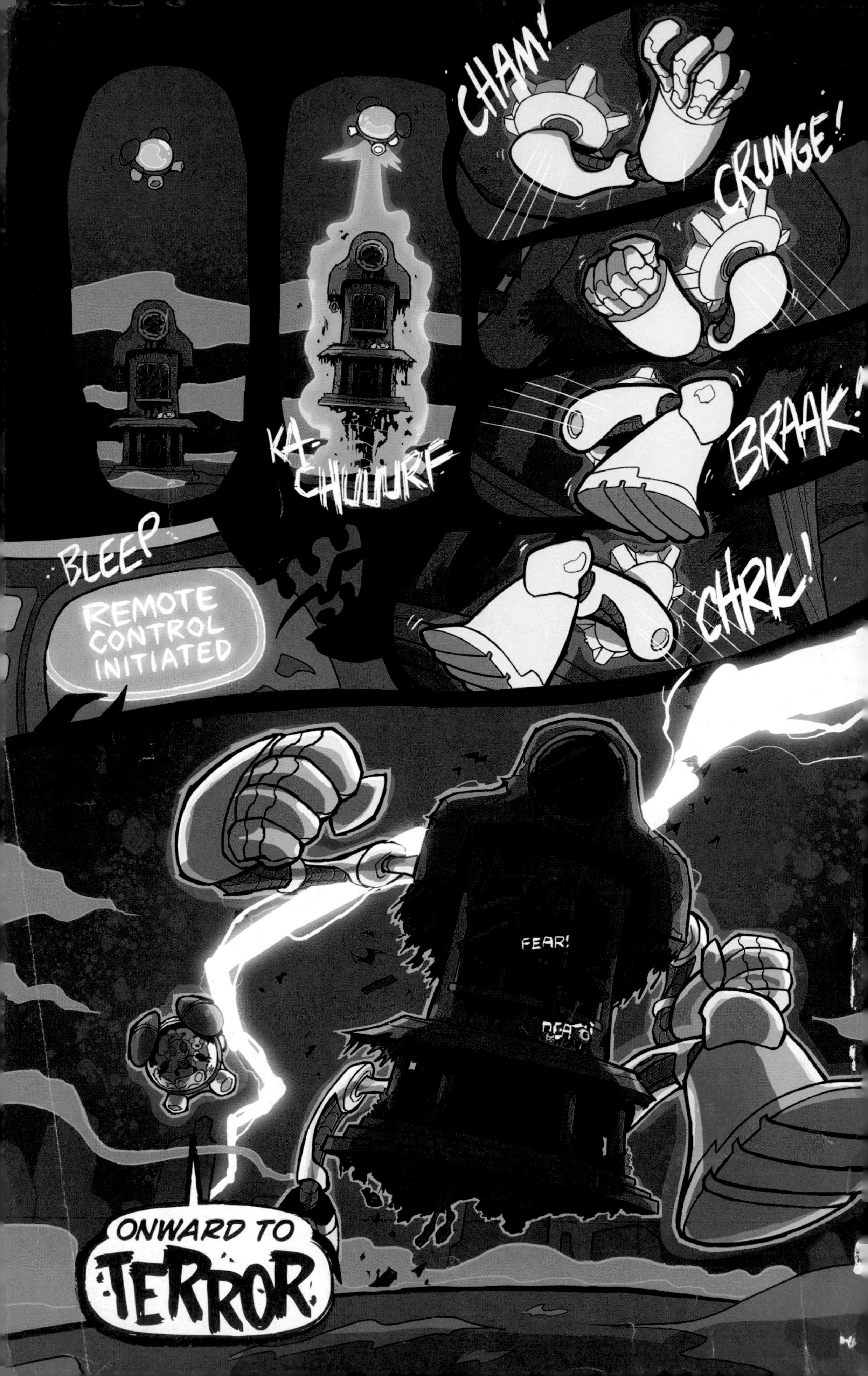
KA-CHUUURF
CHAM!
CRUNGE!
BRAAK!
CHRK!
BLEEP
REMOTE CONTROL INITIATED
FEAR!
ONWARD TO TERROR

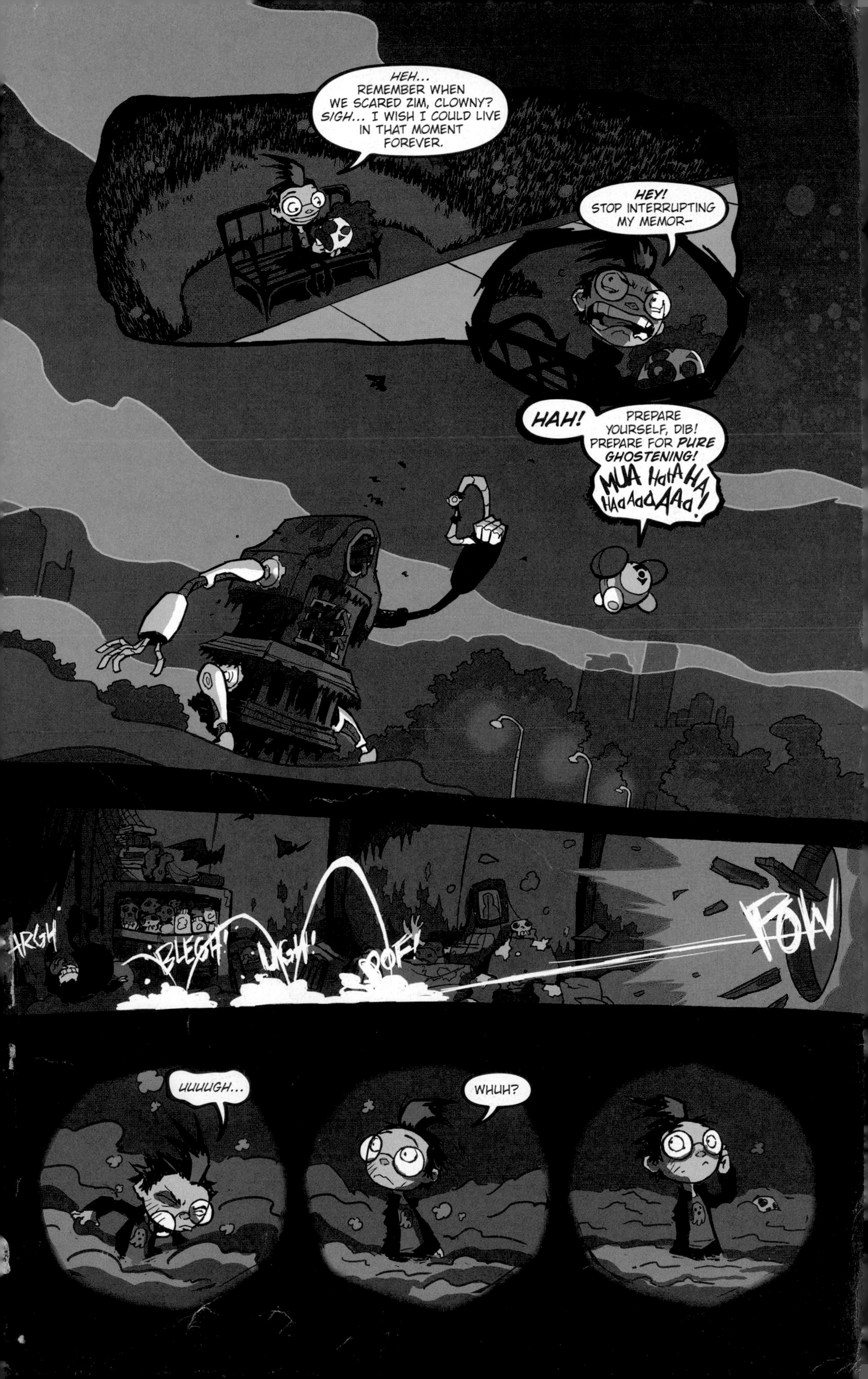
HEH... REMEMBER WHEN WE SCARED ZIM, CLOWNY? SIGH... I WISH I COULD LIVE IN THAT MOMENT FOREVER.
HEY! STOP INTERRUPTING MY MEMOR–
HAH!
PREPARE YOURSELF, DIB! PREPARE FOR PURE GHOSTENING!
MUA HAHAHA, HAAAAAAAA!
ARGH
BLEGH!
UGH!
POOF!
FOW
UUUUGH...
WHUH?

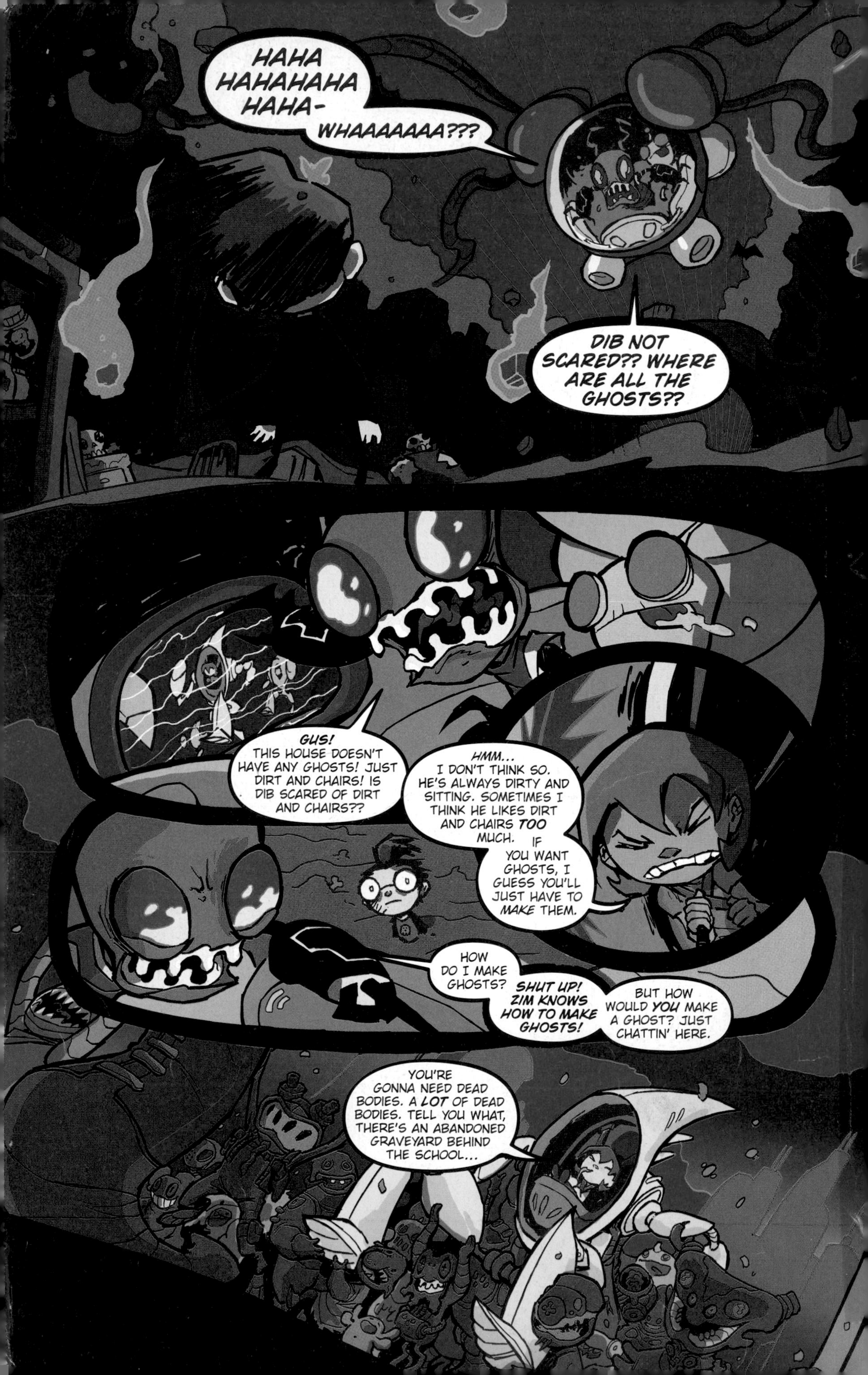
HAHA HAHAHAHA HAHA- WHAAAAAAA???
DIB NOT SCARED?? WHERE ARE ALL THE GHOSTS??
GUS! THIS HOUSE DOESN'T HAVE ANY GHOSTS! JUST DIRT AND CHAIRS! IS DIB SCARED OF DIRT AND CHAIRS??
HMM... I DON'T THINK SO. HE'S ALWAYS DIRTY AND SITTING. SOMETIMES I THINK HE LIKES DIRT AND CHAIRS TOO MUCH.
IF YOU WANT GHOSTS, I GUESS YOU'LL JUST HAVE TO MAKE THEM.
HOW DO I MAKE GHOSTS?
SHUT UP! ZIM KNOWS HOW TO MAKE GHOSTS!
BUT HOW WOULD YOU MAKE A GHOST? JUST CHATTIN' HERE.
YOU'RE GONNA NEED DEAD BODIES. A LOT OF DEAD BODIES. TELL YOU WHAT, THERE'S AN ABANDONED GRAVEYARD BEHIND THE SCHOOL...

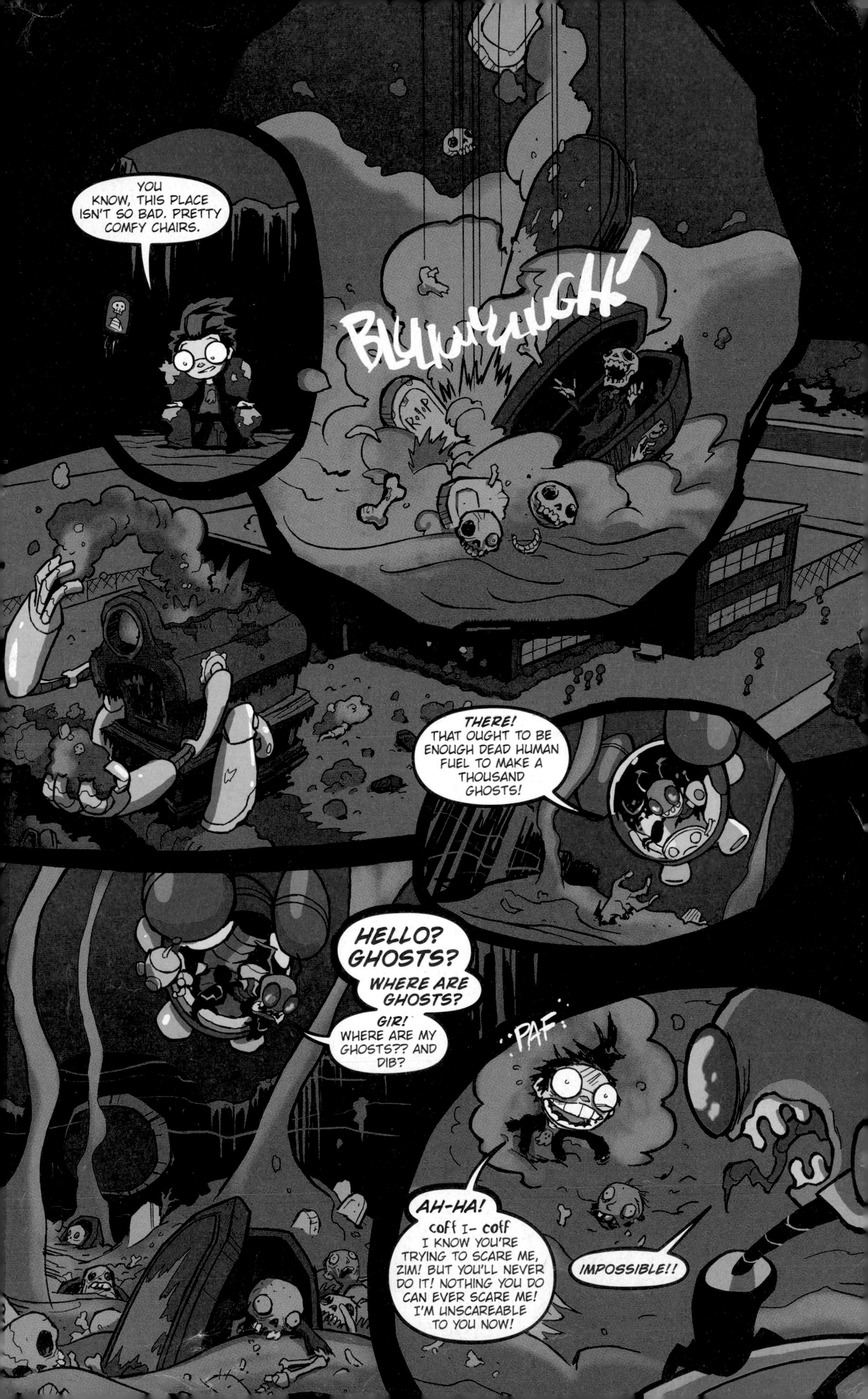

YOU KNOW, THIS PLACE ISN'T SO BAD. PRETTY COMFY CHAIRS.
BLUUURLUGH!
RoloP
THERE! THAT OUGHT TO BE ENOUGH DEAD HUMAN FUEL TO MAKE A THOUSAND GHOSTS!
HELLO? GHOSTS?
WHERE ARE GHOSTS?
GIR! WHERE ARE MY GHOSTS?? AND DIB?
PAF
AH-HA!
coff I- coff
I KNOW YOU'RE TRYING TO SCARE ME, ZIM! BUT YOU'LL NEVER DO IT! NOTHING YOU DO CAN EVER SCARE ME! I'M UNSCAREABLE TO YOU NOW!
IMPOSSIBLE!!

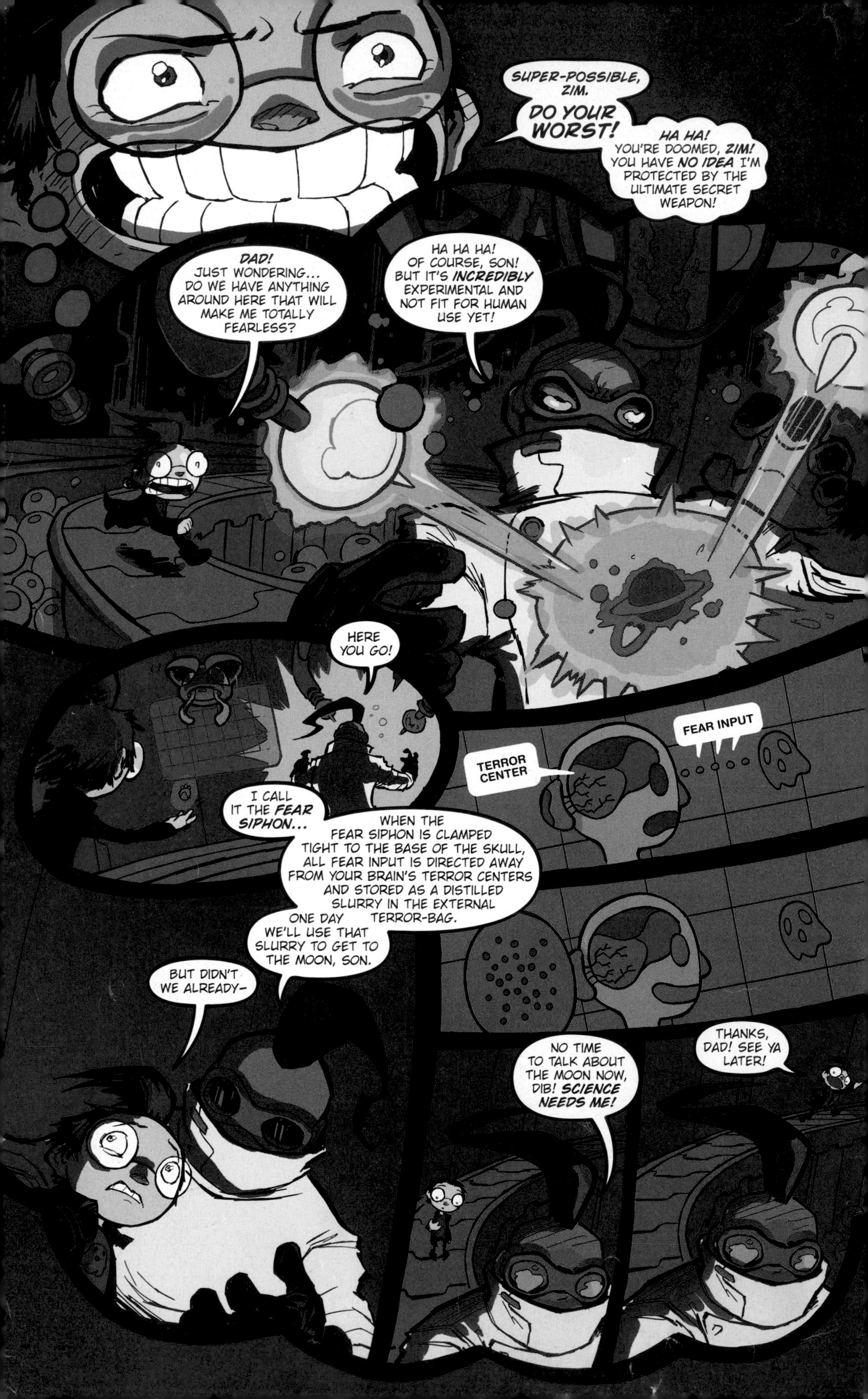
SUPER-POSSIBLE, ZIM. DO YOUR WORST!
HA HA! YOU'RE DOOMED, ZIM! YOU HAVE NO IDEA I'M PROTECTED BY THE ULTIMATE SECRET WEAPON!
DAD! JUST WONDERING... DO WE HAVE ANYTHING AROUND HERE THAT WILL MAKE ME TOTALLY FEARLESS?
HA HA HA! OF COURSE, SON! BUT IT'S INCREDIBLY EXPERIMENTAL AND NOT FIT FOR HUMAN USE YET!
HERE YOU GO!
I CALL IT THE FEAR SIPHON...
TERROR CENTER
FEAR INPUT
WHEN THE FEAR SIPHON IS CLAMPED TIGHT TO THE BASE OF THE SKULL, ALL FEAR INPUT IS DIRECTED AWAY FROM YOUR BRAIN'S TERROR CENTERS AND STORED AS A DISTILLED SLURRY IN THE EXTERNAL TERROR-BAG.
ONE DAY WE'LL USE THAT SLURRY TO GET TO THE MOON, SON.
BUT DIDN'T WE ALREADY-
NO TIME TO TALK ABOUT THE MOON NOW, DIB! SCIENCE NEEDS ME!
THANKS, DAD! SEE YA LATER!

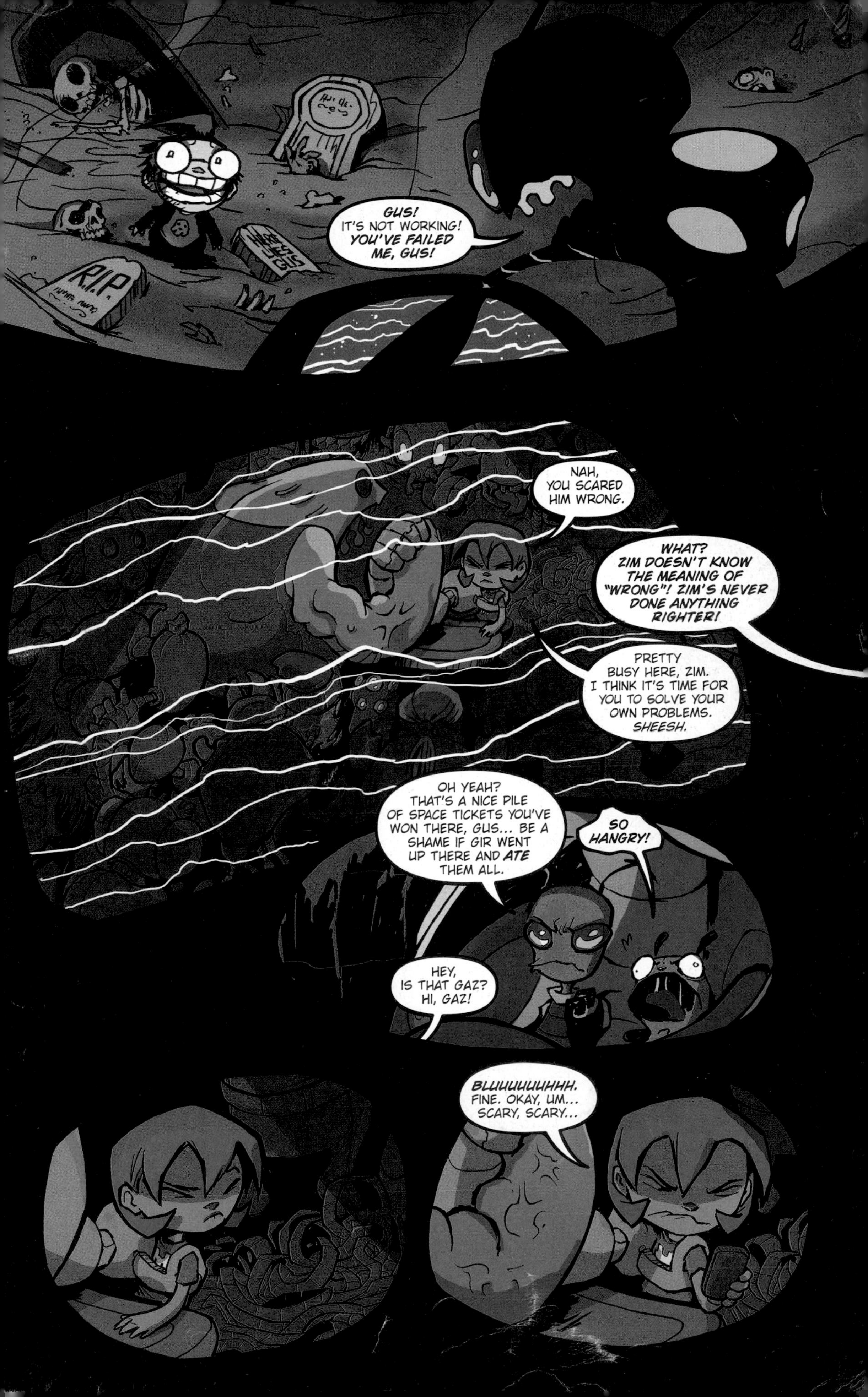
GUS! IT'S NOT WORKING! YOU'VE FAILED ME, GUS!
NAH, YOU SCARED HIM WRONG.
WHAT? ZIM DOESN'T KNOW THE MEANING OF "WRONG"! ZIM'S NEVER DONE ANYTHING RIGHTER!
PRETTY BUSY HERE, ZIM. I THINK IT'S TIME FOR YOU TO SOLVE YOUR OWN PROBLEMS. SHEESH.
OH YEAH? THAT'S A NICE PILE OF SPACE TICKETS YOU'VE WON THERE, GUS... BE A SHAME IF GIR WENT UP THERE AND ATE THEM ALL.
SO HANGRY!
HEY, IS THAT GAZ? HI, GAZ!
BLUUUUUUHHH. FINE. OKAY, UM... SCARY, SCARY...
R.I.P.

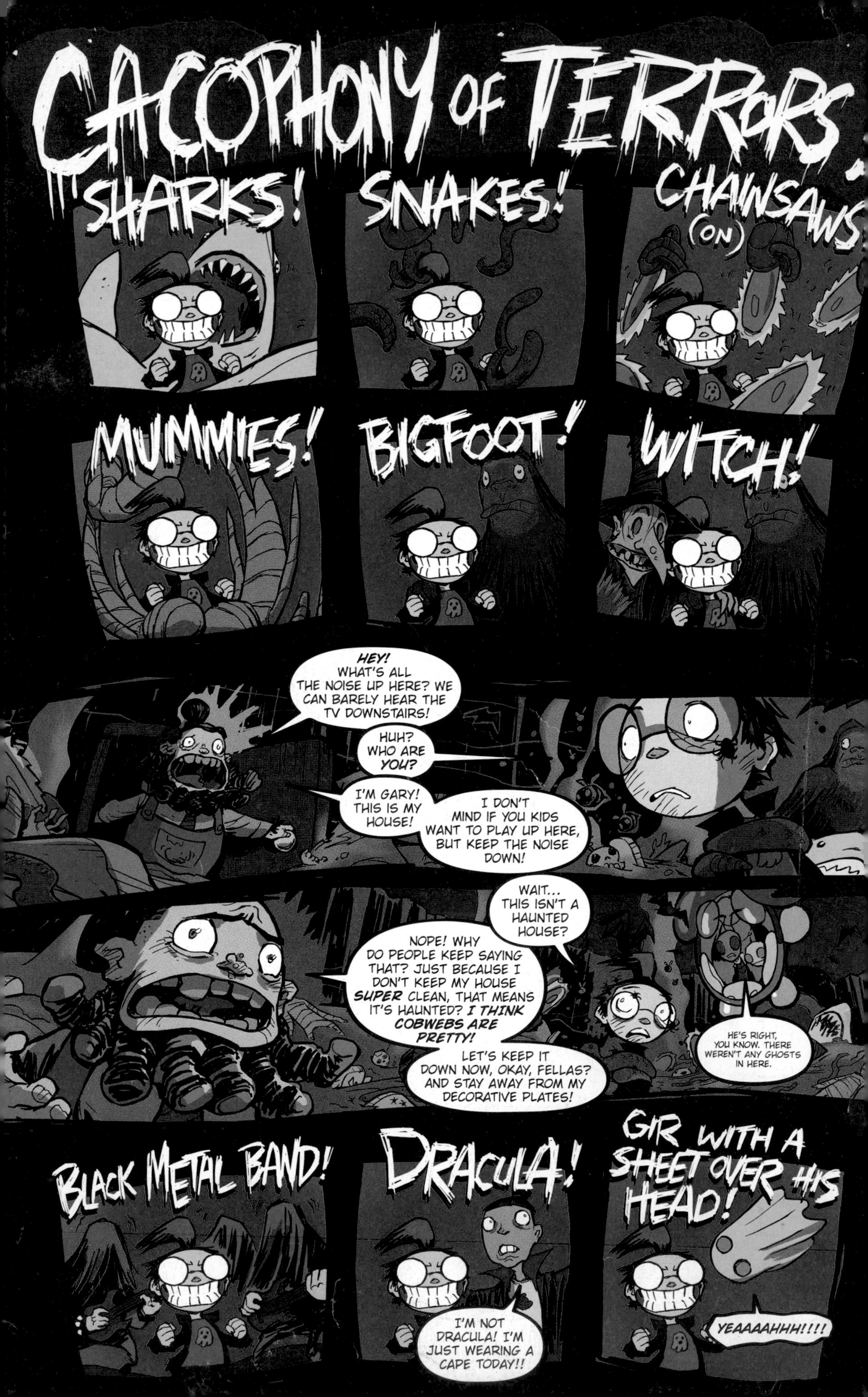
CACOPHONY OF TERRORS:
SHARKS!
SNAKES!
CHAINSAWS (ON)
MUMMIES!
BIGFOOT!
WITCH!
HEY! WHAT'S ALL THE NOISE UP HERE? WE CAN BARELY HEAR THE TV DOWNSTAIRS!
HUH? WHO ARE YOU?
I'M GARY! THIS IS MY HOUSE!
I DON'T MIND IF YOU KIDS WANT TO PLAY UP HERE, BUT KEEP THE NOISE DOWN!
WAIT... THIS ISN'T A HAUNTED HOUSE?
NOPE! WHY DO PEOPLE KEEP SAYING THAT? JUST BECAUSE I DON'T KEEP MY HOUSE SUPER CLEAN, THAT MEANS IT'S HAUNTED? I THINK COBWEBS ARE PRETTY!
HE'S RIGHT, YOU KNOW. THERE WEREN'T ANY GHOSTS IN HERE.
LET'S KEEP IT DOWN NOW, OKAY, FELLAS? AND STAY AWAY FROM MY DECORATIVE PLATES!
BLACK METAL BAND!
DRACULA!
I'M NOT DRACULA! I'M JUST WEARING A CAPE TODAY!!
GIR WITH A SHEET OVER HIS HEAD!
YEAAAAHHH!!!!

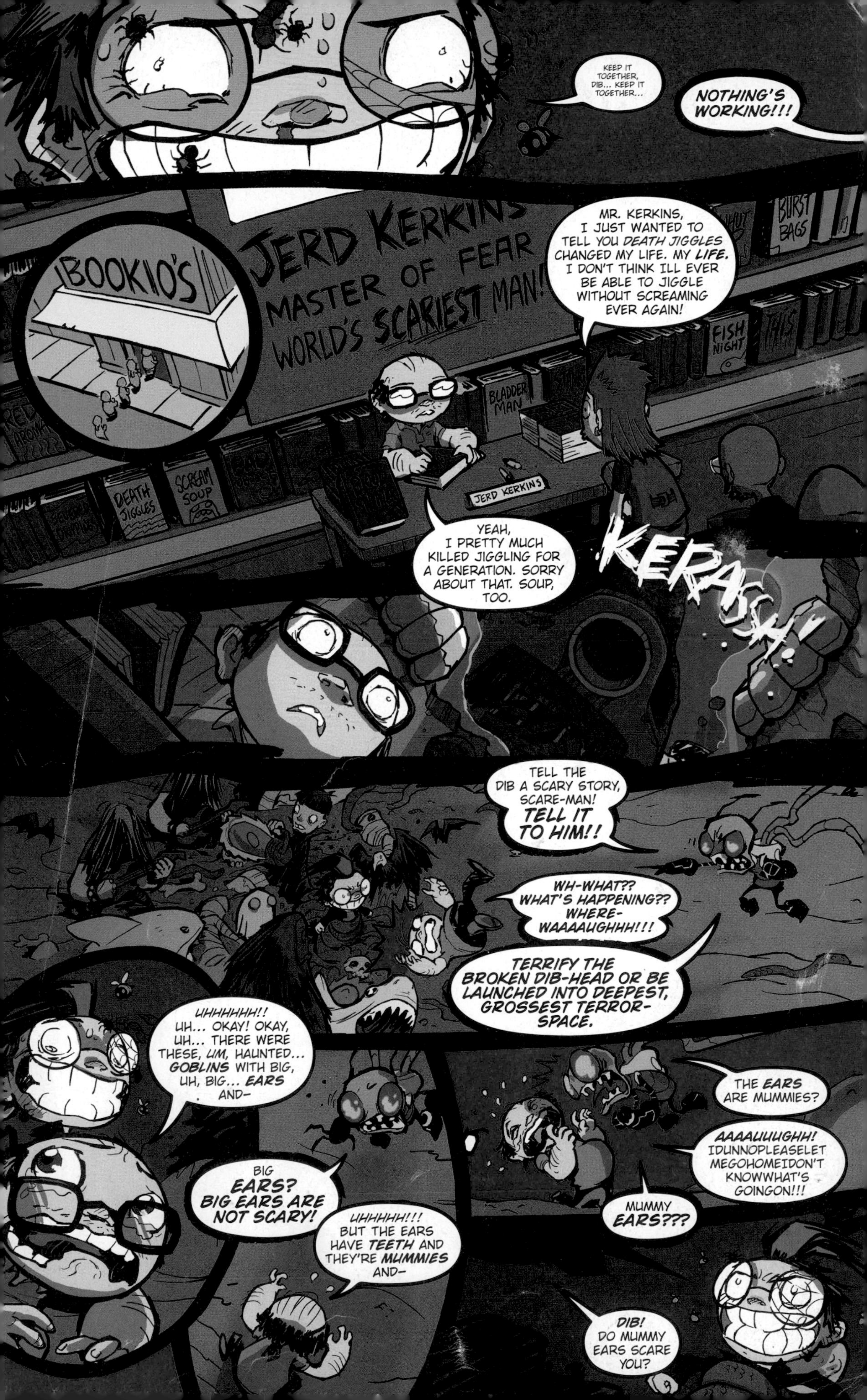
KEEP IT TOGETHER, DIB... KEEP IT TOGETHER...
NOTHING'S WORKING!!!
BOOKIO'S
JERD KERKINS MASTER OF FEAR WORLD'S SCARIEST MAN!
BURST BAGS
FISH NIGHT
BLADDER MAN
DEATH JIGGLES
SCREAM SOUP
JERD KERKINS
MR. KERKINS, I JUST WANTED TO TELL YOU *DEATH JIGGLES* CHANGED MY LIFE. MY ***LIFE.*** I DON'T THINK ILL EVER BE ABLE TO JIGGLE WITHOUT SCREAMING EVER AGAIN!
YEAH, I PRETTY MUCH KILLED JIGGLING FOR A GENERATION. SORRY ABOUT THAT. SOUP, TOO.
KERASH!
TELL THE DIB A SCARY STORY, SCARE-MAN! ***TELL IT TO HIM!!***
WH-WHAT?? WHAT'S HAPPENING?? WHERE- WAAAAUGHHH!!!
TERRIFY THE BROKEN DIB-HEAD OR BE LAUNCHED INTO DEEPEST, GROSSEST TERROR-SPACE.
UHHHHHH!! UH... OKAY! OKAY, UH... THERE WERE THESE, *UM,* HAUNTED... ***GOBLINS*** WITH BIG, UH, BIG... ***EARS*** AND-
BIG ***EARS? BIG EARS ARE NOT SCARY!***
UHHHHH!!! BUT THE EARS HAVE ***TEETH*** AND THEY'RE ***MUMMIES*** AND-
THE *EARS* ARE MUMMIES?
AAAAUUUGHH! IDUNNOPLEASELET MEGOHOMEIDON'T KNOWWHAT'S GOINGON!!!
MUMMY ***EARS???***
DIB! DO MUMMY EARS SCARE YOU?

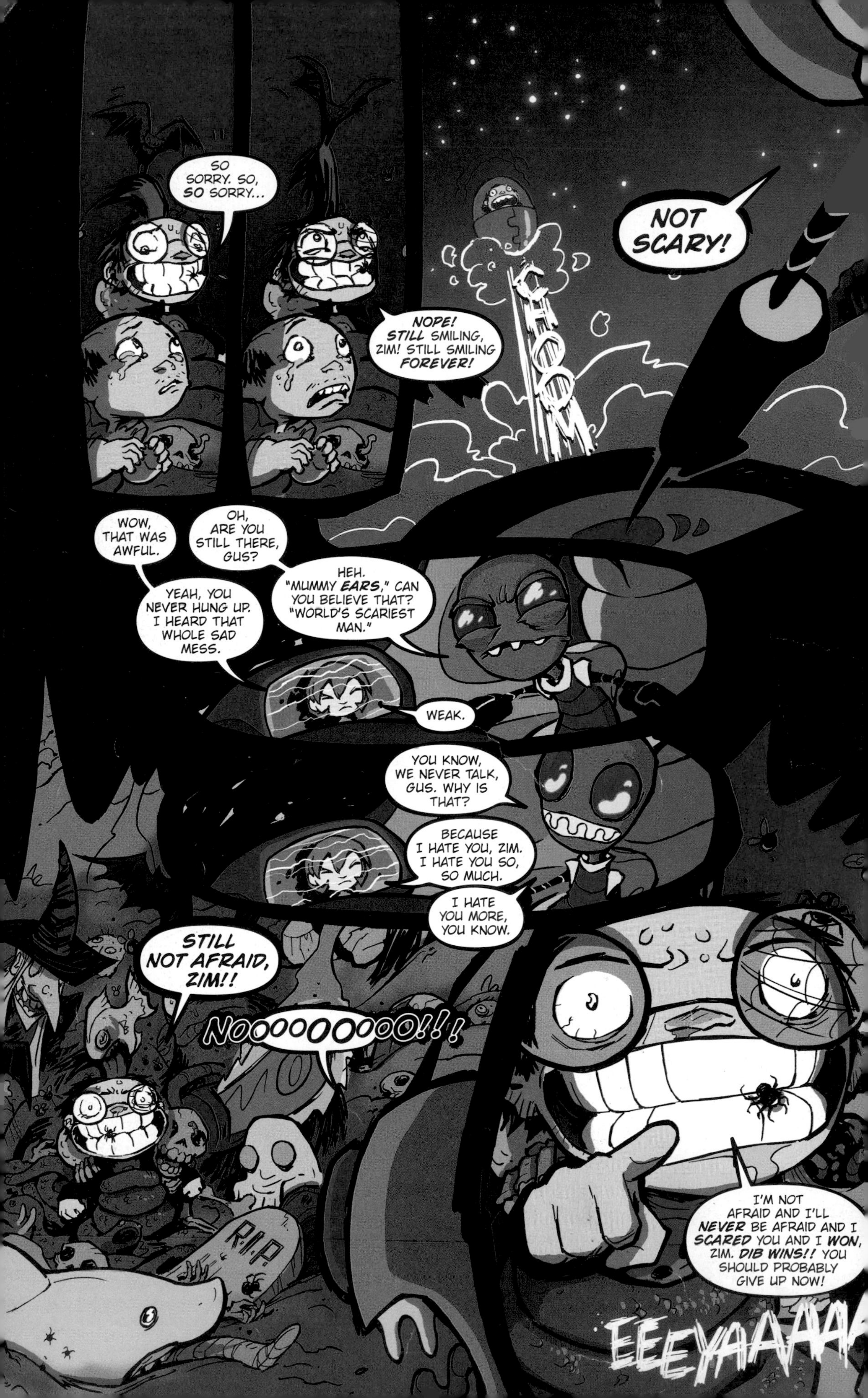
SO SORRY. SO, SO SORRY...
NOPE! STILL SMILING, ZIM! STILL SMILING FOREVER!
NOT SCARY!
WOW, THAT WAS AWFUL.
OH, ARE YOU STILL THERE, GUS?
YEAH, YOU NEVER HUNG UP. I HEARD THAT WHOLE SAD MESS.
HEH. "MUMMY EARS," CAN YOU BELIEVE THAT? "WORLD'S SCARIEST MAN."
WEAK.
YOU KNOW, WE NEVER TALK, GUS. WHY IS THAT?
BECAUSE I HATE YOU, ZIM. I HATE YOU SO, SO MUCH.
I HATE YOU MORE, YOU KNOW.
STILL NOT AFRAID, ZIM!!
NOOOOOOOOOO!!!
I'M NOT AFRAID AND I'LL NEVER BE AFRAID AND I SCARED YOU AND I WON, ZIM. DIB WINS!! YOU SHOULD PROBABLY GIVE UP NOW!
EEEYAAAA

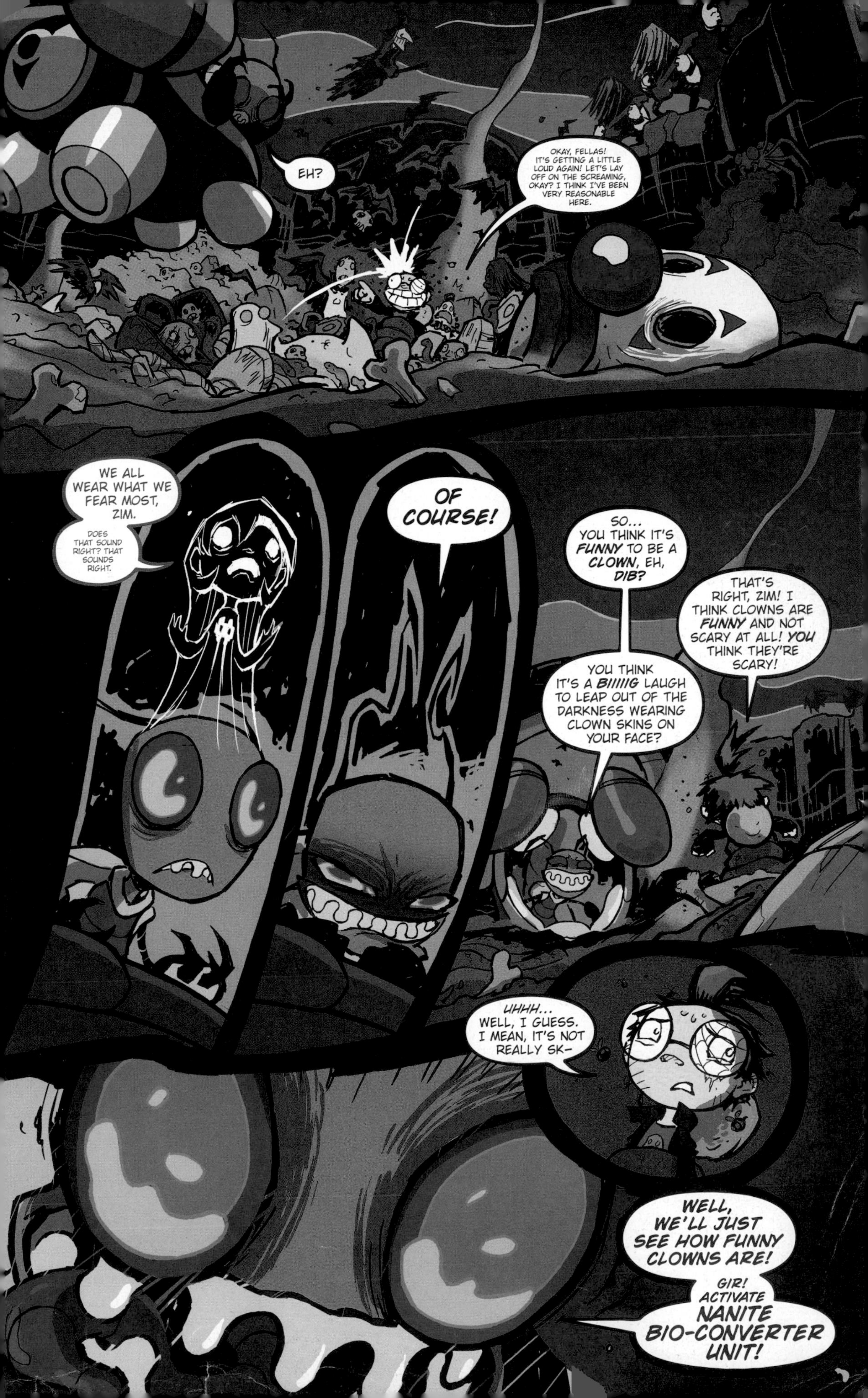
EH?
OKAY, FELLAS! IT'S GETTING A LITTLE LOUD AGAIN! LET'S LAY OFF ON THE SCREAMING, OKAY? I THINK I'VE BEEN VERY REASONABLE HERE.
WE ALL WEAR WHAT WE FEAR MOST, ZIM.
DOES THAT SOUND RIGHT? THAT SOUNDS RIGHT.
OF COURSE!
SO... YOU THINK IT'S FUNNY TO BE A CLOWN, EH, DIB?
YOU THINK IT'S A BIIIIIG LAUGH TO LEAP OUT OF THE DARKNESS WEARING CLOWN SKINS ON YOUR FACE?
THAT'S RIGHT, ZIM! I THINK CLOWNS ARE FUNNY AND NOT SCARY AT ALL! YOU THINK THEY'RE SCARY!
UHHH... WELL, I GUESS. I MEAN, IT'S NOT REALLY SK-
WELL, WE'LL JUST SEE HOW FUNNY CLOWNS ARE!
GIR! ACTIVATE NANITE BIO-CONVERTER UNIT!

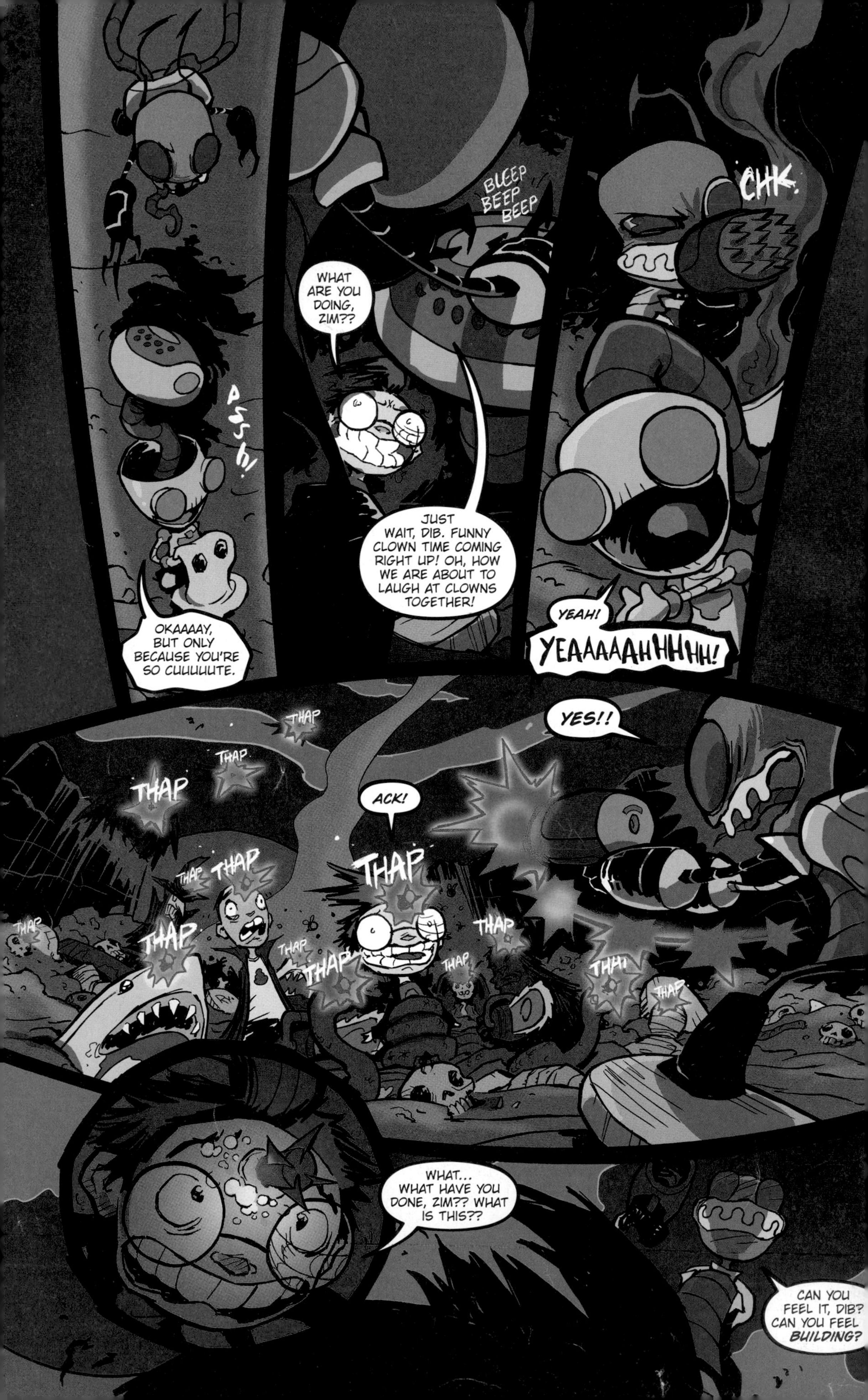

BLEEP BEEP BEEP
CHK
WHAT ARE YOU DOING, ZIM??
PSSSH!
JUST WAIT, DIB. FUNNY CLOWN TIME COMING RIGHT UP! OH, HOW WE ARE ABOUT TO LAUGH AT CLOWNS TOGETHER!
OKAAAAY, BUT ONLY BECAUSE YOU'RE SO CUUUUUTE.
YEAH!
YEAAAAAHHHHH!
YES!!
THAP
THAP
THAP
ACK!
THAP
THAP THAP
THAP
THAP
THAP
THAP
THAP
THAP
THAP
THAP
WHAT... WHAT HAVE YOU DONE, ZIM?? WHAT IS THIS??
CAN YOU FEEL IT, DIB? CAN YOU FEEL *BUILDING?*

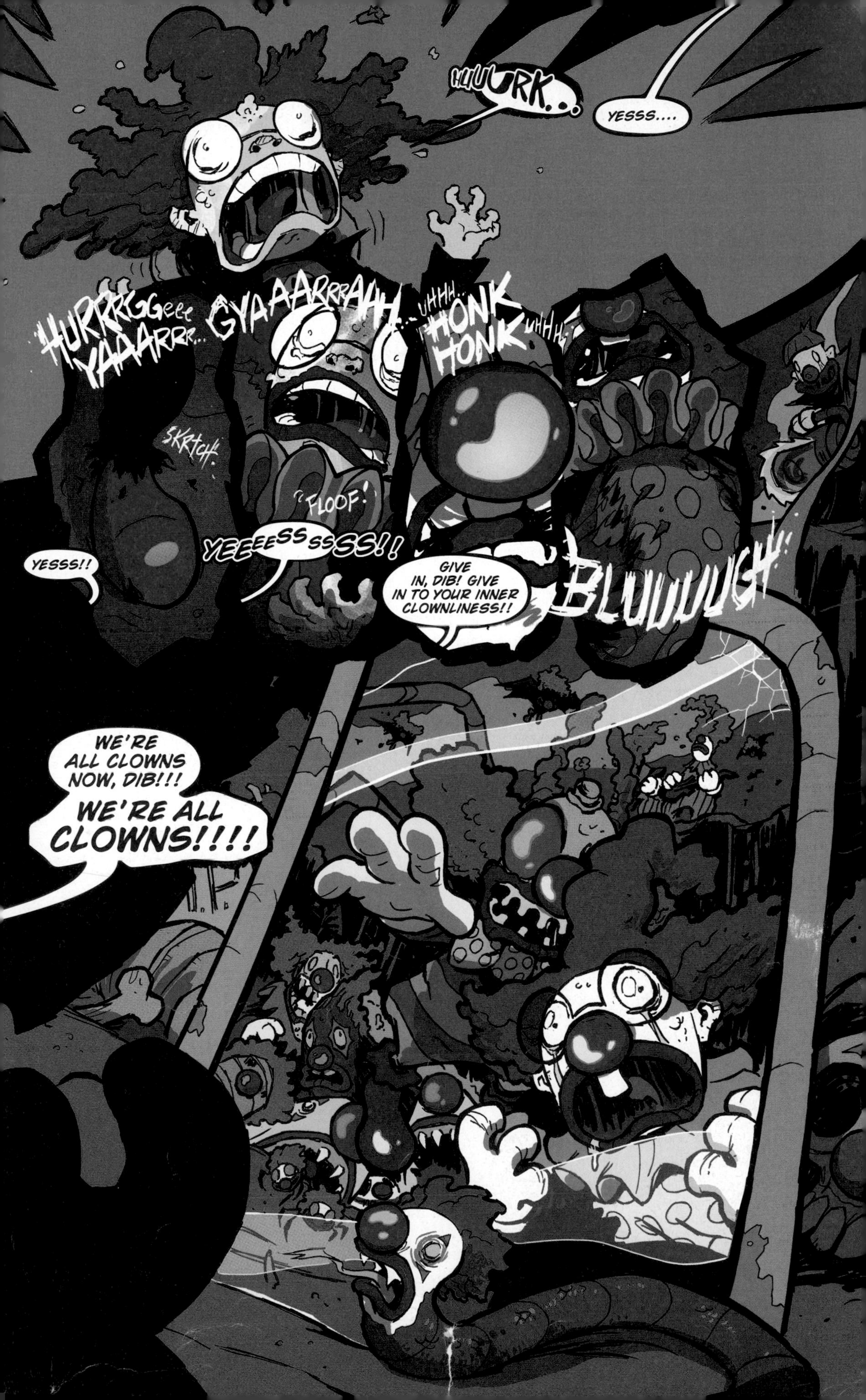
HLUUURK...
YESSS....
HURRRGGeee YAAARRR...
GYAAARRRAHH...
HONK HONK
SKRTCH
FLOOF!
YESSS!!
YEEEEESSSSSS!!
GIVE IN, DIB! GIVE IN TO YOUR INNER CLOWNLINESS!!
BLUUUUGH
WE'RE ALL CLOWNS NOW, DIB!!! WE'RE ALL CLOWNS!!!!

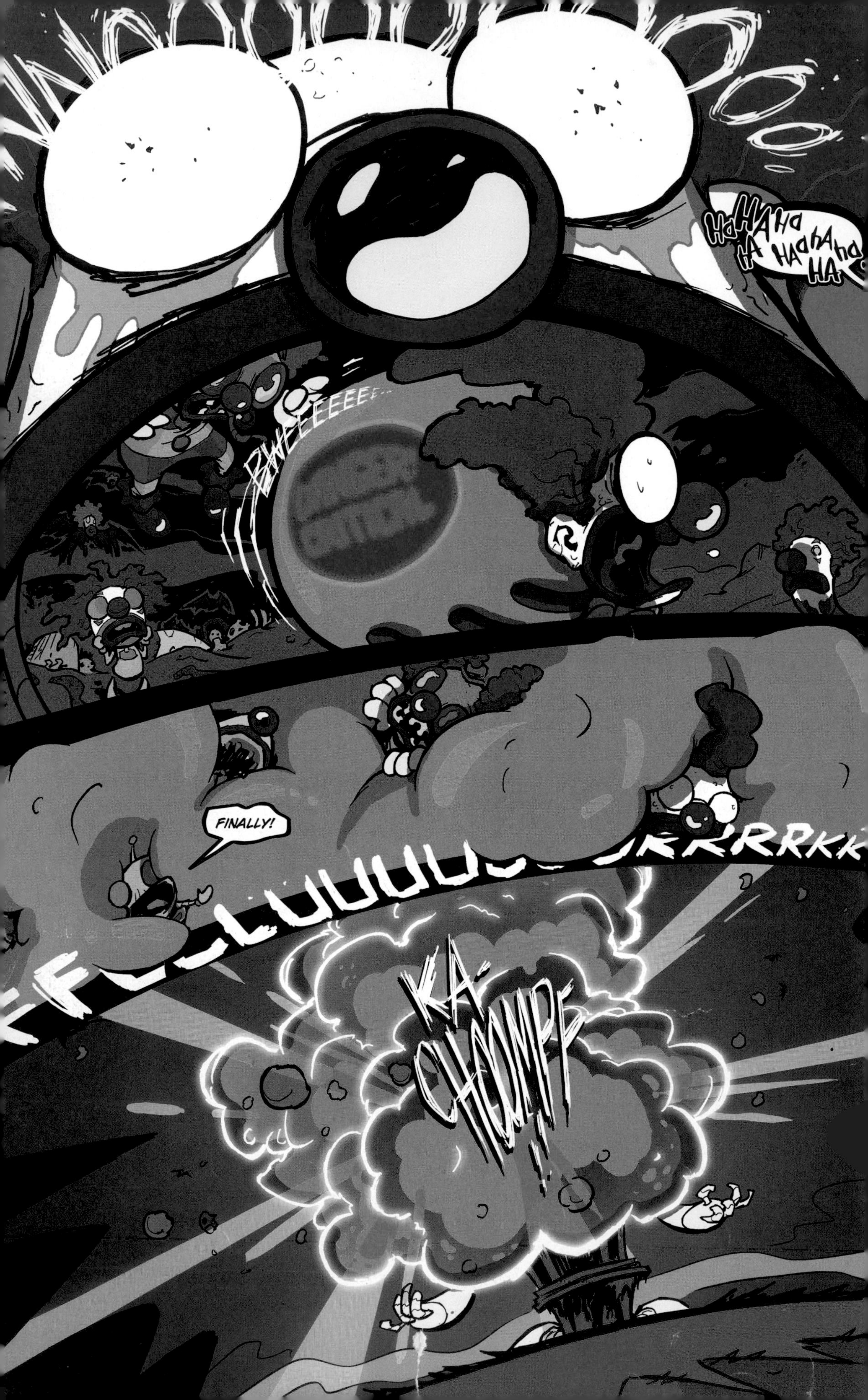
WHOOOOOOOOOO
HAHAHA HA HAHAHAHA HA
BWEEEEEEE...
FINALLY!
FLLUUUUURRRRKK
KA-CHOOMP!

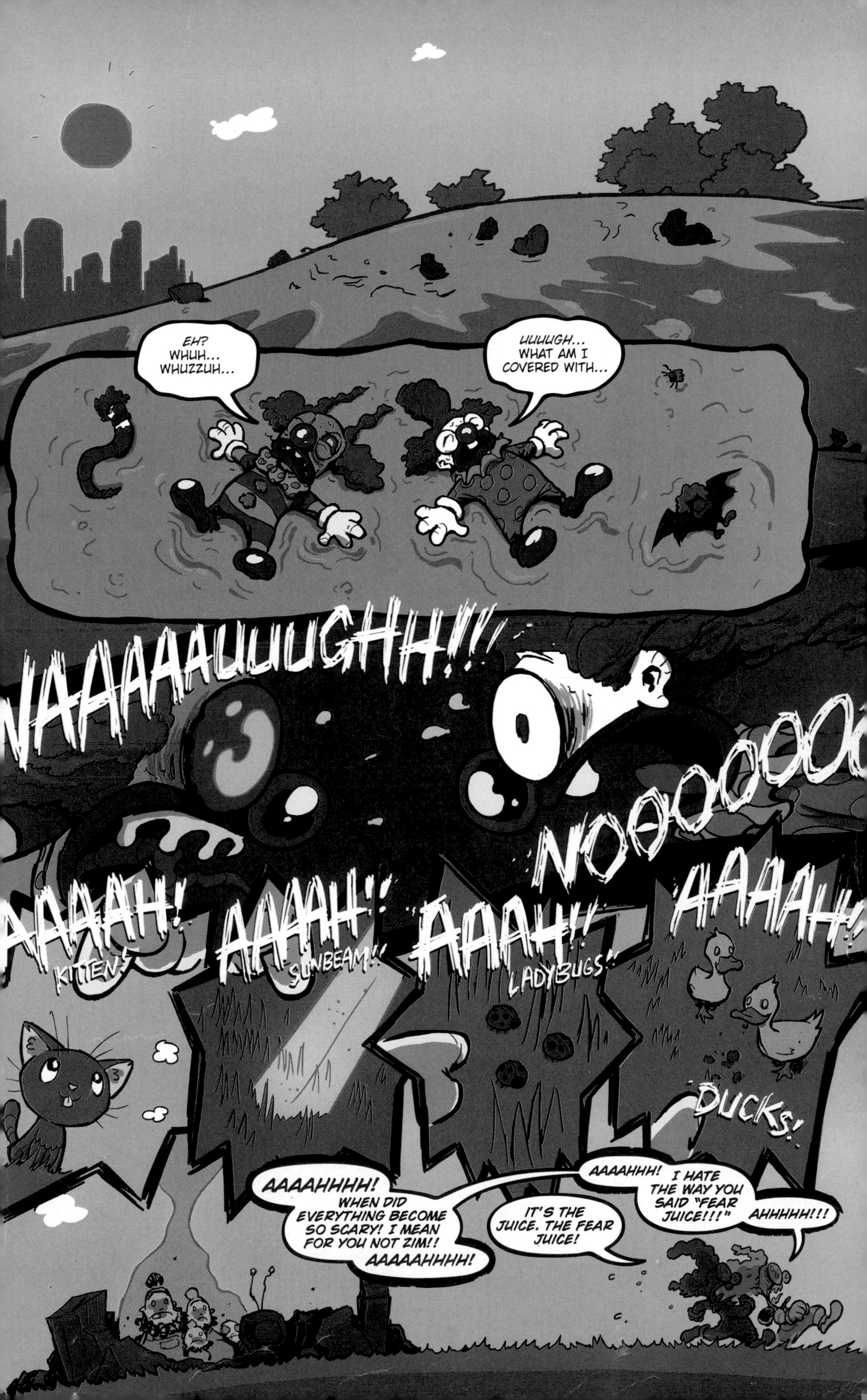
EH? WHUH... WHUZZUH...
UUUUGH... WHAT AM I COVERED WITH...
NAAAAAUUUGHH!!
NOOOOOOO
AAAAH! KITTEN!
AAAH! SUNBEAM!
AAAH! LADYBUGS!
AAAAH! DUCKS!
AAAAHHHH! WHEN DID EVERYTHING BECOME SO SCARY! I MEAN FOR YOU NOT ZIM!! AAAAAHHHH!
IT'S THE JUICE. THE FEAR JUICE!
AAAAHHH! I HATE THE WAY YOU SAID "FEAR JUICE!!!" AHHHHH!!!

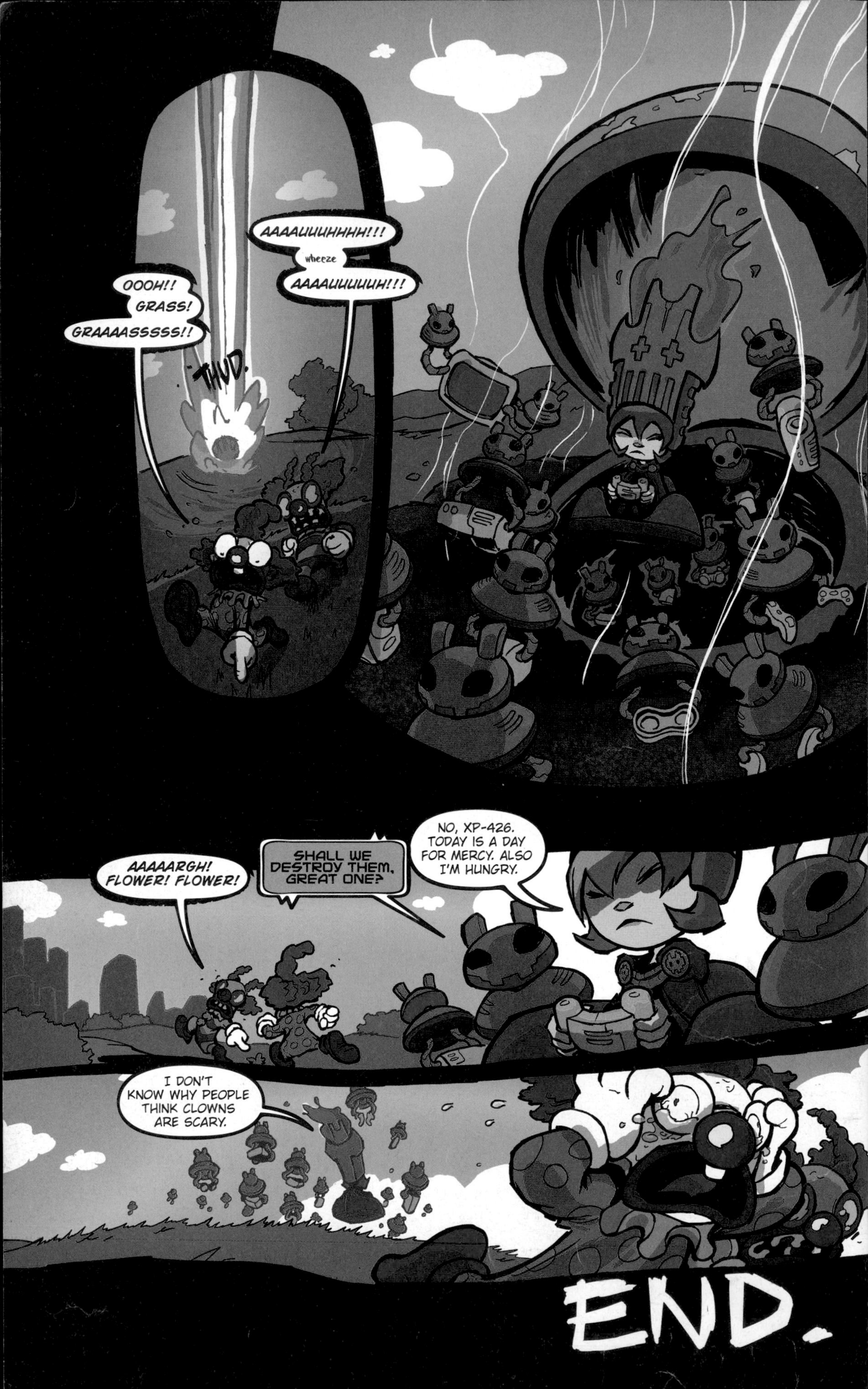

OOOH!! GRASS! GRAAAASSSSS!!
AAAAUUHHHHH!!! wheeze AAAAUUUUUH!!!
THUD.
AAAAARGH! FLOWER! FLOWER!
SHALL WE DESTROY THEM, GREAT ONE?
NO, XP-426. TODAY IS A DAY FOR MERCY. ALSO I'M HUNGRY.
I DON'T KNOW WHY PEOPLE THINK CLOWNS ARE SCARY.
END.

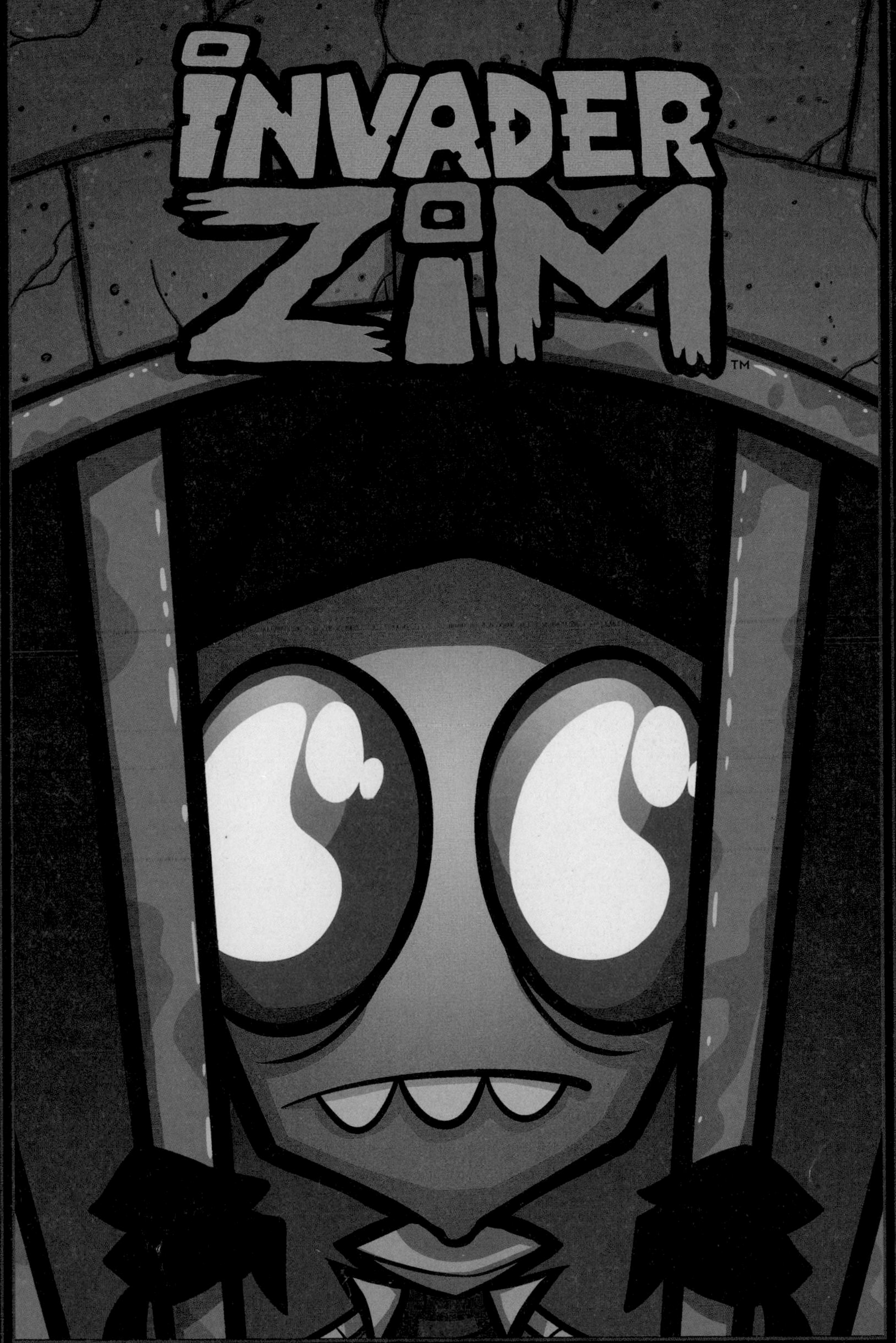
INVADER ZIM™

CHAPTER: 2

illustration by WARREN WUCINICH

Hold onto your seats, everyone! I'm Recap Kid and I'm back! Was I ever even gone? I DUNNO! I mean, I went to go get some chips, and a lot can happen during that time, right? HA HA PROBABLY! Anyway, I won't bore you with that, I'll EXCITE you with the latest ZIM comics! Last issue was about Dib and ZIM trying to scare the pants off each other! I'm not sure that ZIM wears pants, or if they can be scared off... CAN THEY? (I ACTUALLY DON'T KNOW, PLEASE TELL ME!) This next issue is all about ZIM and Dib again, except they've BOTH been kidnapped by aliens! How many times are aliens gonna show up to kidnap someone, anyway? I ate too many chips, guys.

Recap Kid by WARREN WUCINICH

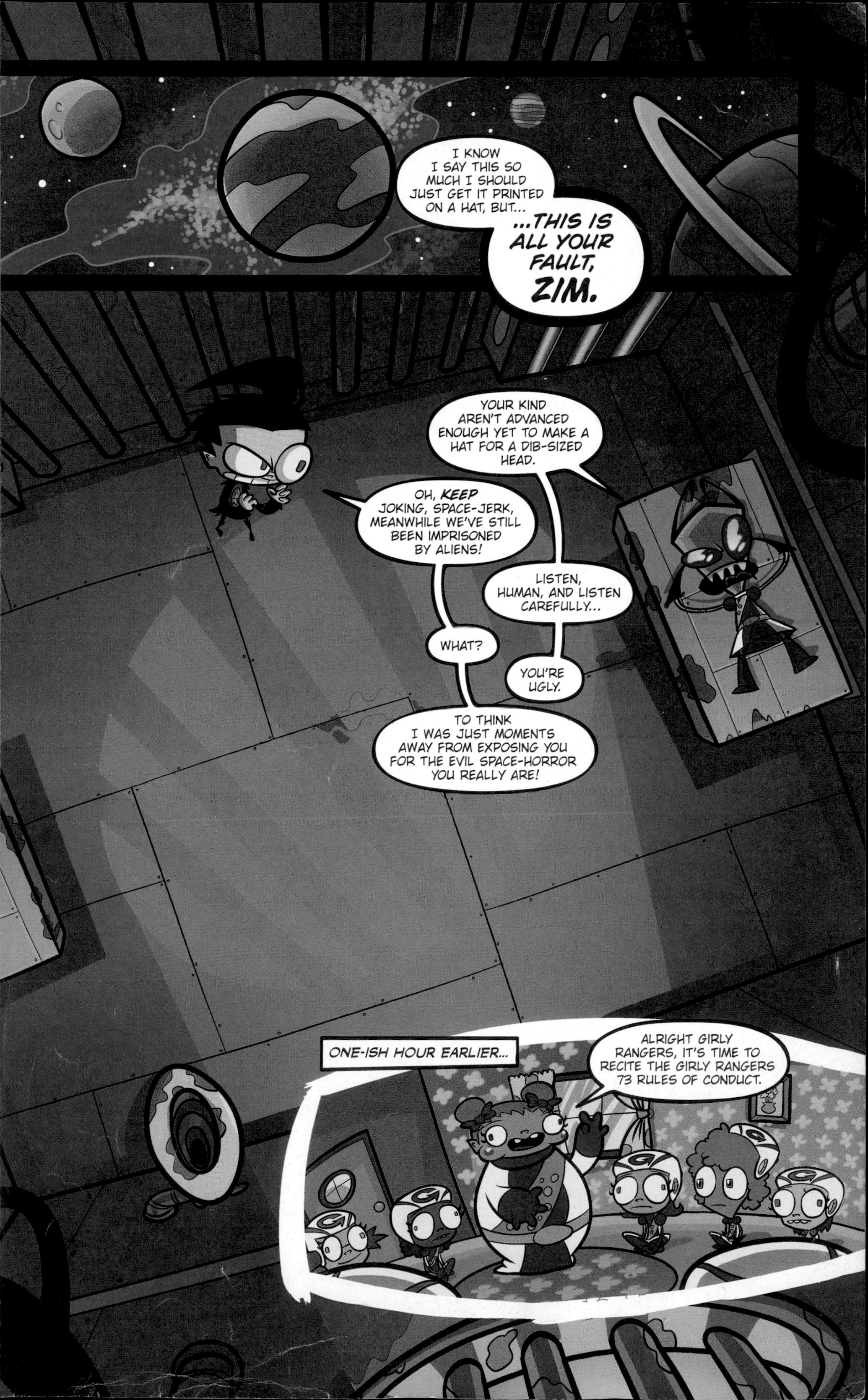
I KNOW I SAY THIS SO MUCH I SHOULD JUST GET IT PRINTED ON A HAT, BUT... ...THIS IS ALL YOUR FAULT, ZIM.
YOUR KIND AREN'T ADVANCED ENOUGH YET TO MAKE A HAT FOR A DIB-SIZED HEAD.
OH, KEEP JOKING, SPACE-JERK, MEANWHILE WE'VE STILL BEEN IMPRISONED BY ALIENS!
LISTEN, HUMAN, AND LISTEN CAREFULLY...
WHAT?
YOU'RE UGLY.
TO THINK I WAS JUST MOMENTS AWAY FROM EXPOSING YOU FOR THE EVIL SPACE-HORROR YOU REALLY ARE!
ONE-ISH HOUR EARLIER...
ALRIGHT GIRLY RANGERS, IT'S TIME TO RECITE THE GIRLY RANGERS 73 RULES OF CONDUCT.

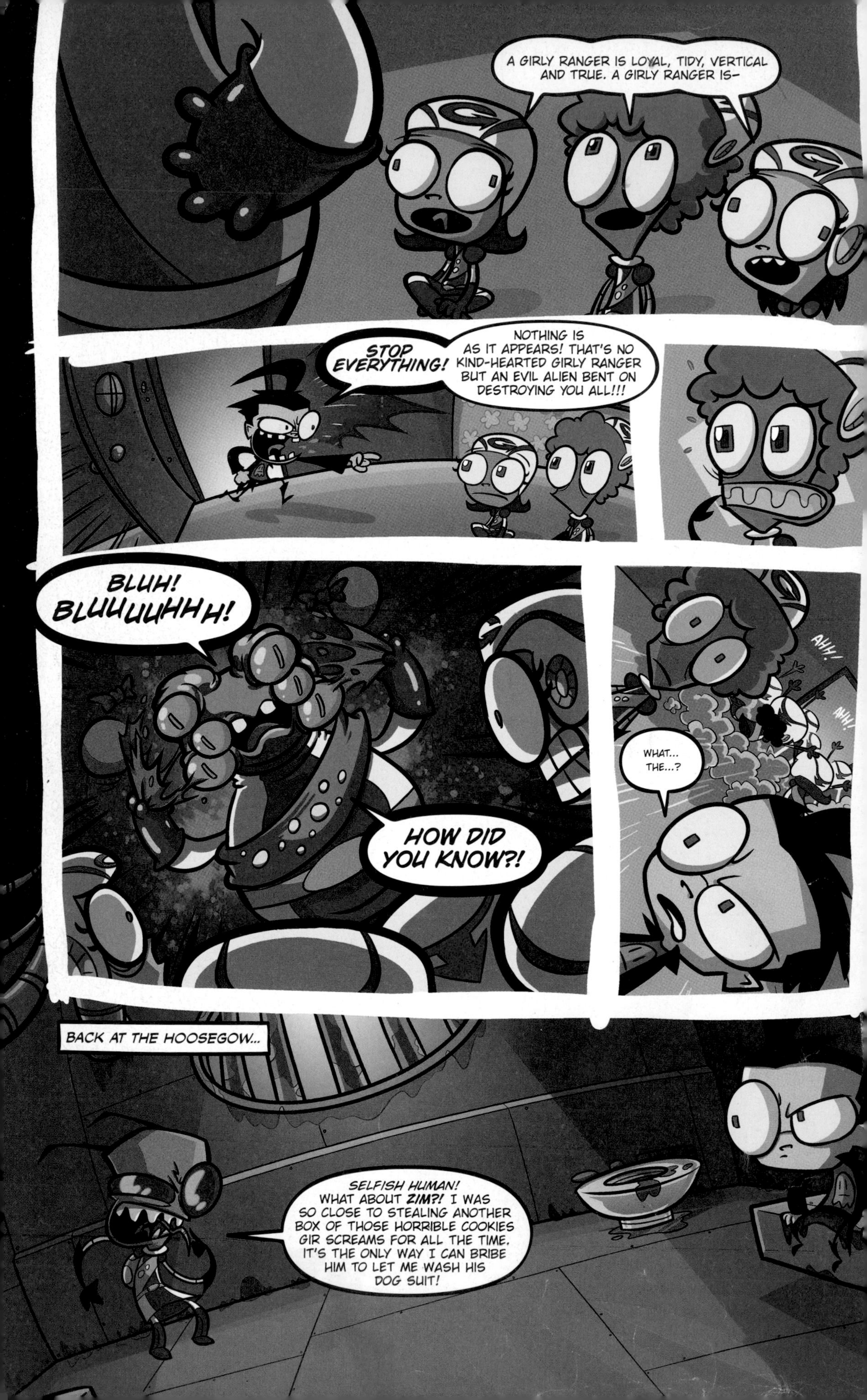
A GIRLY RANGER IS LOYAL, TIDY, VERTICAL AND TRUE. A GIRLY RANGER IS–
STOP EVERYTHING!
NOTHING IS AS IT APPEARS! THAT'S NO KIND-HEARTED GIRLY RANGER BUT AN EVIL ALIEN BENT ON DESTROYING YOU ALL!!!
BLUH! BLUUUUHHH!
HOW DID YOU KNOW?!
AHH!
AHH!
WHAT... THE...?
BACK AT THE HOOSEGOW...
SELFISH HUMAN! WHAT ABOUT ZIM?! I WAS SO CLOSE TO STEALING ANOTHER BOX OF THOSE HORRIBLE COOKIES GIR SCREAMS FOR ALL THE TIME. IT'S THE ONLY WAY I CAN BRIBE HIM TO LET ME WASH HIS DOG SUIT!

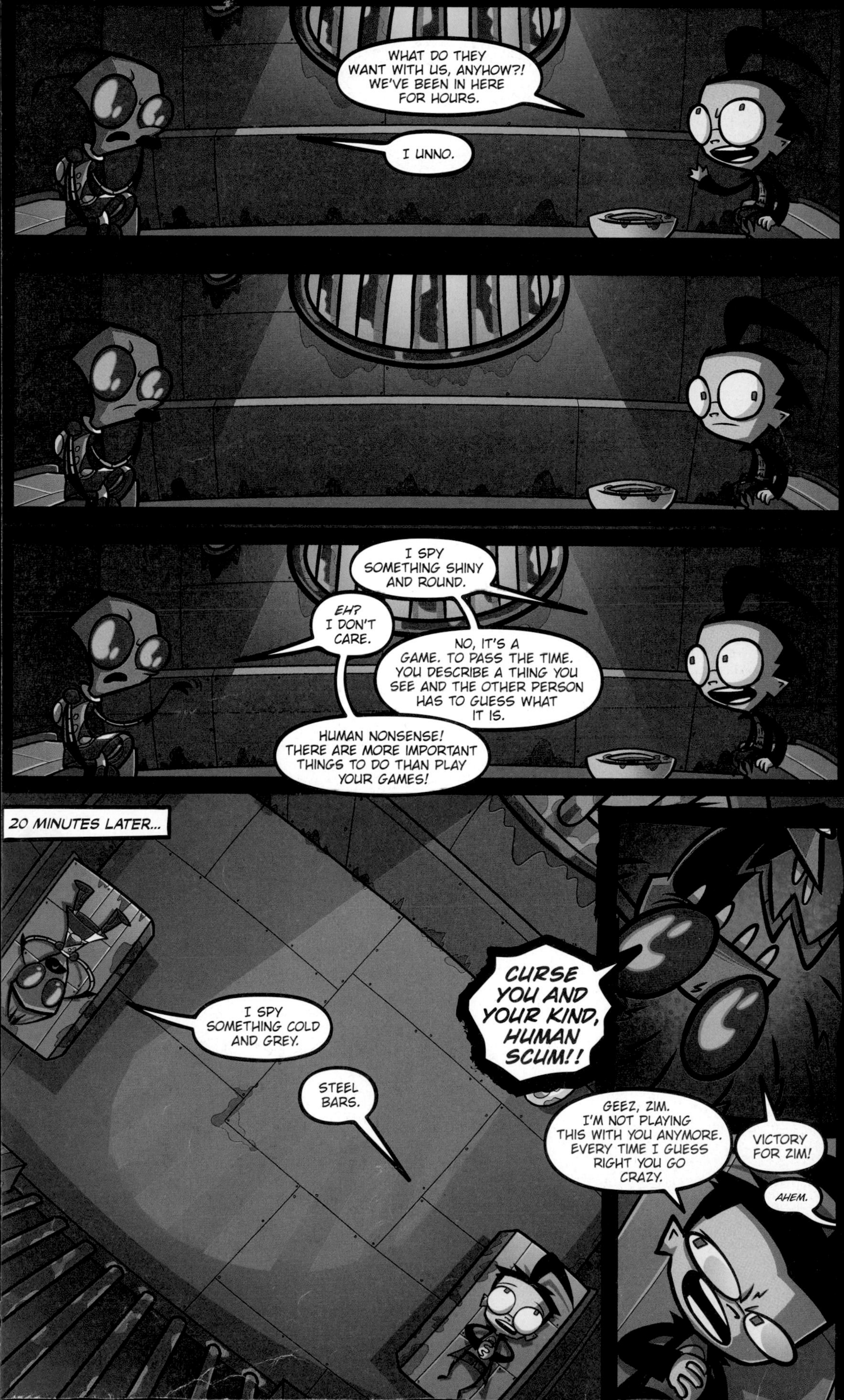
WHAT DO THEY WANT WITH US, ANYHOW?! WE'VE BEEN IN HERE FOR HOURS.
I UNNO.
I SPY SOMETHING SHINY AND ROUND.
EH? I DON'T CARE.
NO, IT'S A GAME. TO PASS THE TIME. YOU DESCRIBE A THING YOU SEE AND THE OTHER PERSON HAS TO GUESS WHAT IT IS.
HUMAN NONSENSE! THERE ARE MORE IMPORTANT THINGS TO DO THAN PLAY YOUR GAMES!
20 MINUTES LATER...
I SPY SOMETHING COLD AND GREY.
STEEL BARS.
CURSE YOU AND YOUR KIND, HUMAN SCUM!!
GEEZ, ZIM. I'M NOT PLAYING THIS WITH YOU ANYMORE. EVERY TIME I GUESS RIGHT YOU GO CRAZY.
VICTORY FOR ZIM!
AHEM.

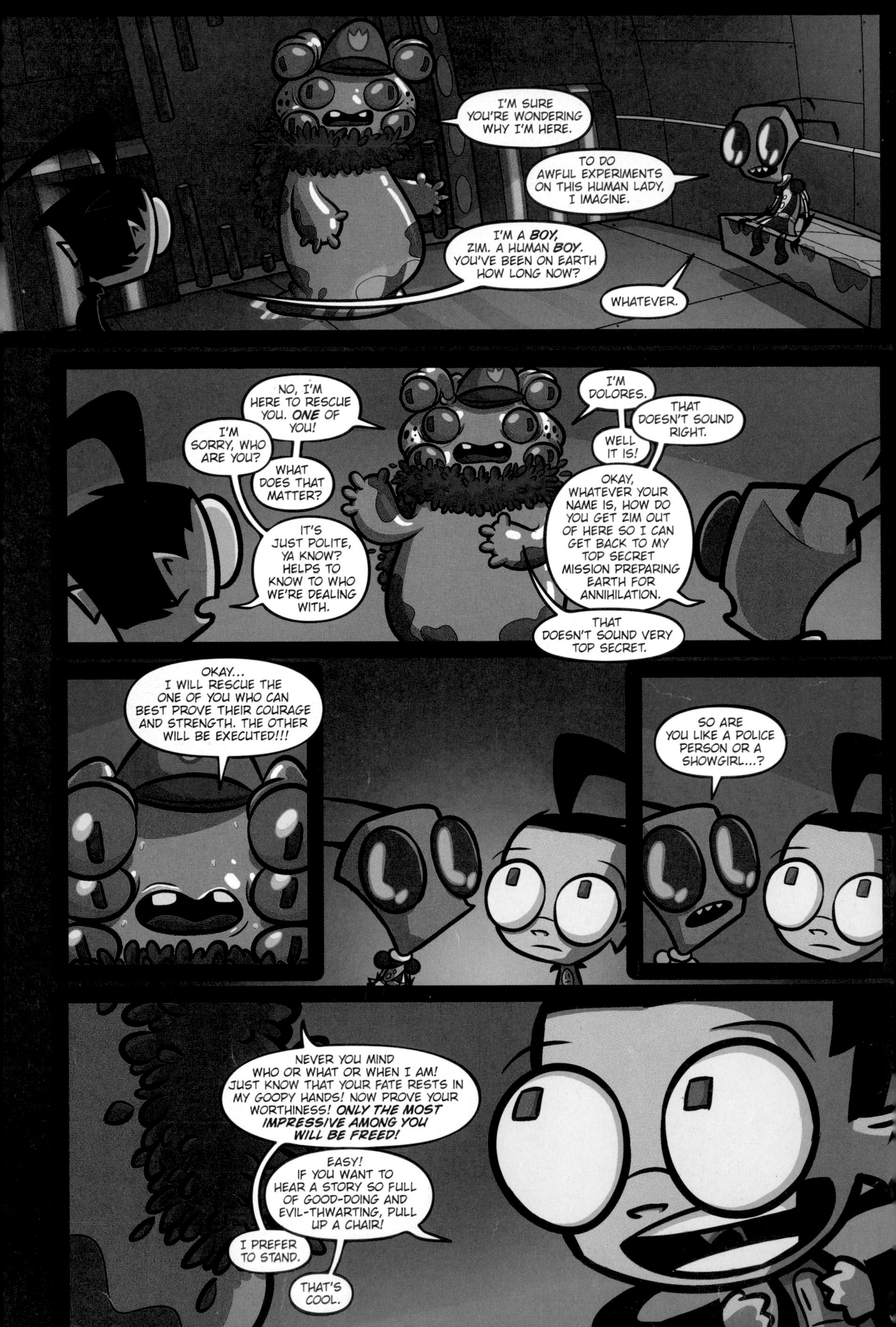
I'M SURE YOU'RE WONDERING WHY I'M HERE.
TO DO AWFUL EXPERIMENTS ON THIS HUMAN LADY, I IMAGINE.
I'M A BOY, ZIM. A HUMAN BOY. YOU'VE BEEN ON EARTH HOW LONG NOW?
WHATEVER.
NO, I'M HERE TO RESCUE YOU. ONE OF YOU!
I'M SORRY, WHO ARE YOU?
WHAT DOES THAT MATTER?
IT'S JUST POLITE, YA KNOW? HELPS TO KNOW TO WHO WE'RE DEALING WITH.
I'M DOLORES.
THAT DOESN'T SOUND RIGHT.
WELL IT IS!
OKAY, WHATEVER YOUR NAME IS, HOW DO YOU GET ZIM OUT OF HERE SO I CAN GET BACK TO MY TOP SECRET MISSION PREPARING EARTH FOR ANNIHILATION.
THAT DOESN'T SOUND VERY TOP SECRET.
OKAY... I WILL RESCUE THE ONE OF YOU WHO CAN BEST PROVE THEIR COURAGE AND STRENGTH. THE OTHER WILL BE EXECUTED!!!
SO ARE YOU LIKE A POLICE PERSON OR A SHOWGIRL...?
NEVER YOU MIND WHO OR WHAT OR WHEN I AM! JUST KNOW THAT YOUR FATE RESTS IN MY GOOPY HANDS! NOW PROVE YOUR WORTHINESS! ONLY THE MOST IMPRESSIVE AMONG YOU WILL BE FREED!
EASY! IF YOU WANT TO HEAR A STORY SO FULL OF GOOD-DOING AND EVIL-THWARTING, PULL UP A CHAIR!
I PREFER TO STAND.
THAT'S COOL.

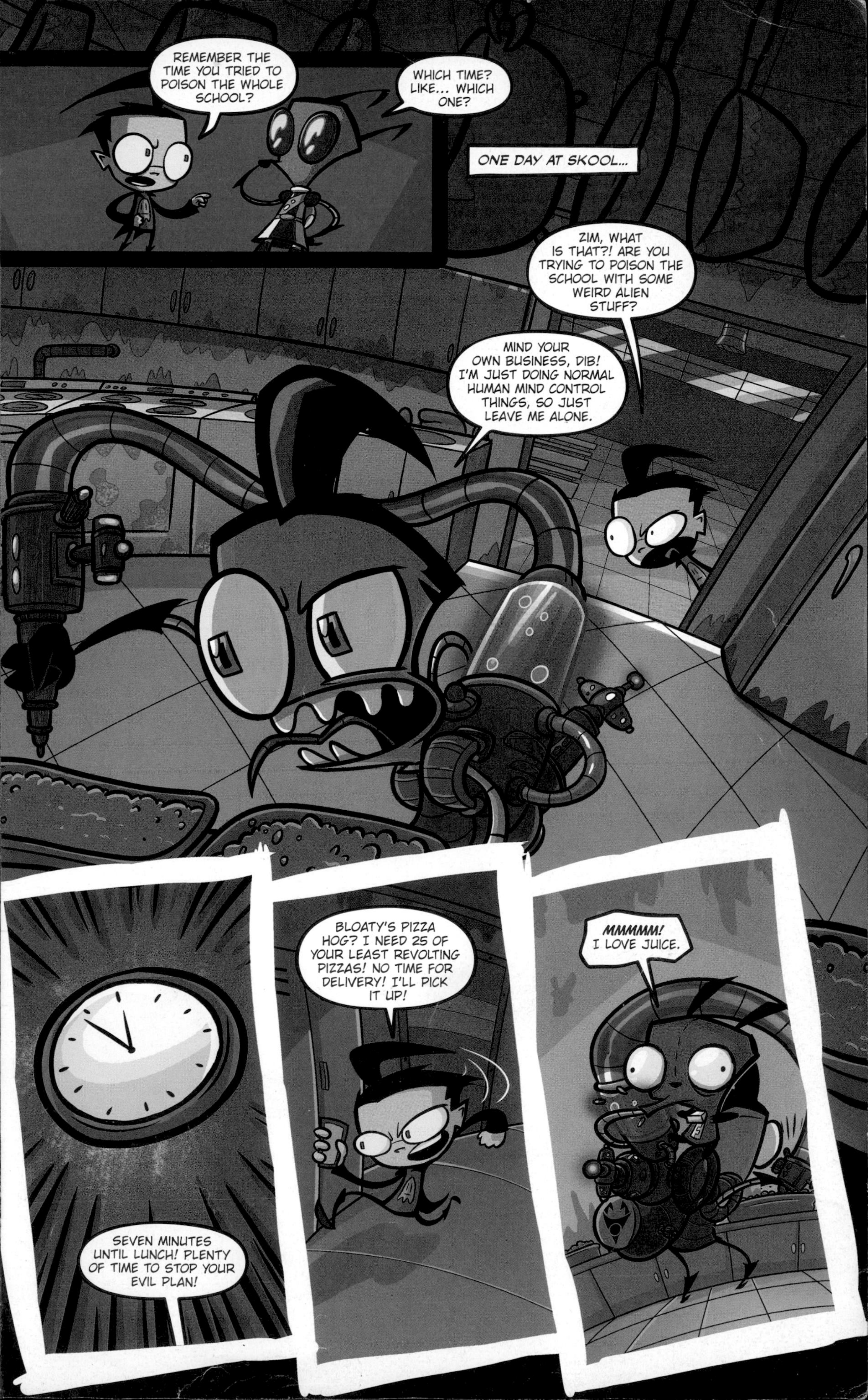
REMEMBER THE TIME YOU TRIED TO POISON THE WHOLE SCHOOL?
WHICH TIME? LIKE... WHICH ONE?
ONE DAY AT SKOOL...
ZIM, WHAT IS THAT?! ARE YOU TRYING TO POISON THE SCHOOL WITH SOME WEIRD ALIEN STUFF?
MIND YOUR OWN BUSINESS, DIB! I'M JUST DOING NORMAL HUMAN MIND CONTROL THINGS, SO JUST LEAVE ME ALONE.
SEVEN MINUTES UNTIL LUNCH! PLENTY OF TIME TO STOP YOUR EVIL PLAN!
BLOATY'S PIZZA HOG? I NEED 25 OF YOUR LEAST REVOLTING PIZZAS! NO TIME FOR DELIVERY! I'LL PICK IT UP!
MMMMM! I LOVE JUICE.

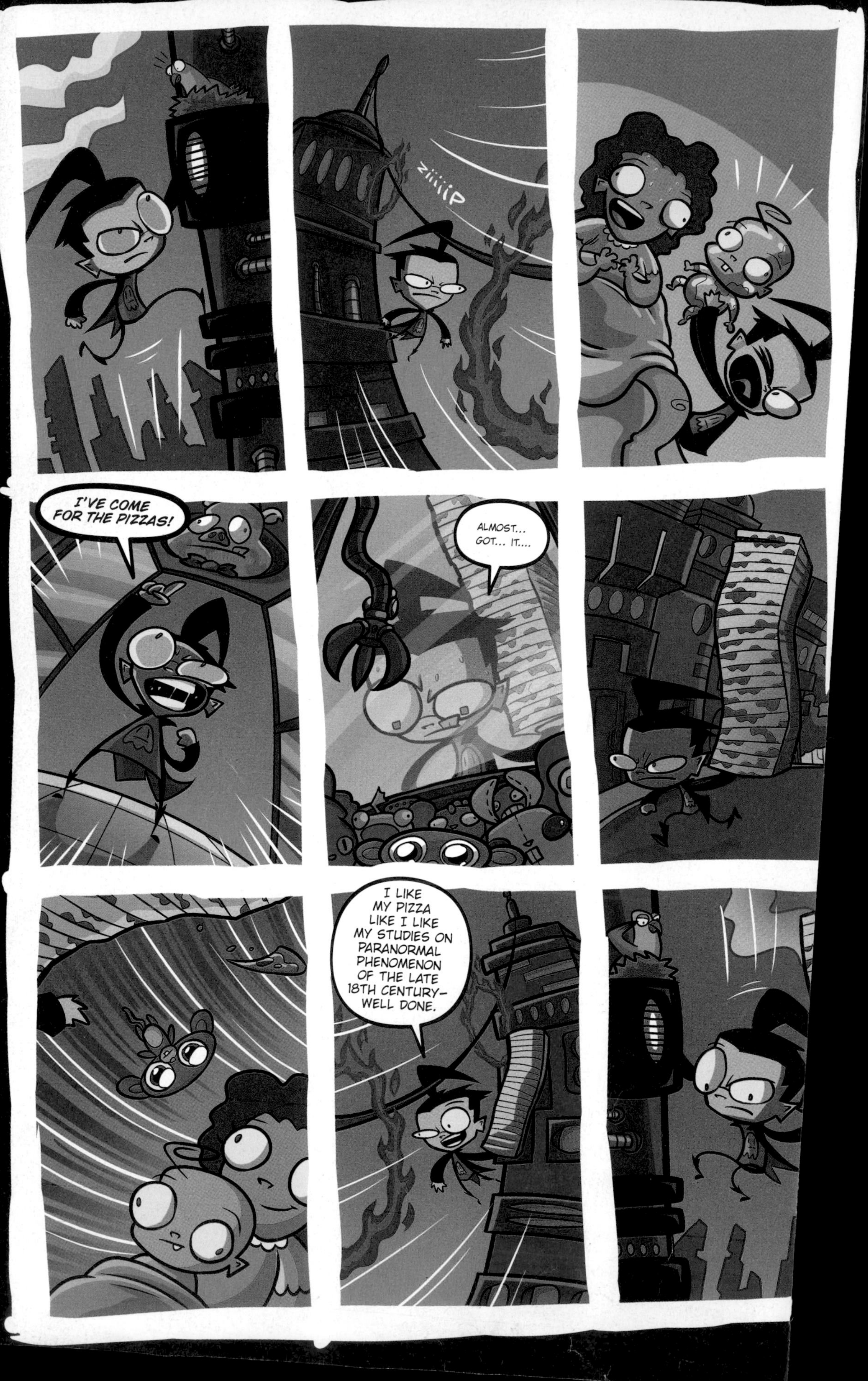
ZiiiiiP
I'VE COME FOR THE PIZZAS!
ALMOST... GOT... IT....
I LIKE MY PIZZA LIKE I LIKE MY STUDIES ON PARANORMAL PHENOMENON OF THE LATE 18TH CENTURY—WELL DONE.

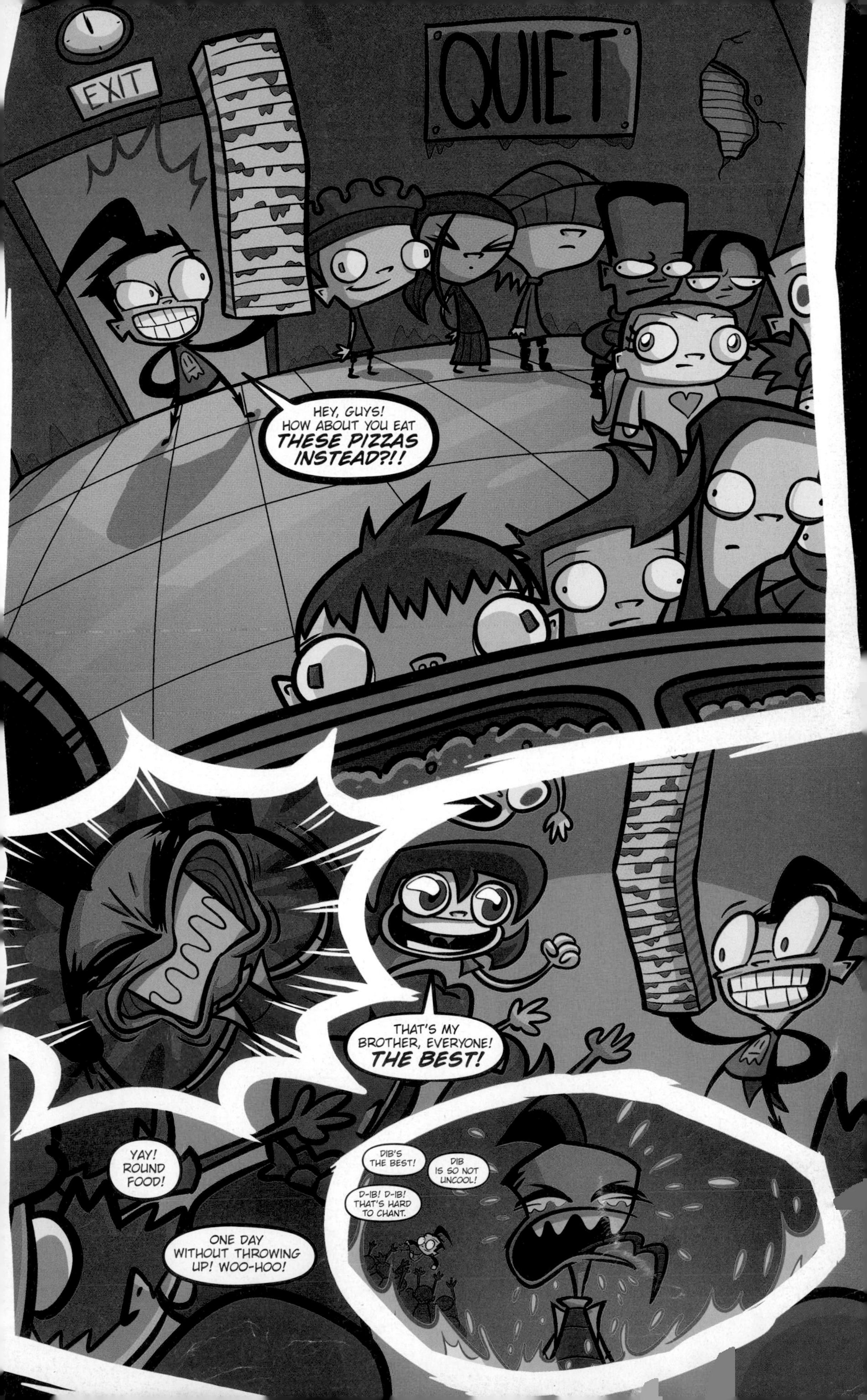
EXIT
QUIET
HEY, GUYS! HOW ABOUT YOU EAT THESE PIZZAS INSTEAD?!!
THAT'S MY BROTHER, EVERYONE! THE BEST!
YAY! ROUND FOOD!
ONE DAY WITHOUT THROWING UP! WOO-HOO!
DIB'S THE BEST!
DIB IS SO NOT UNCOOL!
D-IB! D-IB! THAT'S HARD TO CHANT.

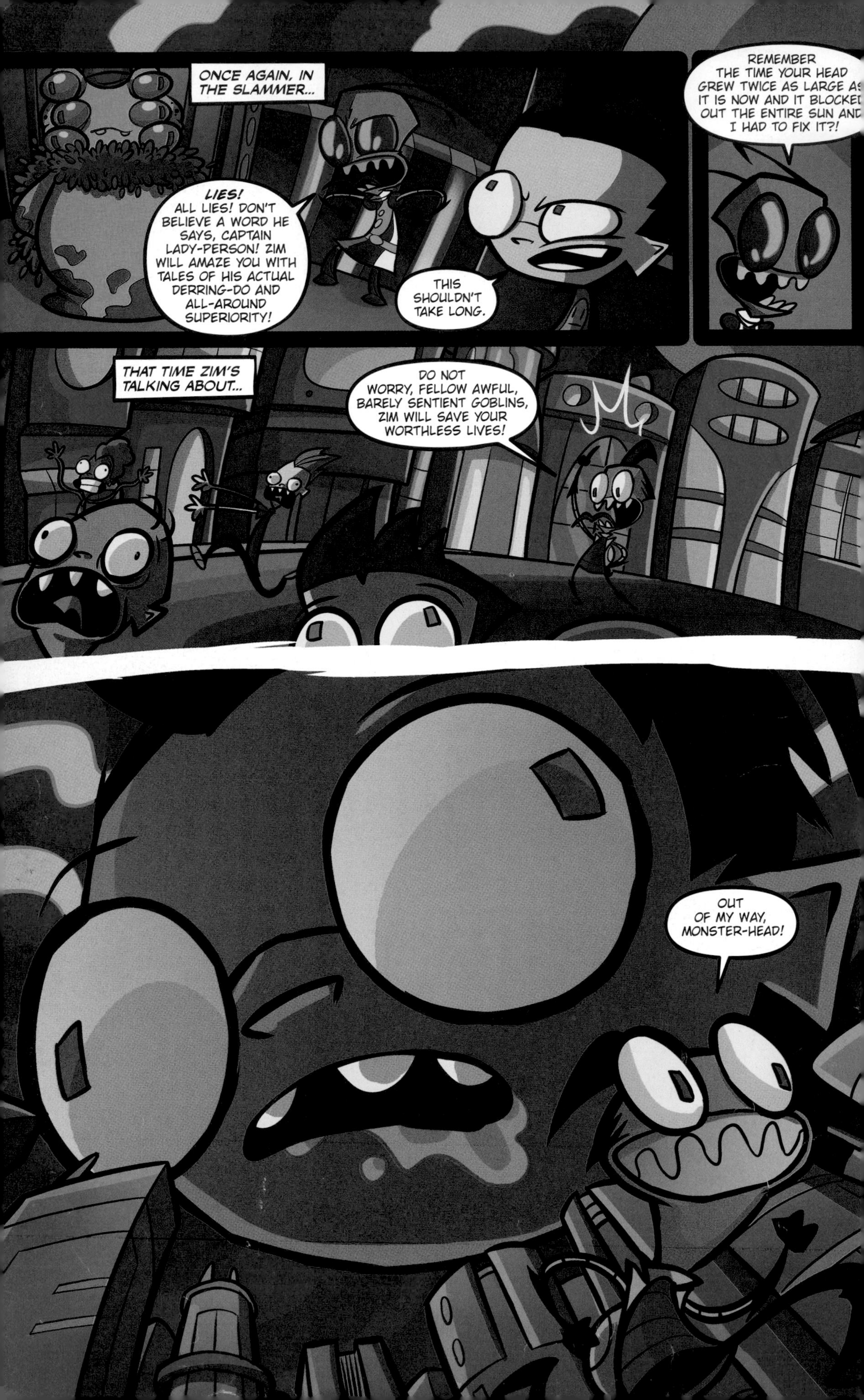
ONCE AGAIN, IN THE SLAMMER...
LIES! ALL LIES! DON'T BELIEVE A WORD HE SAYS, CAPTAIN LADY-PERSON! ZIM WILL AMAZE YOU WITH TALES OF HIS ACTUAL DERRING-DO AND ALL-AROUND SUPERIORITY!
THIS SHOULDN'T TAKE LONG.
REMEMBER THE TIME YOUR HEAD GREW TWICE AS LARGE AS IT IS NOW AND IT BLOCKED OUT THE ENTIRE SUN AND I HAD TO FIX IT?!
THAT TIME ZIM'S TALKING ABOUT...
DO NOT WORRY, FELLOW AWFUL, BARELY SENTIENT GOBLINS, ZIM WILL SAVE YOUR WORTHLESS LIVES!
OUT OF MY WAY, MONSTER-HEAD!

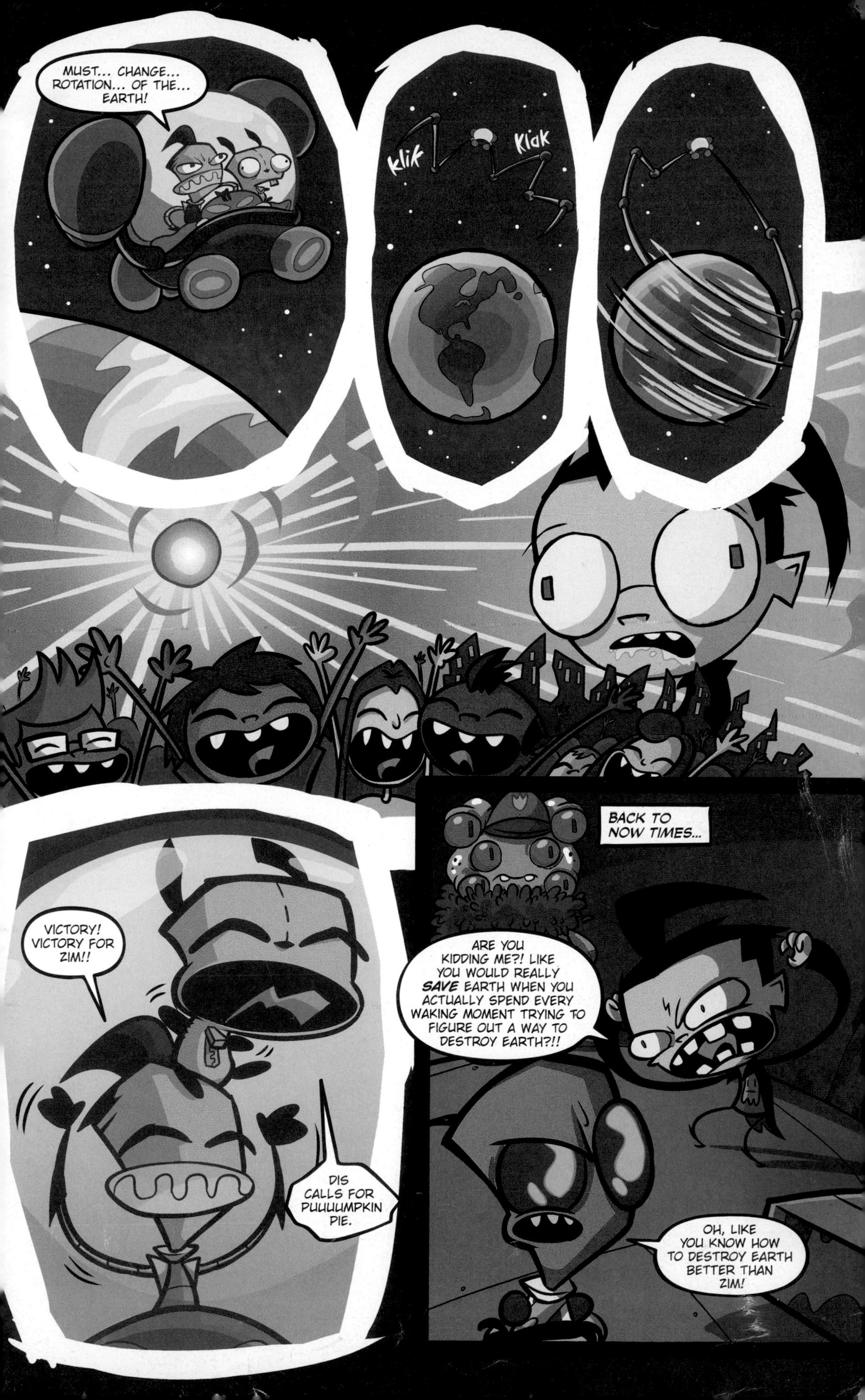
MUST... CHANGE... ROTATION... OF THE... EARTH!
klik
klak
VICTORY! VICTORY FOR ZIM!!
DIS CALLS FOR PUUUUMPKIN PIE.
BACK TO NOW TIMES...
ARE YOU KIDDING ME?! LIKE YOU WOULD REALLY SAVE EARTH WHEN YOU ACTUALLY SPEND EVERY WAKING MOMENT TRYING TO FIGURE OUT A WAY TO DESTROY EARTH?!!
OH, LIKE YOU KNOW HOW TO DESTROY EARTH BETTER THAN ZIM!

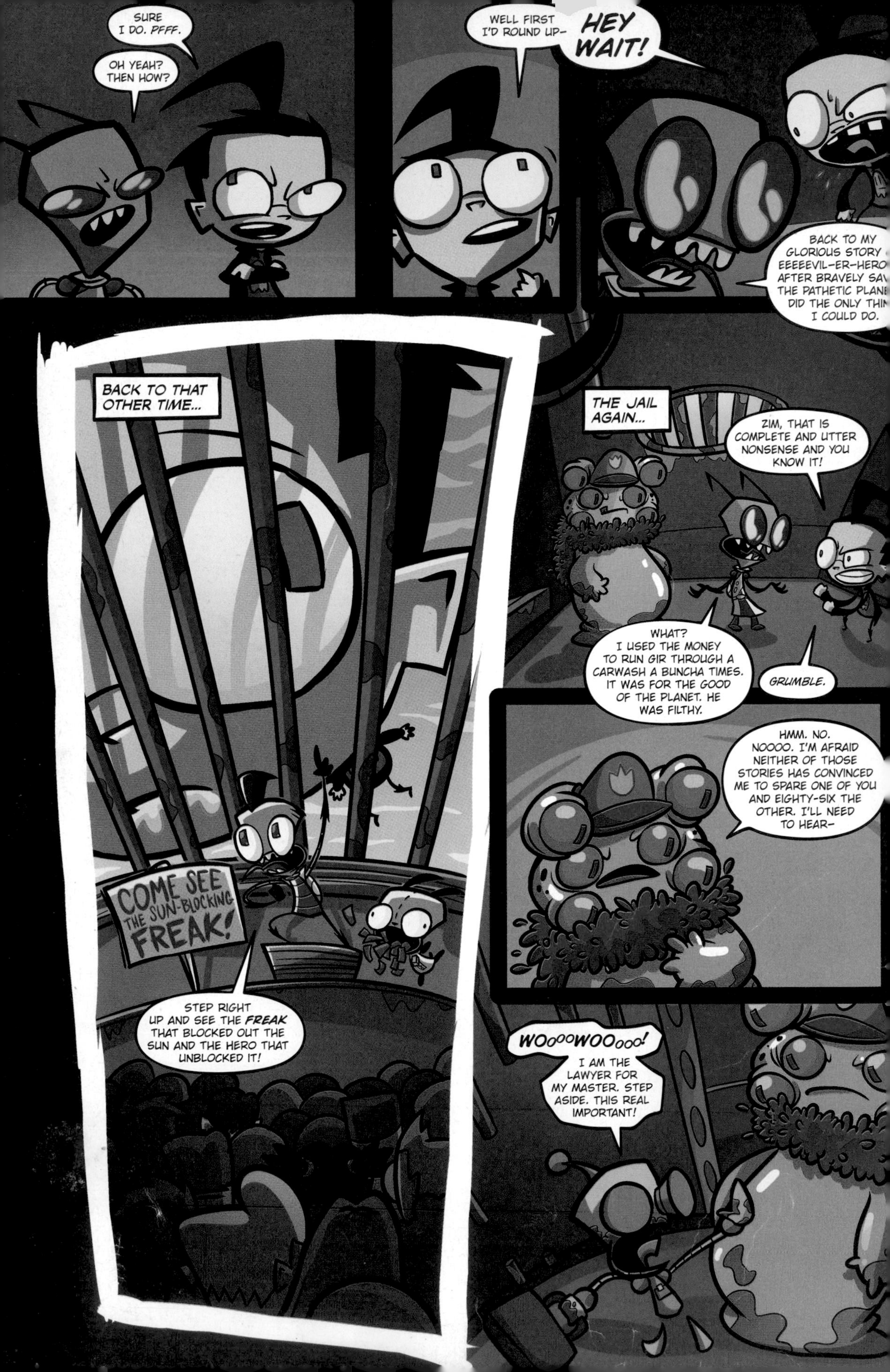
SURE I DO. PFFF.
OH YEAH? THEN HOW?
WELL FIRST I'D ROUND UP-
HEY WAIT!
BACK TO MY GLORIOUS STORY EEEEEVIL-ER-HERO AFTER BRAVELY SAV THE PATHETIC PLANE DID THE ONLY THIN I COULD DO.
BACK TO THAT OTHER TIME...
COME SEE THE SUN-BLOCKING FREAK!
STEP RIGHT UP AND SEE THE FREAK THAT BLOCKED OUT THE SUN AND THE HERO THAT UNBLOCKED IT!
THE JAIL AGAIN...
ZIM, THAT IS COMPLETE AND UTTER NONSENSE AND YOU KNOW IT!
WHAT? I USED THE MONEY TO RUN GIR THROUGH A CARWASH A BUNCHA TIMES. IT WAS FOR THE GOOD OF THE PLANET. HE WAS FILTHY.
GRUMBLE.
HMM. NO. NOOOO. I'M AFRAID NEITHER OF THOSE STORIES HAS CONVINCED ME TO SPARE ONE OF YOU AND EIGHTY-SIX THE OTHER. I'LL NEED TO HEAR-
WOoooWOOooo!
I AM THE LAWYER FOR MY MASTER. STEP ASIDE. THIS REAL IMPORTANT!

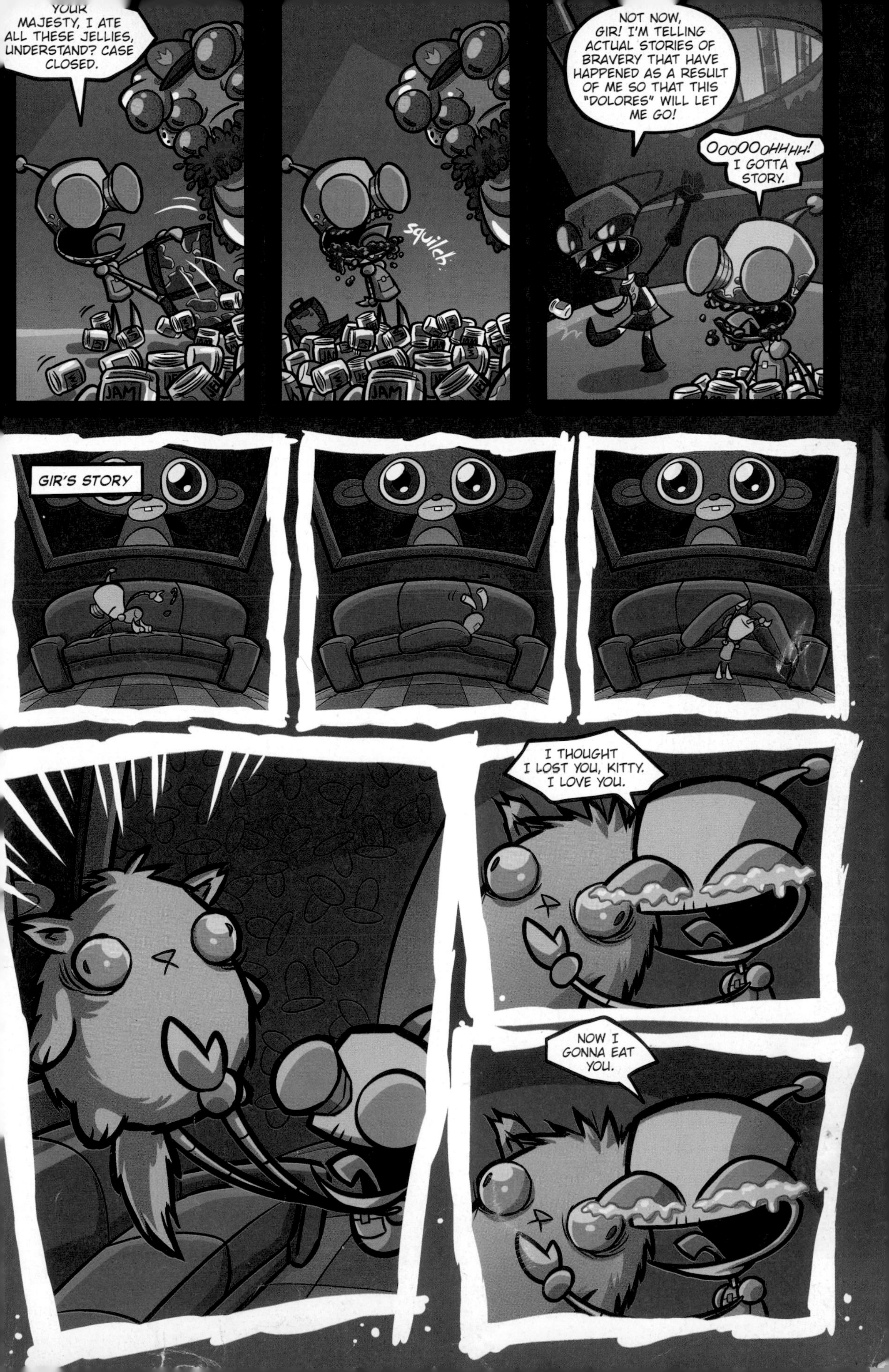
YOUR MAJESTY, I ATE ALL THESE JELLIES, UNDERSTAND? CASE CLOSED.
squilch
NOT NOW, GIR! I'M TELLING ACTUAL STORIES OF BRAVERY THAT HAVE HAPPENED AS A RESULT OF ME SO THAT THIS "DOLORES" WILL LET ME GO!
OooOOoHHHH! I GOTTA STORY.
GIR'S STORY
I THOUGHT I LOST YOU, KITTY. I LOVE YOU.
NOW I GONNA EAT YOU.

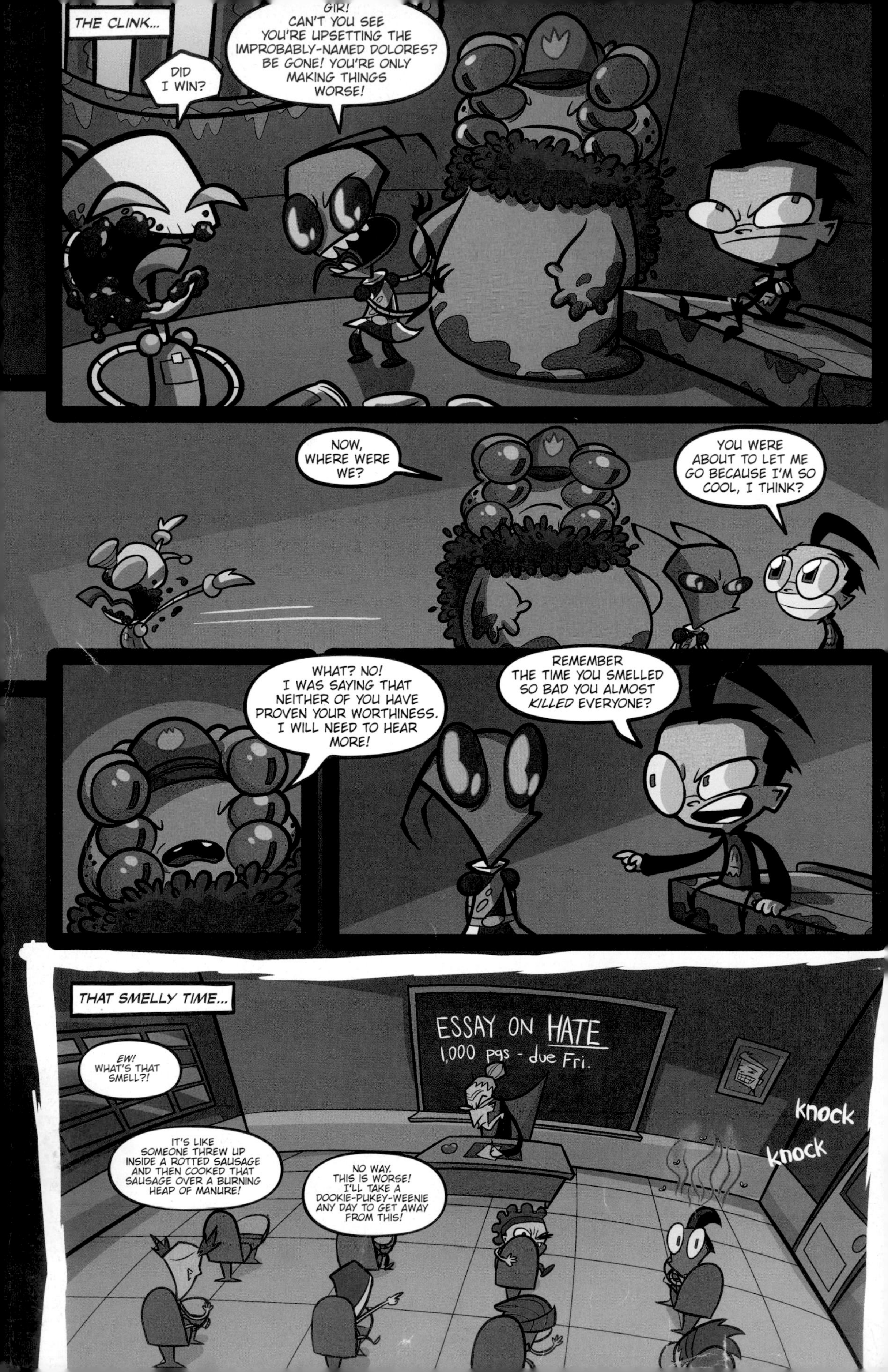
THE CLINK...
DID I WIN?
GIR! CAN'T YOU SEE YOU'RE UPSETTING THE IMPROBABLY-NAMED DOLORES? BE GONE! YOU'RE ONLY MAKING THINGS WORSE!
NOW, WHERE WERE WE?
YOU WERE ABOUT TO LET ME GO BECAUSE I'M SO COOL, I THINK?
WHAT? NO! I WAS SAYING THAT NEITHER OF YOU HAVE PROVEN YOUR WORTHINESS. I WILL NEED TO HEAR MORE!
REMEMBER THE TIME YOU SMELLED SO BAD YOU ALMOST KILLED EVERYONE?
THAT SMELLY TIME...
ESSAY ON HATE
1,000 pgs - due Fri.
EW! WHAT'S THAT SMELL?!
IT'S LIKE SOMEONE THREW UP INSIDE A ROTTED SAUSAGE AND THEN COOKED THAT SAUSAGE OVER A BURNING HEAP OF MANURE!
NO WAY. THIS IS WORSE! I'LL TAKE A DOOKIE-PUKEY-WEENIE ANY DAY TO GET AWAY FROM THIS!
knock
knock

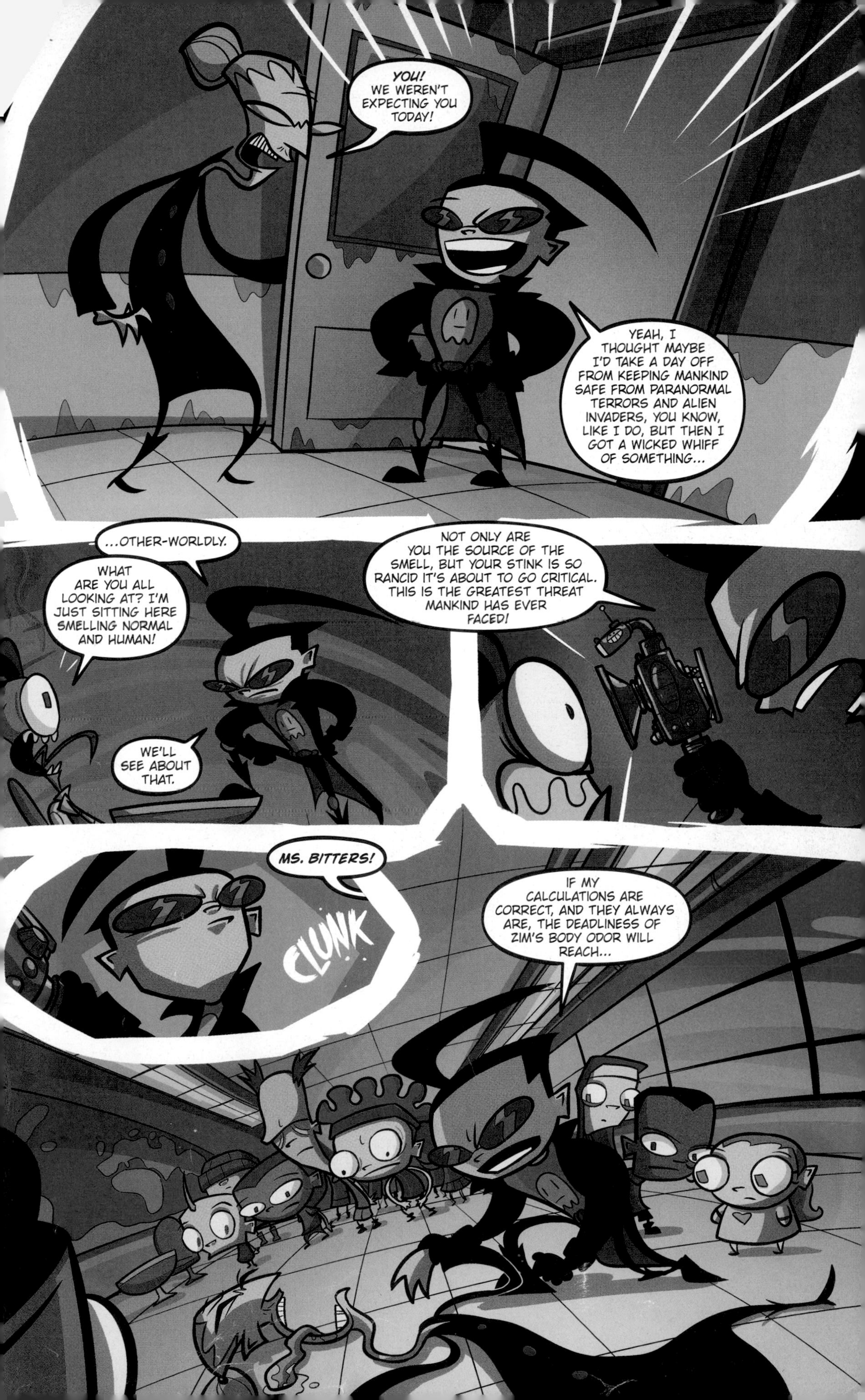
YOU!
WE WEREN'T EXPECTING YOU TODAY!
YEAH, I THOUGHT MAYBE I'D TAKE A DAY OFF FROM KEEPING MANKIND SAFE FROM PARANORMAL TERRORS AND ALIEN INVADERS, YOU KNOW, LIKE I DO, BUT THEN I GOT A WICKED WHIFF OF SOMETHING...
...OTHER-WORLDLY.
WHAT ARE YOU ALL LOOKING AT? I'M JUST SITTING HERE SMELLING NORMAL AND HUMAN!
WE'LL SEE ABOUT THAT.
NOT ONLY ARE YOU THE SOURCE OF THE SMELL, BUT YOUR STINK IS SO RANCID IT'S ABOUT TO GO CRITICAL. THIS IS THE GREATEST THREAT MANKIND HAS EVER FACED!
MS. BITTERS!
CLUNK
IF MY CALCULATIONS ARE CORRECT, AND THEY ALWAYS ARE, THE DEADLINESS OF ZIM'S BODY ODOR WILL REACH...

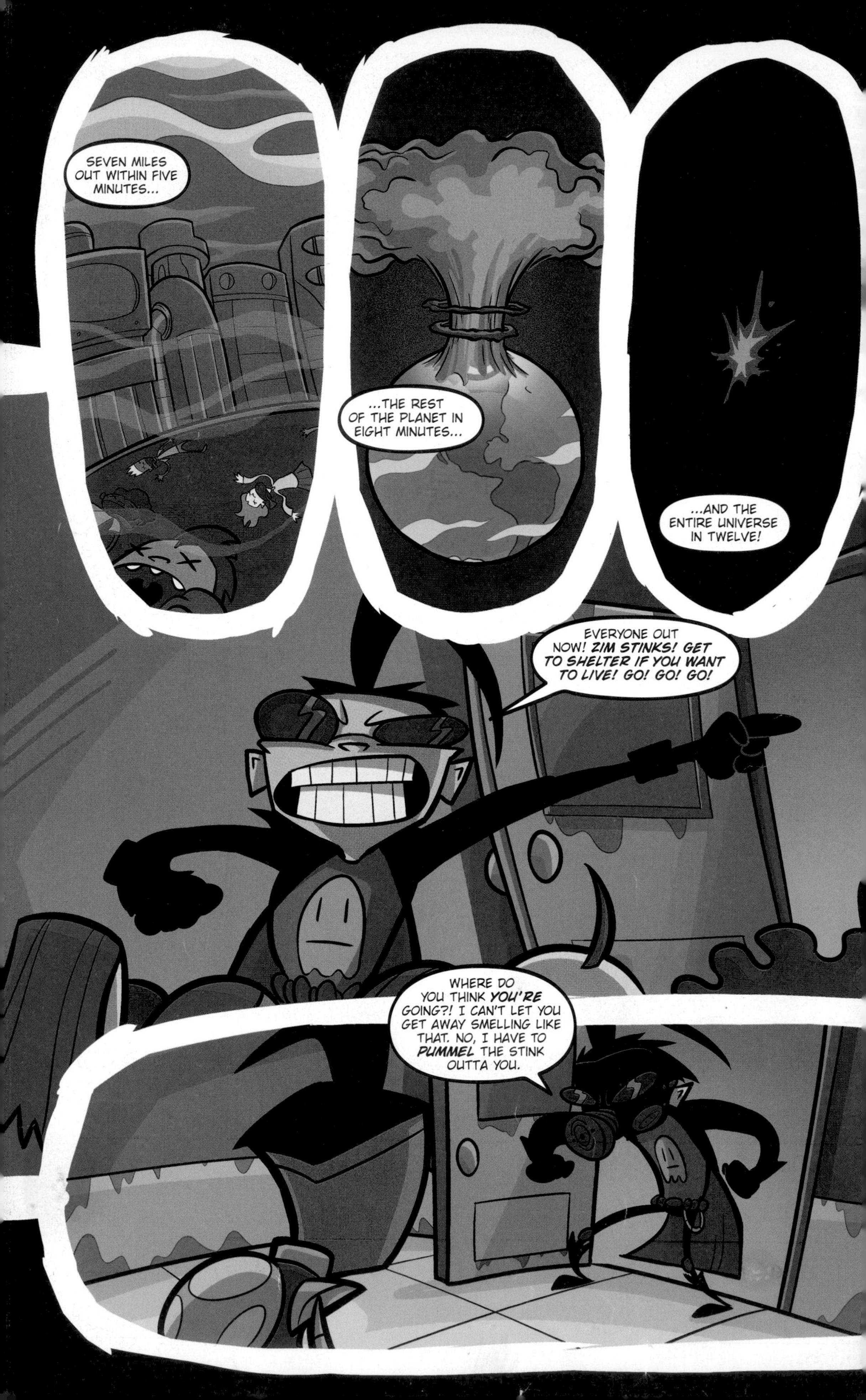
SEVEN MILES OUT WITHIN FIVE MINUTES...
...THE REST OF THE PLANET IN EIGHT MINUTES...
...AND THE ENTIRE UNIVERSE IN TWELVE!
EVERYONE OUT NOW! ZIM STINKS! GET TO SHELTER IF YOU WANT TO LIVE! GO! GO! GO!
WHERE DO YOU THINK YOU'RE GOING?! I CAN'T LET YOU GET AWAY SMELLING LIKE THAT. NO, I HAVE TO PUMMEL THE STINK OUTTA YOU.

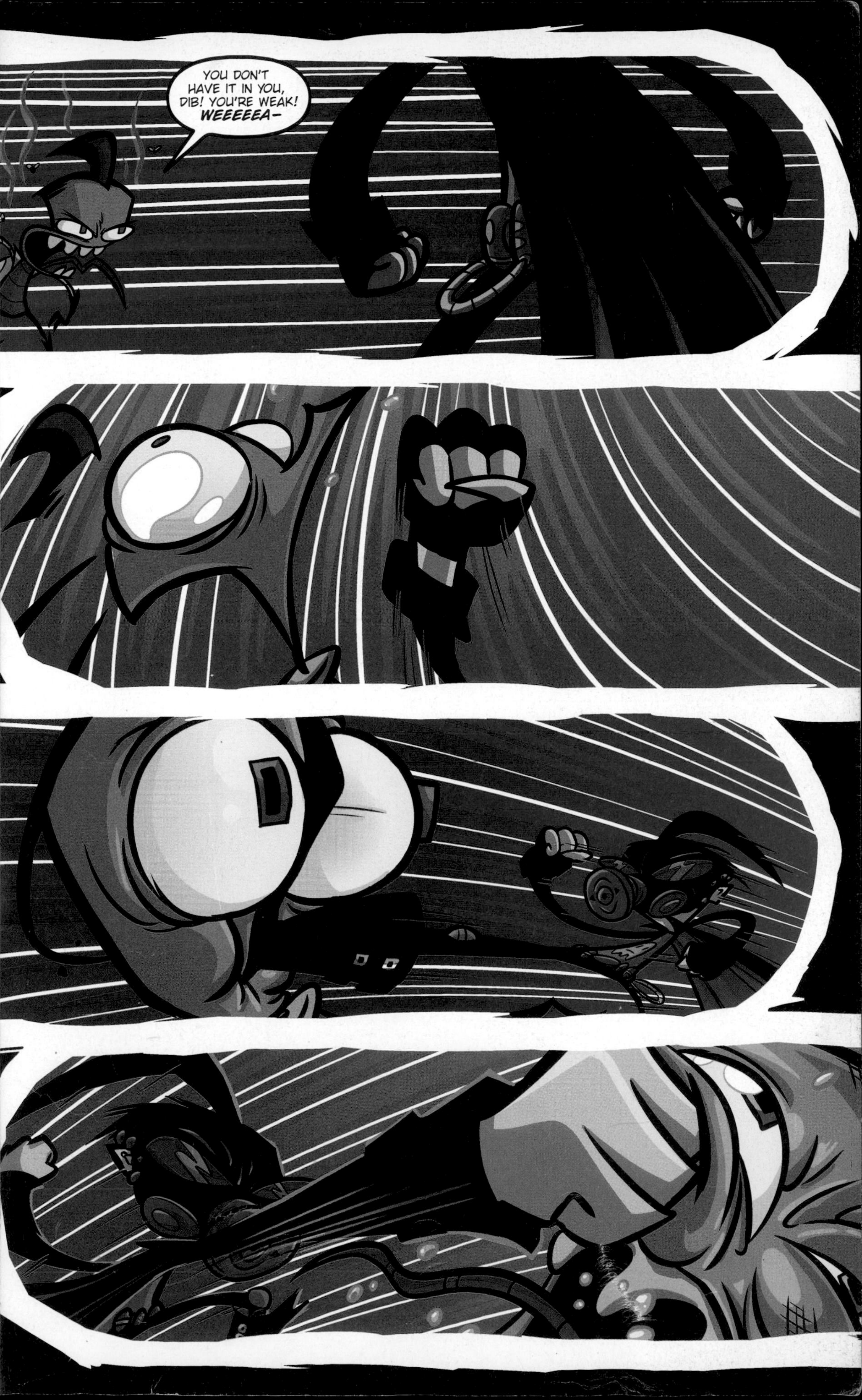
YOU DON'T HAVE IT IN YOU, DIB! YOU'RE WEAK! WEEEEEA-

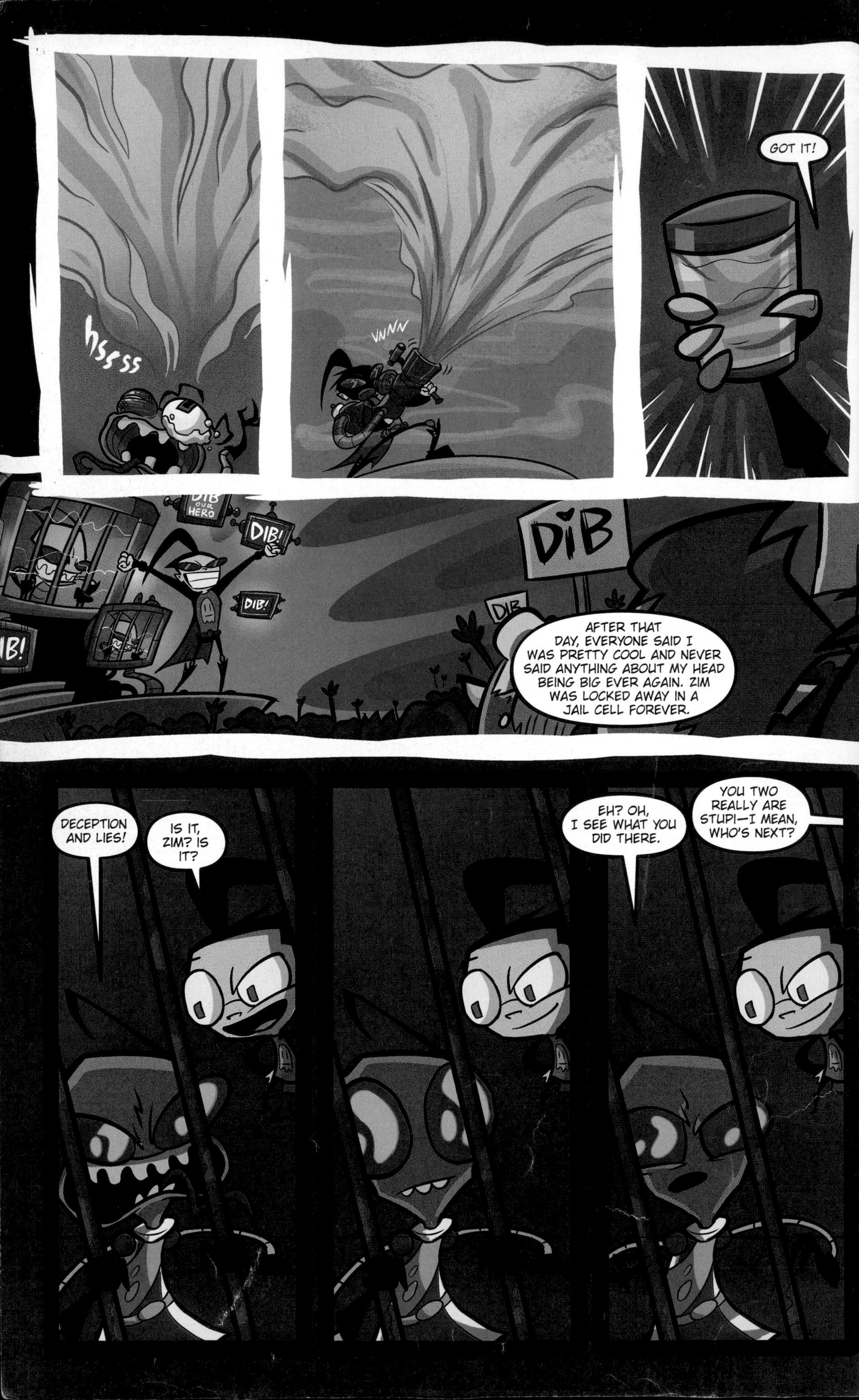
hssss
VNNN
GOT IT!
DIB OUR HERO
DIB!
DIB!
DIB
DIB
AFTER THAT DAY, EVERYONE SAID I WAS PRETTY COOL AND NEVER SAID ANYTHING ABOUT MY HEAD BEING BIG EVER AGAIN. ZIM WAS LOCKED AWAY IN A JAIL CELL FOREVER.
DECEPTION AND LIES!
IS IT, ZIM? IS IT?
EH? OH, I SEE WHAT YOU DID THERE.
YOU TWO REALLY ARE STUPI—I MEAN, WHO'S NEXT?

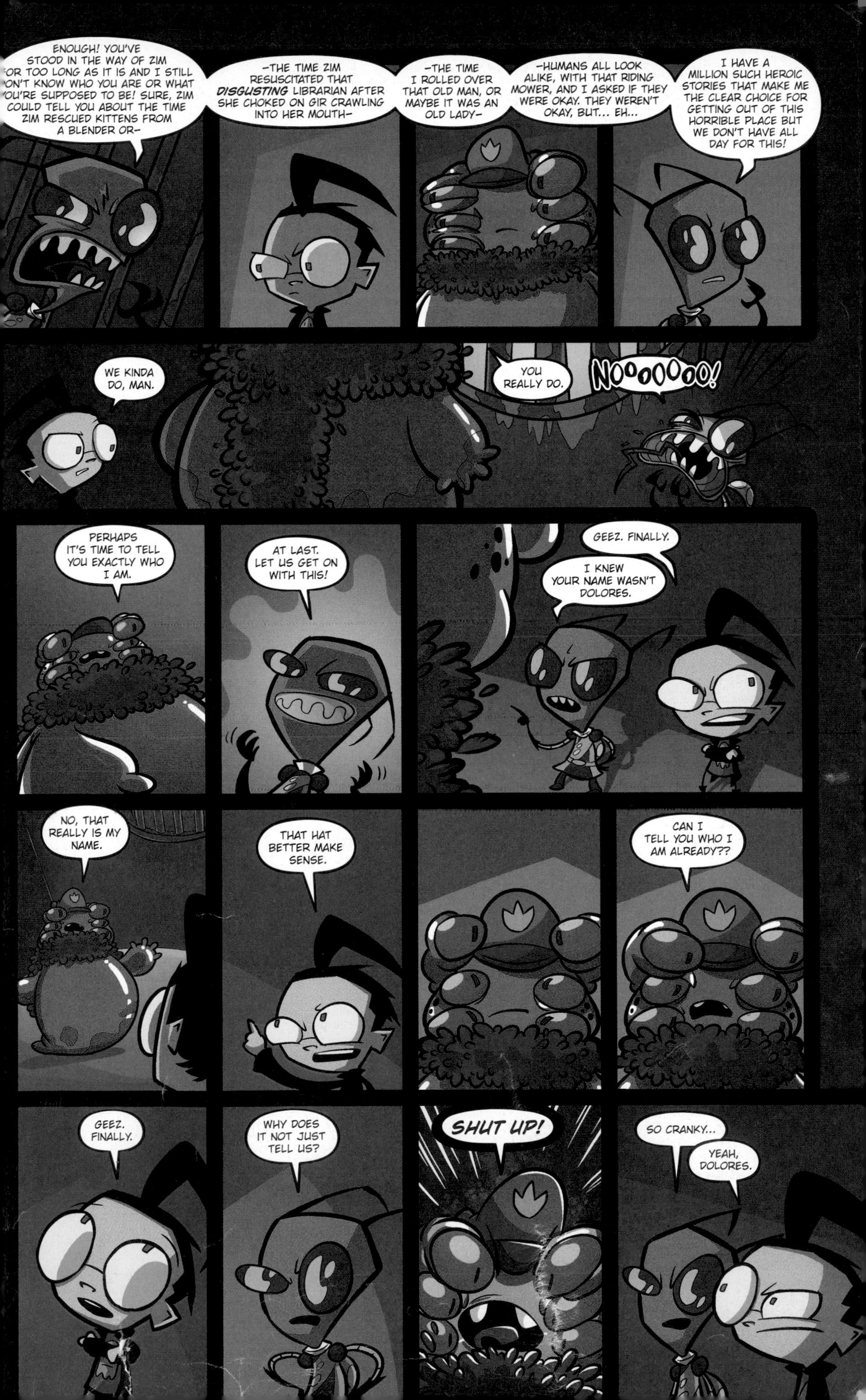
ENOUGH! YOU'VE STOOD IN THE WAY OF ZIM FOR TOO LONG AS IT IS AND I STILL DON'T KNOW WHO YOU ARE OR WHAT YOU'RE SUPPOSED TO BE! SURE, ZIM COULD TELL YOU ABOUT THE TIME ZIM RESCUED KITTENS FROM A BLENDER OR–
–THE TIME ZIM RESUSCITATED THAT DISGUSTING LIBRARIAN AFTER SHE CHOKED ON GIR CRAWLING INTO HER MOUTH–
–THE TIME I ROLLED OVER THAT OLD MAN, OR MAYBE IT WAS AN OLD LADY–
–HUMANS ALL LOOK ALIKE, WITH THAT RIDING MOWER, AND I ASKED IF THEY WERE OKAY. THEY WEREN'T OKAY, BUT... EH...
I HAVE A MILLION SUCH HEROIC STORIES THAT MAKE ME THE CLEAR CHOICE FOR GETTING OUT OF THIS HORRIBLE PLACE BUT WE DON'T HAVE ALL DAY FOR THIS!
WE KINDA DO, MAN.
YOU REALLY DO.
NOOOOOOO!
PERHAPS IT'S TIME TO TELL YOU EXACTLY WHO I AM.
AT LAST. LET US GET ON WITH THIS!
GEEZ. FINALLY.
I KNEW YOUR NAME WASN'T DOLORES.
NO, THAT REALLY IS MY NAME.
THAT HAT BETTER MAKE SENSE.
CAN I TELL YOU WHO I AM ALREADY??
GEEZ. FINALLY.
WHY DOES IT NOT JUST TELL US?
SHUT UP!
SO CRANKY...
YEAH, DOLORES.

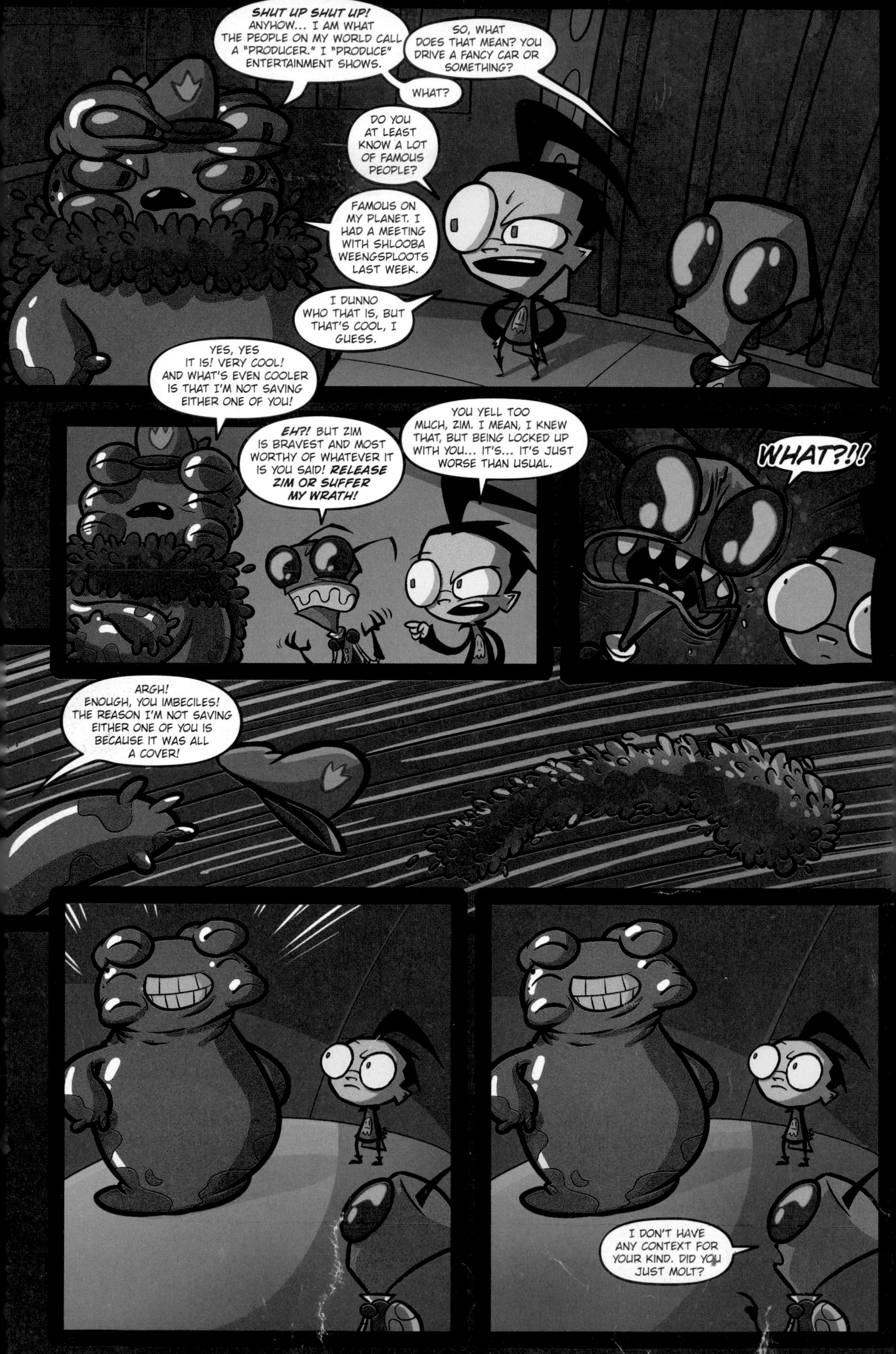
SHUT UP SHUT UP! ANYHOW... I AM WHAT THE PEOPLE ON MY WORLD CALL A "PRODUCER." I "PRODUCE" ENTERTAINMENT SHOWS.
SO, WHAT DOES THAT MEAN? YOU DRIVE A FANCY CAR OR SOMETHING?
WHAT?
DO YOU AT LEAST KNOW A LOT OF FAMOUS PEOPLE?
FAMOUS ON MY PLANET. I HAD A MEETING WITH SHLOOBA WEENGSPLOOTS LAST WEEK.
I DUNNO WHO THAT IS, BUT THAT'S COOL, I GUESS.
YES, YES IT IS! VERY COOL! AND WHAT'S EVEN COOLER IS THAT I'M NOT SAVING EITHER ONE OF YOU!
EH?! BUT ZIM IS BRAVEST AND MOST WORTHY OF WHATEVER IT IS YOU SAID! RELEASE ZIM OR SUFFER MY WRATH!
YOU YELL TOO MUCH, ZIM. I MEAN, I KNEW THAT, BUT BEING LOCKED UP WITH YOU... IT'S... IT'S JUST WORSE THAN USUAL.
WHAT?!!
ARGH! ENOUGH, YOU IMBECILES! THE REASON I'M NOT SAVING EITHER ONE OF YOU IS BECAUSE IT WAS ALL A COVER!
I DON'T HAVE ANY CONTEXT FOR YOUR KIND. DID YOU JUST MOLT?

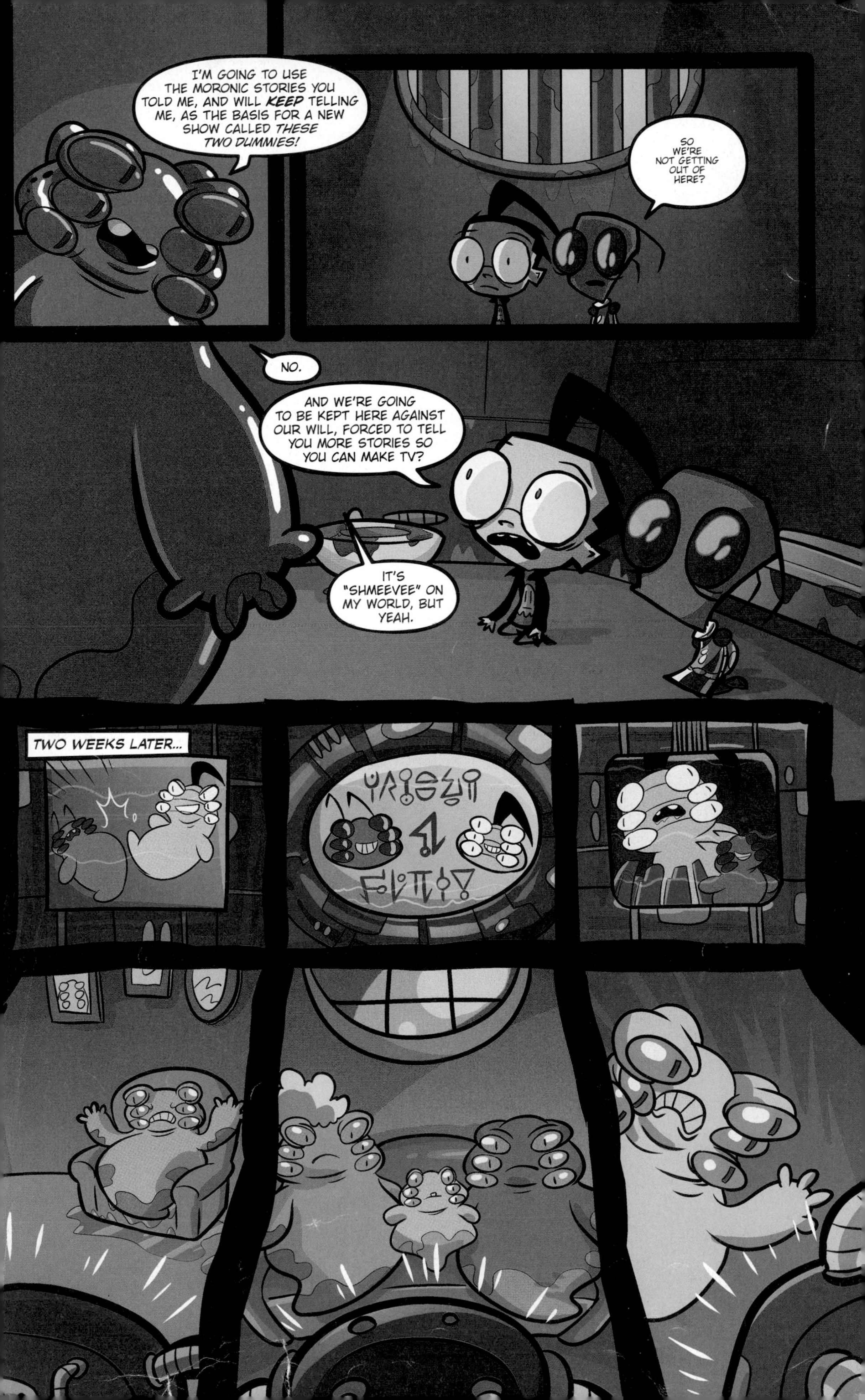
I'M GOING TO USE THE MORONIC STORIES YOU TOLD ME, AND WILL KEEP TELLING ME, AS THE BASIS FOR A NEW SHOW CALLED THESE TWO DUMMIES!
SO WE'RE NOT GETTING OUT OF HERE?
NO.
AND WE'RE GOING TO BE KEPT HERE AGAINST OUR WILL, FORCED TO TELL YOU MORE STORIES SO YOU CAN MAKE TV?
IT'S "SHMEEVEE" ON MY WORLD, BUT YEAH.
TWO WEEKS LATER...

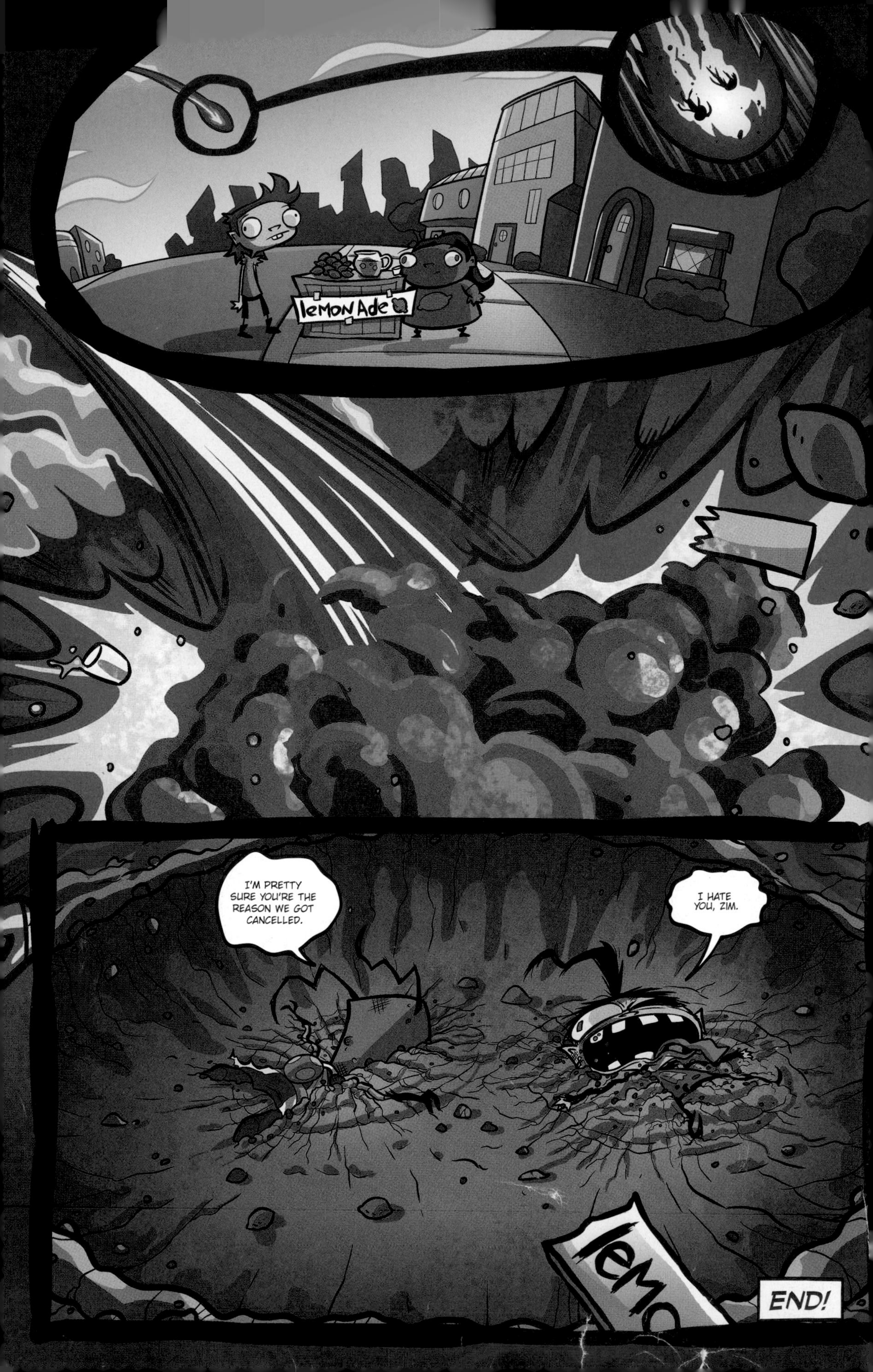
lemON Ade
I'M PRETTY SURE YOU'RE THE REASON WE GOT CANCELLED.
I HATE YOU, ZIM.
lemo
END!

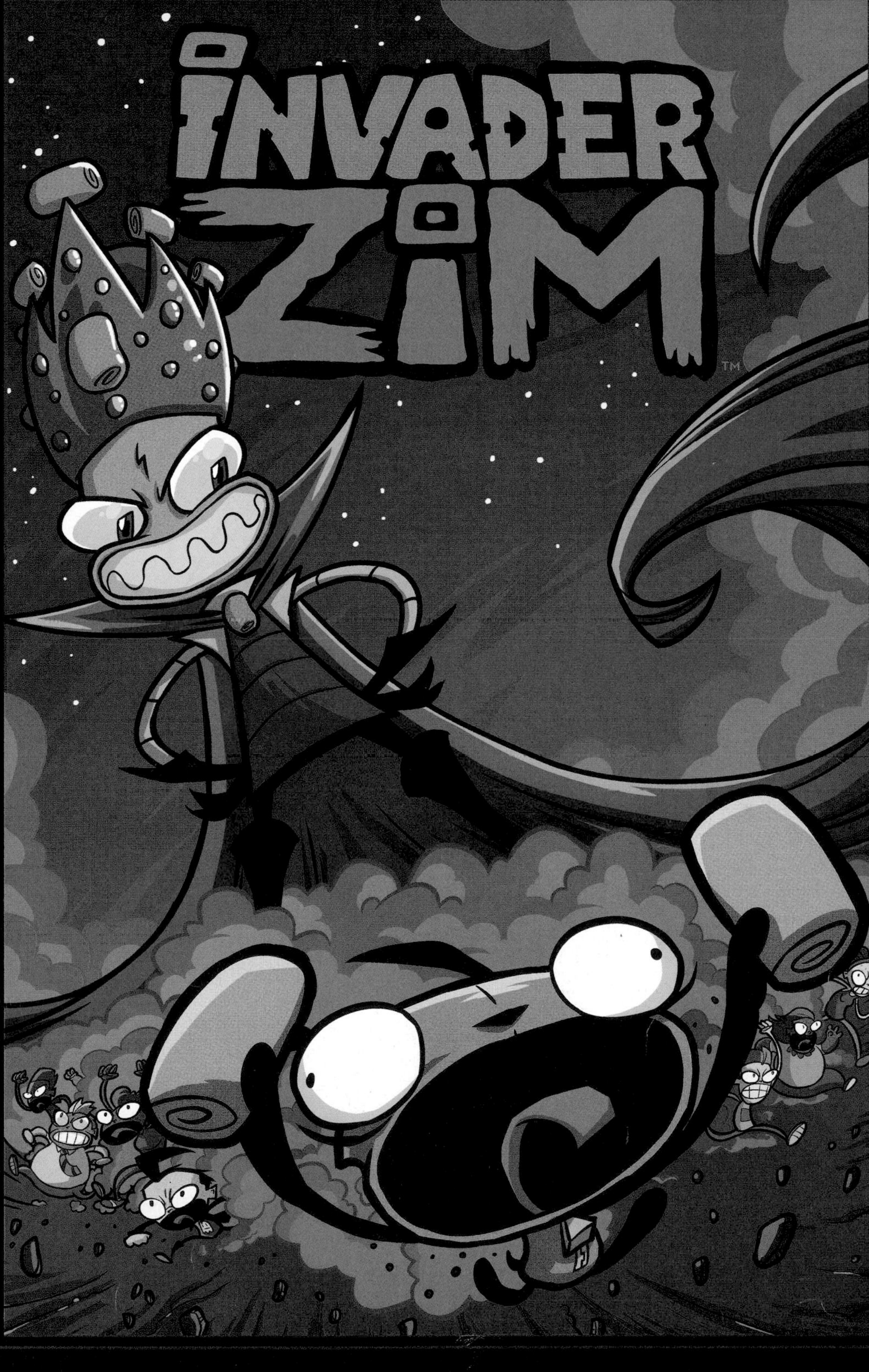
INVADER
ZIM
TM

CHAPTER: 3

illustration by **WARREN WUCINICH**

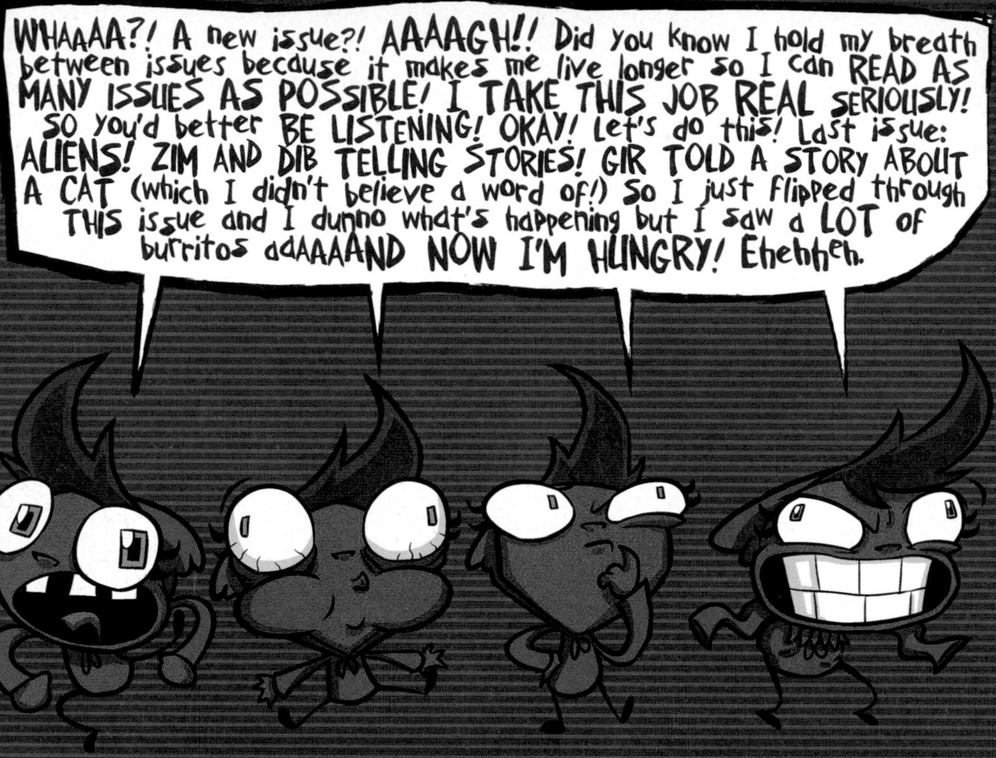
WHAAAA?! A new issue?! AAAAGH!! Did you know I hold my breath between issues because it makes me live longer so I can READ AS MANY ISSUES AS POSSIBLE! I TAKE THIS JOB REAL SERIOUSLY! So you'd better BE LISTENING! OKAY! Let's do this! Last issue: ALIENS! ZIM AND DIB TELLING STORIES! GIR TOLD A STORY ABOUT A CAT (which I didn't believe a word of!) So I just flipped through THIS issue and I dunno what's happening but I saw a LOT of burritos aaAAAAND NOW I'M HUNGRY! Ehehheh.

Recap Kid by **WARREN WUCINICH**

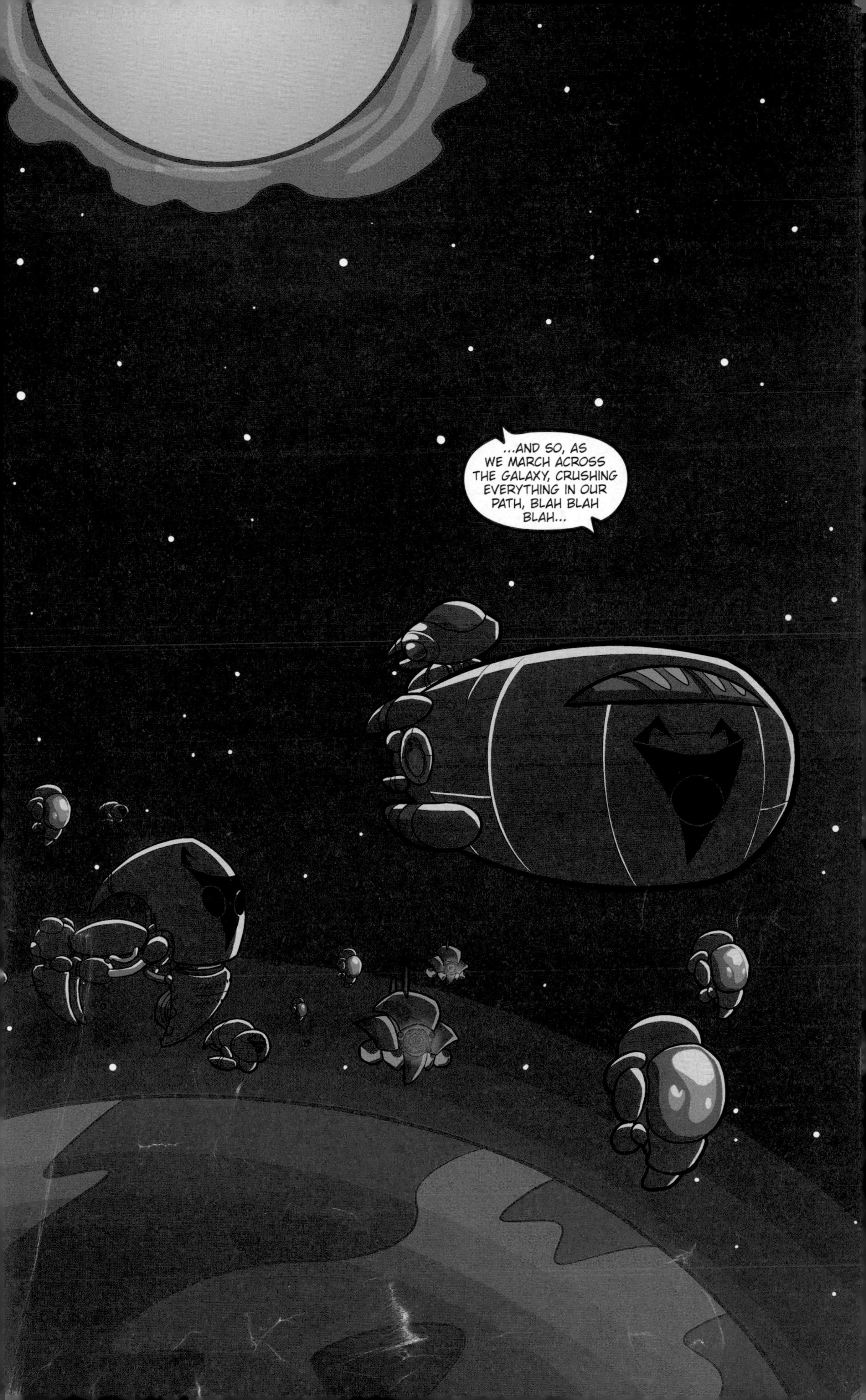
...AND SO, AS WE MARCH ACROSS THE GALAXY, CRUSHING EVERYTHING IN OUR PATH, BLAH BLAH BLAH...

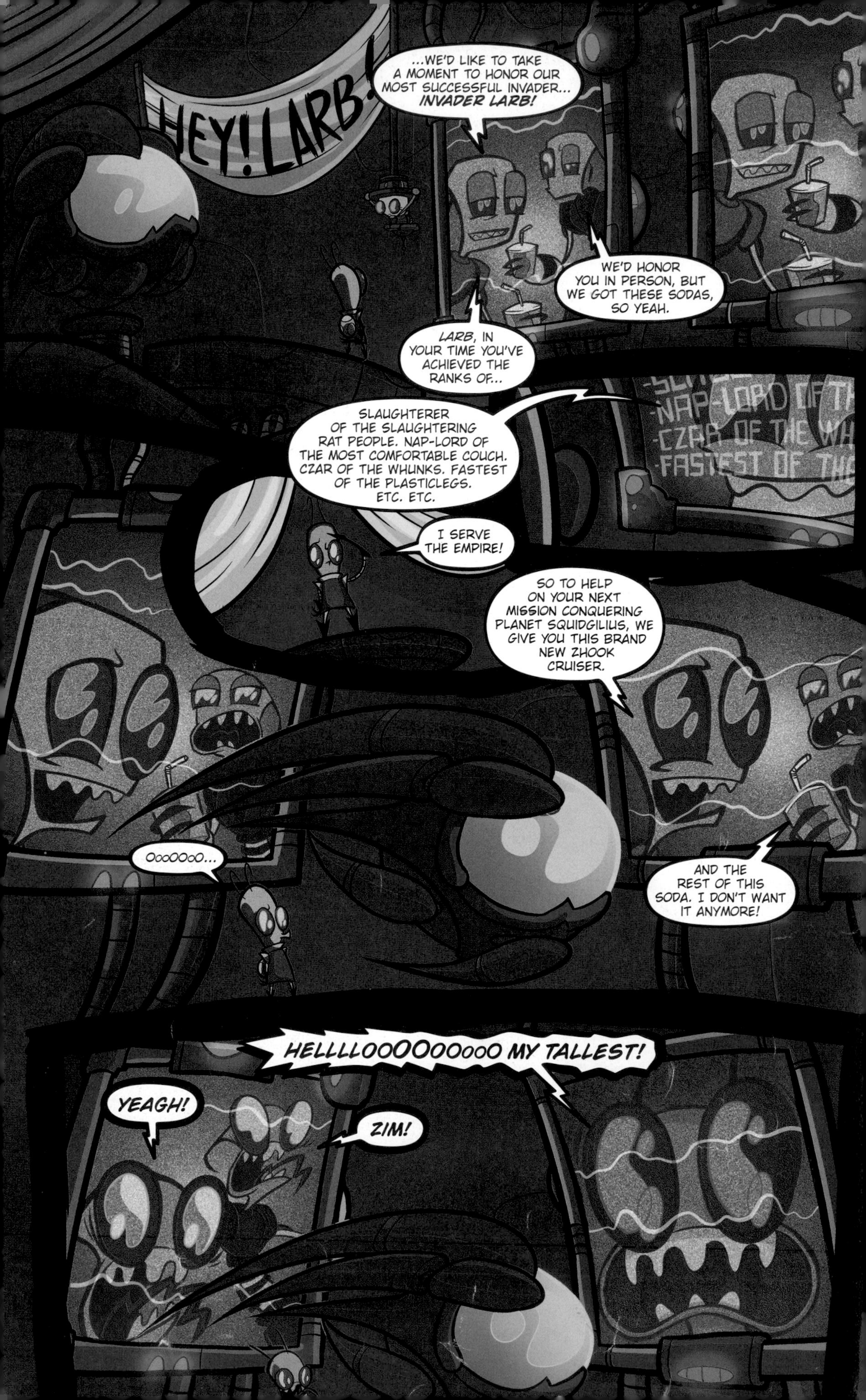
HEY! LARB!
...WE'D LIKE TO TAKE A MOMENT TO HONOR OUR MOST SUCCESSFUL INVADER... INVADER LARB!
WE'D HONOR YOU IN PERSON, BUT WE GOT THESE SODAS, SO YEAH.
LARB, IN YOUR TIME YOU'VE ACHIEVED THE RANKS OF...
SLAUGHTERER OF THE SLAUGHTERING RAT PEOPLE. NAP-LORD OF THE MOST COMFORTABLE COUCH. CZAR OF THE WHUNKS. FASTEST OF THE PLASTICLEGS. ETC. ETC.
I SERVE THE EMPIRE!
SO TO HELP ON YOUR NEXT MISSION CONQUERING PLANET SQUIDGILIUS, WE GIVE YOU THIS BRAND NEW ZHOOK CRUISER.
OooOOoO...
AND THE REST OF THIS SODA. I DON'T WANT IT ANYMORE!
HELLLLOOOOOOoooO MY TALLEST!
YEAGH!
ZIM!

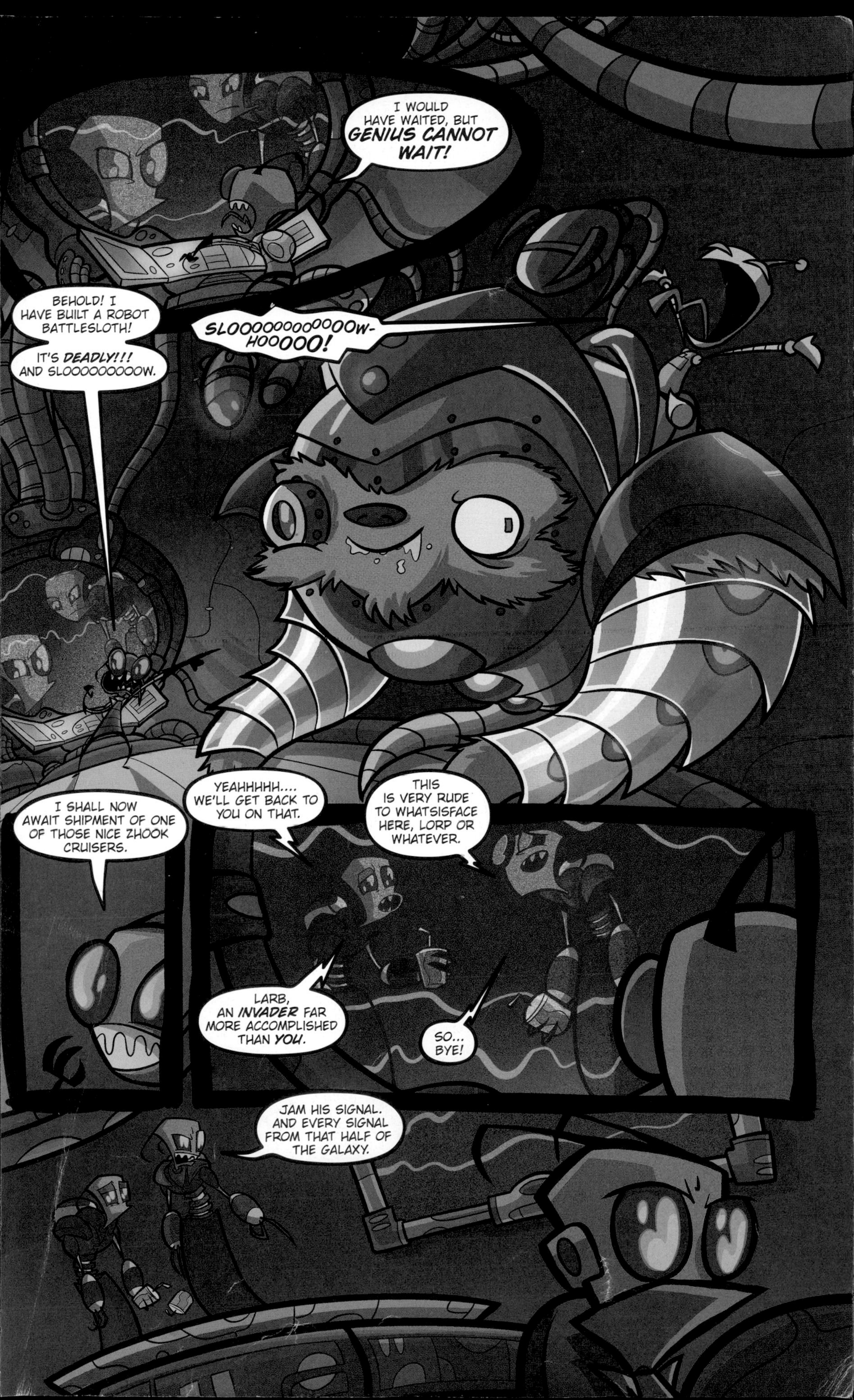
I WOULD HAVE WAITED, BUT GENIUS CANNOT WAIT!
BEHOLD! I HAVE BUILT A ROBOT BATTLESLOTH!
IT'S DEADLY!!! AND SLOOOOOOOOOW.
SLOOOOOOOOOOOOW-HOOOOO!
I SHALL NOW AWAIT SHIPMENT OF ONE OF THOSE NICE ZHOOK CRUISERS.
YEAHHHHH.... WE'LL GET BACK TO YOU ON THAT.
THIS IS VERY RUDE TO WHATSISFACE HERE, LORP OR WHATEVER.
LARB, AN INVADER FAR MORE ACCOMPLISHED THAN YOU.
SO... BYE!
JAM HIS SIGNAL. AND EVERY SIGNAL FROM THAT HALF OF THE GALAXY.

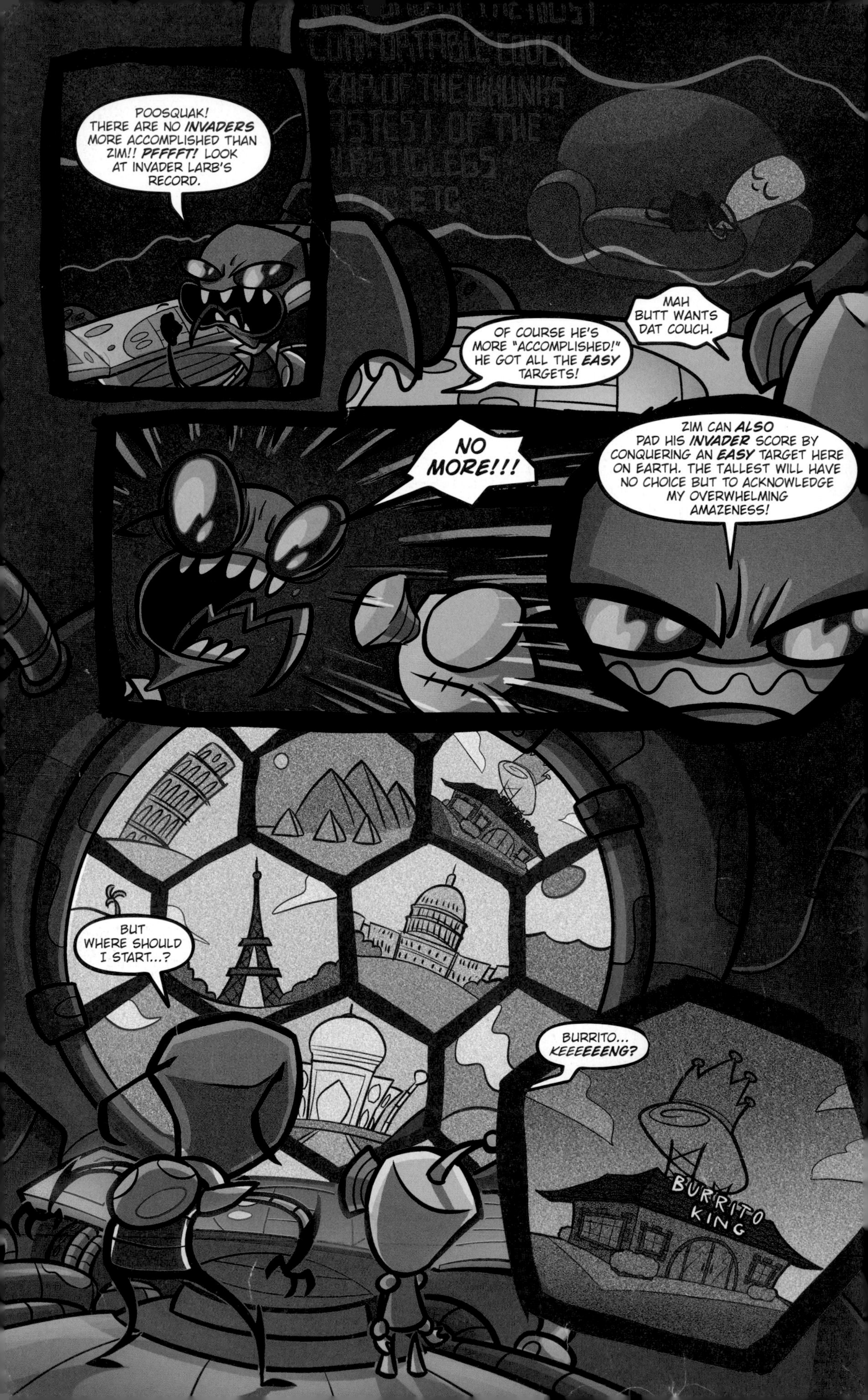
POOSQUAK! THERE ARE NO INVADERS MORE ACCOMPLISHED THAN ZIM!! PFFFFT! LOOK AT INVADER LARB'S RECORD.
OF COURSE HE'S MORE "ACCOMPLISHED!" HE GOT ALL THE EASY TARGETS!
MAH BUTT WANTS DAT COUCH.
NO MORE!!!
ZIM CAN ALSO PAD HIS INVADER SCORE BY CONQUERING AN EASY TARGET HERE ON EARTH. THE TALLEST WILL HAVE NO CHOICE BUT TO ACKNOWLEDGE MY OVERWHELMING AMAZENESS!
BUT WHERE SHOULD I START...?
BURRITO... KEEEEEENG?
BURRITO KING

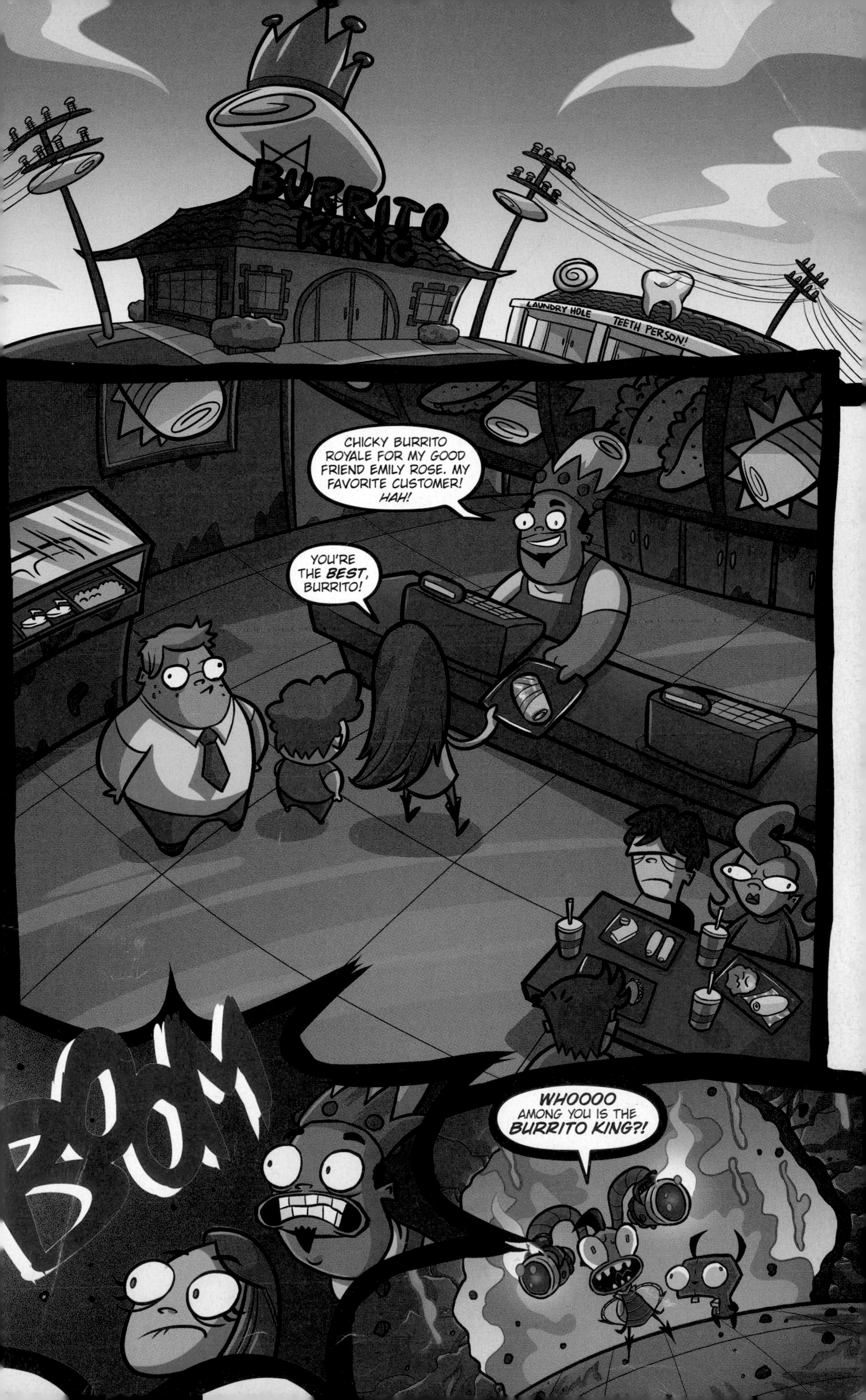
BURRITO KING
LAUNDRY HOLE
TEETH PERSON!
CHICKY BURRITO ROYALE FOR MY GOOD FRIEND EMILY ROSE. MY FAVORITE CUSTOMER! HAH!
YOU'RE THE BEST, BURRITO!
BOOM
WHOOOO AMONG YOU IS THE BURRITO KING?!

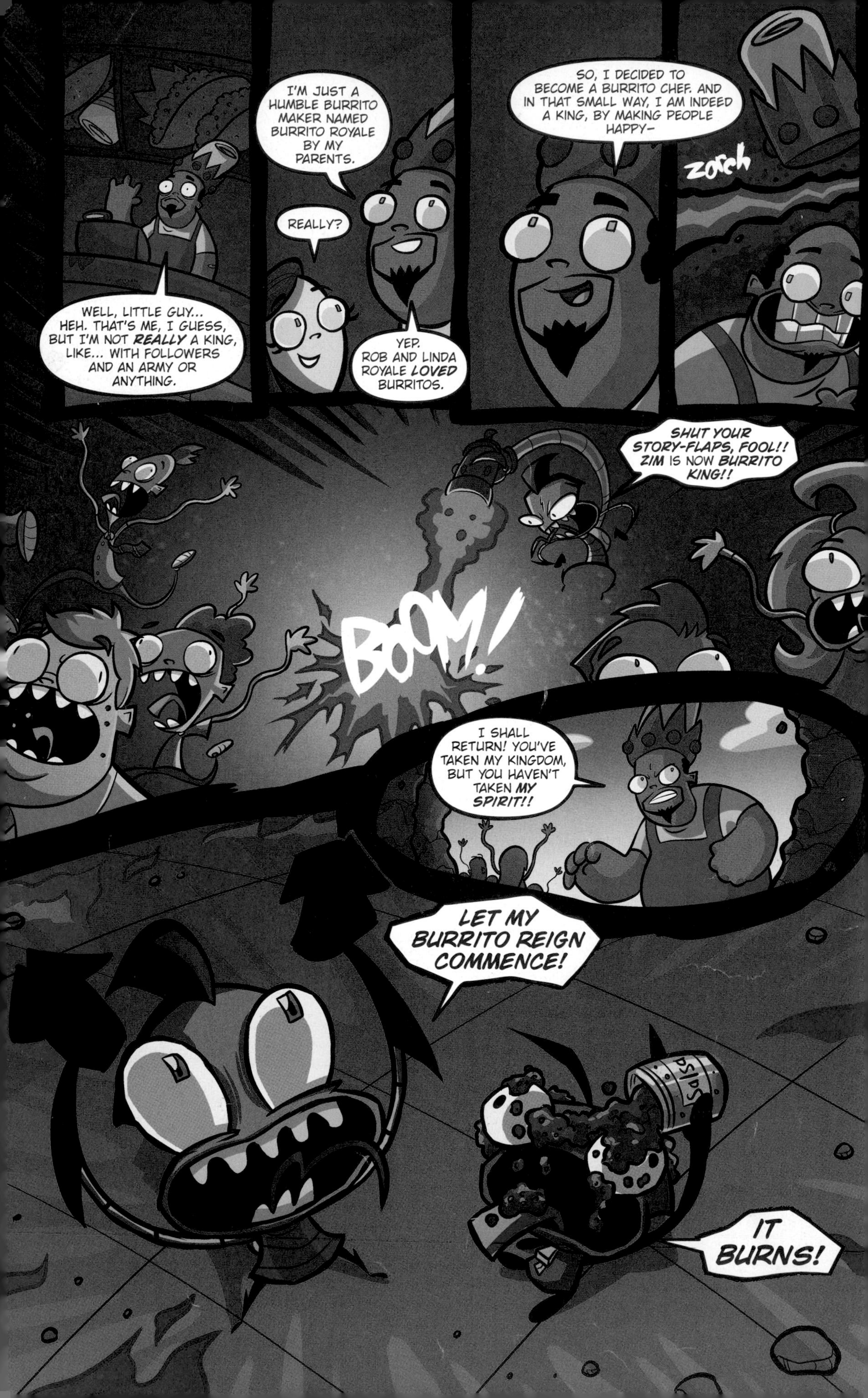
WELL, LITTLE GUY... HEH. THAT'S ME, I GUESS, BUT I'M NOT REALLY A KING, LIKE... WITH FOLLOWERS AND AN ARMY OR ANYTHING.
I'M JUST A HUMBLE BURRITO MAKER NAMED BURRITO ROYALE BY MY PARENTS.
REALLY?
YEP. ROB AND LINDA ROYALE LOVED BURRITOS.
SO, I DECIDED TO BECOME A BURRITO CHEF. AND IN THAT SMALL WAY, I AM INDEED A KING, BY MAKING PEOPLE HAPPY–
ZORCH
SHUT YOUR STORY-FLAPS, FOOL!! ZIM IS NOW BURRITO KING!!
BOOM!
I SHALL RETURN! YOU'VE TAKEN MY KINGDOM, BUT YOU HAVEN'T TAKEN MY SPIRIT!!
LET MY BURRITO REIGN COMMENCE!
IT BURNS!

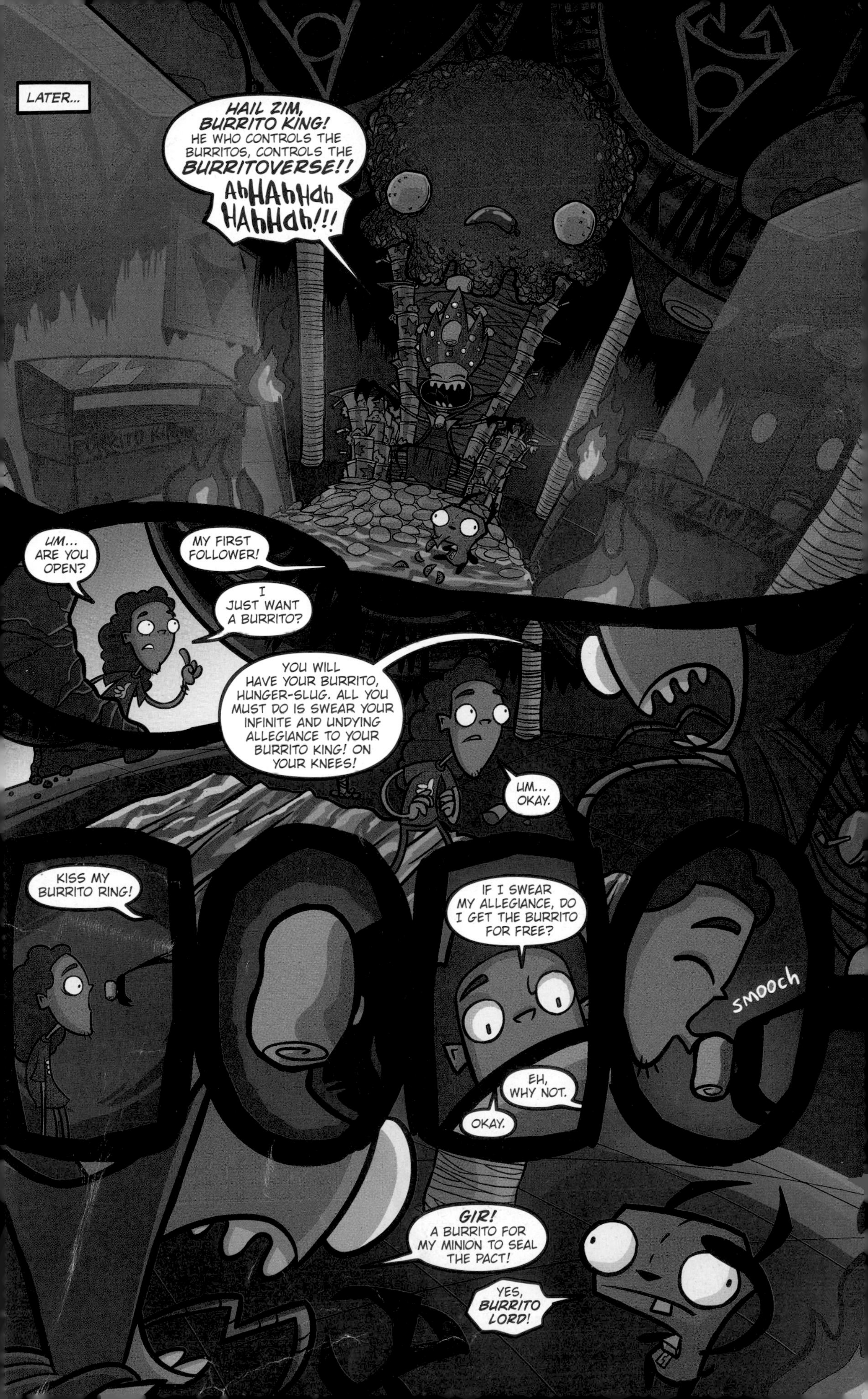
LATER...
HAIL ZIM, BURRITO KING! HE WHO CONTROLS THE BURRITOS, CONTROLS THE BURRITOVERSE!! AhHAhHah HAhHah!!!
UM... ARE YOU OPEN?
MY FIRST FOLLOWER!
I JUST WANT A BURRITO?
YOU WILL HAVE YOUR BURRITO, HUNGER-SLUG. ALL YOU MUST DO IS SWEAR YOUR INFINITE AND UNDYING ALLEGIANCE TO YOUR BURRITO KING! ON YOUR KNEES!
UM... OKAY.
KISS MY BURRITO RING!
IF I SWEAR MY ALLEGIANCE, DO I GET THE BURRITO FOR FREE?
EH, WHY NOT.
OKAY.
SMOOCH
GIR! A BURRITO FOR MY MINION TO SEAL THE PACT!
YES, BURRITO LORD!

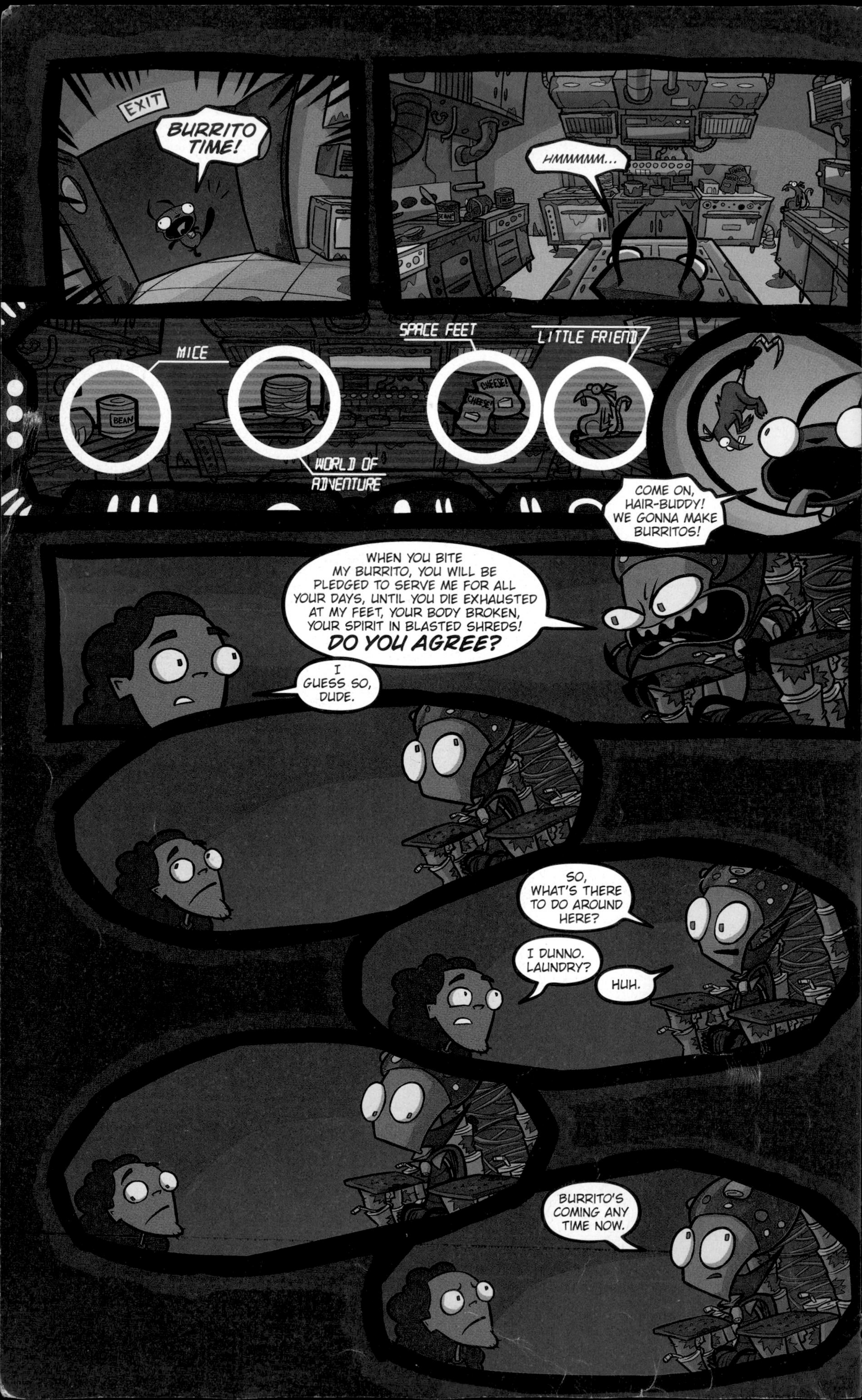
EXIT
BURRITO TIME!
HMMMMM...
BEANS
MICE
WORLD OF ADVENTURE
SPACE FEET
CHEESE!
CHEESE!
LITTLE FRIEND
BEAN
COME ON, HAIR-BUDDY! WE GONNA MAKE BURRITOS!
WHEN YOU BITE MY BURRITO, YOU WILL BE PLEDGED TO SERVE ME FOR ALL YOUR DAYS, UNTIL YOU DIE EXHAUSTED AT MY FEET, YOUR BODY BROKEN, YOUR SPIRIT IN BLASTED SHREDS! DO YOU AGREE?
I GUESS SO, DUDE.
SO, WHAT'S THERE TO DO AROUND HERE?
I DUNNO. LAUNDRY?
HUH.
BURRITO'S COMING ANY TIME NOW.

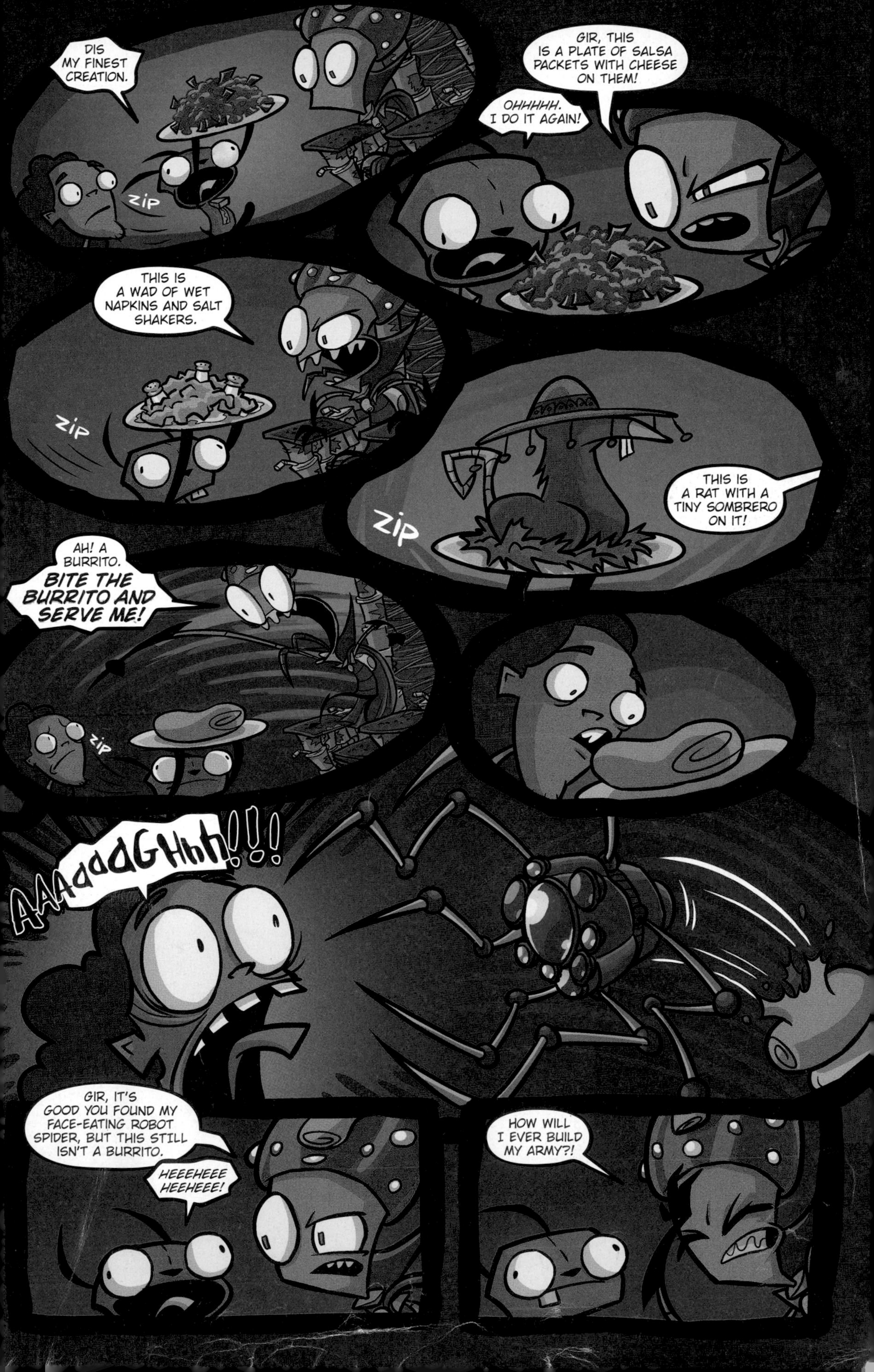
DIS MY FINEST CREATION.
ZIP
GIR, THIS IS A PLATE OF SALSA PACKETS WITH CHEESE ON THEM!
OHHHHH. I DO IT AGAIN!
THIS IS A WAD OF WET NAPKINS AND SALT SHAKERS.
ZIP
ZIP
THIS IS A RAT WITH A TINY SOMBRERO ON IT!
AH! A BURRITO. BITE THE BURRITO AND SERVE ME!
ZIP
AAAaaaGHhh!!!
GIR, IT'S GOOD YOU FOUND MY FACE-EATING ROBOT SPIDER, BUT THIS STILL ISN'T A BURRITO.
HEEEHEEE HEEHEEE!
HOW WILL I EVER BUILD MY ARMY?!

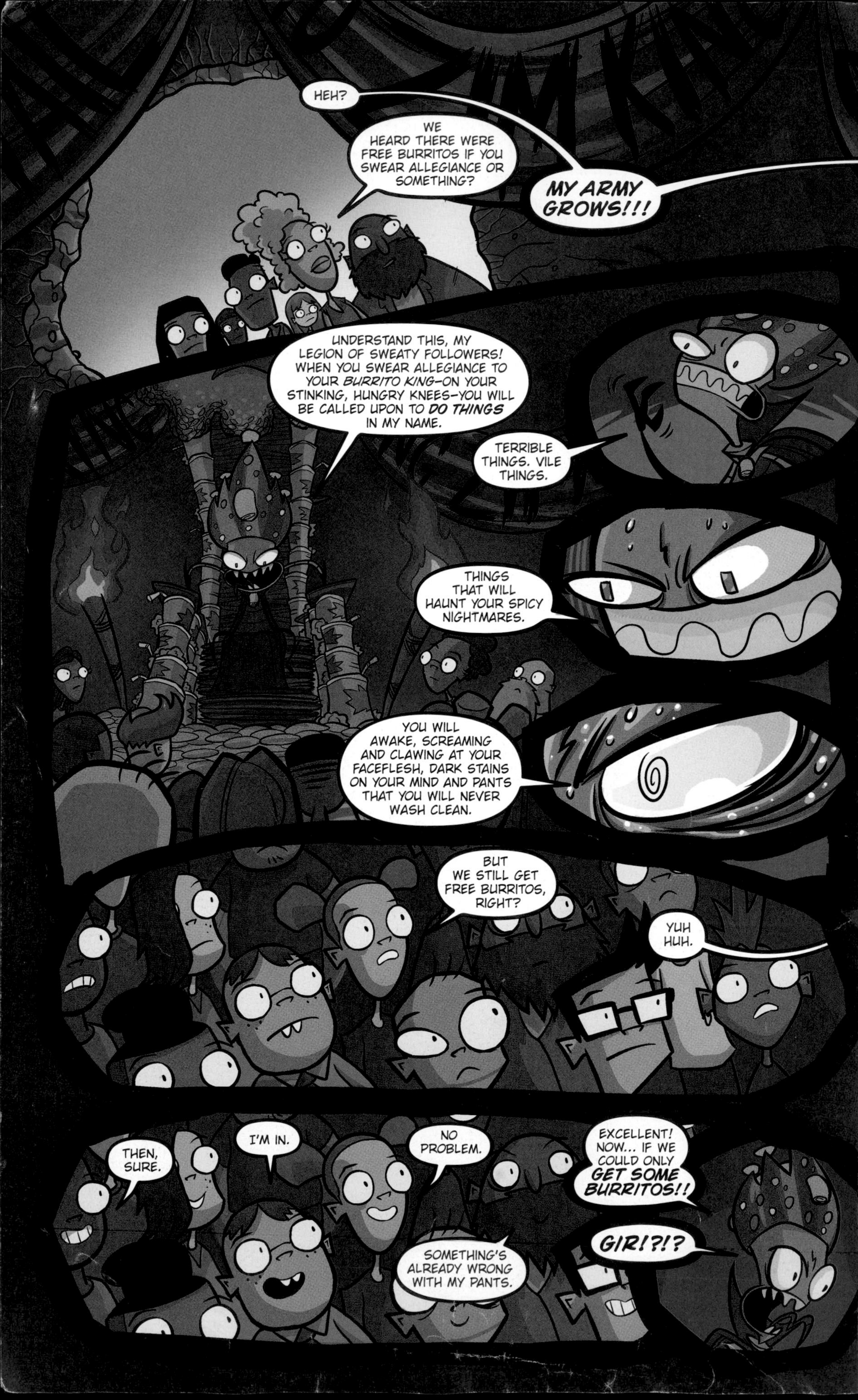
HEH?
WE HEARD THERE WERE FREE BURRITOS IF YOU SWEAR ALLEGIANCE OR SOMETHING?
MY ARMY GROWS!!!
UNDERSTAND THIS, MY LEGION OF SWEATY FOLLOWERS! WHEN YOU SWEAR ALLEGIANCE TO YOUR BURRITO KING—ON YOUR STINKING, HUNGRY KNEES—YOU WILL BE CALLED UPON TO DO THINGS IN MY NAME.
TERRIBLE THINGS. VILE THINGS.
THINGS THAT WILL HAUNT YOUR SPICY NIGHTMARES.
YOU WILL AWAKE, SCREAMING AND CLAWING AT YOUR FACEFLESH, DARK STAINS ON YOUR MIND AND PANTS THAT YOU WILL NEVER WASH CLEAN.
BUT WE STILL GET FREE BURRITOS, RIGHT?
YUH HUH.
THEN, SURE.
I'M IN.
NO PROBLEM.
EXCELLENT! NOW... IF WE COULD ONLY GET SOME BURRITOS!!
SOMETHING'S ALREADY WRONG WITH MY PANTS.
GIR!?!?

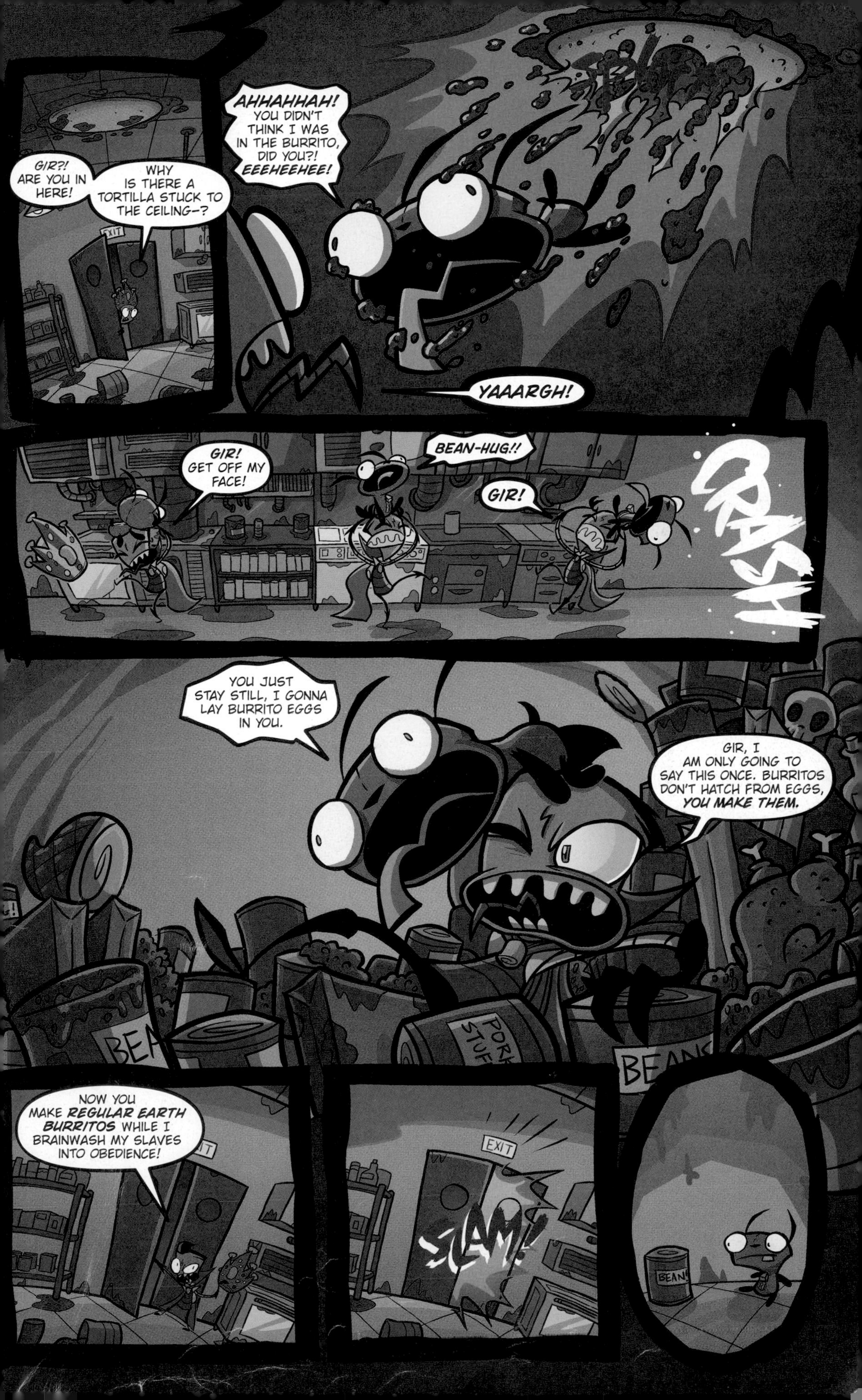
GIR?! ARE YOU IN HERE!
WHY IS THERE A TORTILLA STUCK TO THE CEILING–?
EXIT
AHHAHHAH! YOU DIDN'T THINK I WAS IN THE BURRITO, DID YOU?! EEEHEEHEE!
YAAARGH!
GIR! GET OFF MY FACE!
BEAN-HUG!!
GIR!
CRASH
YOU JUST STAY STILL, I GONNA LAY BURRITO EGGS IN YOU.
GIR, I AM ONLY GOING TO SAY THIS ONCE. BURRITOS DON'T HATCH FROM EGGS, YOU MAKE THEM.
PORK STUFF
NOW YOU MAKE REGULAR EARTH BURRITOS WHILE I BRAINWASH MY SLAVES INTO OBEDIENCE!
EXIT
SLAM!

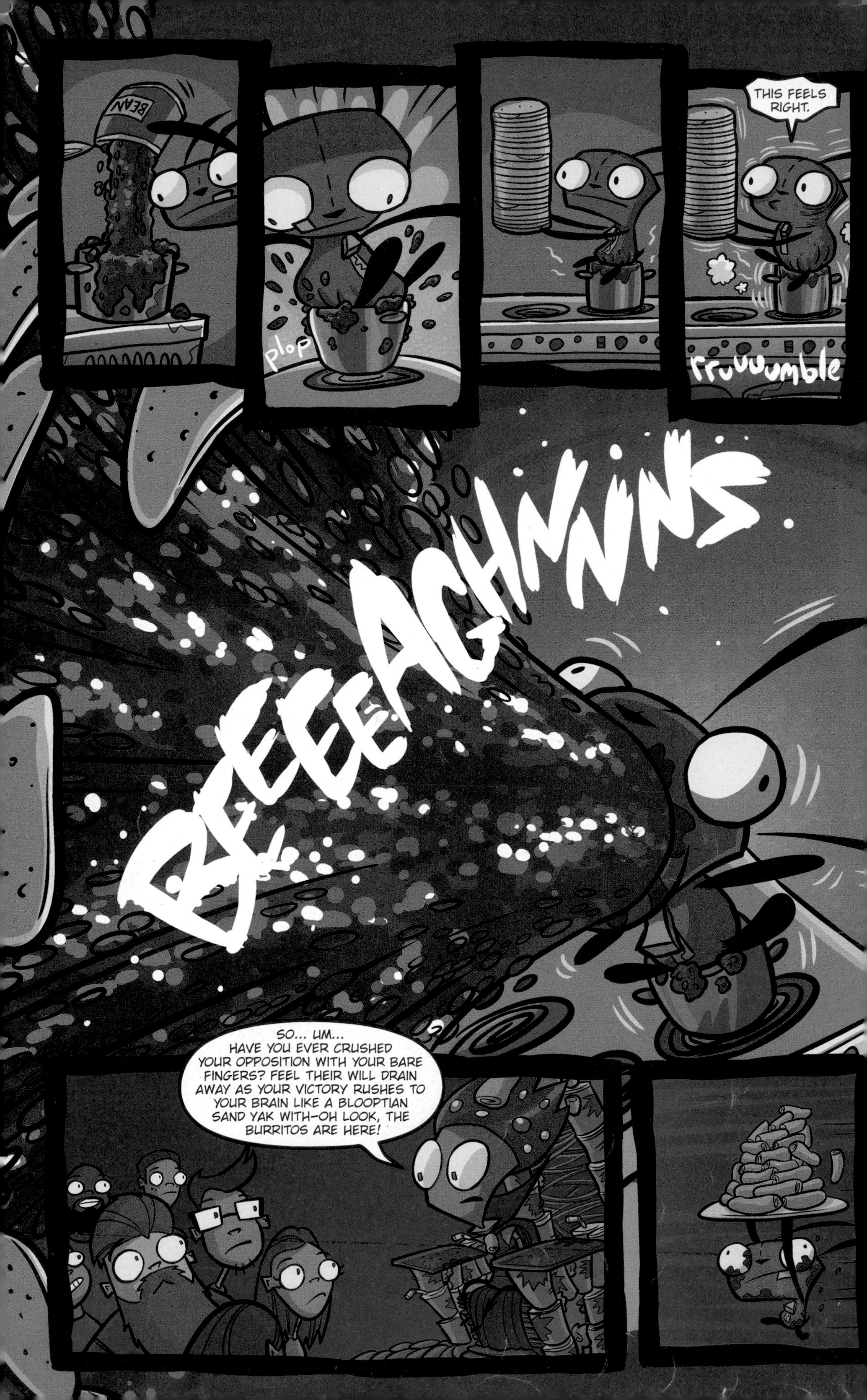
BEAN
plop
THIS FEELS RIGHT.
rruuuumble
BEEEAGHNNNS
SO... UM... HAVE YOU EVER CRUSHED YOUR OPPOSITION WITH YOUR BARE FINGERS? FEEL THEIR WILL DRAIN AWAY AS YOUR VICTORY RUSHES TO YOUR BRAIN LIKE A BLOOPTIAN SAND YAK WITH–OH LOOK, THE BURRITOS ARE HERE!

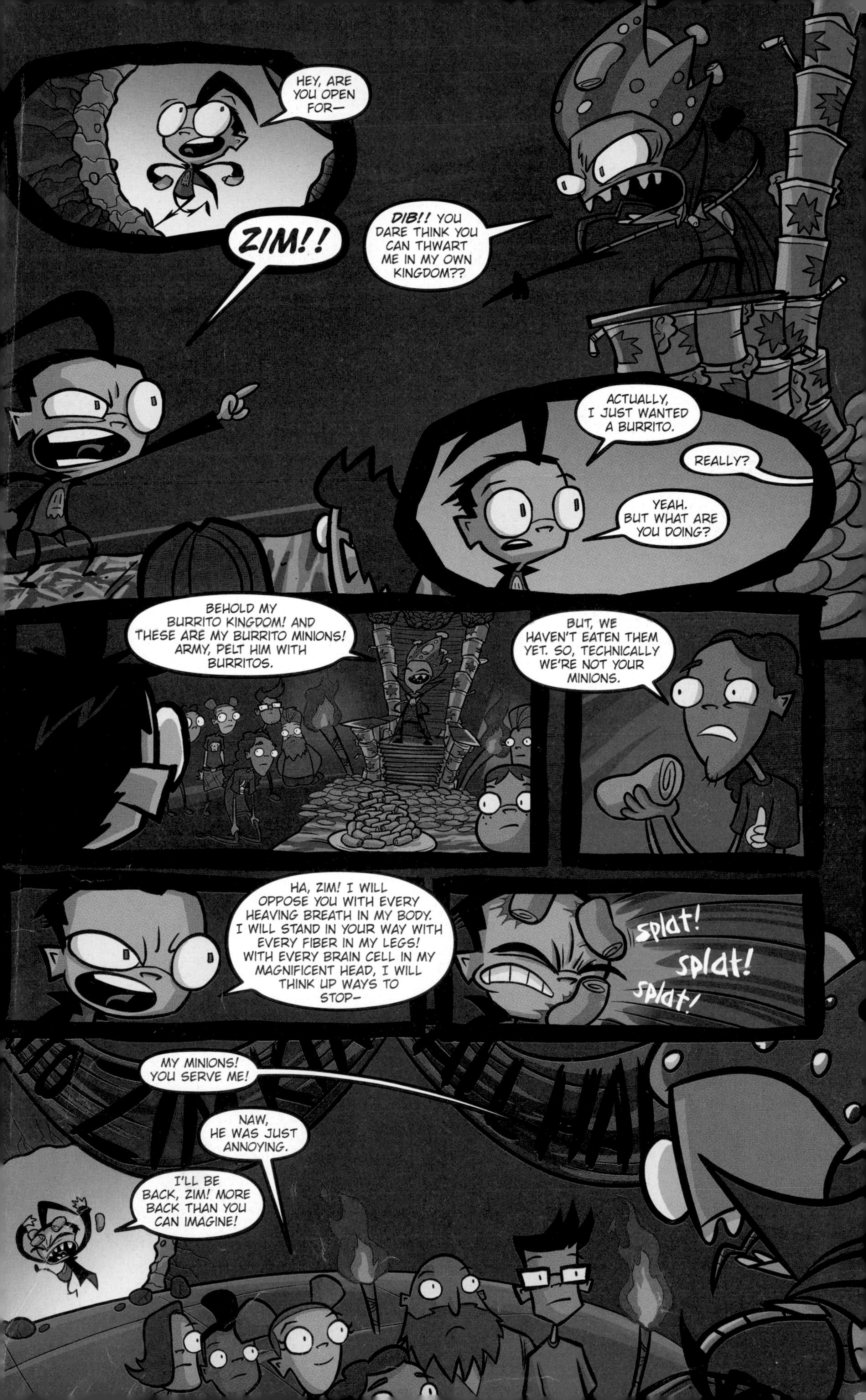
HEY, ARE YOU OPEN FOR—
ZIM!!
DIB!! YOU DARE THINK YOU CAN THWART ME IN MY OWN KINGDOM??
ACTUALLY, I JUST WANTED A BURRITO.
REALLY?
YEAH. BUT WHAT ARE YOU DOING?
BEHOLD MY BURRITO KINGDOM! AND THESE ARE MY BURRITO MINIONS! ARMY, PELT HIM WITH BURRITOS.
BUT, WE HAVEN'T EATEN THEM YET. SO, TECHNICALLY WE'RE NOT YOUR MINIONS.
HA, ZIM! I WILL OPPOSE YOU WITH EVERY HEAVING BREATH IN MY BODY. I WILL STAND IN YOUR WAY WITH EVERY FIBER IN MY LEGS! WITH EVERY BRAIN CELL IN MY MAGNIFICENT HEAD, I WILL THINK UP WAYS TO STOP—
splat!
splat!
splat!
MY MINIONS! YOU SERVE ME!
NAW, HE WAS JUST ANNOYING.
I'LL BE BACK, ZIM! MORE BACK THAN YOU CAN IMAGINE!

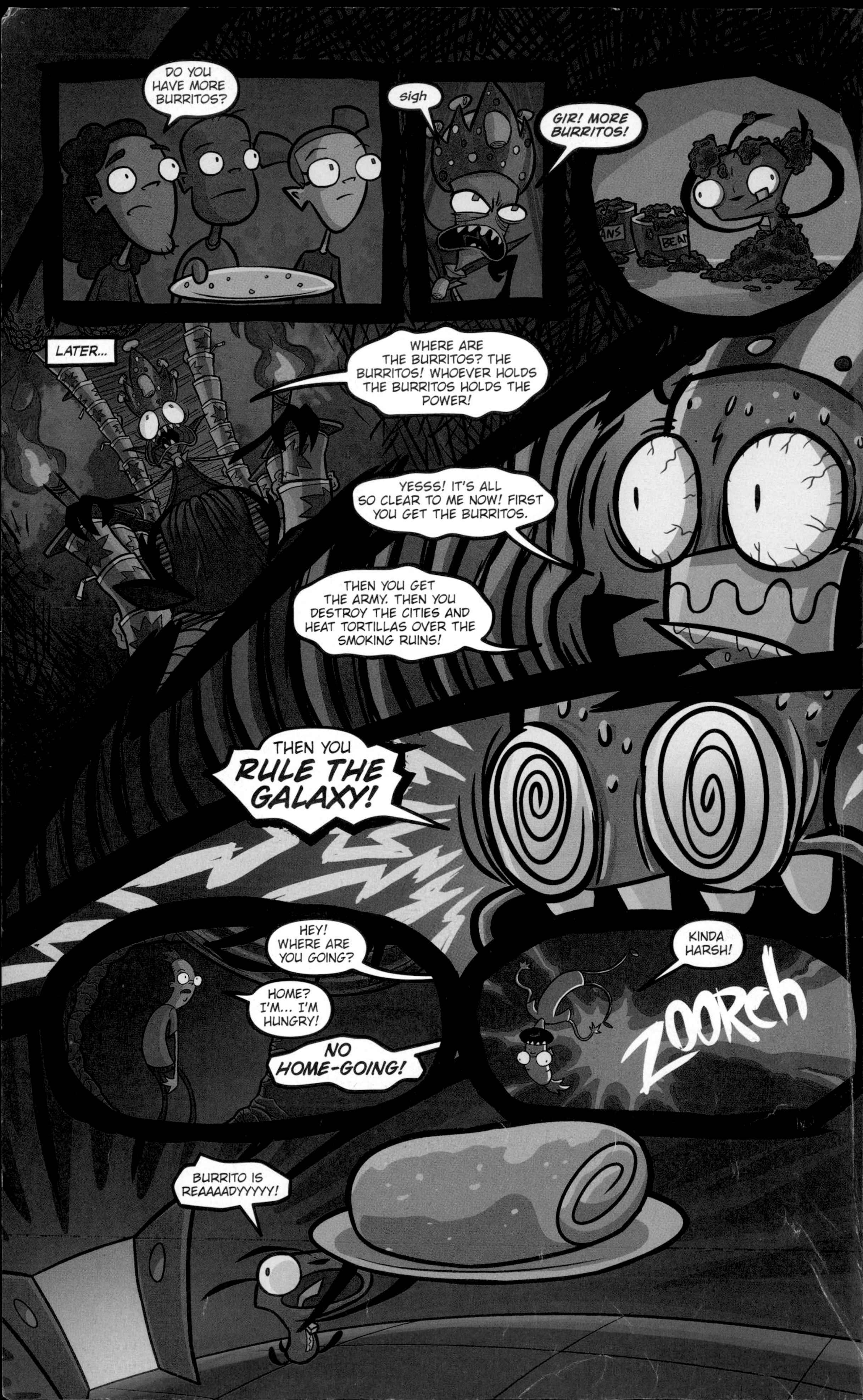
DO YOU HAVE MORE BURRITOS?
sigh
GIR! MORE BURRITOS!
BEANS
BEANS
LATER...
WHERE ARE THE BURRITOS? THE BURRITOS! WHOEVER HOLDS THE BURRITOS HOLDS THE POWER!
YESSS! IT'S ALL SO CLEAR TO ME NOW! FIRST YOU GET THE BURRITOS.
THEN YOU GET THE ARMY. THEN YOU DESTROY THE CITIES AND HEAT TORTILLAS OVER THE SMOKING RUINS!
THEN YOU RULE THE GALAXY!
HEY! WHERE ARE YOU GOING?
HOME? I'M... I'M HUNGRY!
NO HOME-GOING!
KINDA HARSH!
ZOORCH
BURRITO IS REAAAADYYYYY!

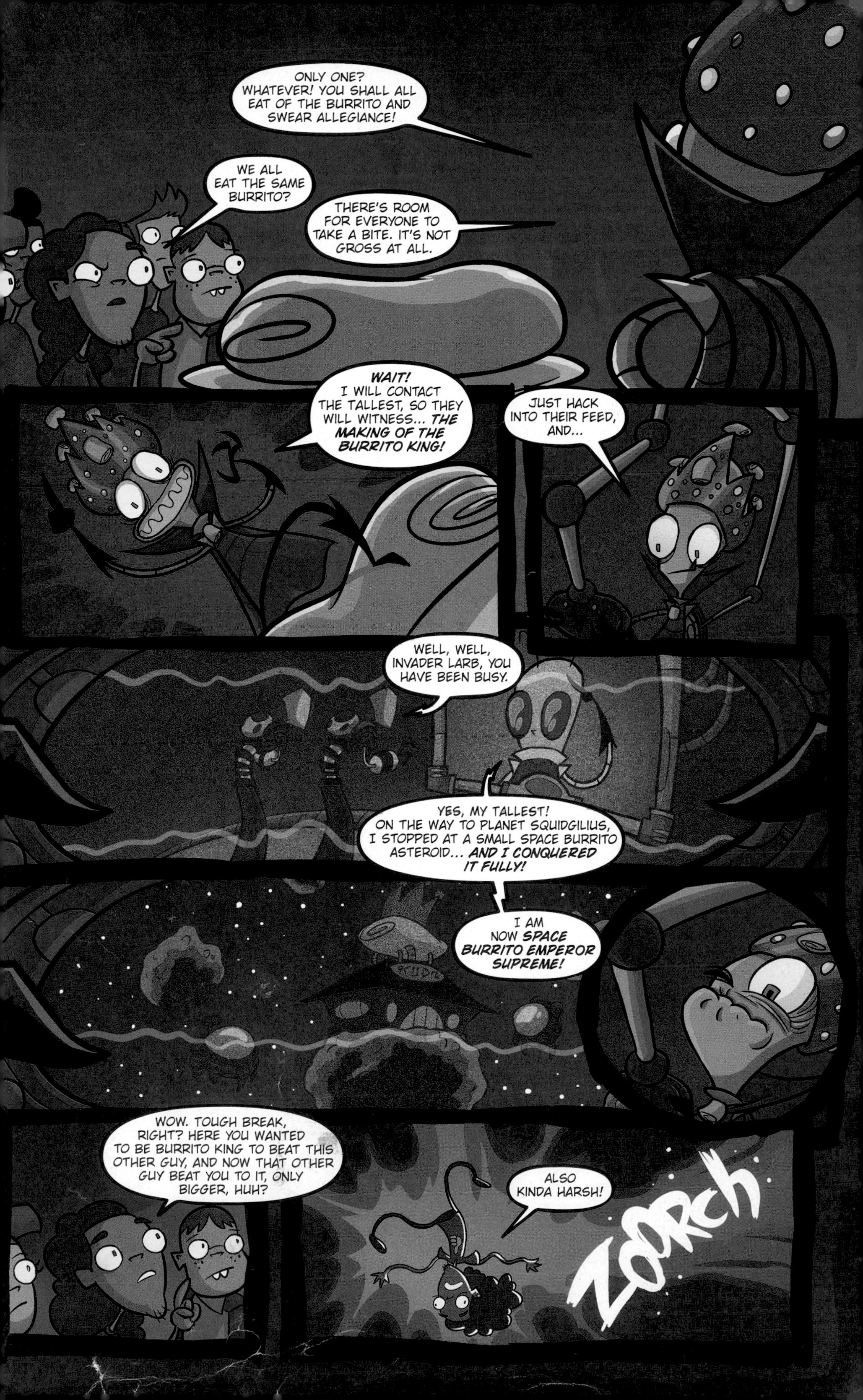
ONLY ONE? WHATEVER! YOU SHALL ALL EAT OF THE BURRITO AND SWEAR ALLEGIANCE!
WE ALL EAT THE SAME BURRITO?
THERE'S ROOM FOR EVERYONE TO TAKE A BITE. IT'S NOT GROSS AT ALL.
WAIT! I WILL CONTACT THE TALLEST, SO THEY WILL WITNESS... THE MAKING OF THE BURRITO KING!
JUST HACK INTO THEIR FEED, AND...
WELL, WELL, INVADER LARB, YOU HAVE BEEN BUSY.
YES, MY TALLEST! ON THE WAY TO PLANET SQUIDGILIUS, I STOPPED AT A SMALL SPACE BURRITO ASTEROID... AND I CONQUERED IT FULLY!
I AM NOW SPACE BURRITO EMPEROR SUPREME!
WOW. TOUGH BREAK, RIGHT? HERE YOU WANTED TO BE BURRITO KING TO BEAT THIS OTHER GUY, AND NOW THAT OTHER GUY BEAT YOU TO IT, ONLY BIGGER, HUH?
ALSO KINDA HARSH!
ZOORCH

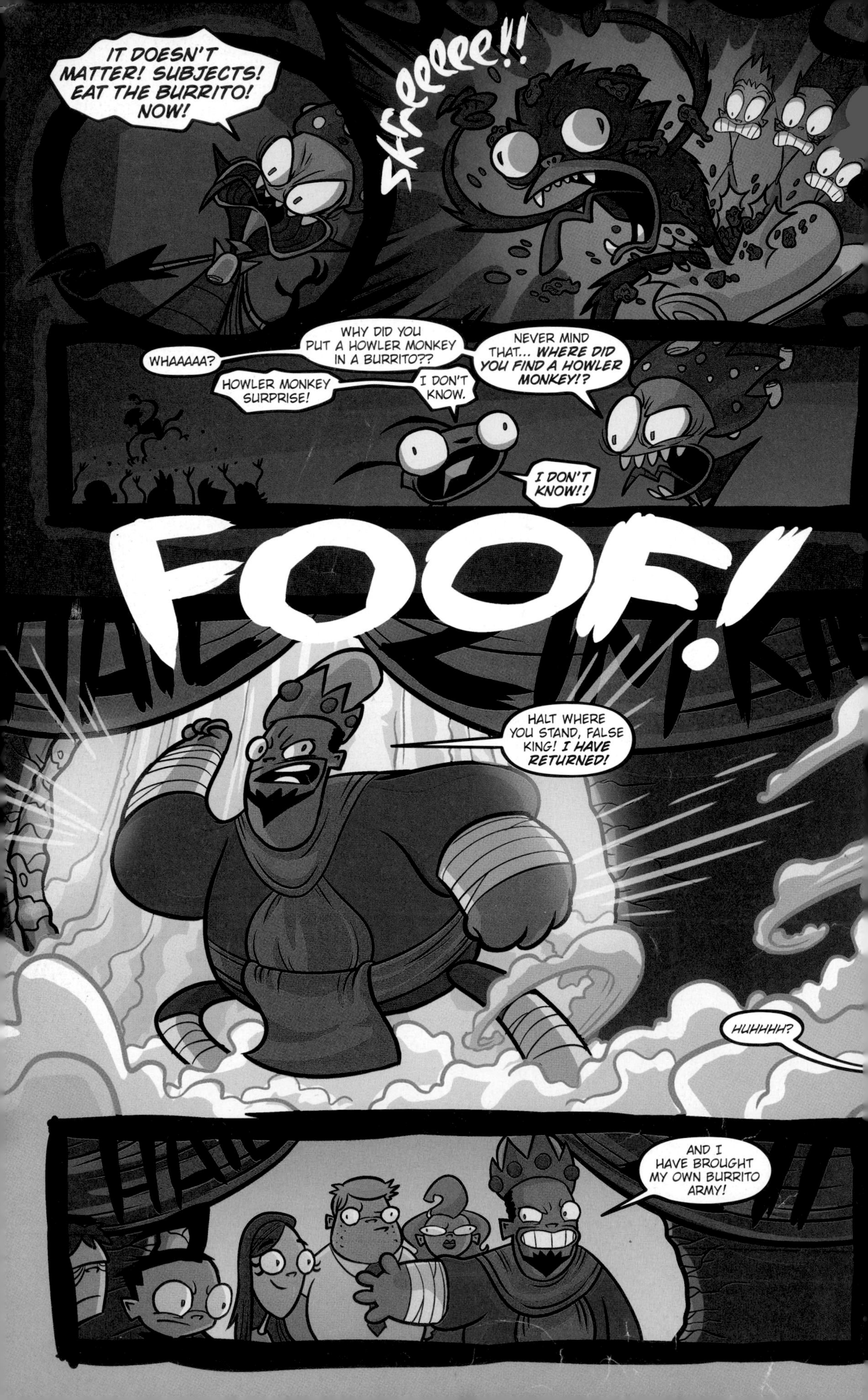
IT DOESN'T MATTER! SUBJECTS! EAT THE BURRITO! NOW!
SKREEEEE!!
WHAAAAA?
WHY DID YOU PUT A HOWLER MONKEY IN A BURRITO??
NEVER MIND THAT... WHERE DID YOU FIND A HOWLER MONKEY!?
HOWLER MONKEY SURPRISE!
I DON'T KNOW.
I DON'T KNOW!!
FOOF!
HALT WHERE YOU STAND, FALSE KING! I HAVE RETURNED!
HUHHHH?
AND I HAVE BROUGHT MY OWN BURRITO ARMY!

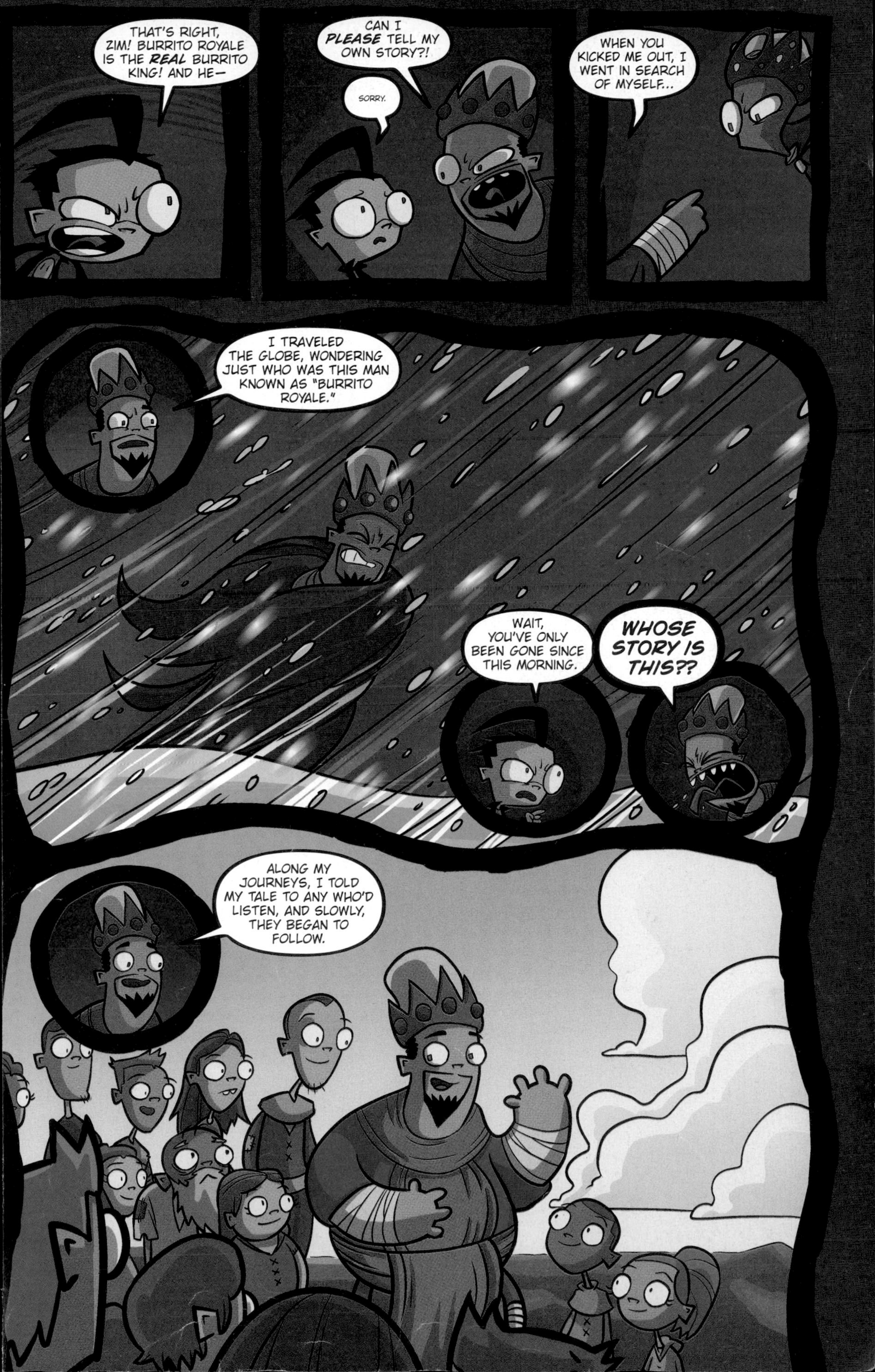
THAT'S RIGHT, ZIM! BURRITO ROYALE IS THE REAL BURRITO KING! AND HE—
CAN I PLEASE TELL MY OWN STORY?!
SORRY.
WHEN YOU KICKED ME OUT, I WENT IN SEARCH OF MYSELF...
I TRAVELED THE GLOBE, WONDERING JUST WHO WAS THIS MAN KNOWN AS "BURRITO ROYALE."
WAIT, YOU'VE ONLY BEEN GONE SINCE THIS MORNING.
WHOSE STORY IS THIS??
ALONG MY JOURNEYS, I TOLD MY TALE TO ANY WHO'D LISTEN, AND SLOWLY, THEY BEGAN TO FOLLOW.

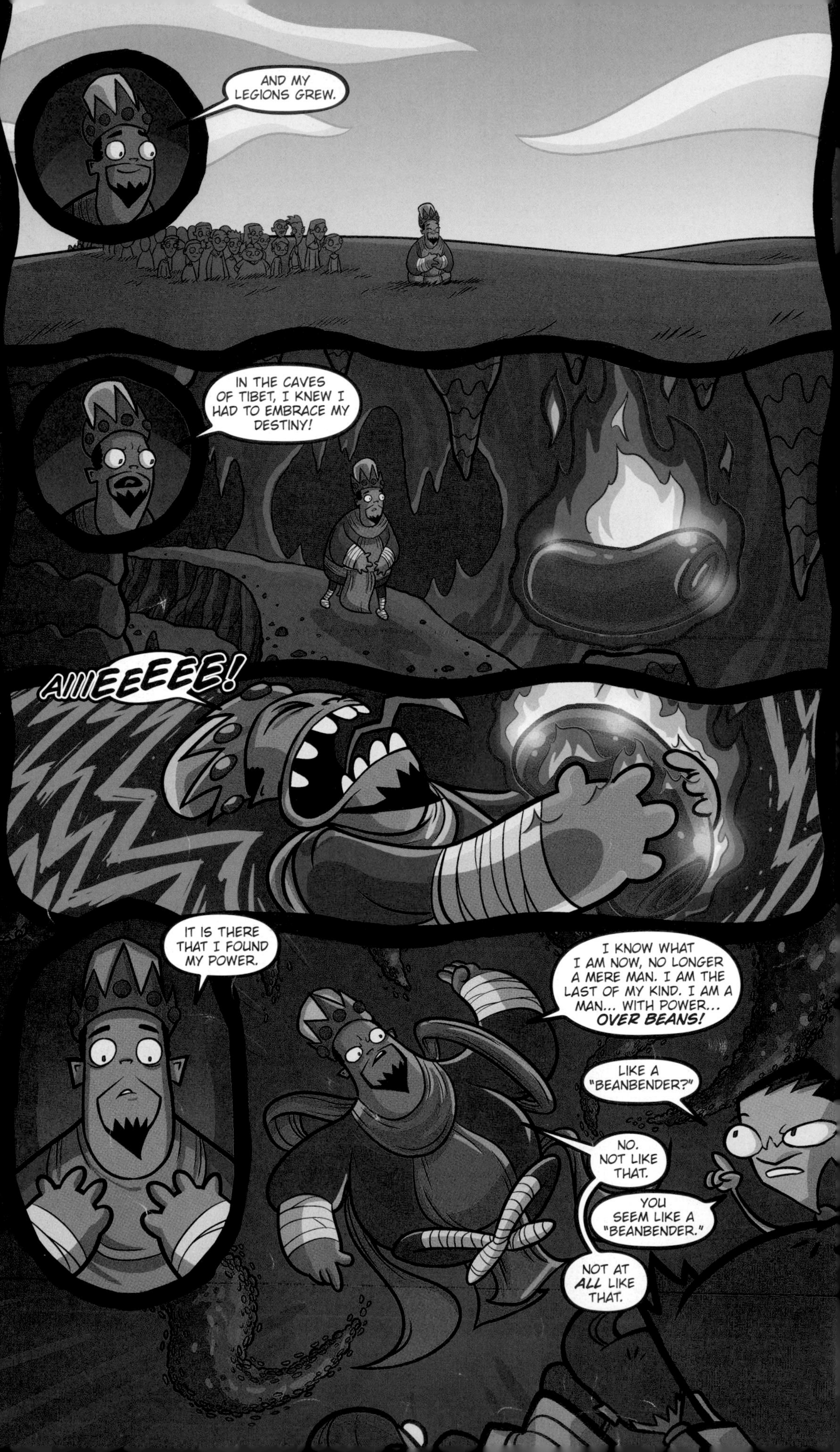
AND MY LEGIONS GREW.
IN THE CAVES OF TIBET, I KNEW I HAD TO EMBRACE MY DESTINY!
AIIIEEEEEE!
IT IS THERE THAT I FOUND MY POWER.
I KNOW WHAT I AM NOW, NO LONGER A MERE MAN. I AM THE LAST OF MY KIND. I AM A MAN... WITH POWER... OVER BEANS!
LIKE A "BEANBENDER?"
NO. NOT LIKE THAT.
YOU SEEM LIKE A "BEANBENDER."
NOT AT ALL LIKE THAT.

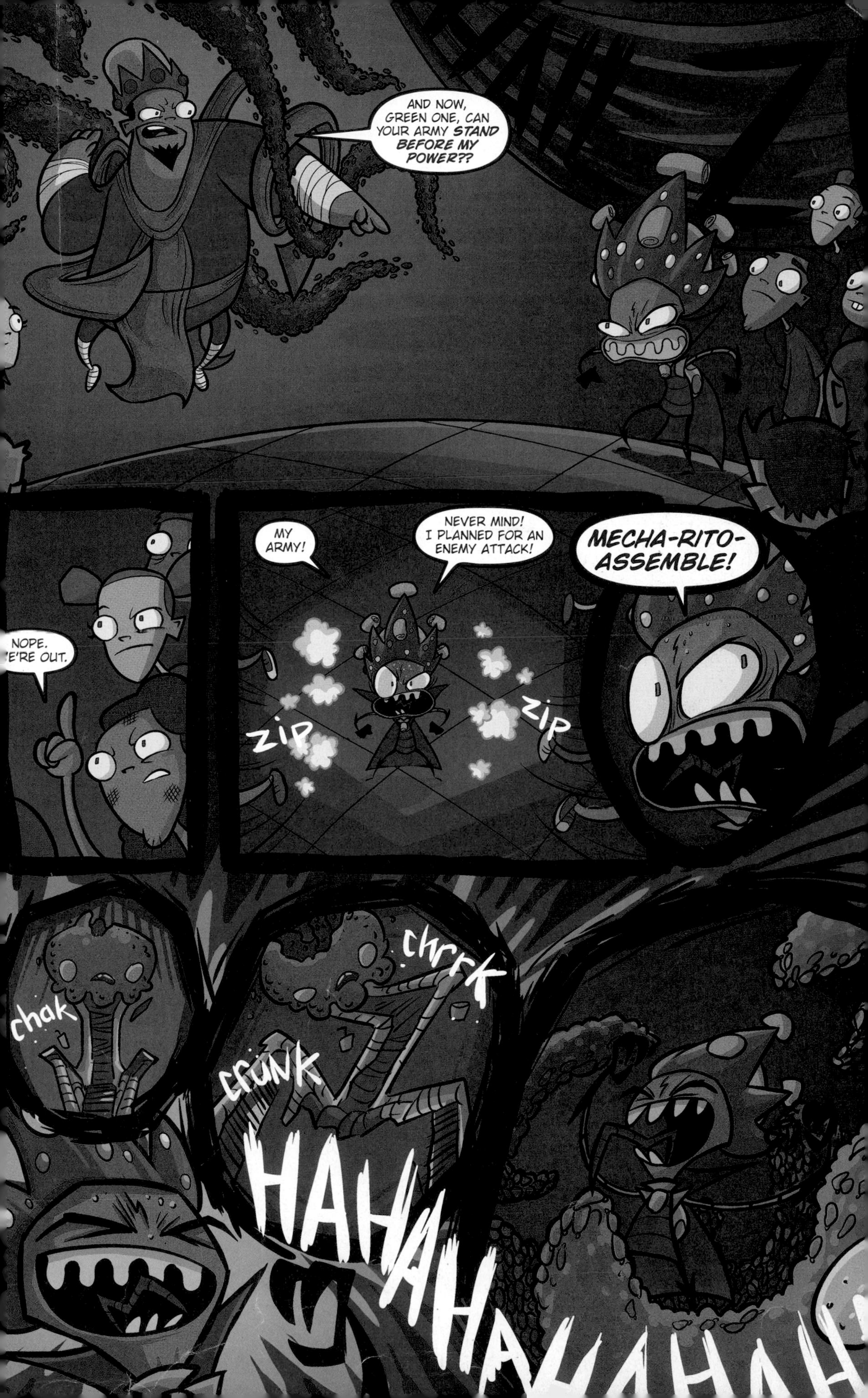
AND NOW, GREEN ONE, CAN YOUR ARMY STAND BEFORE MY POWER??
NOPE. 'E'RE OUT.
MY ARMY!
NEVER MIND! I PLANNED FOR AN ENEMY ATTACK!
zip
zip
MECHA-RITO-ASSEMBLE!
chak
chrrk
crunk
HAHAHAHAHAHAH

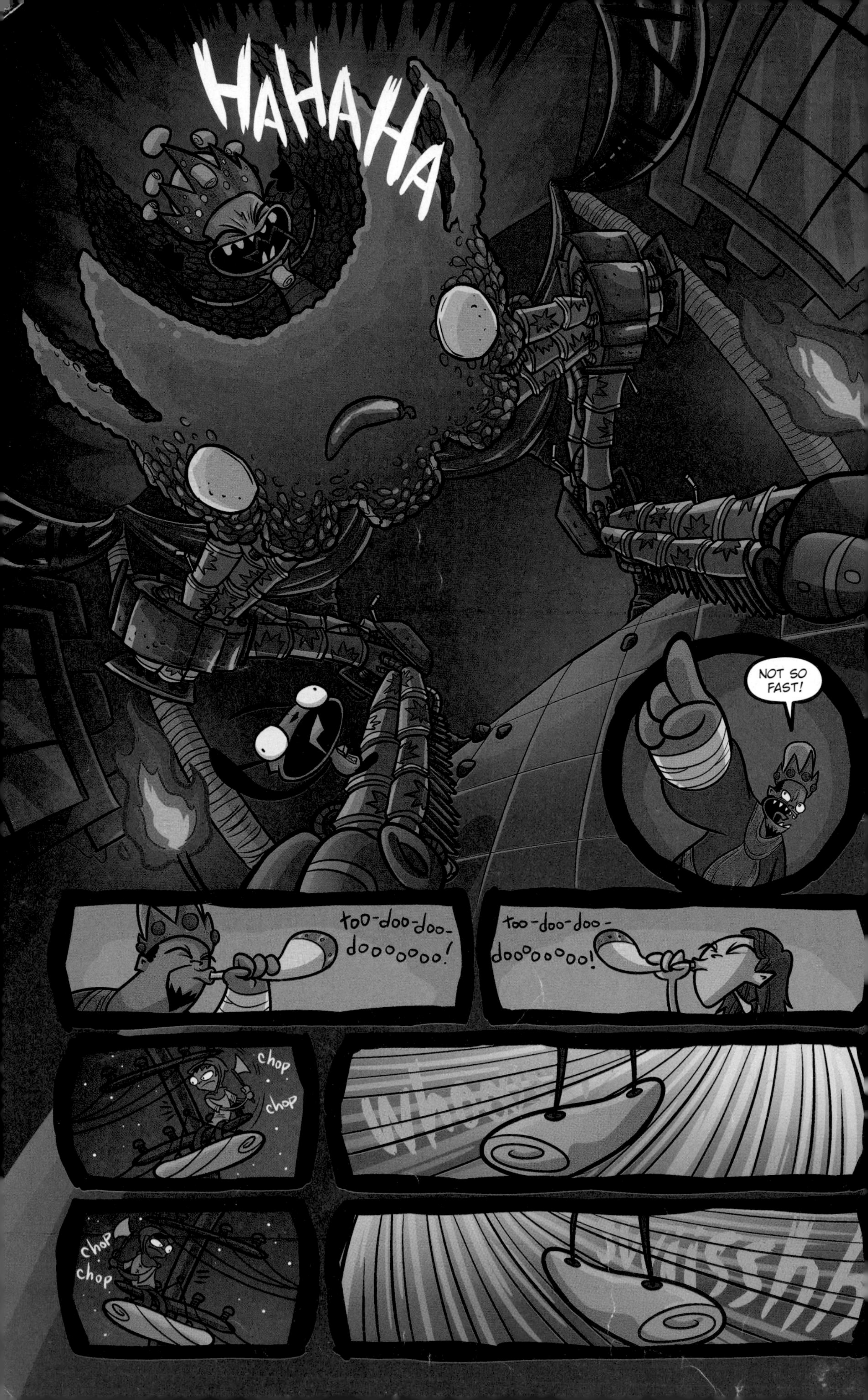

HAHAHA
NOT SO FAST!
too-doo-doo-doooooooo!
too-doo-doo-dooooooo!
chop
chop
chop
chop

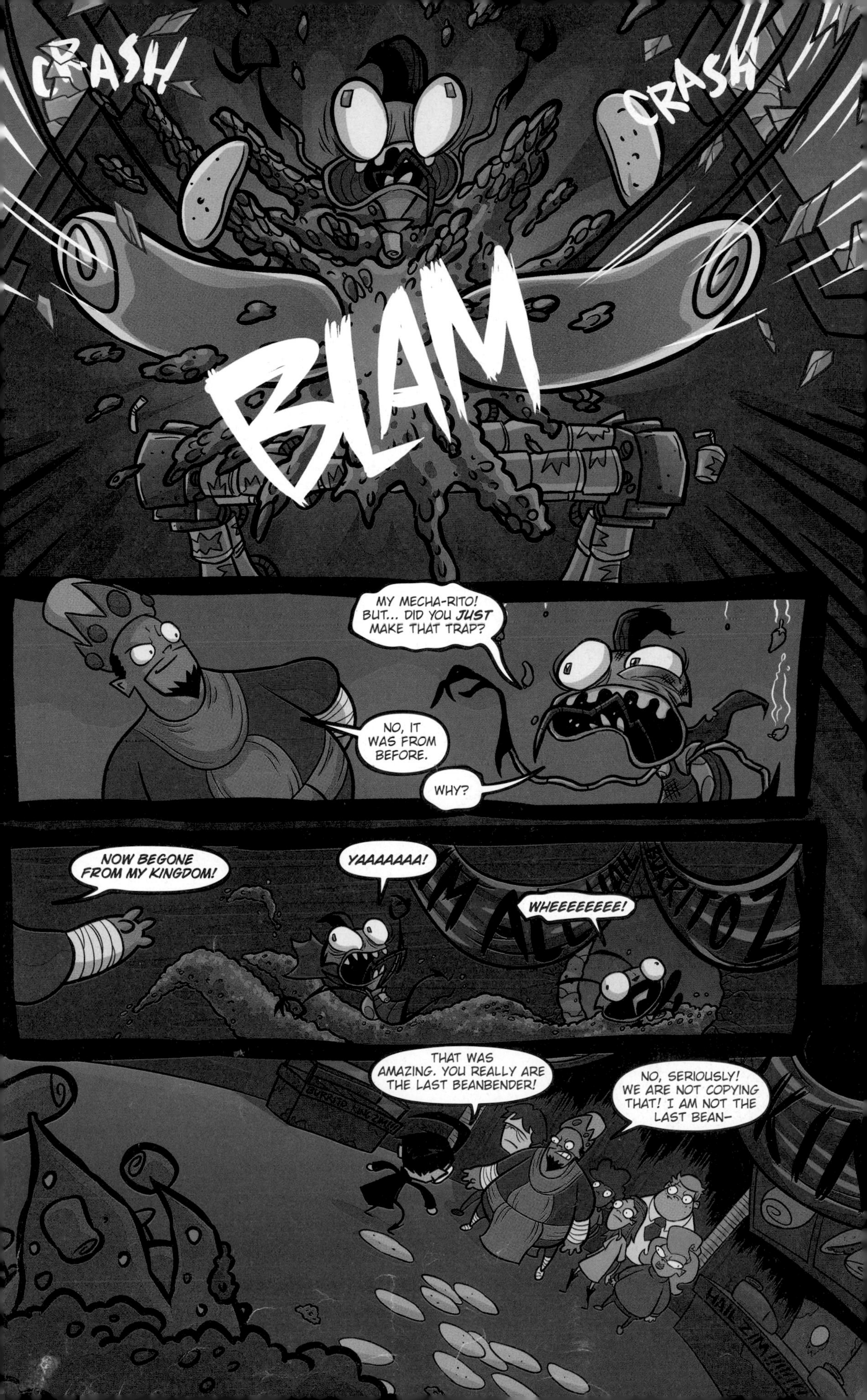
CRASH
CRASH
BLAM
MY MECHA-RITO! BUT... DID YOU *JUST* MAKE THAT TRAP?
NO, IT WAS FROM BEFORE.
WHY?
NOW BEGONE FROM MY KINGDOM!
YAAAAAAA!
WHEEEEEEEE!
THAT WAS AMAZING. YOU REALLY ARE THE LAST BEANBENDER!
NO, SERIOUSLY! WE ARE NOT COPYING THAT! I AM NOT THE LAST BEAN-

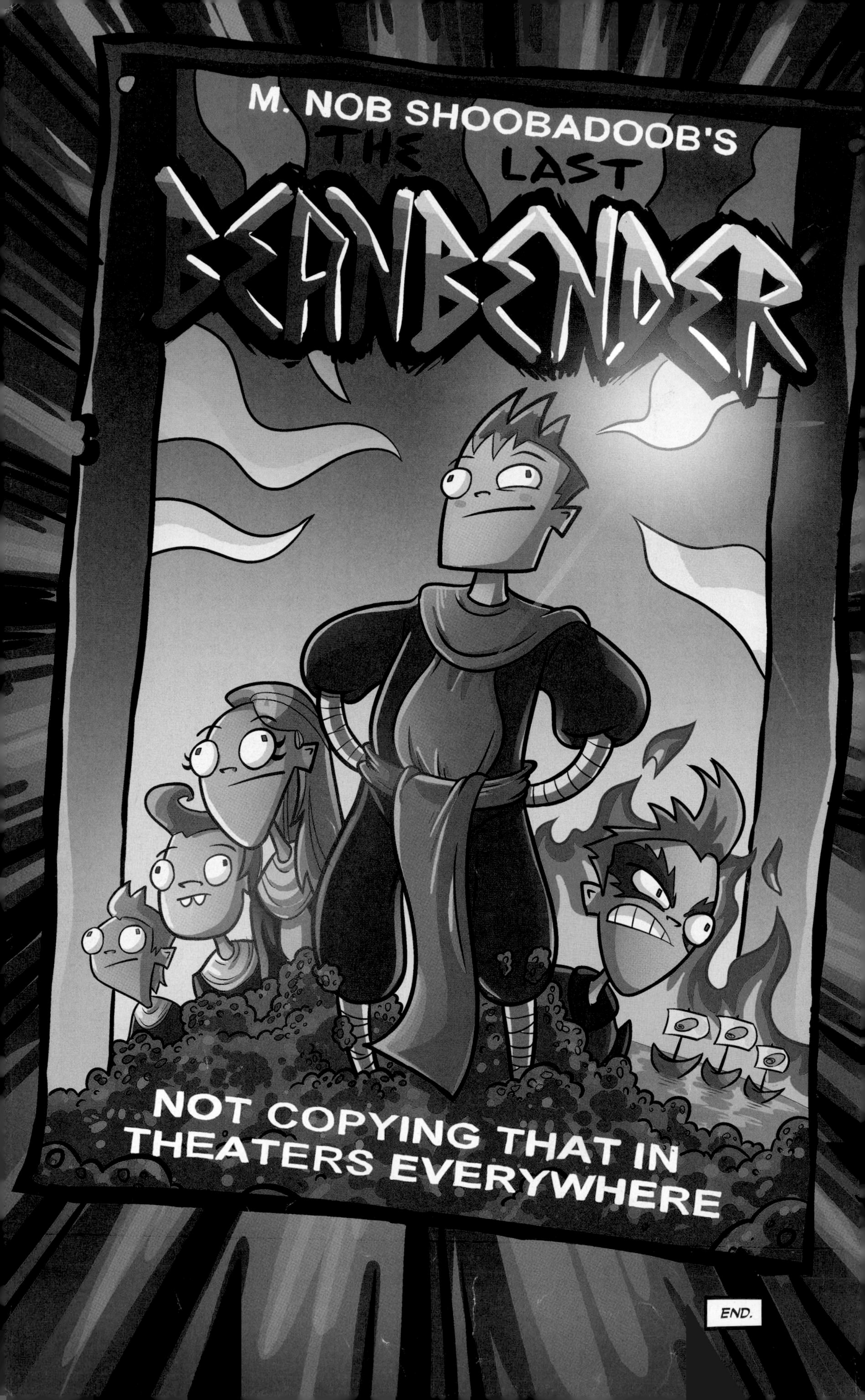

M. NOB SHOOBADOOB'S
THE LAST
BEANBENDER
NOT COPYING THAT IN THEATERS EVERYWHERE
END.

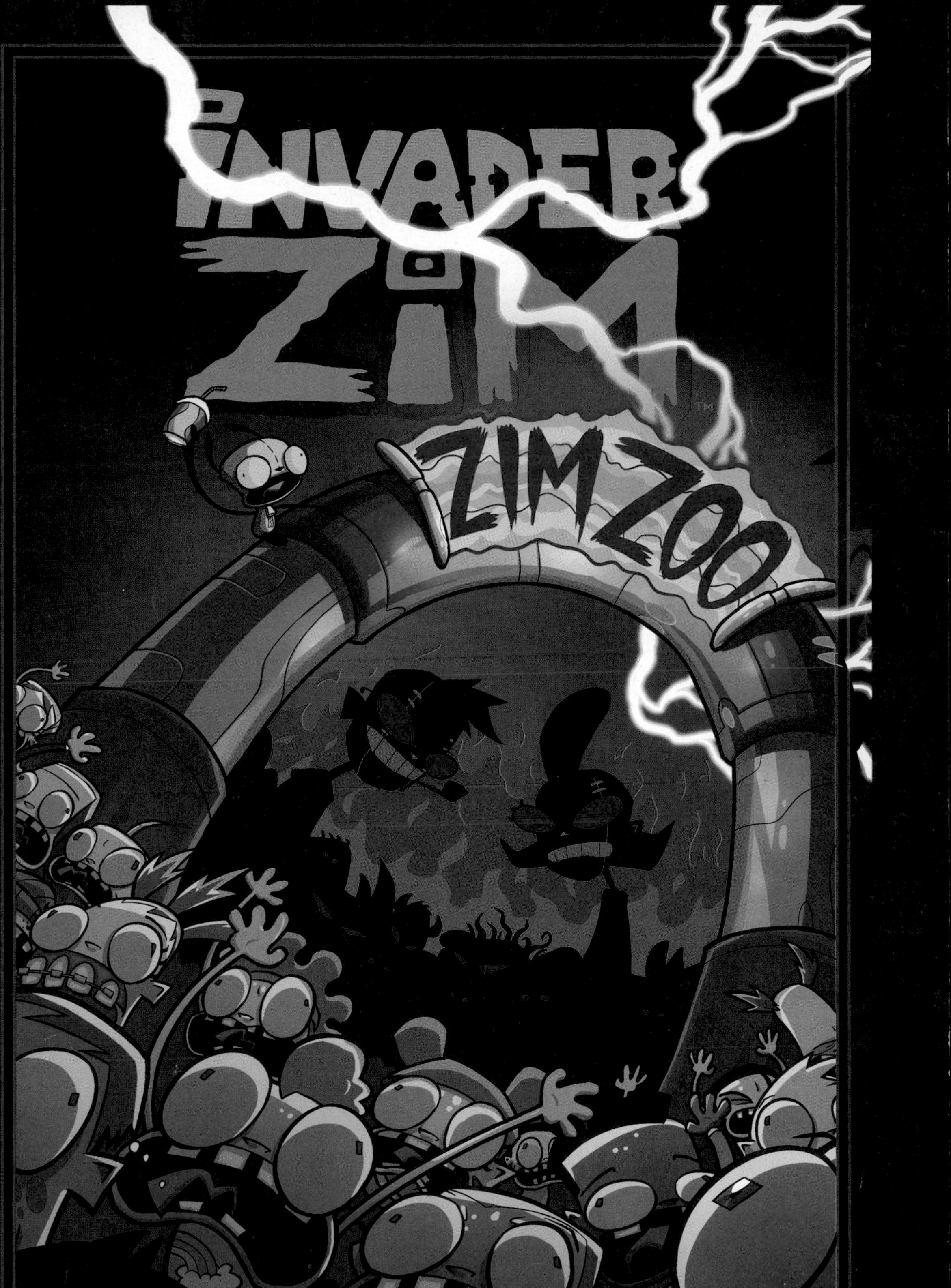
INVADER ZIM
ZIM ZOO

CHAPTER: 4

illustration by WARREN WUCINICH

WHUHH?! A new issue of INVADER ZIM, mah favorite comic OF ALL TIME?! UH MUH GUH! ZIM's in this one! YESSSS! And GIR is here too! AHAHAHAH ALRIGHT! And DIIIIB?! This issue's gonna be SO GOOD! LAST issue was about burritos, and ZIM went mad with burrito power— THE POWER TO MAKE ME HUNGRY FOR BURRITOS, AM I RIGHT?! Anyhow, I DID get a burrito and my hands are still all greasy. Ehhehhe. OKAY! SORRY! THIS issue's about a zoo and there's all kindsa funny-lookin' animals! I hope there's a walrus in here. IF THERE'S NO WALRUS I'M QUITTING MY JOB AS NUMBER ONE ZIM FAN! I'M JUST KIDDING!! I'll probably just get really mad is all. OKAY SEE YA!

Recap Kid by **WARREN WUCINICH**

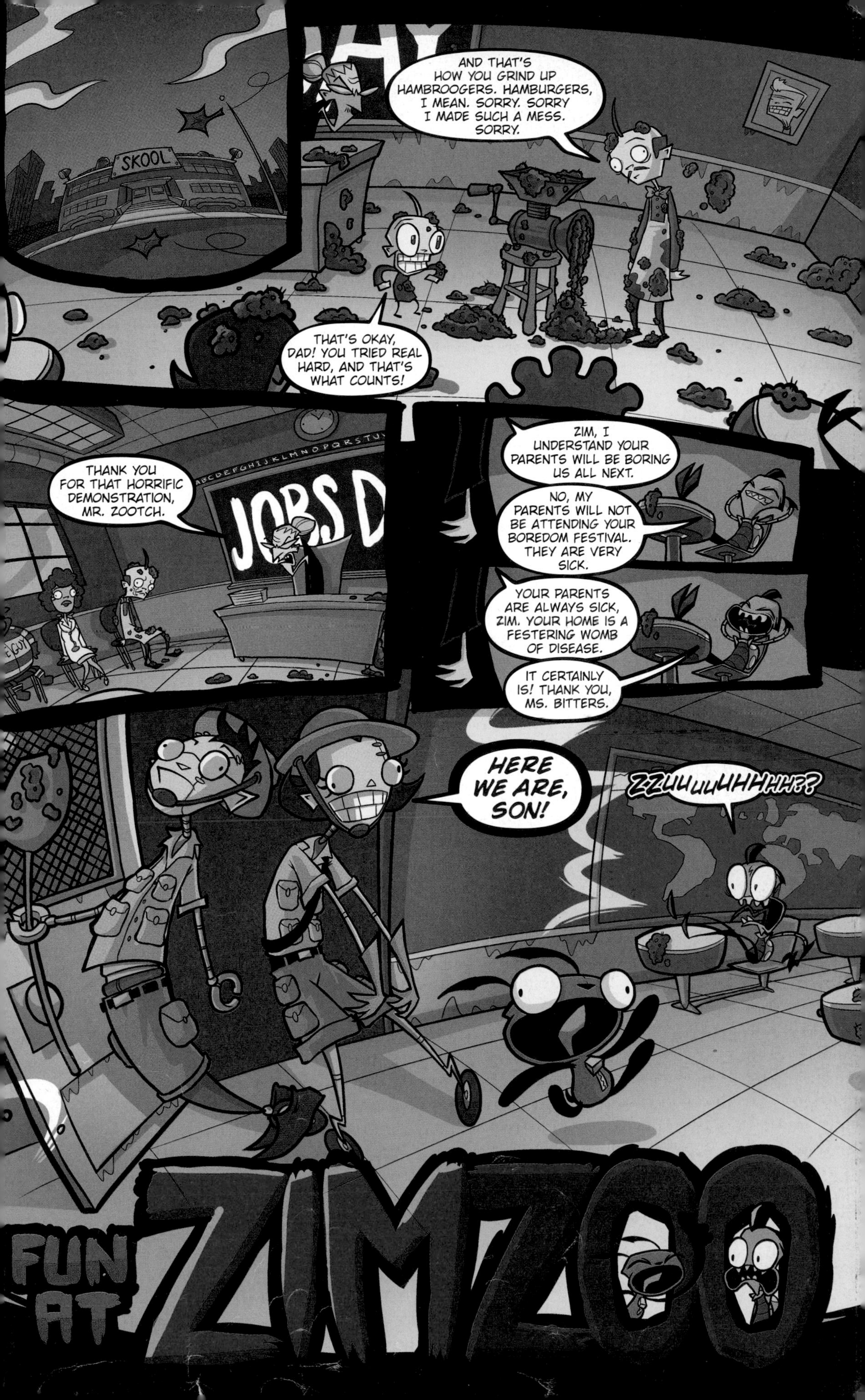

SKOOL
AND THAT'S HOW YOU GRIND UP HAMBROOGERS. HAMBURGERS, I MEAN. SORRY. SORRY I MADE SUCH A MESS. SORRY.
THAT'S OKAY, DAD! YOU TRIED REAL HARD, AND THAT'S WHAT COUNTS!
THANK YOU FOR THAT HORRIFIC DEMONSTRATION, MR. ZOOTCH.
JOBS D
ZIM, I UNDERSTAND YOUR PARENTS WILL BE BORING US ALL NEXT.
NO, MY PARENTS WILL NOT BE ATTENDING YOUR BOREDOM FESTIVAL. THEY ARE VERY SICK.
YOUR PARENTS ARE ALWAYS SICK, ZIM. YOUR HOME IS A FESTERING WOMB OF DISEASE.
IT CERTAINLY IS! THANK YOU, MS. BITTERS.
HERE WE ARE, SON!
ZZUHuuUHHHH??
FUN AT ZIM ZOO

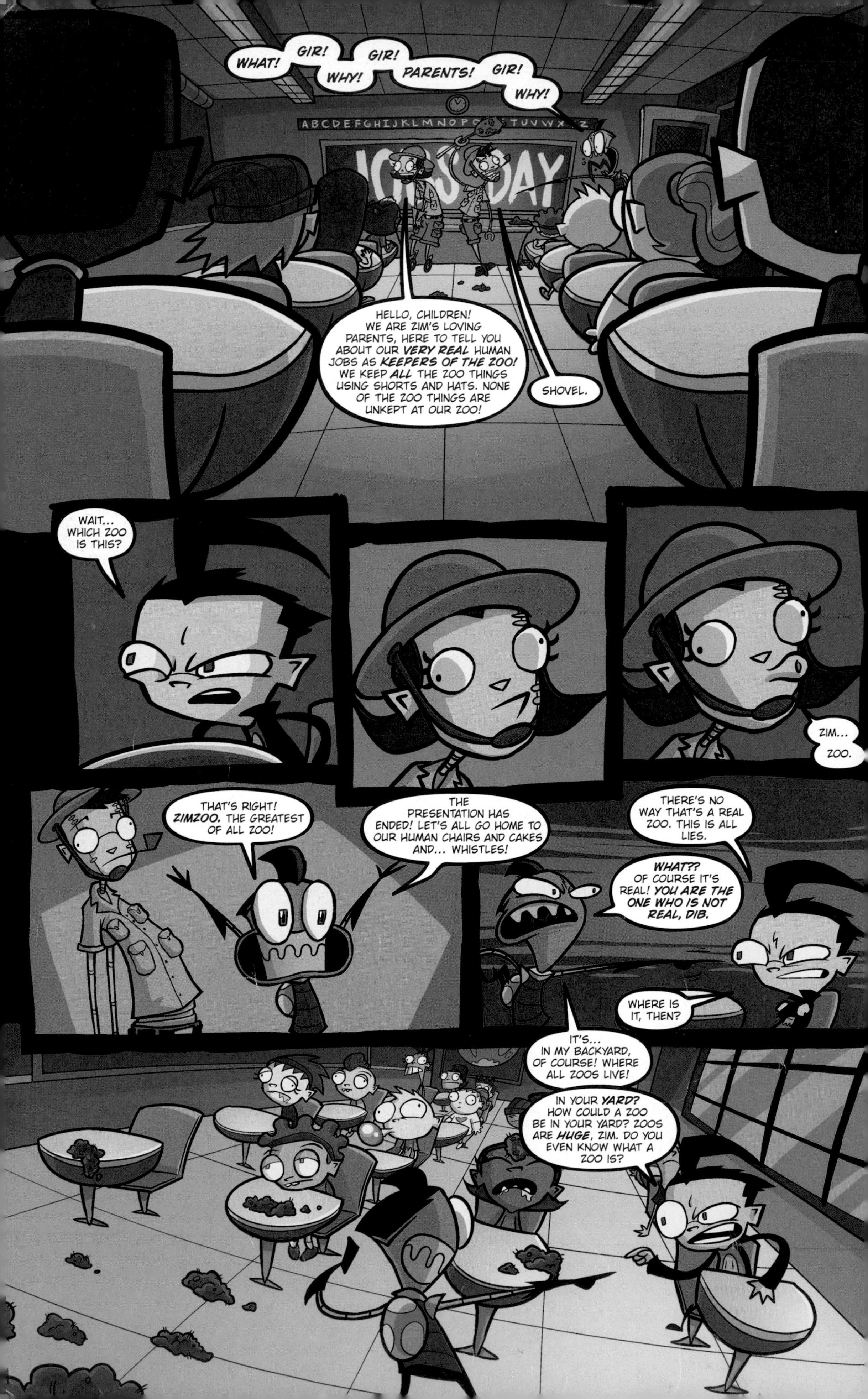
WHAT!
GIR!
WHY!
GIR!
PARENTS!
GIR!
WHY!
ABCDEFGHIJKLMNOP
TUVWX
HELLO, CHILDREN! WE ARE ZIM'S LOVING PARENTS, HERE TO TELL YOU ABOUT OUR VERY REAL HUMAN JOBS AS KEEPERS OF THE ZOO! WE KEEP ALL THE ZOO THINGS USING SHORTS AND HATS. NONE OF THE ZOO THINGS ARE UNKEPT AT OUR ZOO!
SHOVEL.
WAIT... WHICH ZOO IS THIS?
ZIM...
ZOO.
THAT'S RIGHT! ZIMZOO. THE GREATEST OF ALL ZOO!
THE PRESENTATION HAS ENDED! LET'S ALL GO HOME TO OUR HUMAN CHAIRS AND CAKES AND... WHISTLES!
THERE'S NO WAY THAT'S A REAL ZOO. THIS IS ALL LIES.
WHAT?? OF COURSE IT'S REAL! YOU ARE THE ONE WHO IS NOT REAL, DIB.
WHERE IS IT, THEN?
IT'S... IN MY BACKYARD, OF COURSE! WHERE ALL ZOOS LIVE!
IN YOUR YARD? HOW COULD A ZOO BE IN YOUR YARD? ZOOS ARE HUGE, ZIM. DO YOU EVEN KNOW WHAT A ZOO IS?

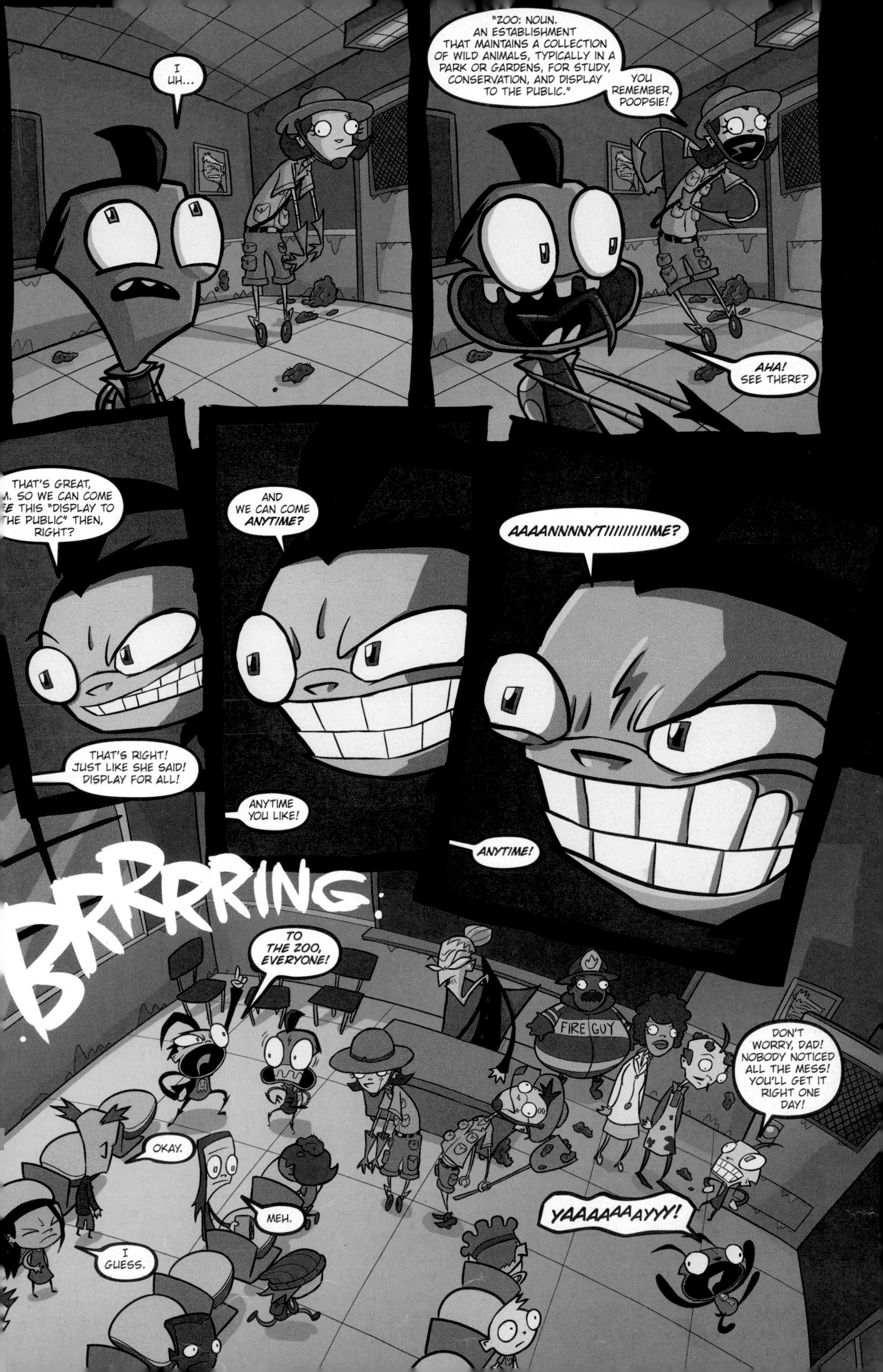

I UH...
"ZOO: NOUN. AN ESTABLISHMENT THAT MAINTAINS A COLLECTION OF WILD ANIMALS, TYPICALLY IN A PARK OR GARDENS, FOR STUDY, CONSERVATION, AND DISPLAY TO THE PUBLIC."
YOU REMEMBER, POOPSIE!
AHA! SEE THERE?
THAT'S GREAT, M. SO WE CAN COME E THIS "DISPLAY TO THE PUBLIC" THEN, RIGHT?
THAT'S RIGHT! JUST LIKE SHE SAID! DISPLAY FOR ALL!
AND WE CAN COME ANYTIME?
ANYTIME YOU LIKE!
AAAANNNNYTIIIIIIIIIIIME?
ANYTIME!
BRRRRING
TO THE ZOO, EVERYONE!
FIRE GUY
DON'T WORRY, DAD! NOBODY NOTICED ALL THE MESS! YOU'LL GET IT RIGHT ONE DAY!
OKAY.
MEH.
I GUESS.
YAAAAAAAYYY!

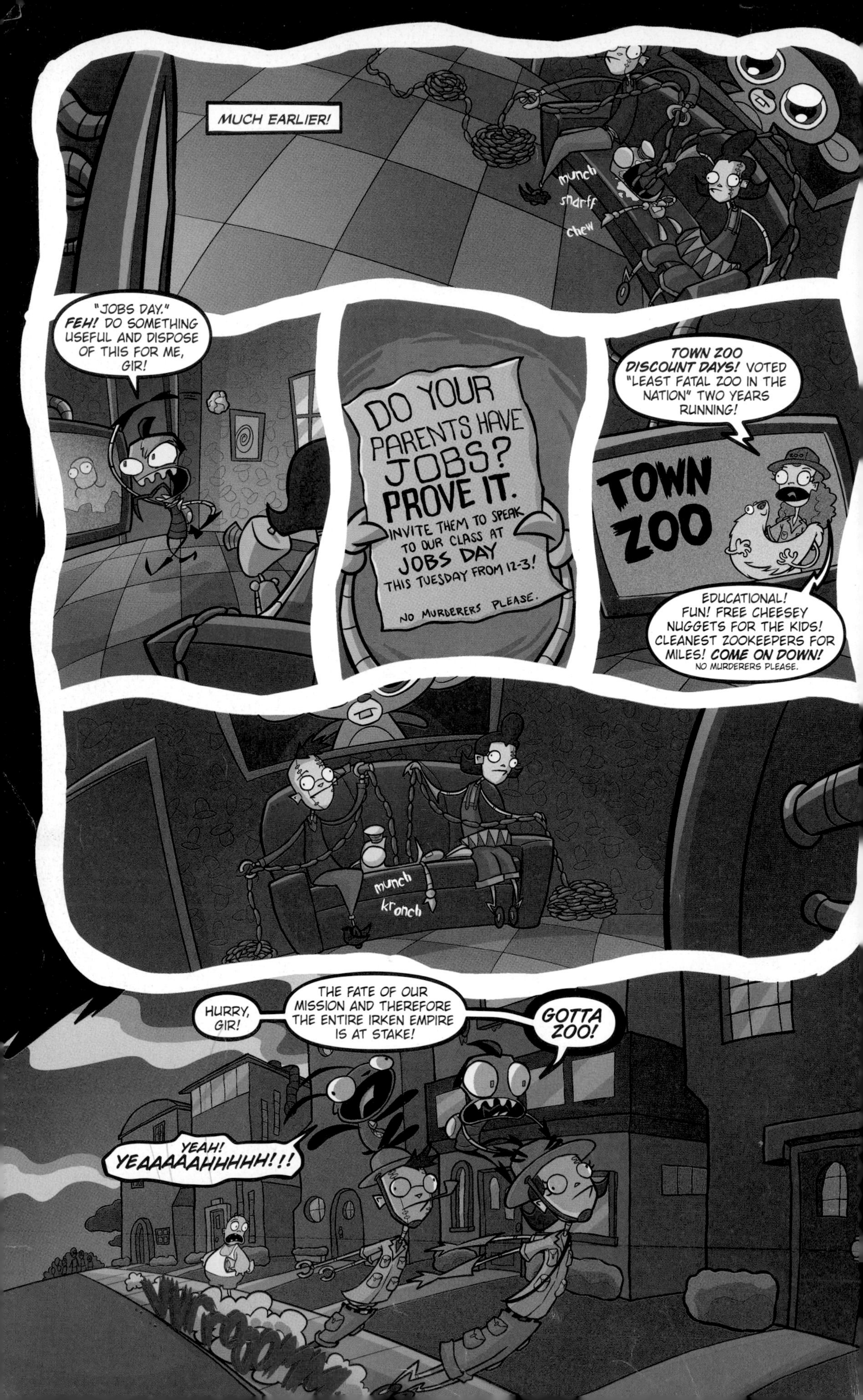
MUCH EARLIER!
munch
snarff
chew
"JOBS DAY." FEH! DO SOMETHING USEFUL AND DISPOSE OF THIS FOR ME, GIR!
DO YOUR PARENTS HAVE JOBS? PROVE IT.
INVITE THEM TO SPEAK TO OUR CLASS AT JOBS DAY THIS TUESDAY FROM 12-3!
NO MURDERERS PLEASE.
TOWN ZOO DISCOUNT DAYS! VOTED "LEAST FATAL ZOO IN THE NATION" TWO YEARS RUNNING!
TOWN ZOO
EDUCATIONAL! FUN! FREE CHEESEY NUGGETS FOR THE KIDS! CLEANEST ZOOKEEPERS FOR MILES! COME ON DOWN!
NO MURDERERS PLEASE.
munch
kronch
HURRY, GIR!
THE FATE OF OUR MISSION AND THEREFORE THE ENTIRE IRKEN EMPIRE IS AT STAKE!
GOTTA ZOO!
YEAH! YEAAAAAHHHHH!!!

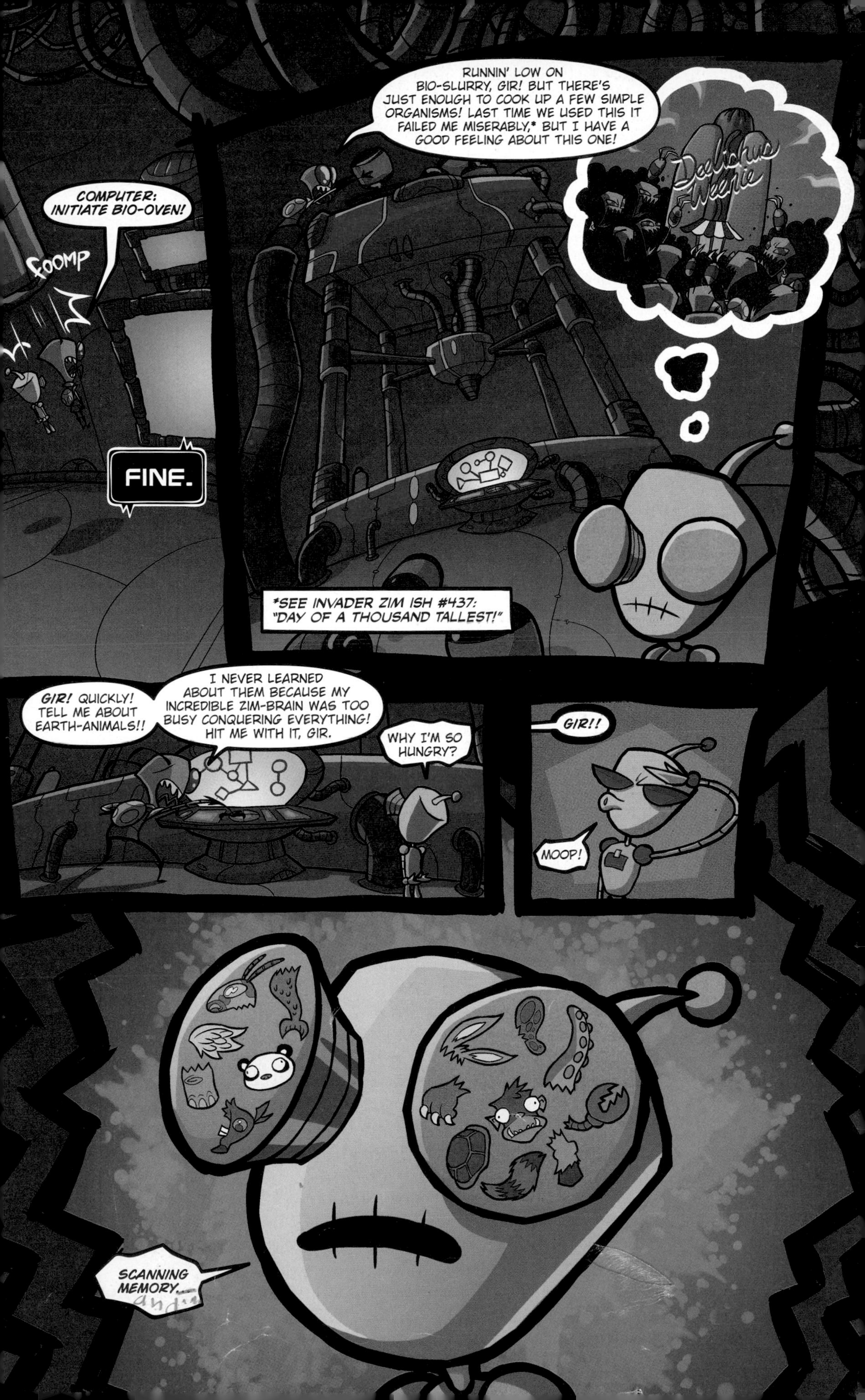
COMPUTER: INITIATE BIO-OVEN!
FOOMP
FINE.
RUNNIN' LOW ON BIO-SLURRY, GIR! BUT THERE'S JUST ENOUGH TO COOK UP A FEW SIMPLE ORGANISMS! LAST TIME WE USED THIS IT FAILED ME MISERABLY,* BUT I HAVE A GOOD FEELING ABOUT THIS ONE!
*SEE INVADER ZIM ISH #437: "DAY OF A THOUSAND TALLEST!"
GIR! QUICKLY! TELL ME ABOUT EARTH-ANIMALS!!
I NEVER LEARNED ABOUT THEM BECAUSE MY INCREDIBLE ZIM-BRAIN WAS TOO BUSY CONQUERING EVERYTHING! HIT ME WITH IT, GIR.
WHY I'M SO HUNGRY?
GIR!!
MOOP!
SCANNING MEMORY...

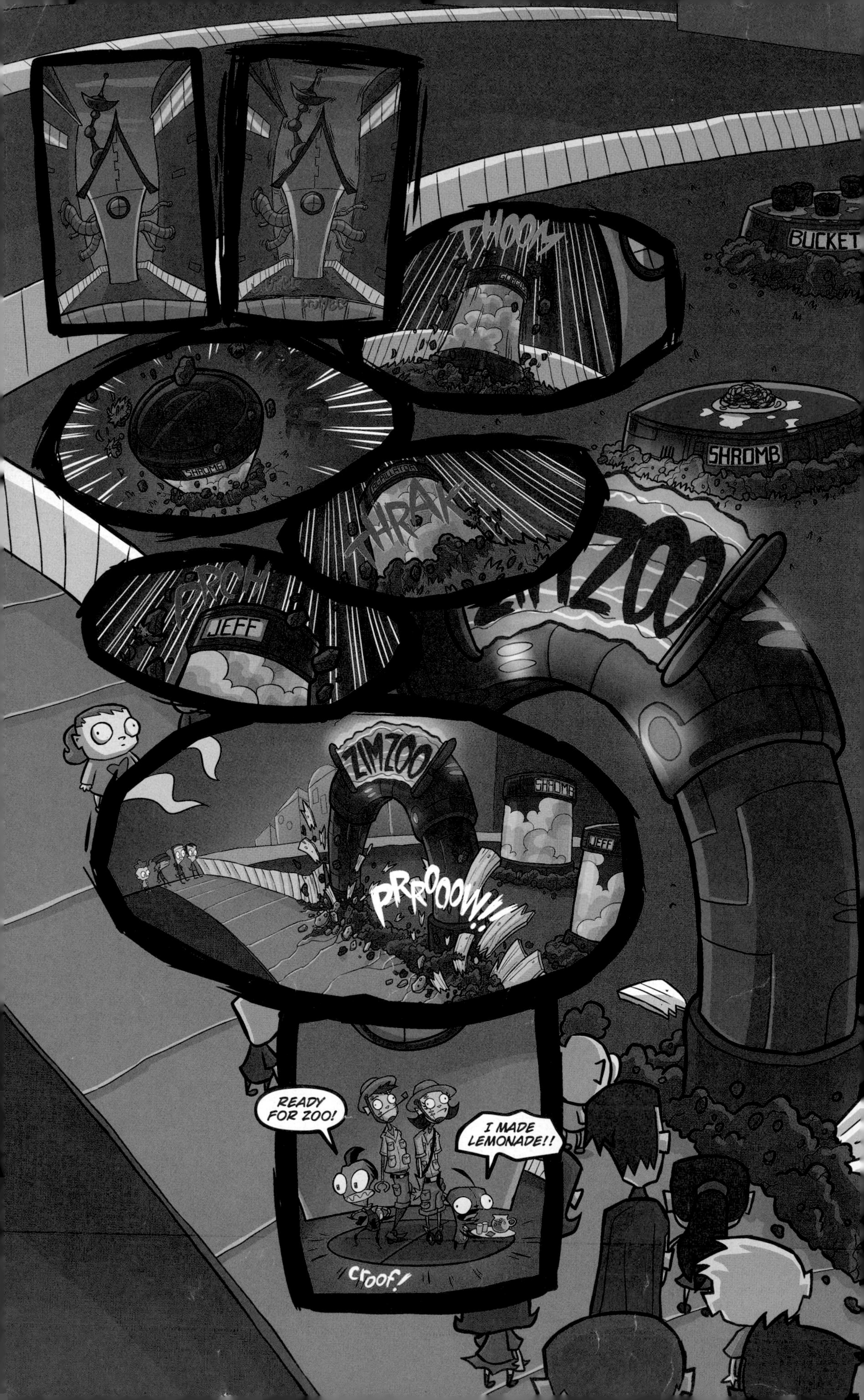
THOOM
BUCKET
SHROMB
THRAK
PROH
JEFF
ZIMZOO
ZIMZOO
SHROMB
JEFF
PRROOOW!!!
READY FOR ZOO!
I MADE LEMONADE!!
croof!

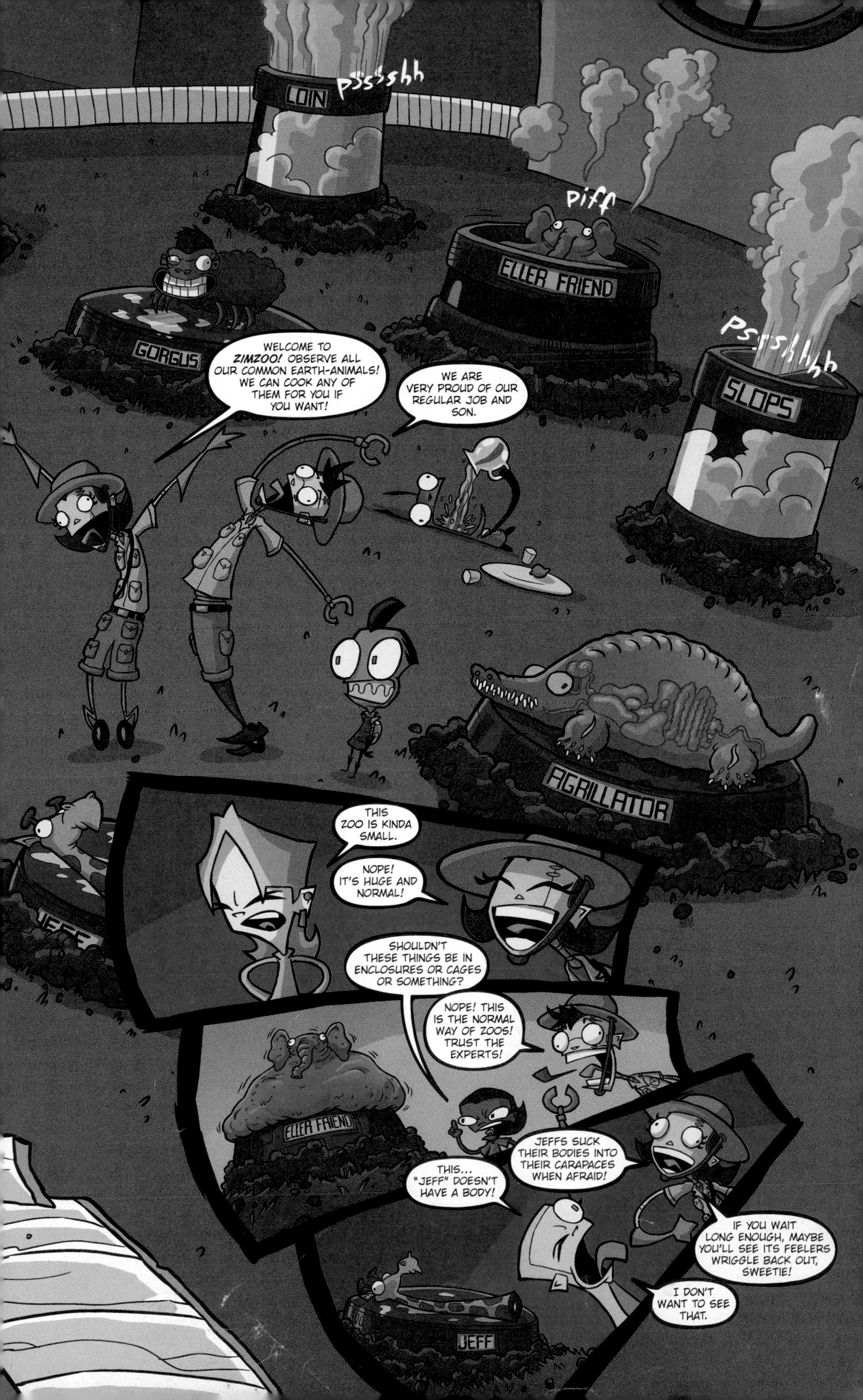
LOIN
PSSSSHH
PIFF
ELLER FRIEND
GORGUS
PSSSHHHH
SLOPS
WELCOME TO ZIMZOO! OBSERVE ALL OUR COMMON EARTH-ANIMALS! WE CAN COOK ANY OF THEM FOR YOU IF YOU WANT!
WE ARE VERY PROUD OF OUR REGULAR JOB AND SON.
AGRILLATOR
THIS ZOO IS KINDA SMALL.
NOPE! IT'S HUGE AND NORMAL!
SHOULDN'T THESE THINGS BE IN ENCLOSURES OR CAGES OR SOMETHING?
NOPE! THIS IS THE NORMAL WAY OF ZOOS! TRUST THE EXPERTS!
ELLER FRIEND
JEFFS SUCK THEIR BODIES INTO THEIR CARAPACES WHEN AFRAID!
THIS... "JEFF" DOESN'T HAVE A BODY!
IF YOU WAIT LONG ENOUGH, MAYBE YOU'LL SEE ITS FEELERS WRIGGLE BACK OUT, SWEETIE!
I DON'T WANT TO SEE THAT.
JEFF

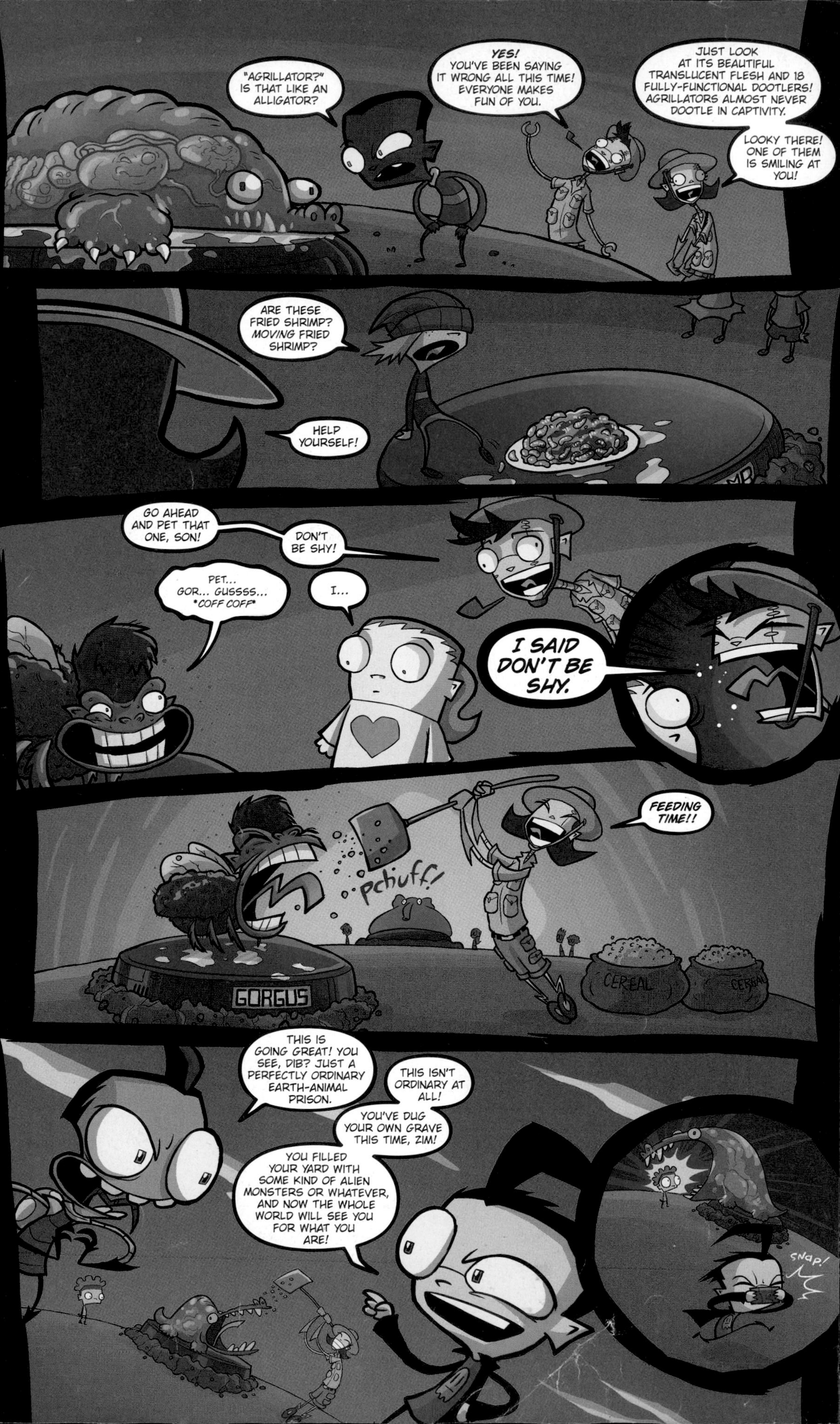
"AGRILLATOR?" IS THAT LIKE AN ALLIGATOR?
YES! YOU'VE BEEN SAYING IT WRONG ALL THIS TIME! EVERYONE MAKES FUN OF YOU.
JUST LOOK AT ITS BEAUTIFUL TRANSLUCENT FLESH AND 18 FULLY-FUNCTIONAL DOOTLERS! AGRILLATORS ALMOST NEVER DOOTLE IN CAPTIVITY.
LOOKY THERE! ONE OF THEM IS SMILING AT YOU!
ARE THESE FRIED SHRIMP? MOVING FRIED SHRIMP?
HELP YOURSELF!
GO AHEAD AND PET THAT ONE, SON!
DON'T BE SHY!
PET... GOR... GUSSSS... *COFF COFF*
I...
I SAID DON'T BE SHY.
FEEDING TIME!!
pchuff!
GORGUS
CEREAL
CEREAL
THIS IS GOING GREAT! YOU SEE, DIB? JUST A PERFECTLY ORDINARY EARTH-ANIMAL PRISON.
THIS ISN'T ORDINARY AT ALL!
YOU'VE DUG YOUR OWN GRAVE THIS TIME, ZIM!
YOU FILLED YOUR YARD WITH SOME KIND OF ALIEN MONSTERS OR WHATEVER, AND NOW THE WHOLE WORLD WILL SEE YOU FOR WHAT YOU ARE!
SNAP!

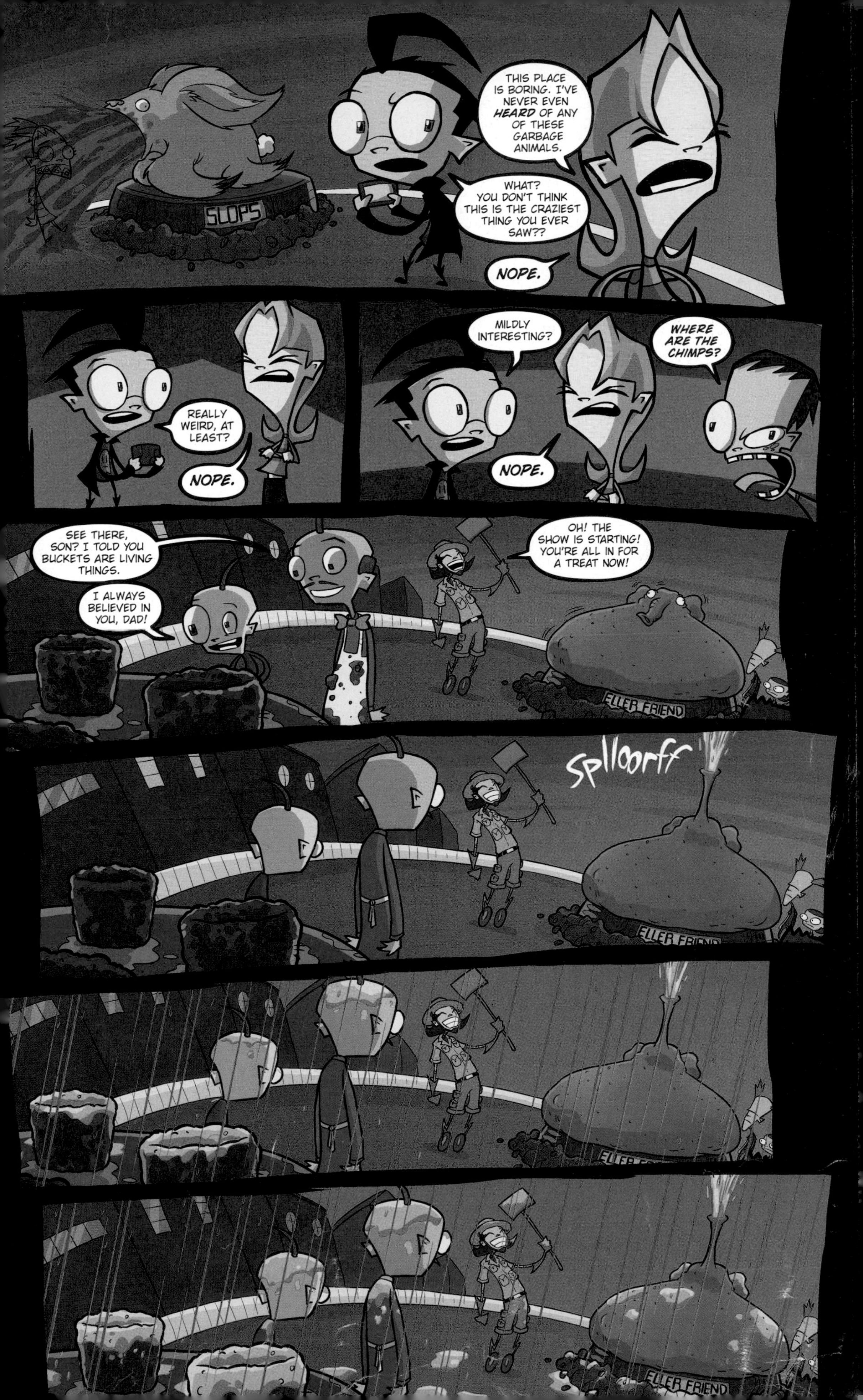
SLOPS
THIS PLACE IS BORING. I'VE NEVER EVEN HEARD OF ANY OF THESE GARBAGE ANIMALS.
WHAT? YOU DON'T THINK THIS IS THE CRAZIEST THING YOU EVER SAW??
NOPE.
REALLY WEIRD, AT LEAST?
NOPE.
MILDLY INTERESTING?
NOPE.
WHERE ARE THE CHIMPS?
SEE THERE, SON? I TOLD YOU BUCKETS ARE LIVING THINGS.
I ALWAYS BELIEVED IN YOU, DAD!
OH! THE SHOW IS STARTING! YOU'RE ALL IN FOR A TREAT NOW!
ELLER FRIEND
spllooorff
ELLER FRIEND

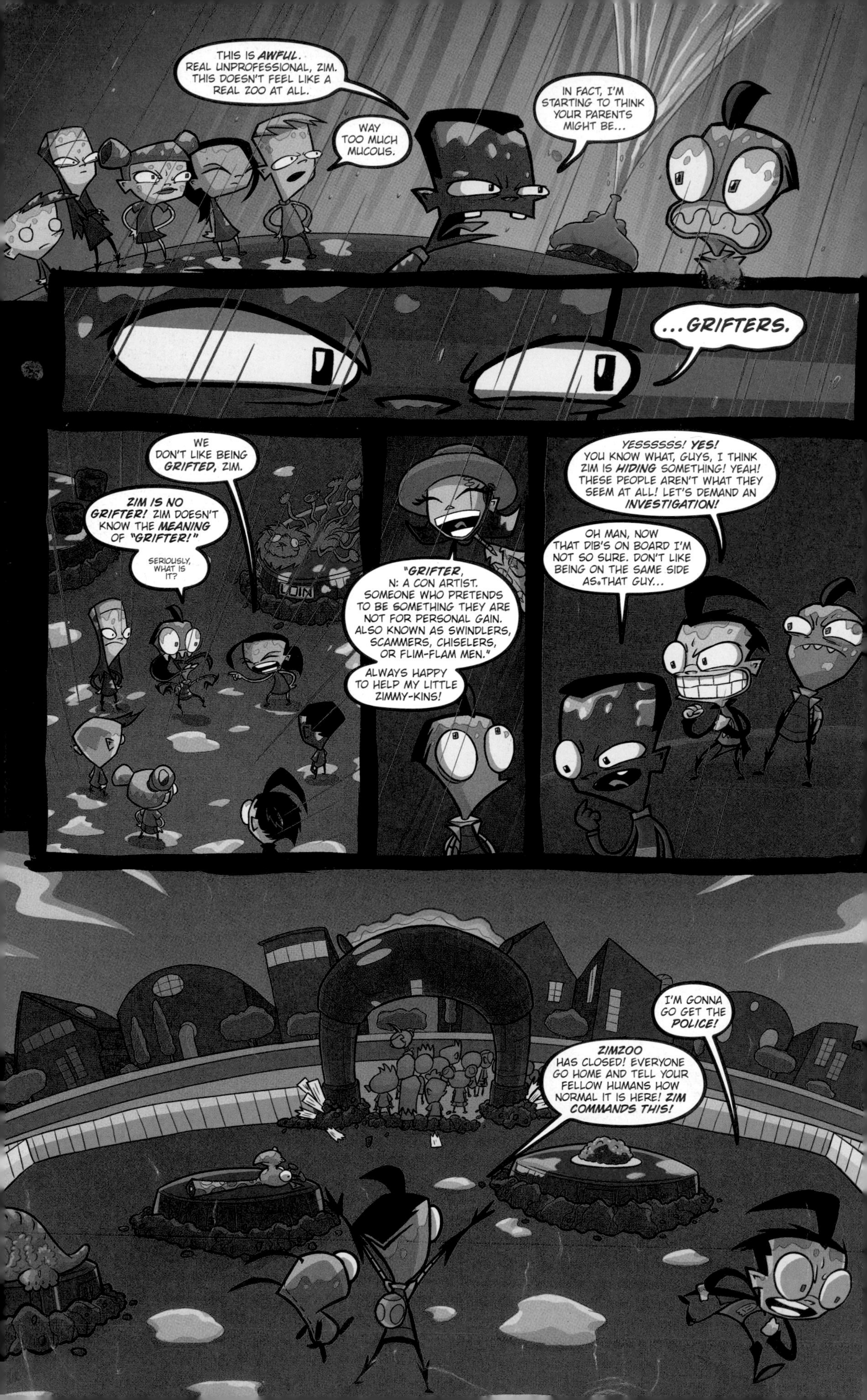

THIS IS AWFUL. REAL UNPROFESSIONAL, ZIM. THIS DOESN'T FEEL LIKE A REAL ZOO AT ALL.
WAY TOO MUCH MUCOUS.
IN FACT, I'M STARTING TO THINK YOUR PARENTS MIGHT BE...
...GRIFTERS.
WE DON'T LIKE BEING GRIFTED, ZIM.
ZIM IS NO GRIFTER! ZIM DOESN'T KNOW THE MEANING OF "GRIFTER!"
SERIOUSLY, WHAT IS IT?
"GRIFTER, N: A CON ARTIST. SOMEONE WHO PRETENDS TO BE SOMETHING THEY ARE NOT FOR PERSONAL GAIN. ALSO KNOWN AS SWINDLERS, SCAMMERS, CHISELERS, OR FLIM-FLAM MEN."
ALWAYS HAPPY TO HELP MY LITTLE ZIMMY-KINS!
YESSSSSS! YES! YOU KNOW WHAT, GUYS, I THINK ZIM IS HIDING SOMETHING! YEAH! THESE PEOPLE AREN'T WHAT THEY SEEM AT ALL! LET'S DEMAND AN INVESTIGATION!
OH MAN, NOW THAT DIB'S ON BOARD I'M NOT SO SURE. DON'T LIKE BEING ON THE SAME SIDE AS THAT GUY...
I'M GONNA GO GET THE POLICE!
ZIMZOO HAS CLOSED! EVERYONE GO HOME AND TELL YOUR FELLOW HUMANS HOW NORMAL IT IS HERE! ZIM COMMANDS THIS!

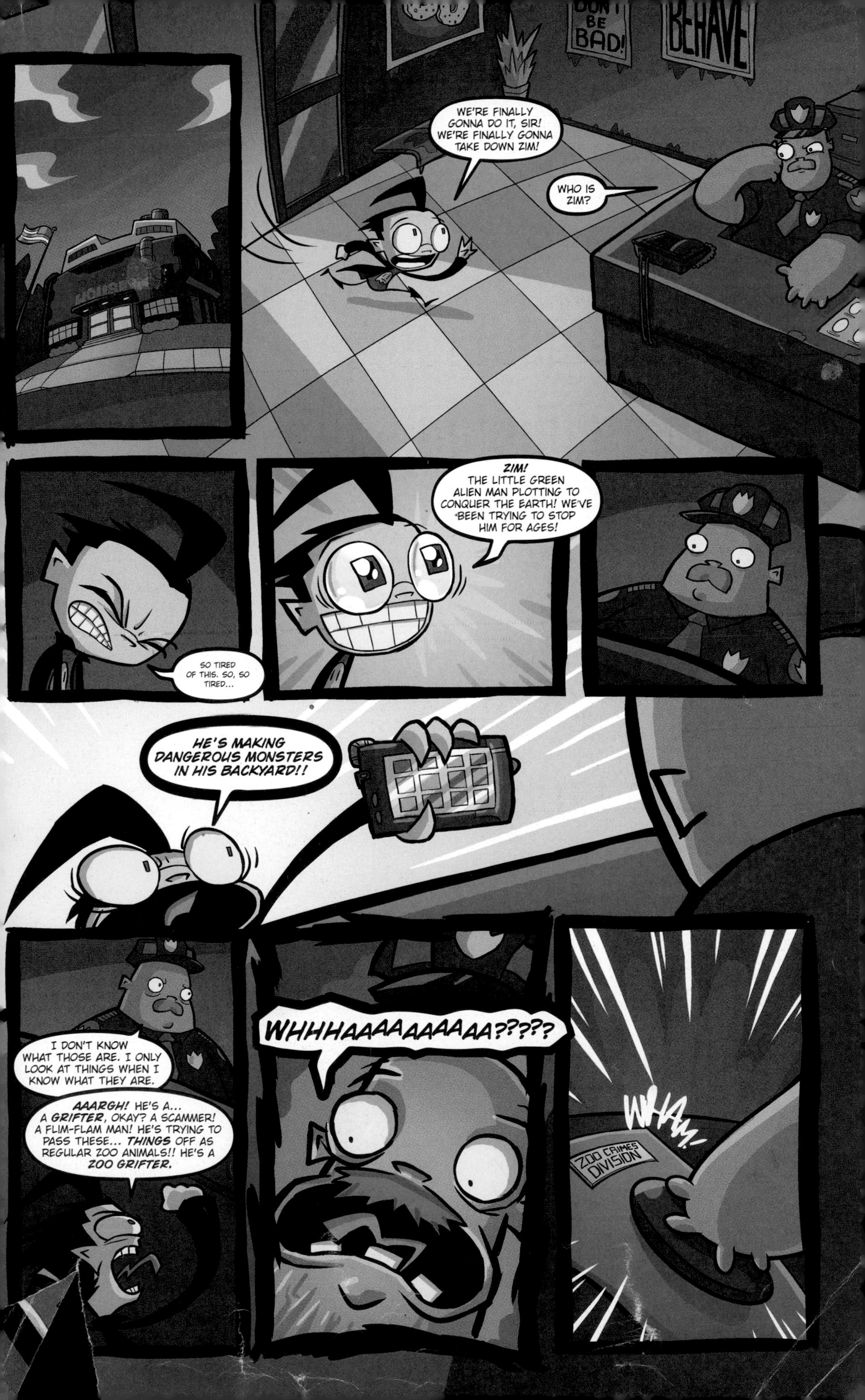

DON'T BE BAD!
BEHAVE
WE'RE FINALLY GONNA DO IT, SIR! WE'RE FINALLY GONNA TAKE DOWN ZIM!
WHO IS ZIM?
SO TIRED OF THIS. SO, SO TIRED...
ZIM! THE LITTLE GREEN ALIEN MAN PLOTTING TO CONQUER THE EARTH! WE'VE BEEN TRYING TO STOP HIM FOR AGES!
HE'S MAKING DANGEROUS MONSTERS IN HIS BACKYARD!!
I DON'T KNOW WHAT THOSE ARE. I ONLY LOOK AT THINGS WHEN I KNOW WHAT THEY ARE.
AAARGH! HE'S A... A GRIFTER, OKAY? A SCAMMER! A FLIM-FLAM MAN! HE'S TRYING TO PASS THESE... THINGS OFF AS REGULAR ZOO ANIMALS!! HE'S A ZOO GRIFTER.
WHHHAAAAAAAAAA????
WHAM!
ZOO CRIMES DIVISION

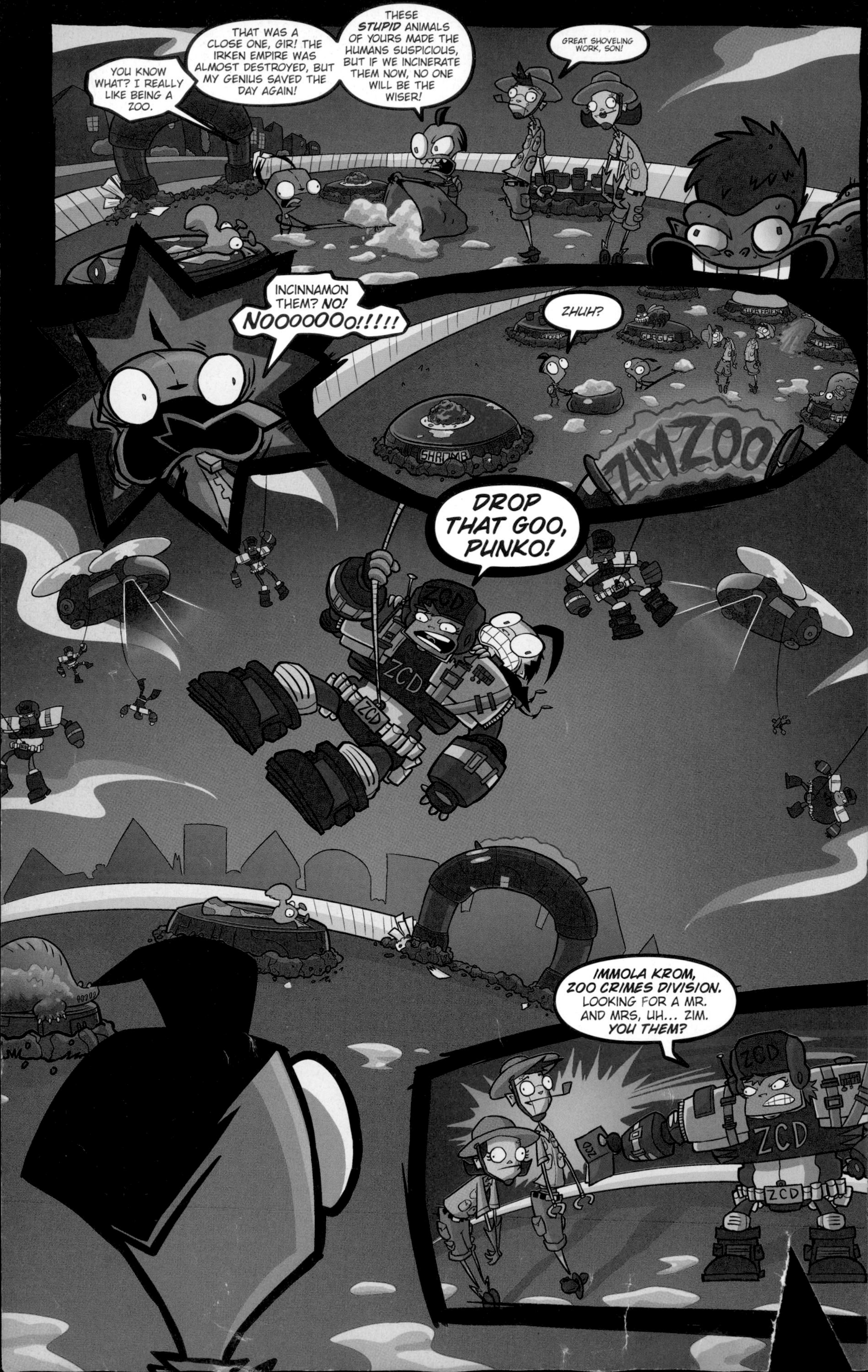
YOU KNOW WHAT? I REALLY LIKE BEING A ZOO.
THAT WAS A CLOSE ONE, GIR! THE IRKEN EMPIRE WAS ALMOST DESTROYED, BUT MY GENIUS SAVED THE DAY AGAIN!
THESE STUPID ANIMALS OF YOURS MADE THE HUMANS SUSPICIOUS, BUT IF WE INCINERATE THEM NOW, NO ONE WILL BE THE WISER!
GREAT SHOVELING WORK, SON!
INCINNAMON THEM? NO! NOOOOOOo!!!!!
ZHUH?
SHROMB
GORGUS
ZIM ZOO
DROP THAT GOO, PUNKO!
ZCD
IMMOLA KROM, ZOO CRIMES DIVISION. LOOKING FOR A MR. AND MRS, UH... ZIM. YOU THEM?

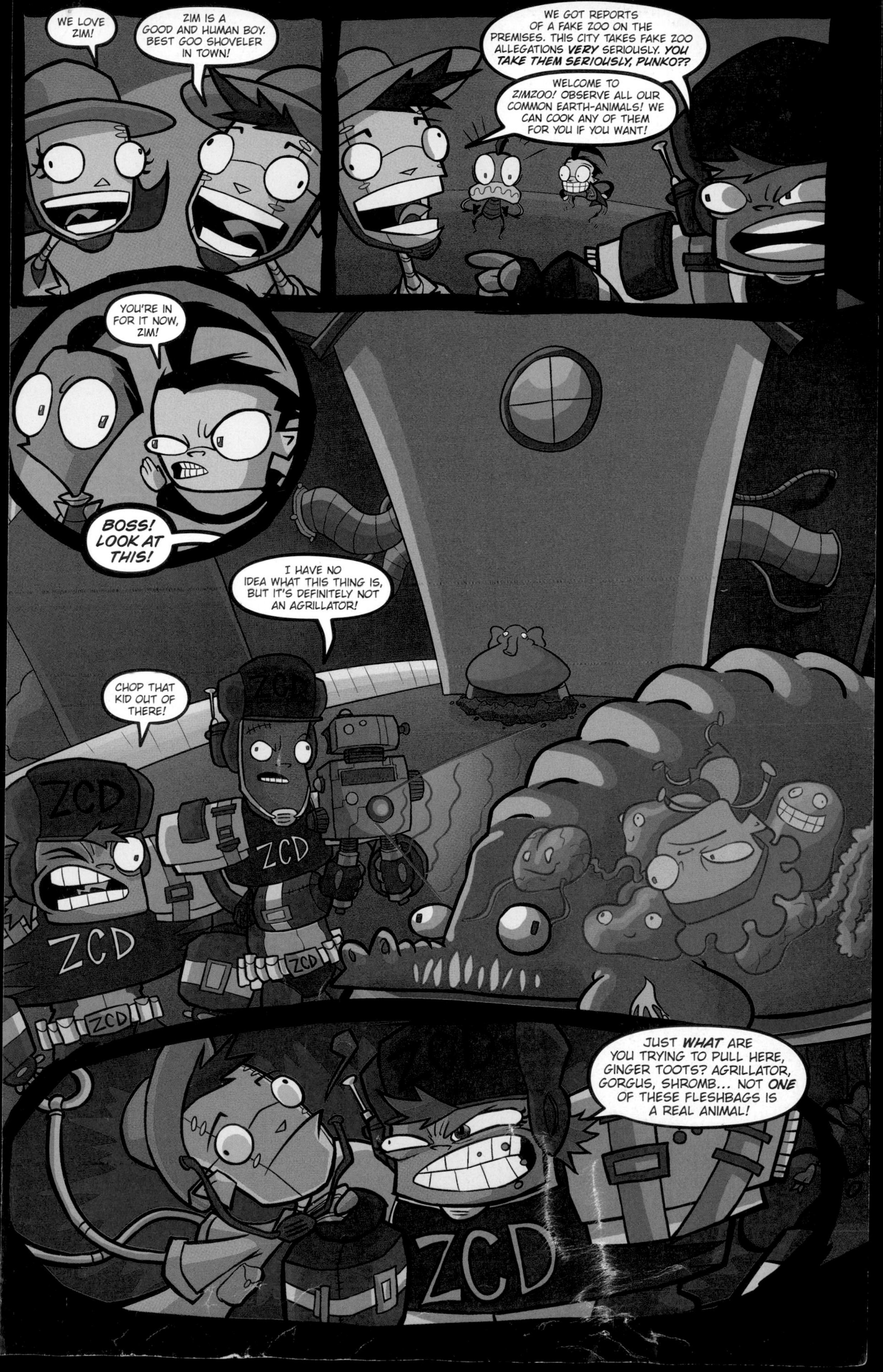
WE LOVE ZIM!
ZIM IS A GOOD AND HUMAN BOY. BEST GOO SHOVELER IN TOWN!
WE GOT REPORTS OF A FAKE ZOO ON THE PREMISES. THIS CITY TAKES FAKE ZOO ALLEGATIONS VERY SERIOUSLY. YOU TAKE THEM SERIOUSLY, PUNKO??
WELCOME TO ZIMZOO! OBSERVE ALL OUR COMMON EARTH-ANIMALS! WE CAN COOK ANY OF THEM FOR YOU IF YOU WANT!
YOU'RE IN FOR IT NOW, ZIM!
BOSS! LOOK AT THIS!
I HAVE NO IDEA WHAT THIS THING IS, BUT IT'S DEFINITELY NOT AN AGRILLATOR!
CHOP THAT KID OUT OF THERE!
ZCD
ZCD
ZCD
JUST WHAT ARE YOU TRYING TO PULL HERE, GINGER TOOTS? AGRILLATOR, GORGUS, SHROMB... NOT ONE OF THESE FLESHBAGS IS A REAL ANIMAL!
ZCD

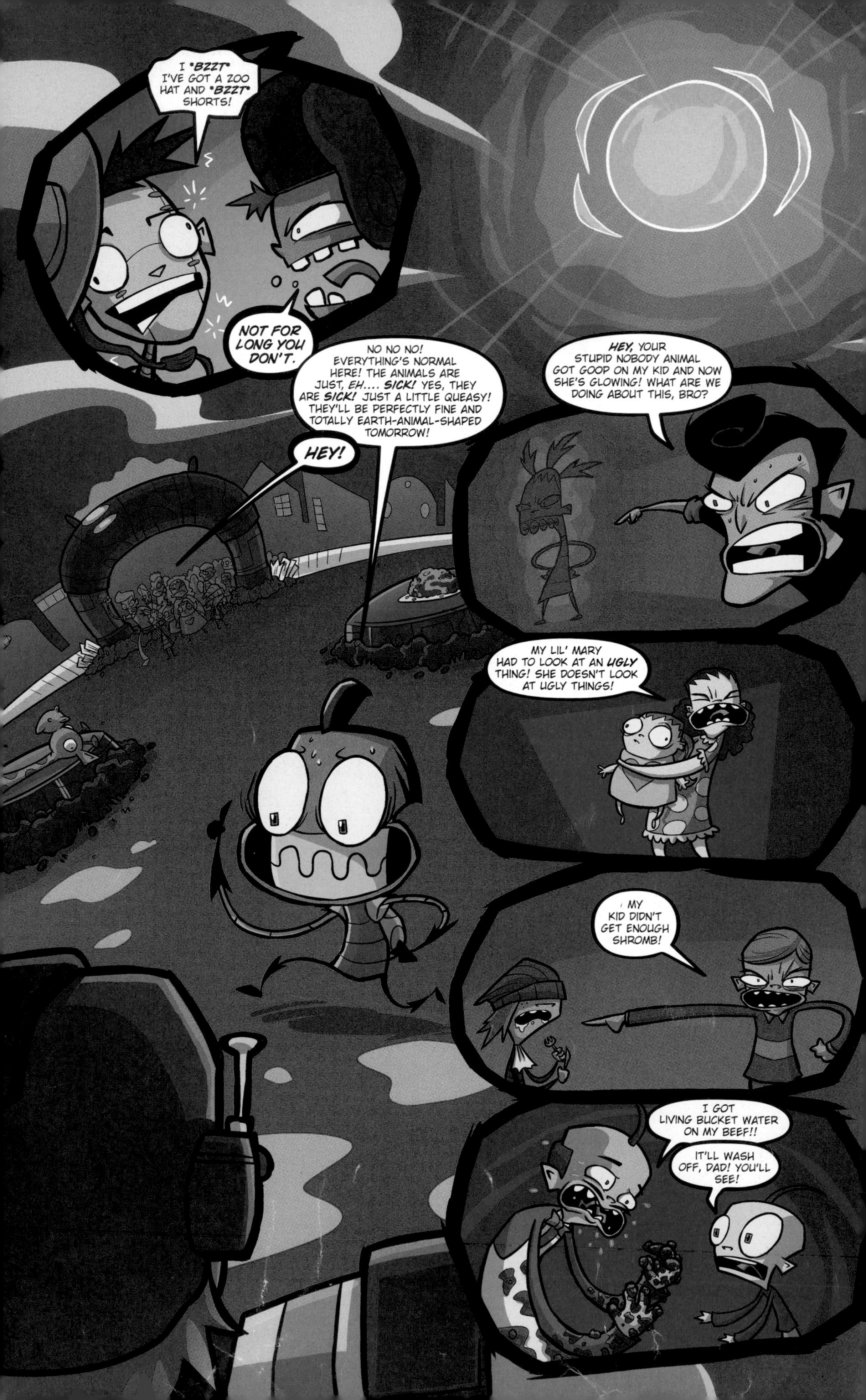
I *BZZT* I'VE GOT A ZOO HAT AND *BZZT* SHORTS!
NOT FOR LONG YOU DON'T.
NO NO NO! EVERYTHING'S NORMAL HERE! THE ANIMALS ARE JUST, EH.... SICK! YES, THEY ARE SICK! JUST A LITTLE QUEASY! THEY'LL BE PERFECTLY FINE AND TOTALLY EARTH-ANIMAL-SHAPED TOMORROW!
HEY!
HEY, YOUR STUPID NOBODY ANIMAL GOT GOOP ON MY KID AND NOW SHE'S GLOWING! WHAT ARE WE DOING ABOUT THIS, BRO?
MY LIL' MARY HAD TO LOOK AT AN UGLY THING! SHE DOESN'T LOOK AT UGLY THINGS!
MY KID DIDN'T GET ENOUGH SHROMB!
I GOT LIVING BUCKET WATER ON MY BEEF!!
IT'LL WASH OFF, DAD! YOU'LL SEE!

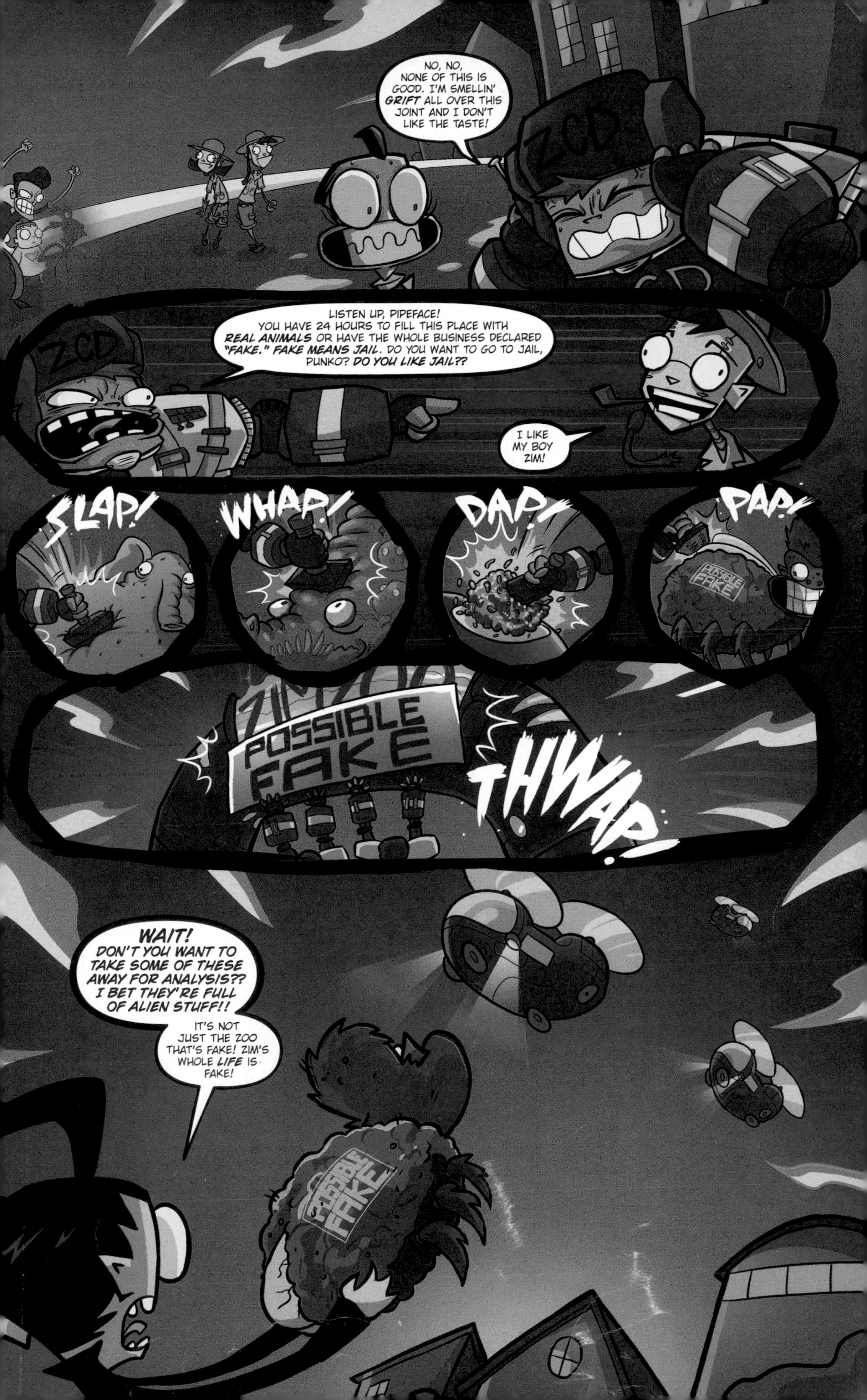
NO, NO, NONE OF THIS IS GOOD. I'M SMELLIN' GRIFT ALL OVER THIS JOINT AND I DON'T LIKE THE TASTE!
ZCD
LISTEN UP, PIPEFACE! YOU HAVE 24 HOURS TO FILL THIS PLACE WITH REAL ANIMALS OR HAVE THE WHOLE BUSINESS DECLARED "FAKE." FAKE MEANS JAIL. DO YOU WANT TO GO TO JAIL, PUNKO? DO YOU LIKE JAIL??
I LIKE MY BOY ZIM!
SLAP!
WHAP!
DAP!
PAP!
POSSIBLE FAKE
POSSIBLE FAKE
THWAP!
WAIT! DON'T YOU WANT TO TAKE SOME OF THESE AWAY FOR ANALYSIS?? I BET THEY'RE FULL OF ALIEN STUFF!!
IT'S NOT JUST THE ZOO THAT'S FAKE! ZIM'S WHOLE LIFE IS FAKE!
POSSIBLE FAKE

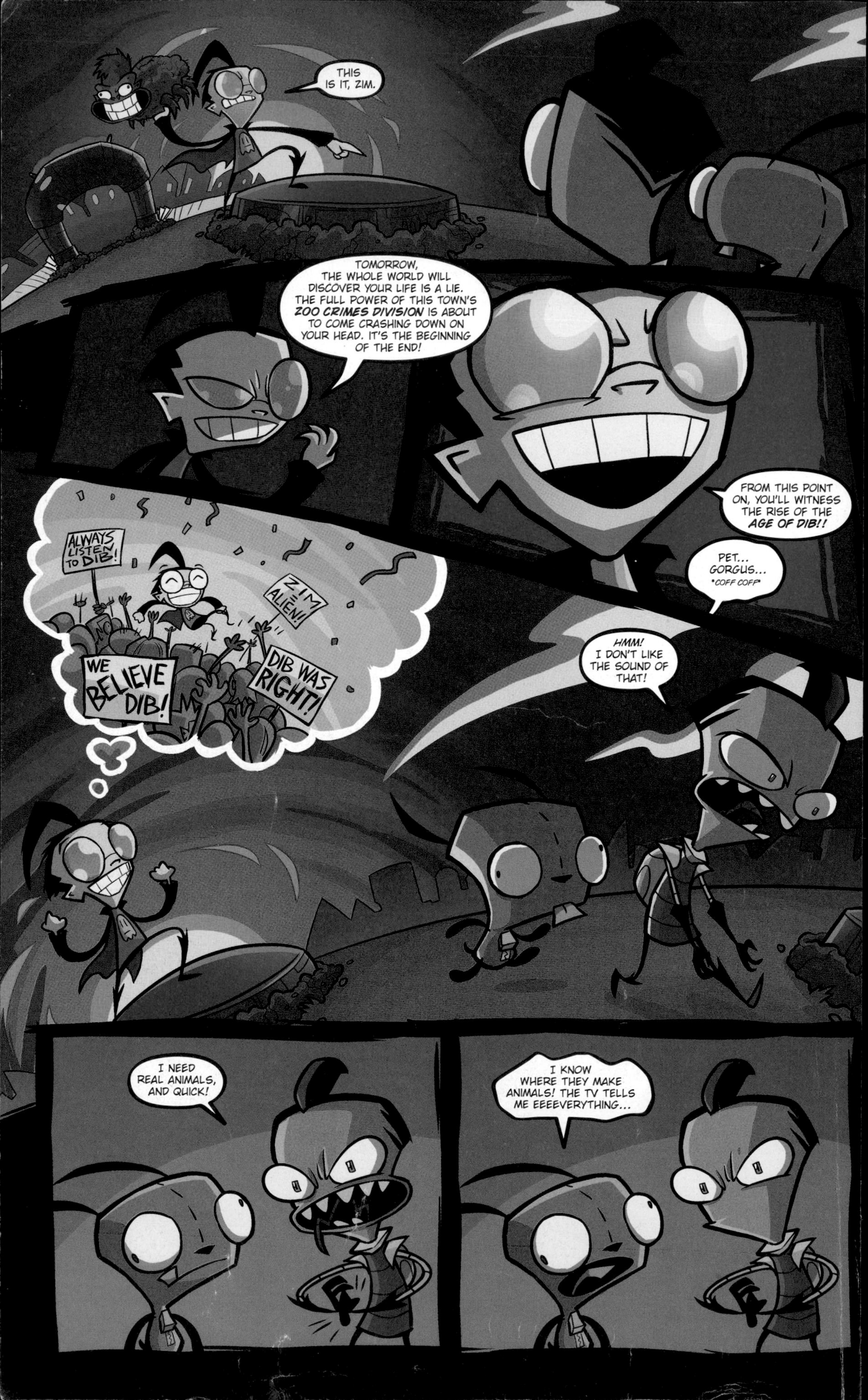
THIS IS IT, ZIM.
TOMORROW, THE WHOLE WORLD WILL DISCOVER YOUR LIFE IS A LIE. THE FULL POWER OF THIS TOWN'S ***ZOO CRIMES DIVISION*** IS ABOUT TO COME CRASHING DOWN ON YOUR HEAD. IT'S THE BEGINNING OF THE END!
FROM THIS POINT ON, YOU'LL WITNESS THE RISE OF THE ***AGE OF DIB!!***
ALWAYS LISTEN TO DIB!
ZIM = ALIEN!!
WE BELIEVE DIB!
DIB WAS RIGHT!
PET... GORGUS... *COFF COFF*
HMM! I DON'T LIKE THE SOUND OF THAT!
I NEED REAL ANIMALS, AND QUICK!
I KNOW WHERE THEY MAKE ANIMALS! THE TV TELLS ME EEEEVERYTHING...

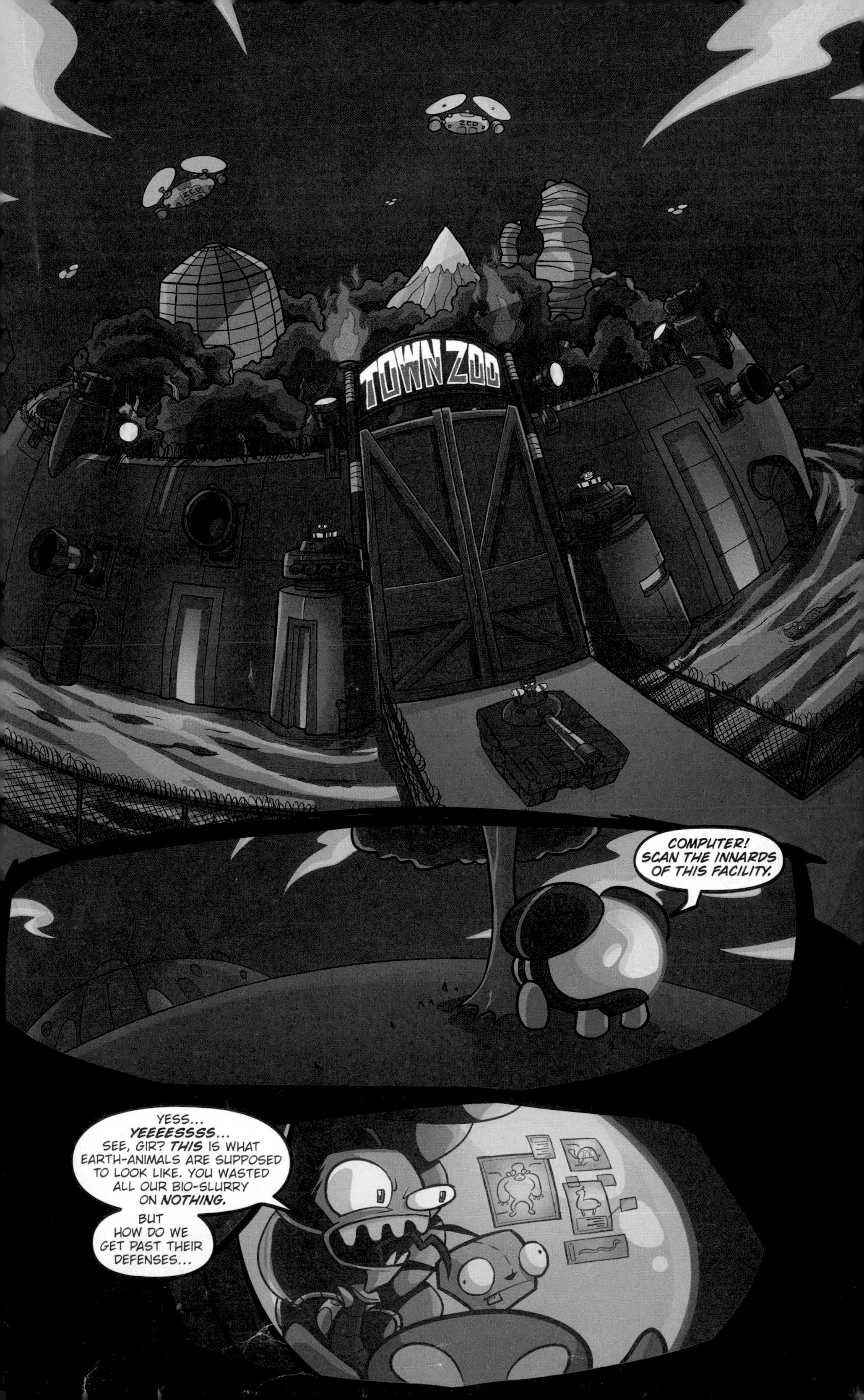
TOWN ZOO
ZCD
COMPUTER! SCAN THE INNARDS OF THIS FACILITY.
YESS... YEEEESSSS... SEE, GIR? THIS IS WHAT EARTH-ANIMALS ARE SUPPOSED TO LOOK LIKE. YOU WASTED ALL OUR BIO-SLURRY ON NOTHING.
BUT HOW DO WE GET PAST THEIR DEFENSES...

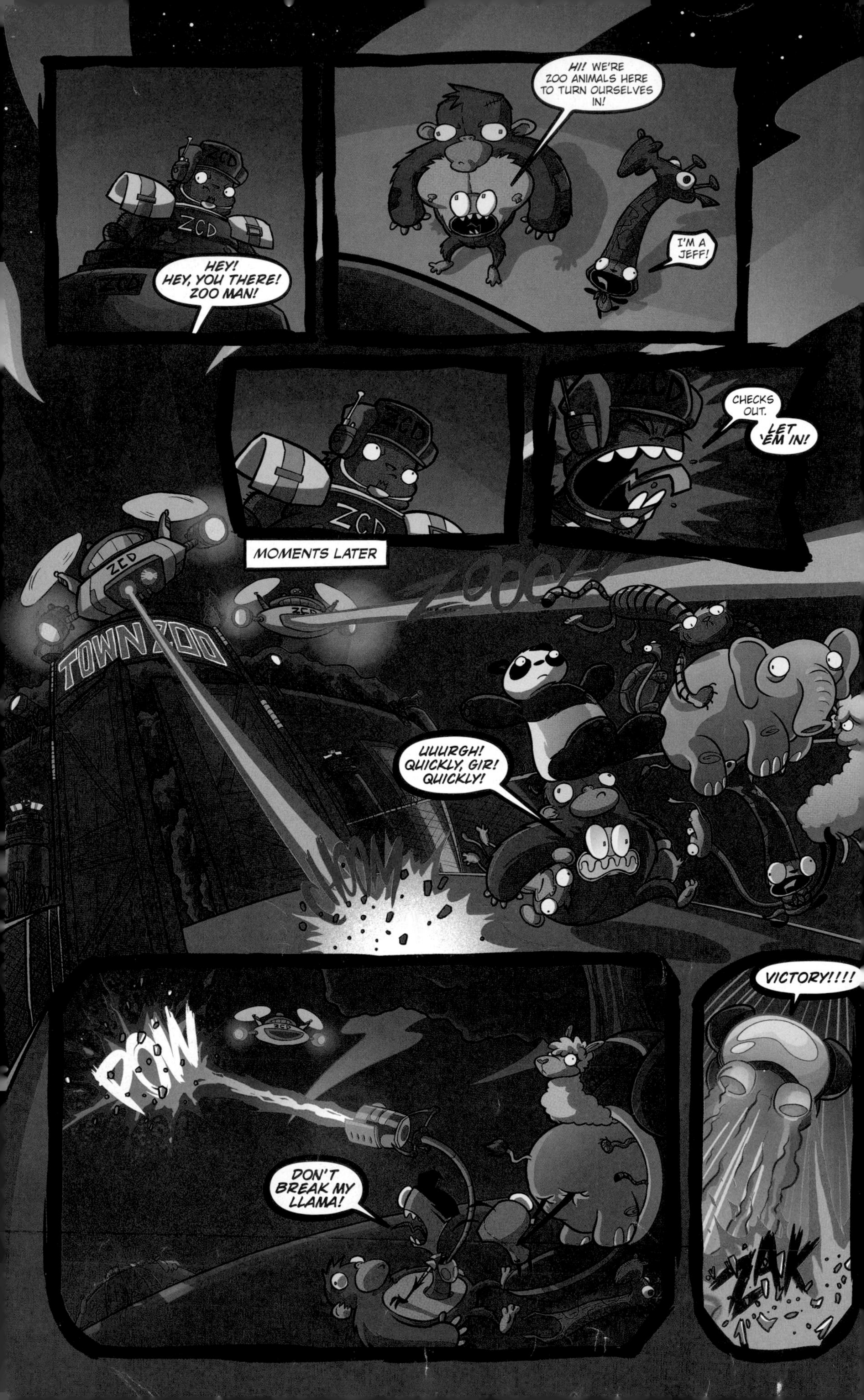
HEY!
HEY, YOU THERE!
ZOO MAN!
HI! WE'RE ZOO ANIMALS HERE TO TURN OURSELVES IN!
I'M A JEFF!
CHECKS OUT.
LET 'EM IN!
MOMENTS LATER
TOWN ZOO
UUURGH! QUICKLY, GIR! QUICKLY!
POW
DON'T BREAK MY LLAMA!
VICTORY!!!!
ZAK

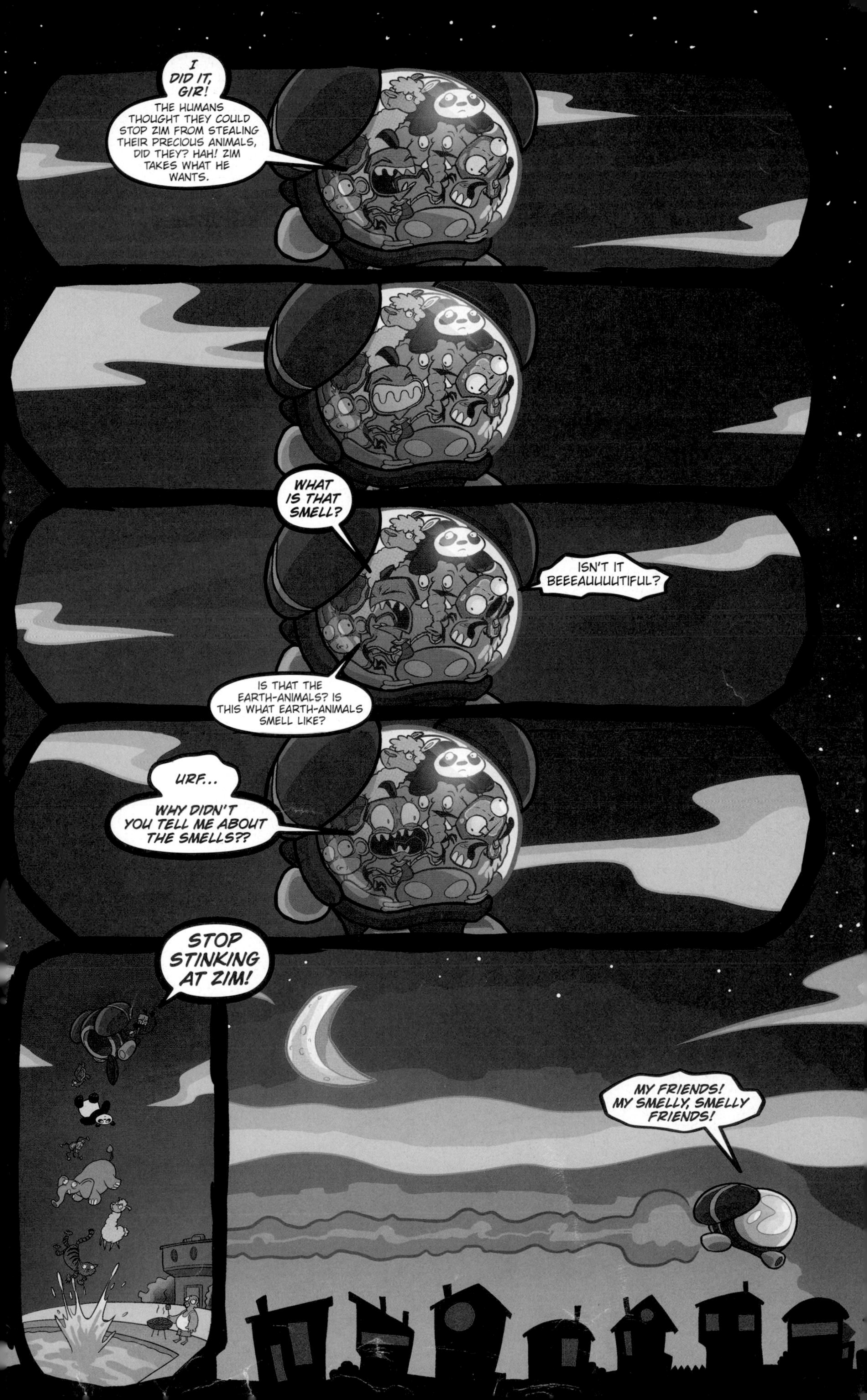
I DID IT, GIR!
THE HUMANS THOUGHT THEY COULD STOP ZIM FROM STEALING THEIR PRECIOUS ANIMALS, DID THEY? HAH! ZIM TAKES WHAT HE WANTS.
WHAT IS THAT SMELL?
ISN'T IT BEEEAUUUUTIFUL?
IS THAT THE EARTH-ANIMALS? IS THIS WHAT EARTH-ANIMALS SMELL LIKE?
URF...
WHY DIDN'T YOU TELL ME ABOUT THE SMELLS??
STOP STINKING AT ZIM!
MY FRIENDS! MY SMELLY, SMELLY FRIENDS!

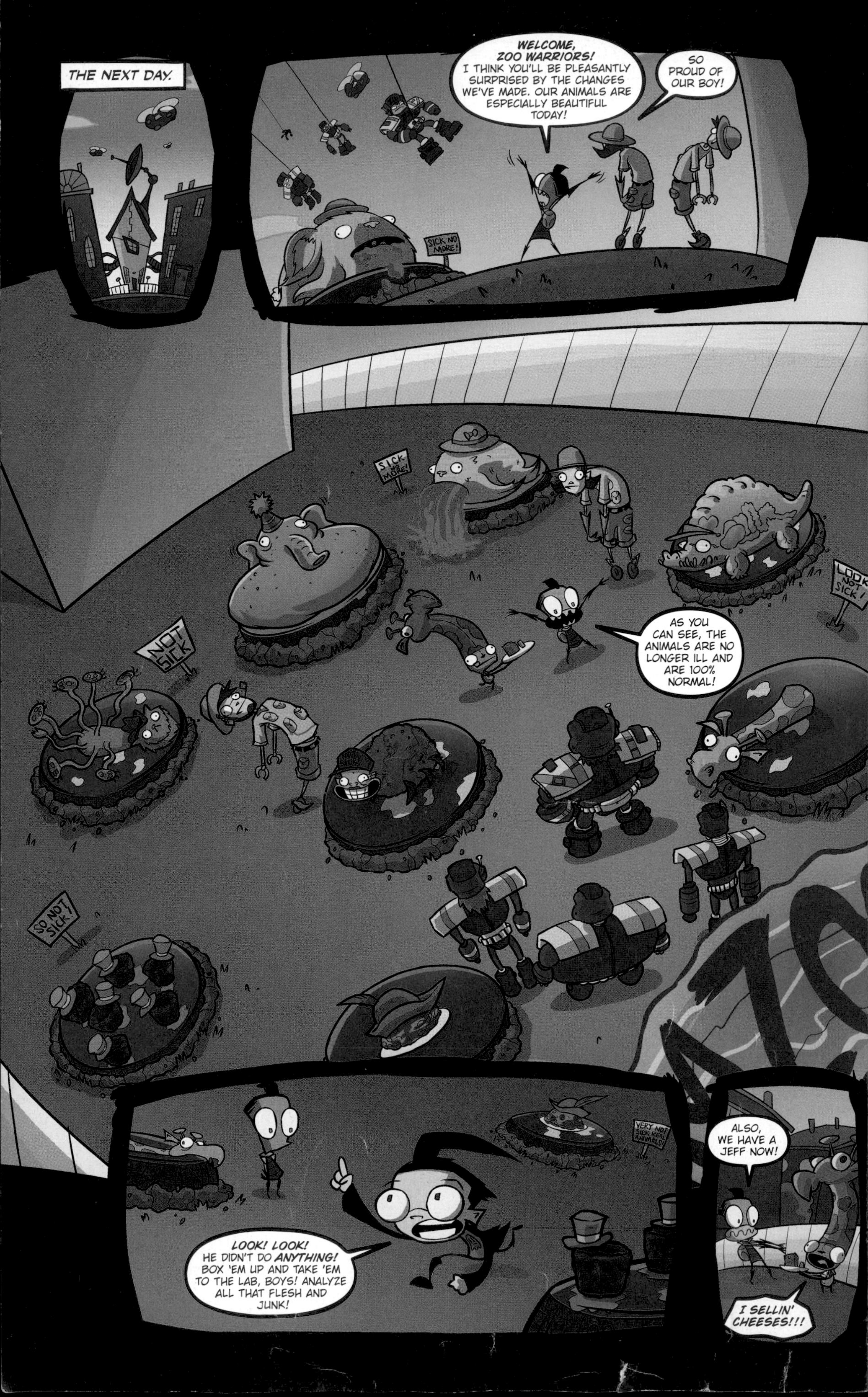

THE NEXT DAY.
WELCOME, ZOO WARRIORS! I THINK YOU'LL BE PLEASANTLY SURPRISED BY THE CHANGES WE'VE MADE. OUR ANIMALS ARE ESPECIALLY BEAUTIFUL TODAY!
SO PROUD OF OUR BOY!
SICK NO MORE!
SICK NO MORE!
LOOK! NOT SICK!
NOT SICK
AS YOU CAN SEE, THE ANIMALS ARE NO LONGER ILL AND ARE 100% NORMAL!
SO NOT SICK!
VERY NOT SICK REAL ANIMALS
LOOK! LOOK! HE DIDN'T DO ANYTHING! BOX 'EM UP AND TAKE 'EM TO THE LAB, BOYS! ANALYZE ALL THAT FLESH AND JUNK!
ALSO, WE HAVE A JEFF NOW!
I SELLIN' CHEESES!!!

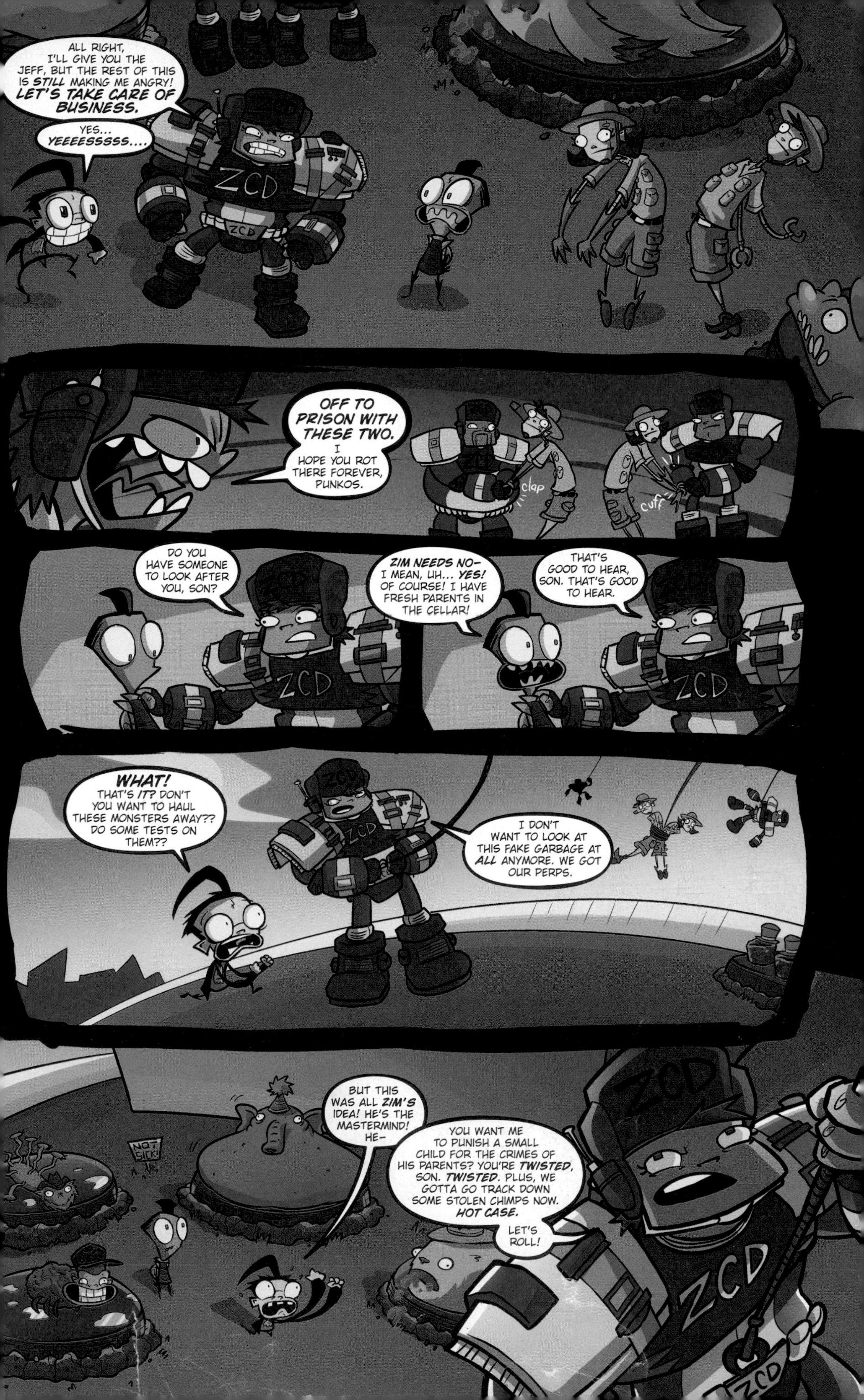
ALL RIGHT, I'LL GIVE YOU THE JEFF, BUT THE REST OF THIS IS STILL MAKING ME ANGRY! LET'S TAKE CARE OF BUSINESS.
YES... YEEEESSSSS....
OFF TO PRISON WITH THESE TWO. I HOPE YOU ROT THERE FOREVER, PUNKOS.
clap
cuff
DO YOU HAVE SOMEONE TO LOOK AFTER YOU, SON?
ZIM NEEDS NO— I MEAN, UH... YES! OF COURSE! I HAVE FRESH PARENTS IN THE CELLAR!
THAT'S GOOD TO HEAR, SON. THAT'S GOOD TO HEAR.
WHAT! THAT'S IT? DON'T YOU WANT TO HAUL THESE MONSTERS AWAY?? DO SOME TESTS ON THEM??
I DON'T WANT TO LOOK AT THIS FAKE GARBAGE AT ALL ANYMORE. WE GOT OUR PERPS.
BUT THIS WAS ALL ZIM'S IDEA! HE'S THE MASTERMIND! HE-
NOT SICK!
YOU WANT ME TO PUNISH A SMALL CHILD FOR THE CRIMES OF HIS PARENTS? YOU'RE TWISTED, SON. TWISTED. PLUS, WE GOTTA GO TRACK DOWN SOME STOLEN CHIMPS NOW. HOT CASE.
LET'S ROLL!

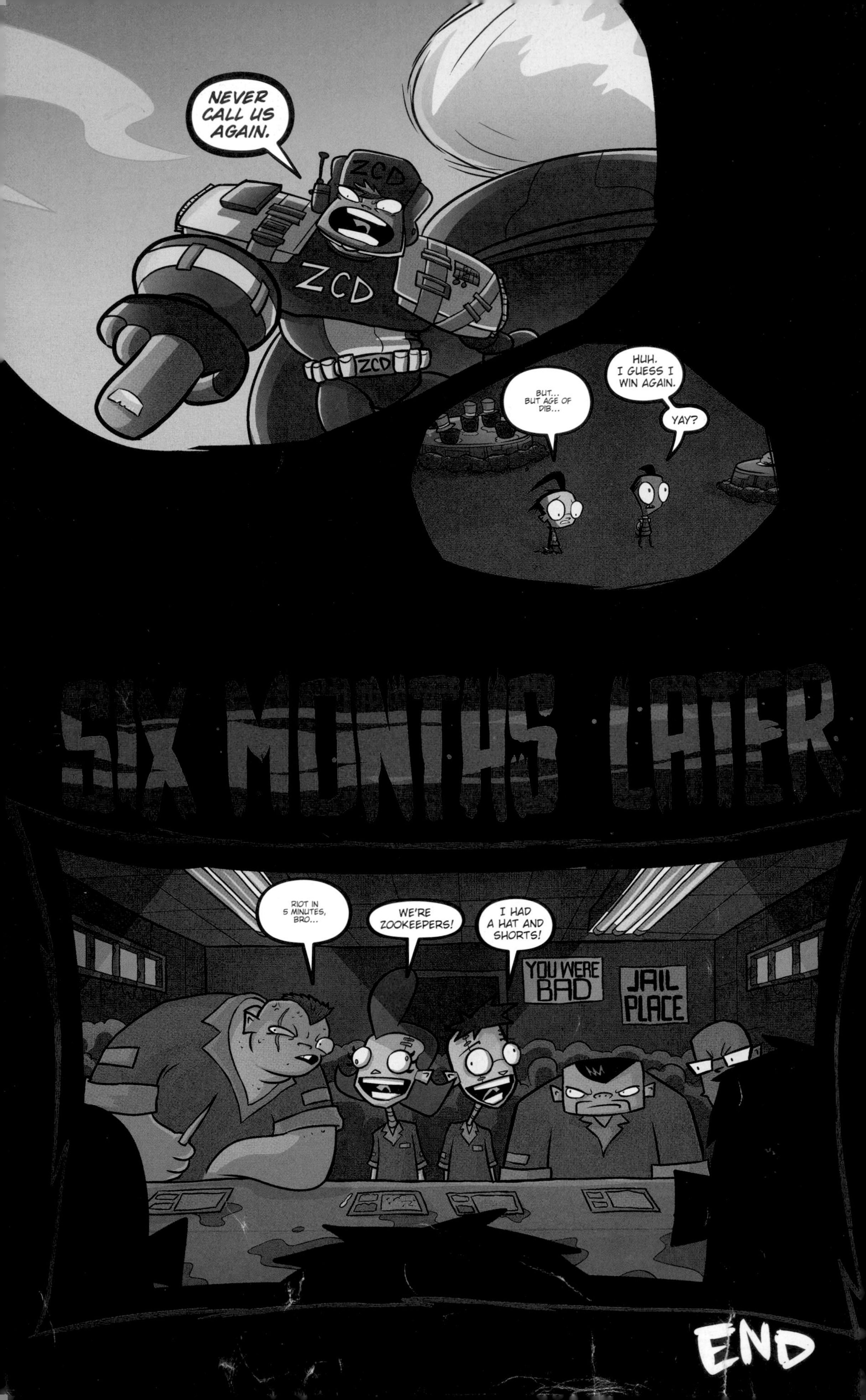
NEVER CALL US AGAIN.
ZCD
ZCD
ZCD
BUT... BUT AGE OF DIB...
HUH. I GUESS I WIN AGAIN.
YAY?
SIX MONTHS LATER
RIOT IN 5 MINUTES, BRO...
WE'RE ZOOKEEPERS!
I HAD A HAT AND SHORTS!
YOU WERE BAD
JAIL PLACE
END

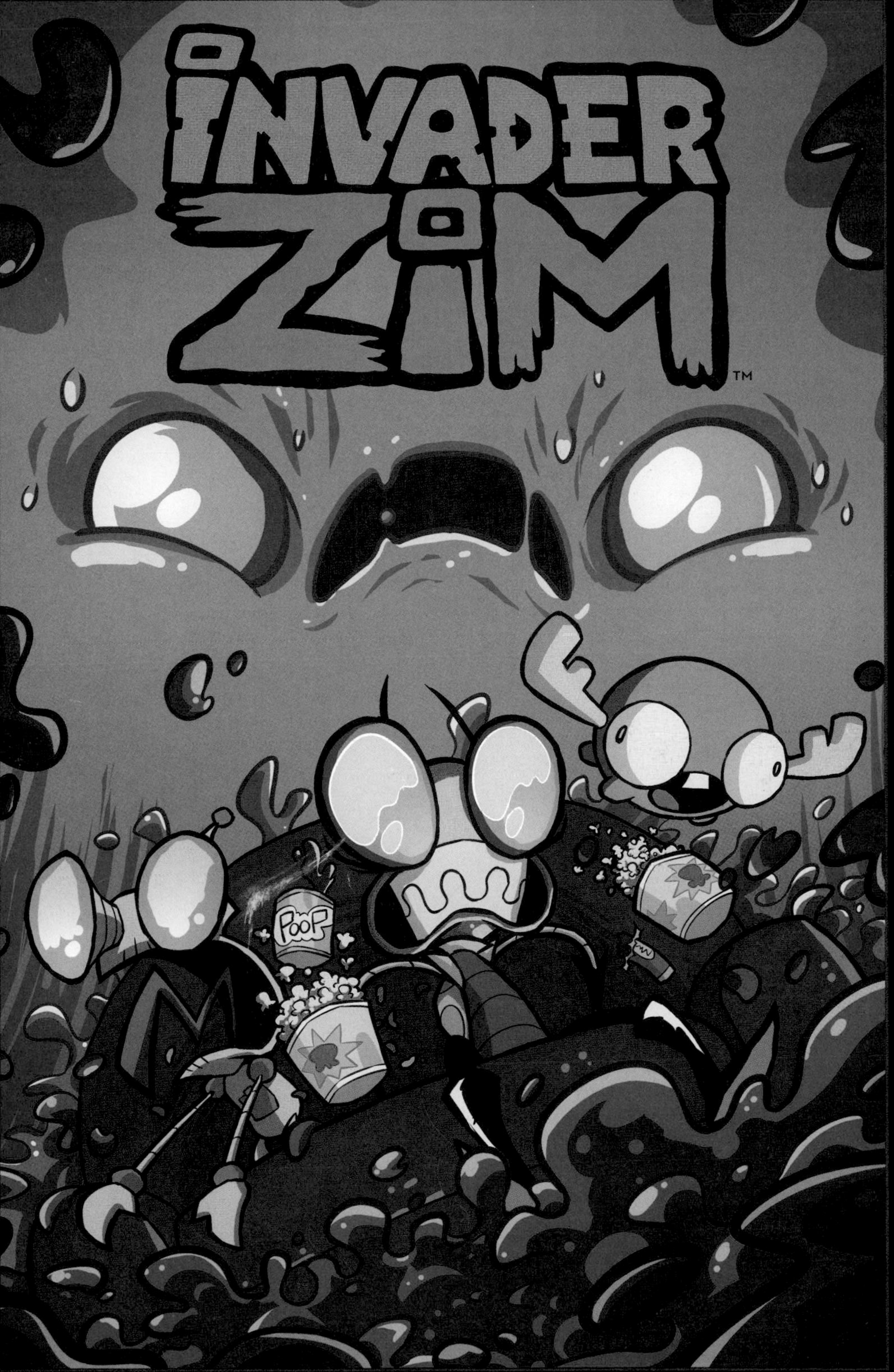
INVADER ZIM™
POOP

CHAPTER: 5

illustration by WARREN WUCINICH

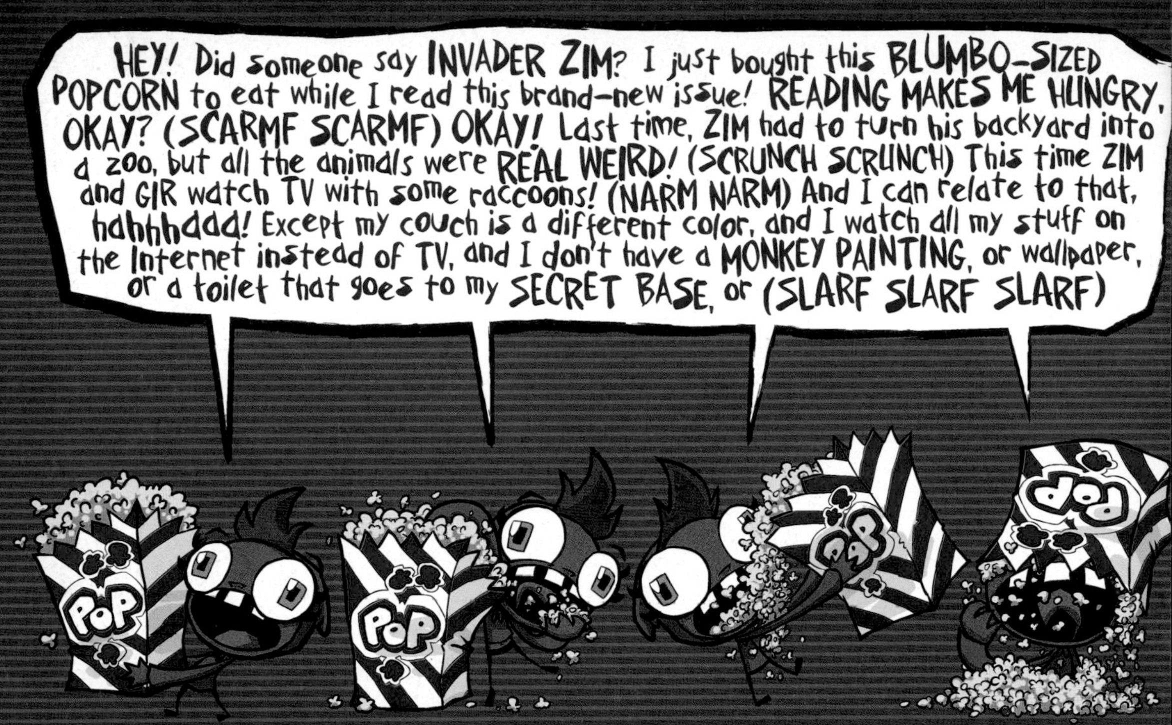
HEY! Did someone say INVADER ZIM? I just bought this BLUMBO-SIZED POPCORN to eat while I read this brand-new issue! READING MAKES ME HUNGRY, OKAY? (SCARMF SCARMF) OKAY! Last time, ZIM had to turn his backyard into a zoo, but all the animals were REAL WEIRD! (SCRUNCH SCRUNCH) This time ZIM and GIR watch TV with some raccoons! (NARM NARM) And I can relate to that, hahhhaaa! Except my couch is a different color, and I watch all my stuff on the Internet instead of TV, and I don't have a MONKEY PAINTING, or wallpaper, or a toilet that goes to my SECRET BASE, or (SLARF SLARF SLARF)
POP
POP
POP
POP

Recap Kid by WARREN WUCINICH

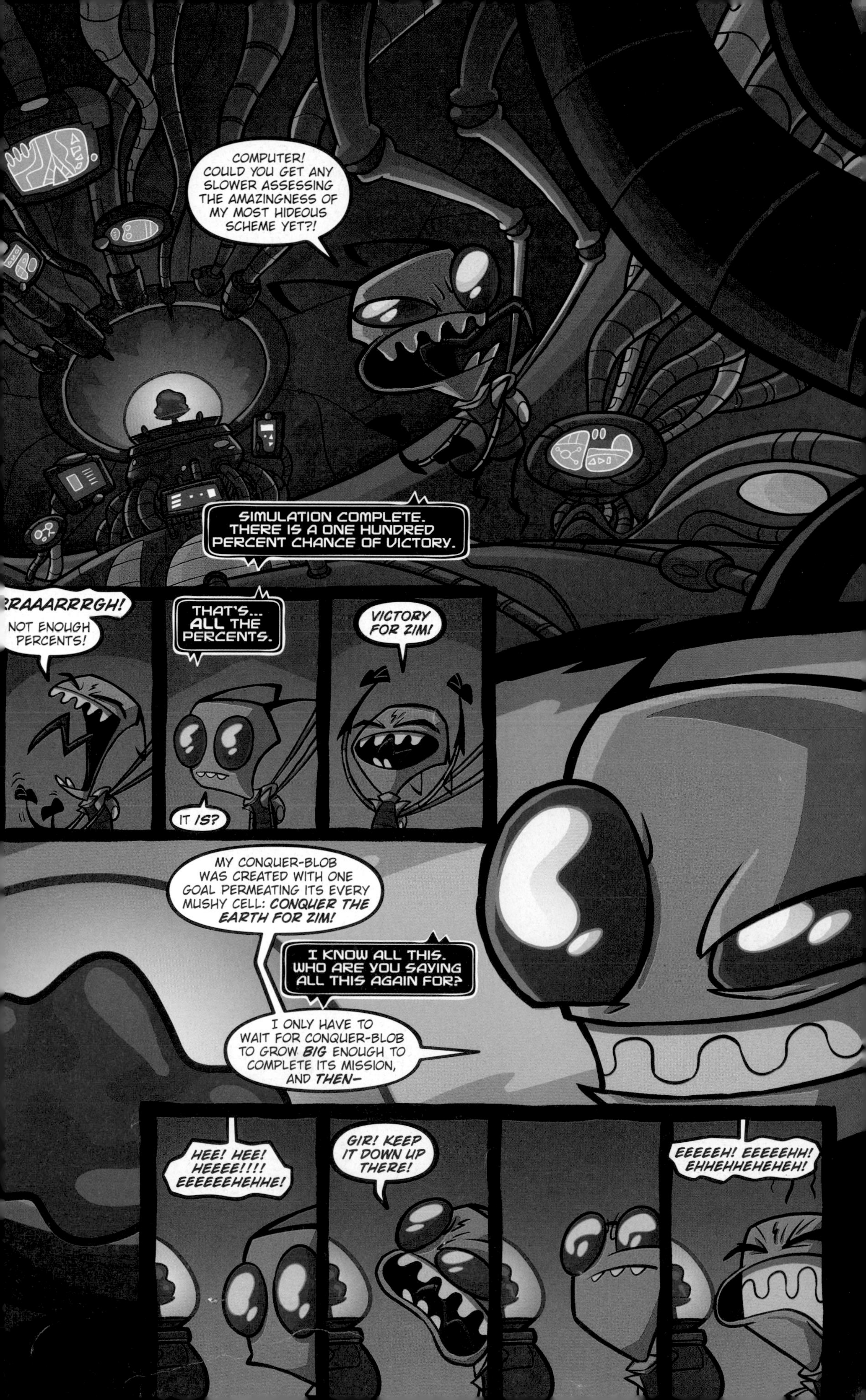
COMPUTER! COULD YOU GET ANY SLOWER ASSESSING THE AMAZINGNESS OF MY MOST HIDEOUS SCHEME YET?!
SIMULATION COMPLETE. THERE IS A ONE HUNDRED PERCENT CHANCE OF VICTORY.
RRAAARRRGH! NOT ENOUGH PERCENTS!
THAT'S... ALL THE PERCENTS.
IT IS?
VICTORY FOR ZIM!
MY CONQUER-BLOB WAS CREATED WITH ONE GOAL PERMEATING ITS EVERY MUSHY CELL: CONQUER THE EARTH FOR ZIM!
I KNOW ALL THIS. WHO ARE YOU SAYING ALL THIS AGAIN FOR?
I ONLY HAVE TO WAIT FOR CONQUER-BLOB TO GROW BIG ENOUGH TO COMPLETE ITS MISSION, AND THEN—
HEE! HEE! HEEEE!!!! EEEEEEHEHHE!
GIR! KEEP IT DOWN UP THERE!
EEEEEH! EEEEEHH! EHHEHHEHEHEH!

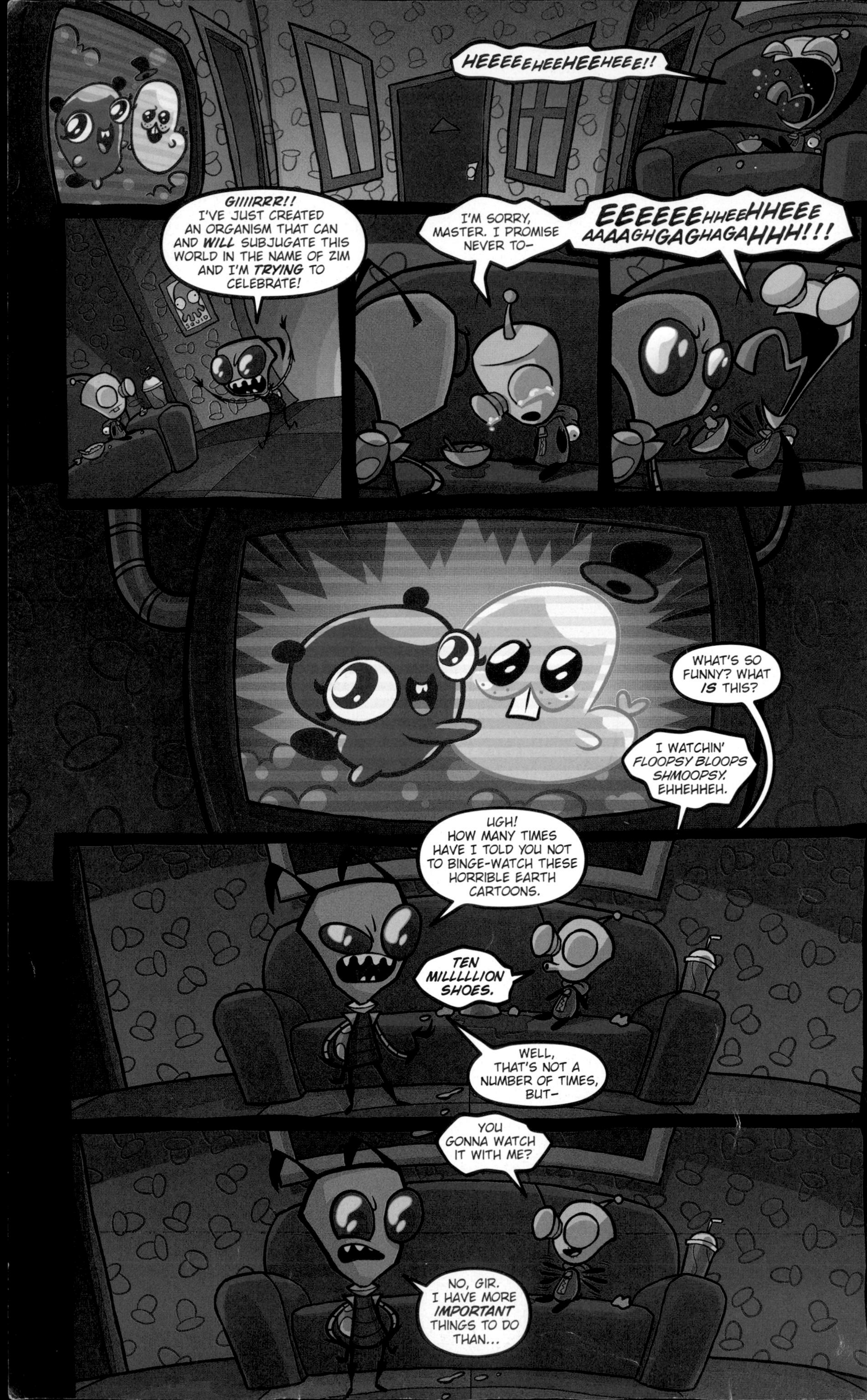
HEEEEEHEEHEEHEEE!!
GIIIIRRR!! I'VE JUST CREATED AN ORGANISM THAT CAN AND WILL SUBJUGATE THIS WORLD IN THE NAME OF ZIM AND I'M TRYING TO CELEBRATE!
SQUID
I'M SORRY, MASTER. I PROMISE NEVER TO-
EEEEEEHHEEHHEEE AAAAGHGAGHAGAHHH!!!
WHAT'S SO FUNNY? WHAT IS THIS?
I WATCHIN' FLOOPSY BLOOPS SHMOOPSY. EHHEHHEH.
UGH! HOW MANY TIMES HAVE I TOLD YOU NOT TO BINGE-WATCH THESE HORRIBLE EARTH CARTOONS.
TEN MILLLLLION SHOES.
WELL, THAT'S NOT A NUMBER OF TIMES, BUT-
YOU GONNA WATCH IT WITH ME?
NO, GIR. I HAVE MORE IMPORTANT THINGS TO DO THAN...

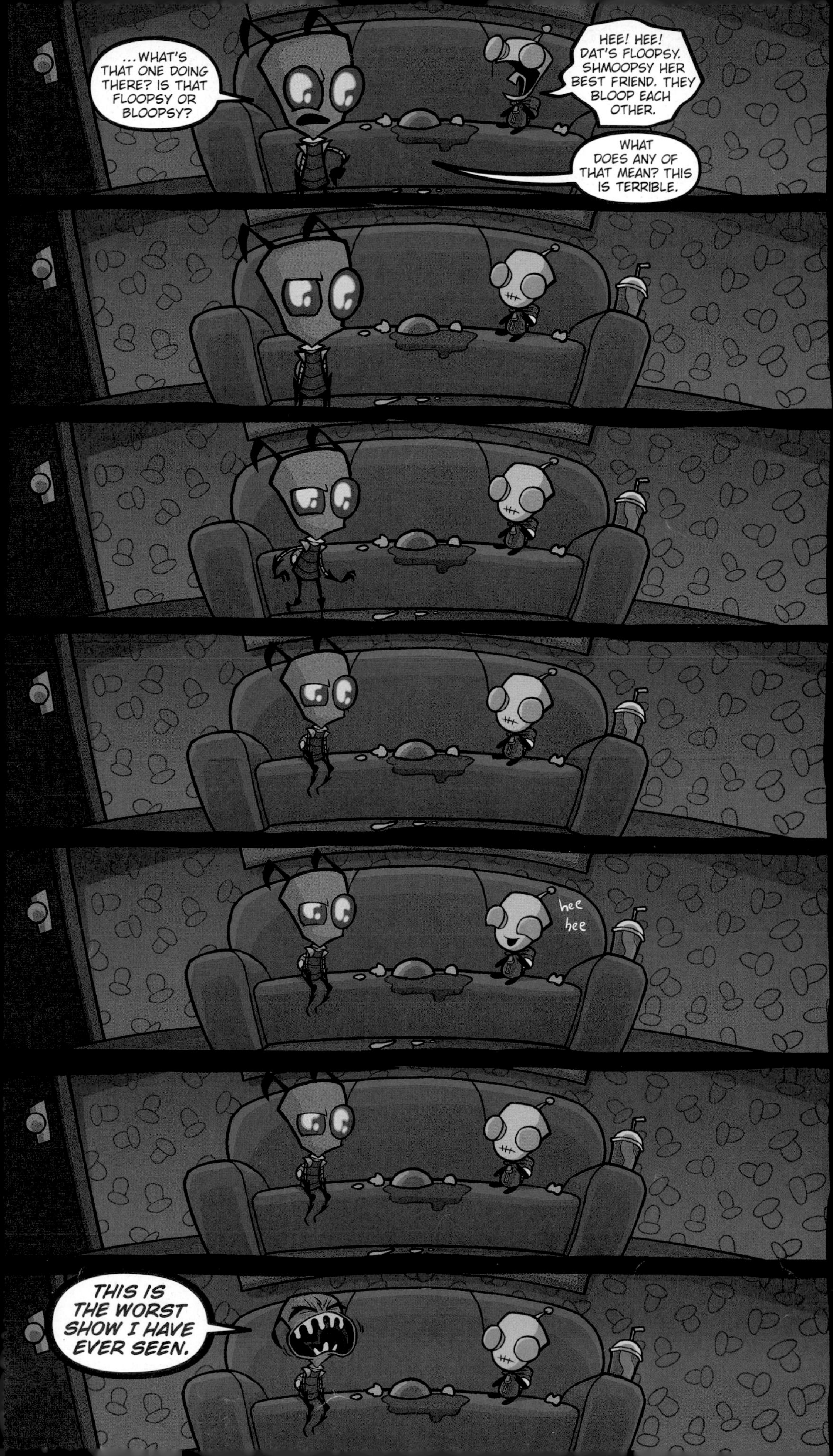
...WHAT'S THAT ONE DOING THERE? IS THAT FLOOPSY OR BLOOPSY?
HEE! HEE! DAT'S FLOOPSY. SHMOOPSY HER BEST FRIEND. THEY BLOOP EACH OTHER.
WHAT DOES ANY OF THAT MEAN? THIS IS TERRIBLE.
hee hee
THIS IS THE WORST SHOW I HAVE EVER SEEN.

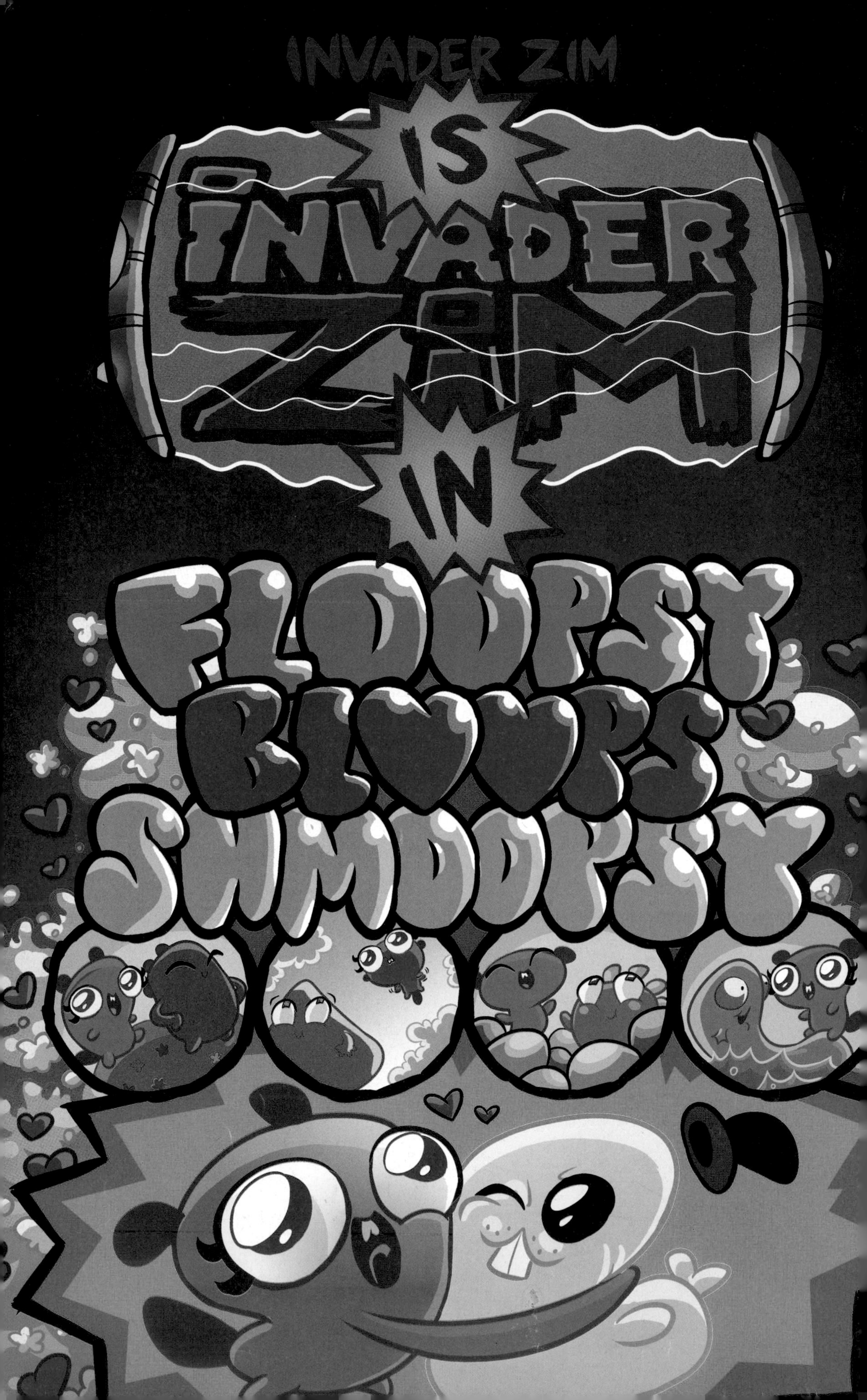
INVADER ZIM
IS
INVADER ZIM
IN
FLOOPSY BLOOPS SHMOOPSY

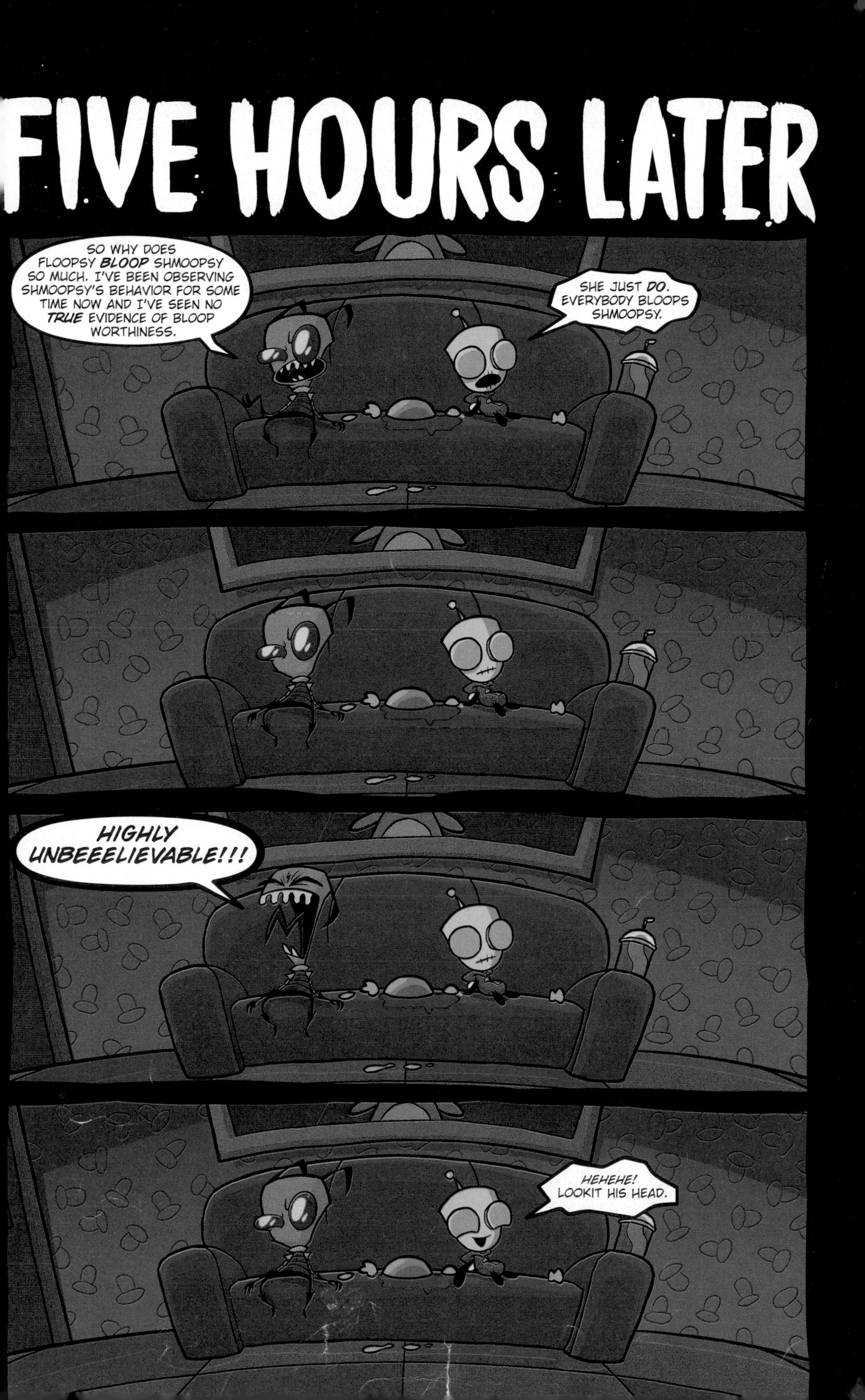
FIVE HOURS LATER
SO WHY DOES FLOOPSY BLOOP SHMOOPSY SO MUCH. I'VE BEEN OBSERVING SHMOOPSY'S BEHAVIOR FOR SOME TIME NOW AND I'VE SEEN NO TRUE EVIDENCE OF BLOOP WORTHINESS.
SHE JUST DO. EVERYBODY BLOOPS SHMOOPSY.
HIGHLY UNBEEELIEVABLE!!!
HEHEHE! LOOKIT HIS HEAD.

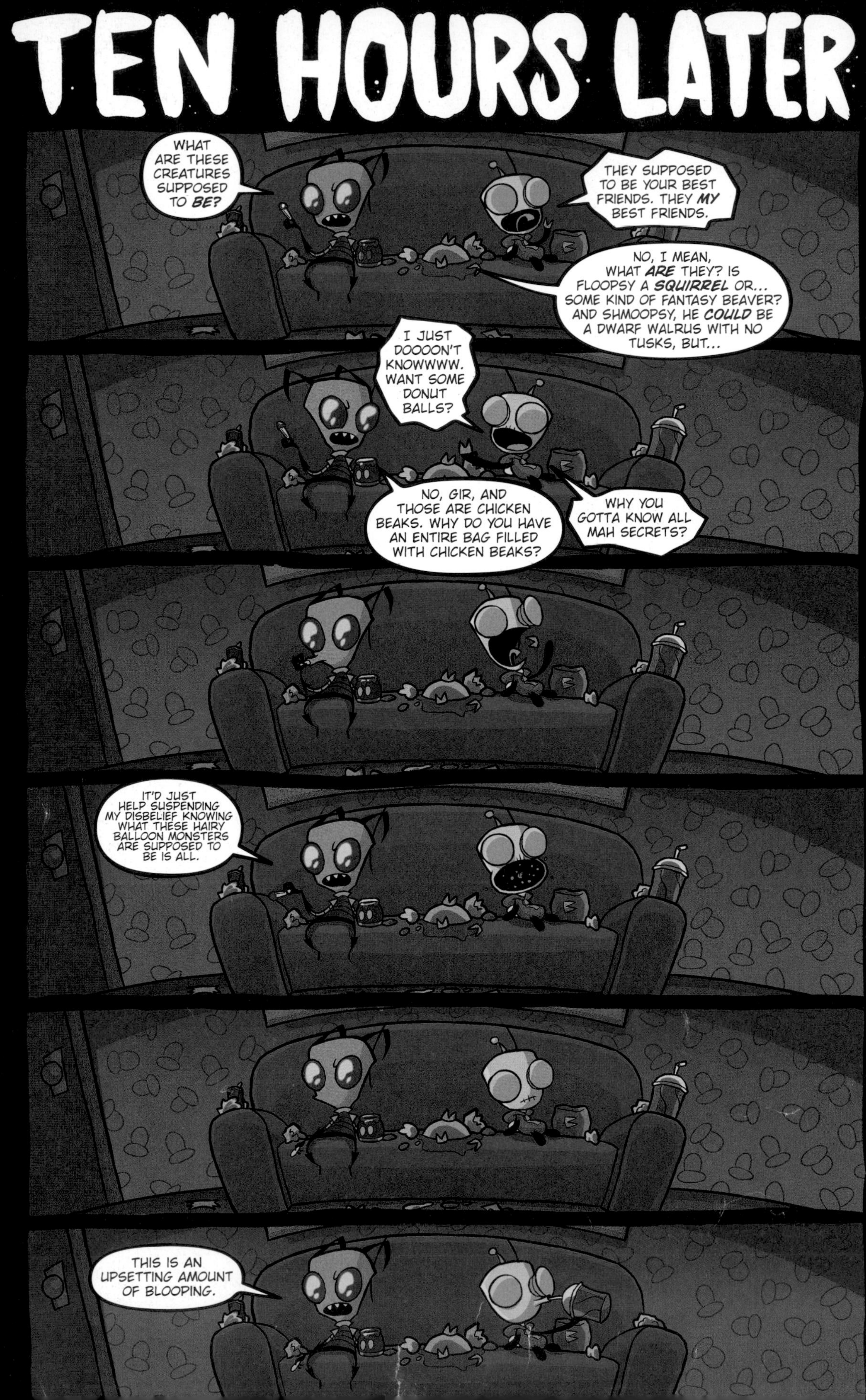
TEN HOURS LATER
WHAT ARE THESE CREATURES SUPPOSED TO BE?
THEY SUPPOSED TO BE YOUR BEST FRIENDS. THEY MY BEST FRIENDS.
NO, I MEAN, WHAT ARE THEY? IS FLOOPSY A SQUIRREL OR... SOME KIND OF FANTASY BEAVER? AND SHMOOPSY, HE COULD BE A DWARF WALRUS WITH NO TUSKS, BUT...
I JUST DOOOOON'T KNOWWWW. WANT SOME DONUT BALLS?
NO, GIR, AND THOSE ARE CHICKEN BEAKS. WHY DO YOU HAVE AN ENTIRE BAG FILLED WITH CHICKEN BEAKS?
WHY YOU GOTTA KNOW ALL MAH SECRETS?
IT'D JUST HELP SUSPENDING MY DISBELIEF KNOWING WHAT THESE HAIRY BALLOON MONSTERS ARE SUPPOSED TO BE IS ALL.
THIS IS AN UPSETTING AMOUNT OF BLOOPING.

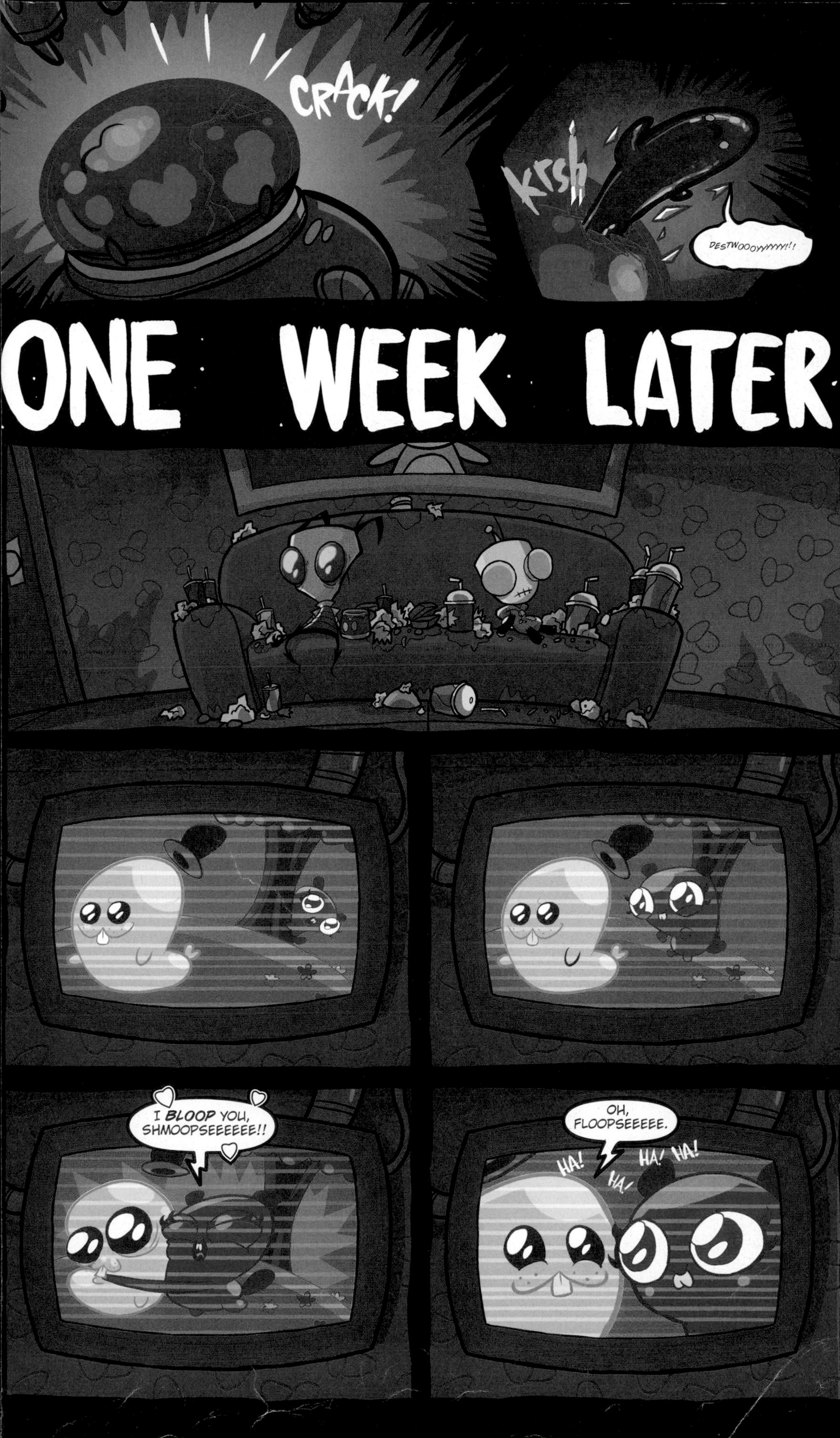
CRACK!
KRSH
DESTWOOOYYYYYY!!!
ONE WEEK LATER
I BLOOP YOU, SHMOOPSEEEEEE!!
OH, FLOOPSEEEEE.
HA! HA! HA! HA!

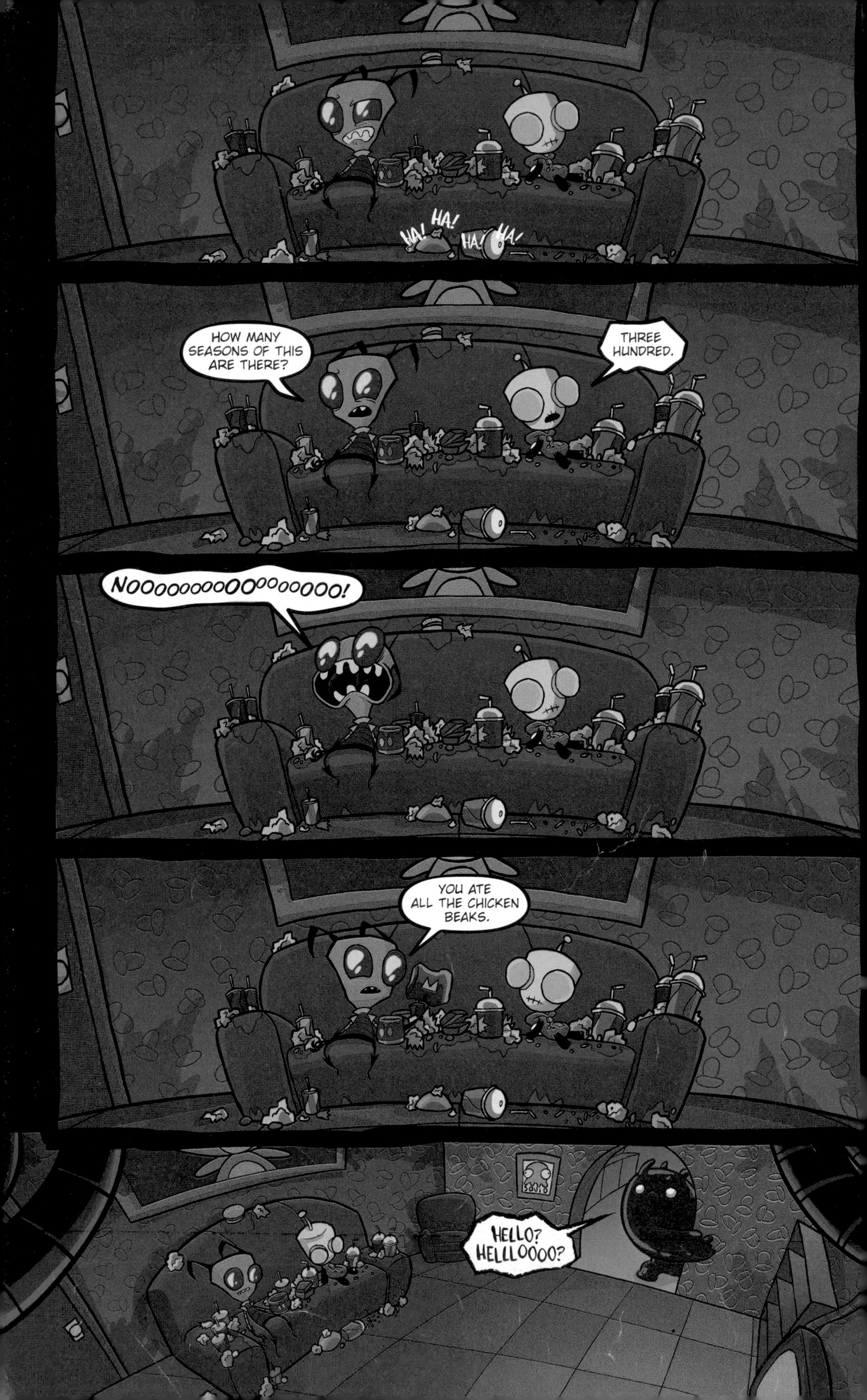
HA! HA! HA! HA!
HOW MANY SEASONS OF THIS ARE THERE?
THREE HUNDRED.
NOOOOOOOOOOOOOOOOOO!
YOU ATE ALL THE CHICKEN BEAKS.
SQUID
HELLO? HELLLOOOO?

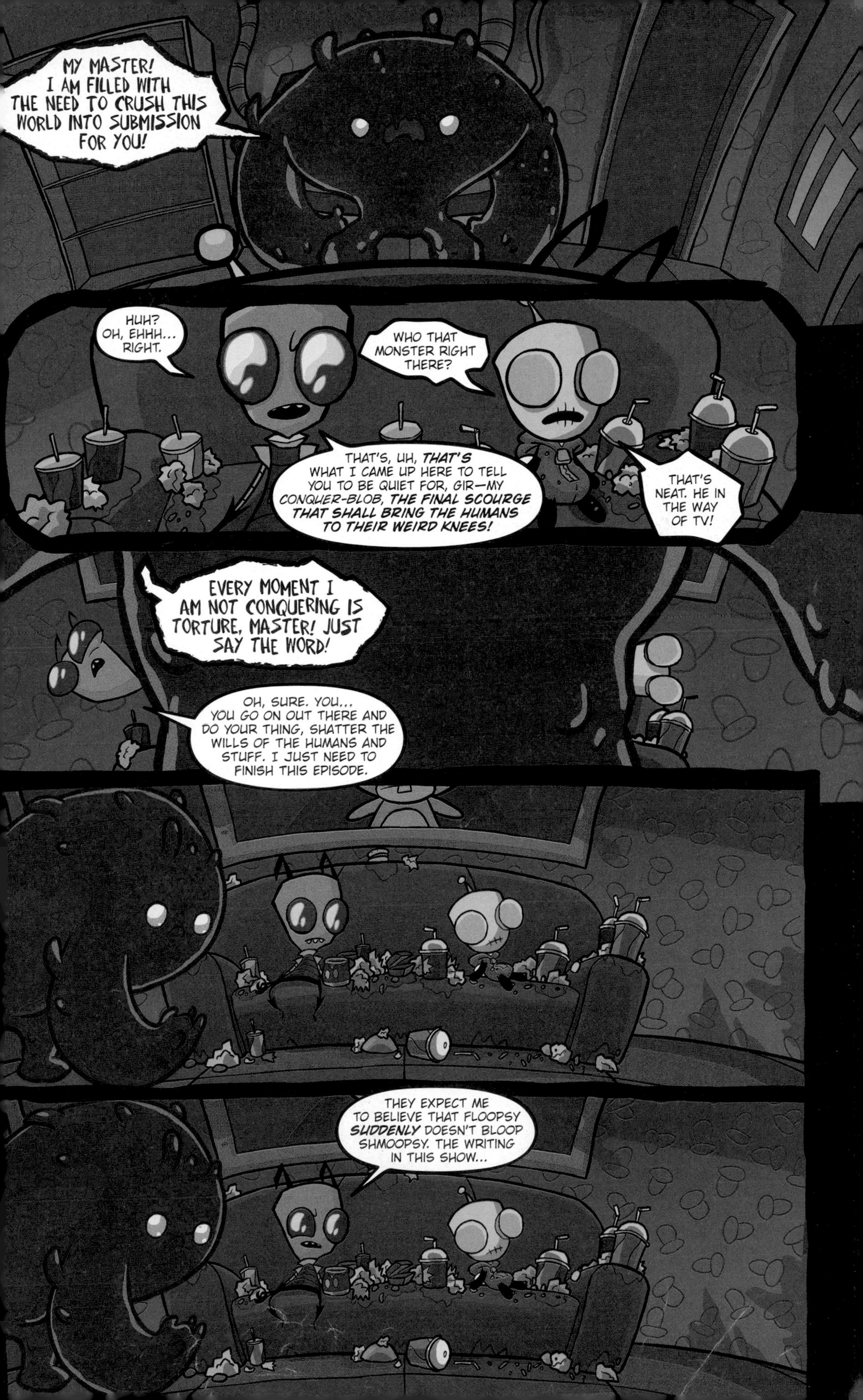
MY MASTER! I AM FILLED WITH THE NEED TO CRUSH THIS WORLD INTO SUBMISSION FOR YOU!
HUH? OH, EHHH... RIGHT.
WHO THAT MONSTER RIGHT THERE?
THAT'S, UH, THAT'S WHAT I CAME UP HERE TO TELL YOU TO BE QUIET FOR, GIR—MY CONQUER-BLOB, THE FINAL SCOURGE THAT SHALL BRING THE HUMANS TO THEIR WEIRD KNEES!
THAT'S NEAT. HE IN THE WAY OF TV!
EVERY MOMENT I AM NOT CONQUERING IS TORTURE, MASTER! JUST SAY THE WORD!
OH, SURE. YOU... YOU GO ON OUT THERE AND DO YOUR THING, SHATTER THE WILLS OF THE HUMANS AND STUFF. I JUST NEED TO FINISH THIS EPISODE.
THEY EXPECT ME TO BELIEVE THAT FLOOPSY SUDDENLY DOESN'T BLOOP SHMOOPSY. THE WRITING IN THIS SHOW...

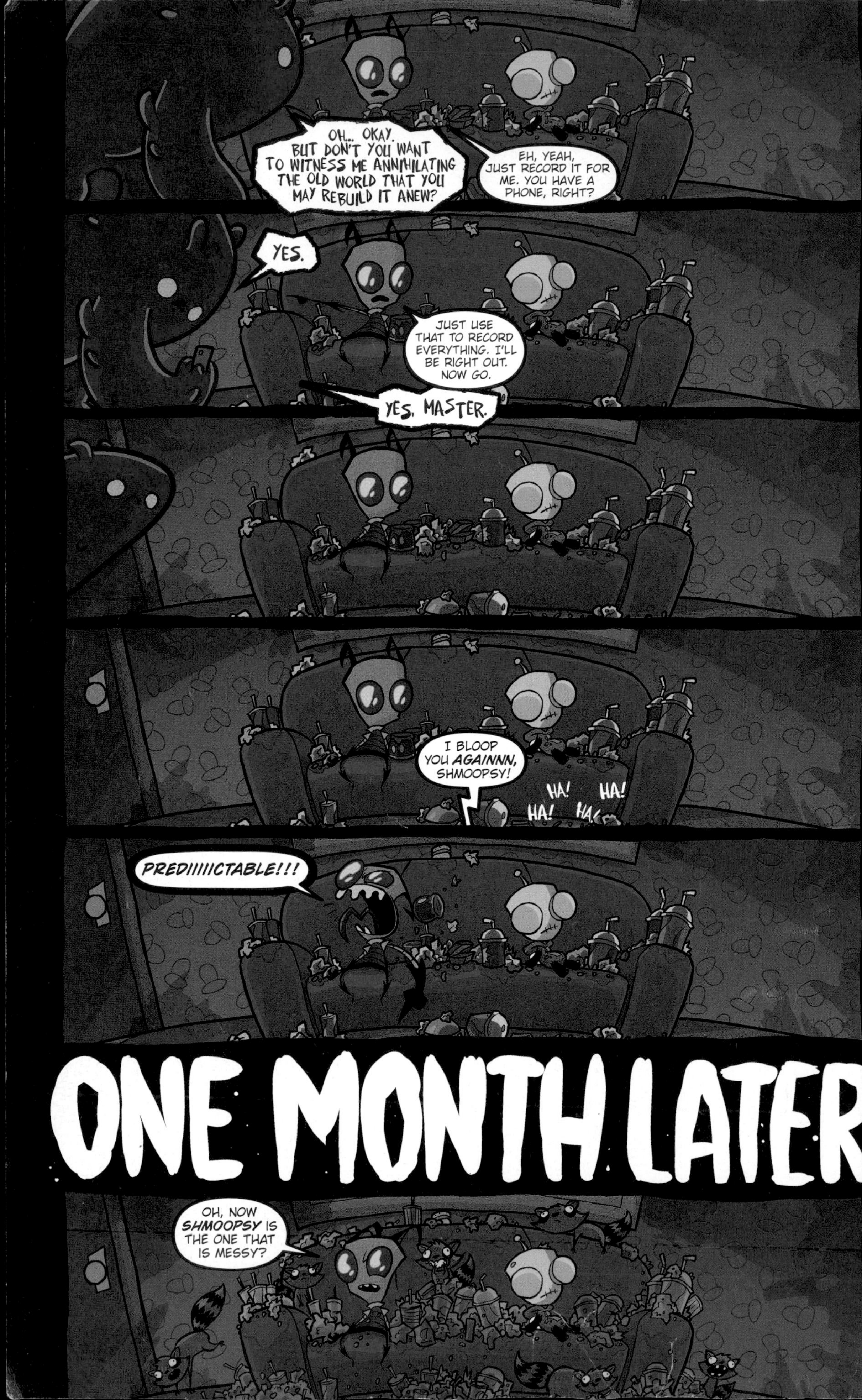
OH... OKAY. BUT DON'T YOU WANT TO WITNESS ME ANNIHILATING THE OLD WORLD THAT YOU MAY REBUILD IT ANEW?
EH, YEAH, JUST RECORD IT FOR ME. YOU HAVE A PHONE, RIGHT?
YES.
JUST USE THAT TO RECORD EVERYTHING. I'LL BE RIGHT OUT. NOW GO.
YES. MASTER.
I BLOOP YOU AGAINNN, SHMOOPSY!
HA! HA! HA!
PREDIIIIIICTABLE!!!
ONE MONTH LATER
OH, NOW SHMOOPSY IS THE ONE THAT IS MESSY?

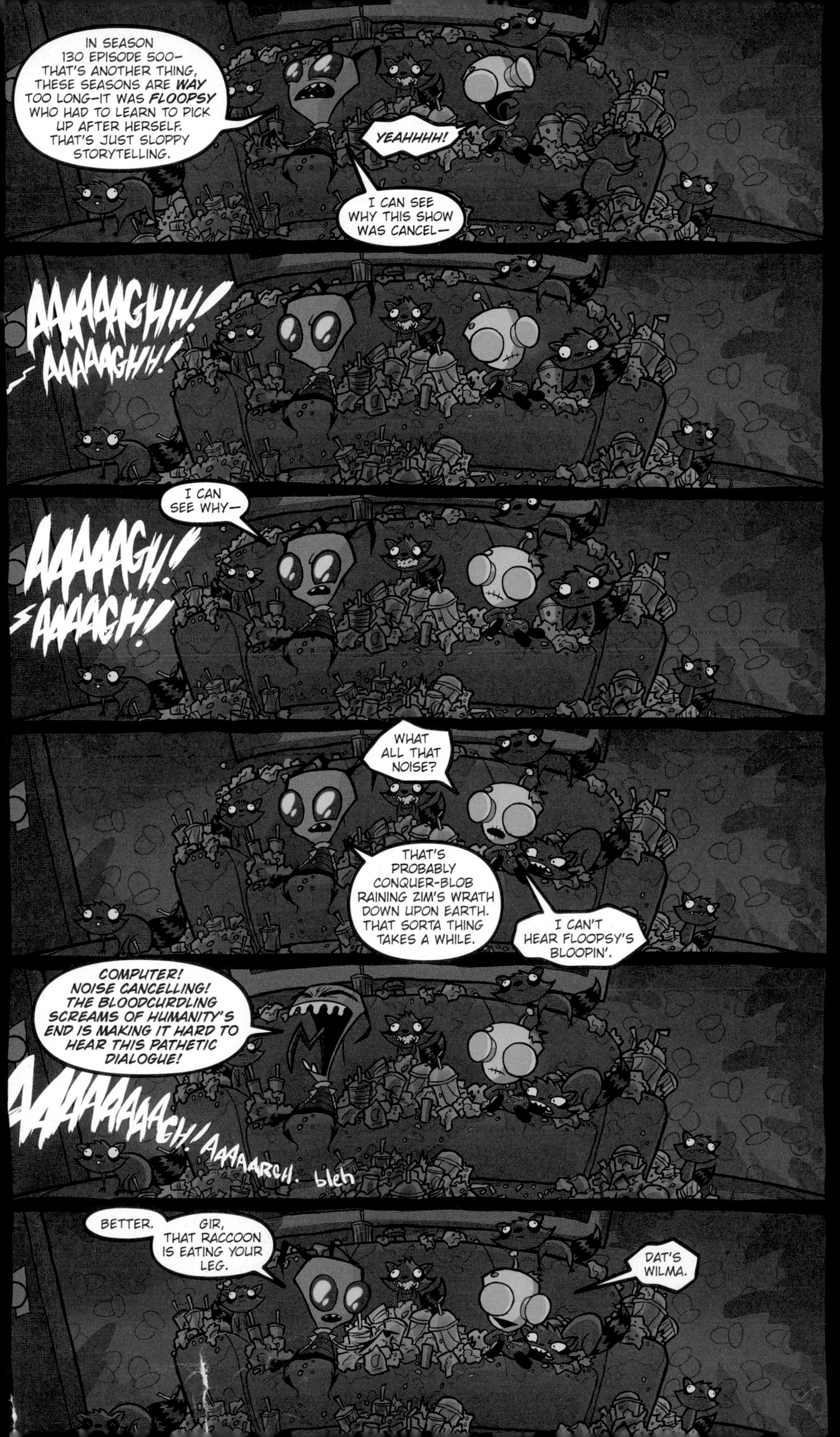

IN SEASON 130 EPISODE 500—THAT'S ANOTHER THING, THESE SEASONS ARE WAY TOO LONG—IT WAS FLOOPSY WHO HAD TO LEARN TO PICK UP AFTER HERSELF. THAT'S JUST SLOPPY STORYTELLING.
YEAHHHH!
I CAN SEE WHY THIS SHOW WAS CANCEL—
AAAAAGHH!
AAAAAGHH!
I CAN SEE WHY—
AAAAAGH!
AAAAGH!
WHAT ALL THAT NOISE?
THAT'S PROBABLY CONQUER-BLOB RAINING ZIM'S WRATH DOWN UPON EARTH. THAT SORTA THING TAKES A WHILE.
I CAN'T HEAR FLOOPSY'S BLOOPIN'.
COMPUTER! NOISE CANCELLING! THE BLOODCURDLING SCREAMS OF HUMANITY'S END IS MAKING IT HARD TO HEAR THIS PATHETIC DIALOGUE!
AAAAAAAAAGH! AAAAARCH. bleh
BETTER.
GIR, THAT RACCOON IS EATING YOUR LEG.
DAT'S WILMA.

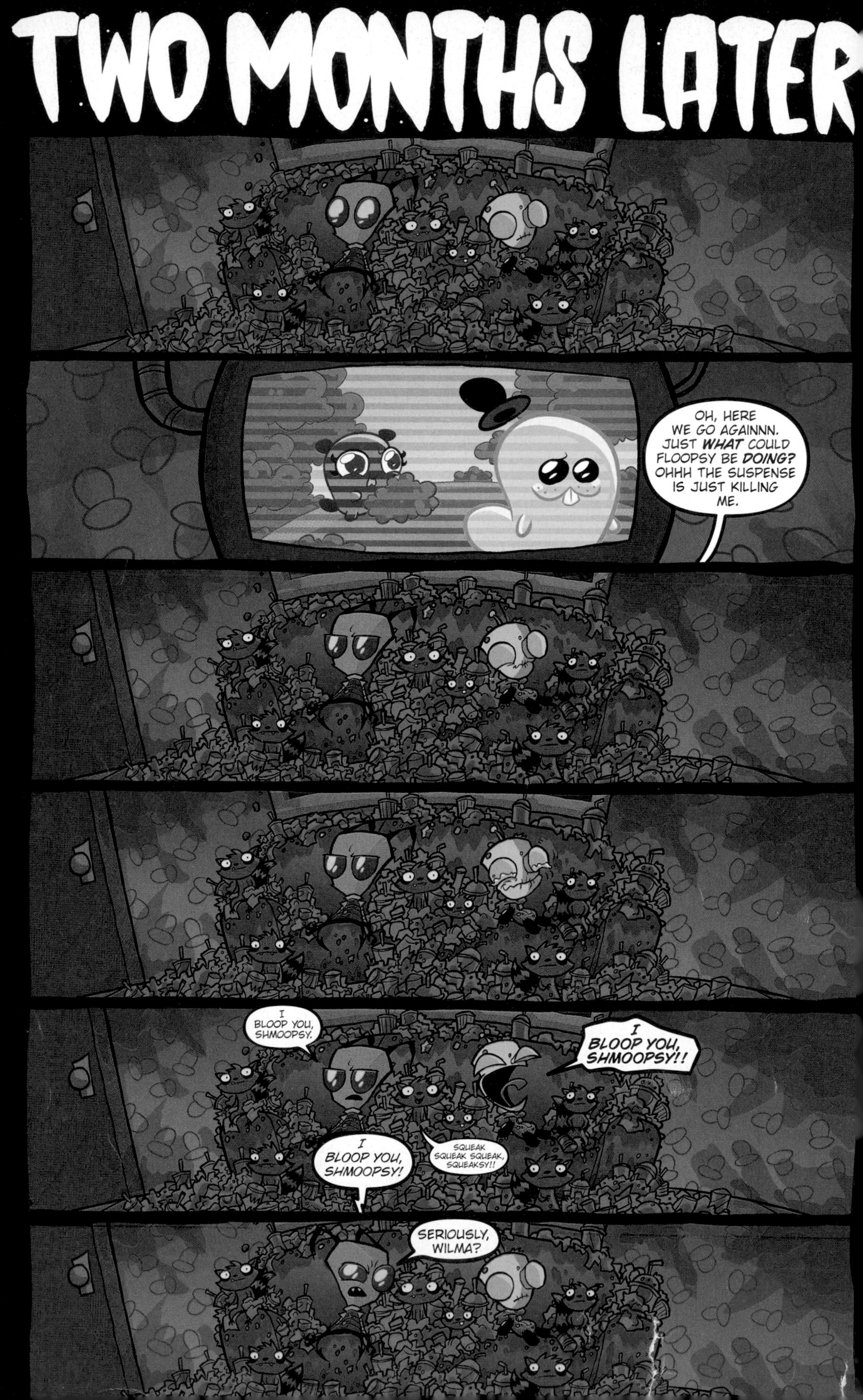
TWO MONTHS LATER
OH, HERE WE GO AGAINNN. JUST WHAT COULD FLOOPSY BE DOING? OHHH THE SUSPENSE IS JUST KILLING ME.
I BLOOP YOU, SHMOOPSY.
I BLOOP YOU, SHMOOPSY!!
I BLOOP YOU, SHMOOPSY!
SQUEAK SQUEAK SQUEAK, SQUEAKSY!!
SERIOUSLY, WILMA?

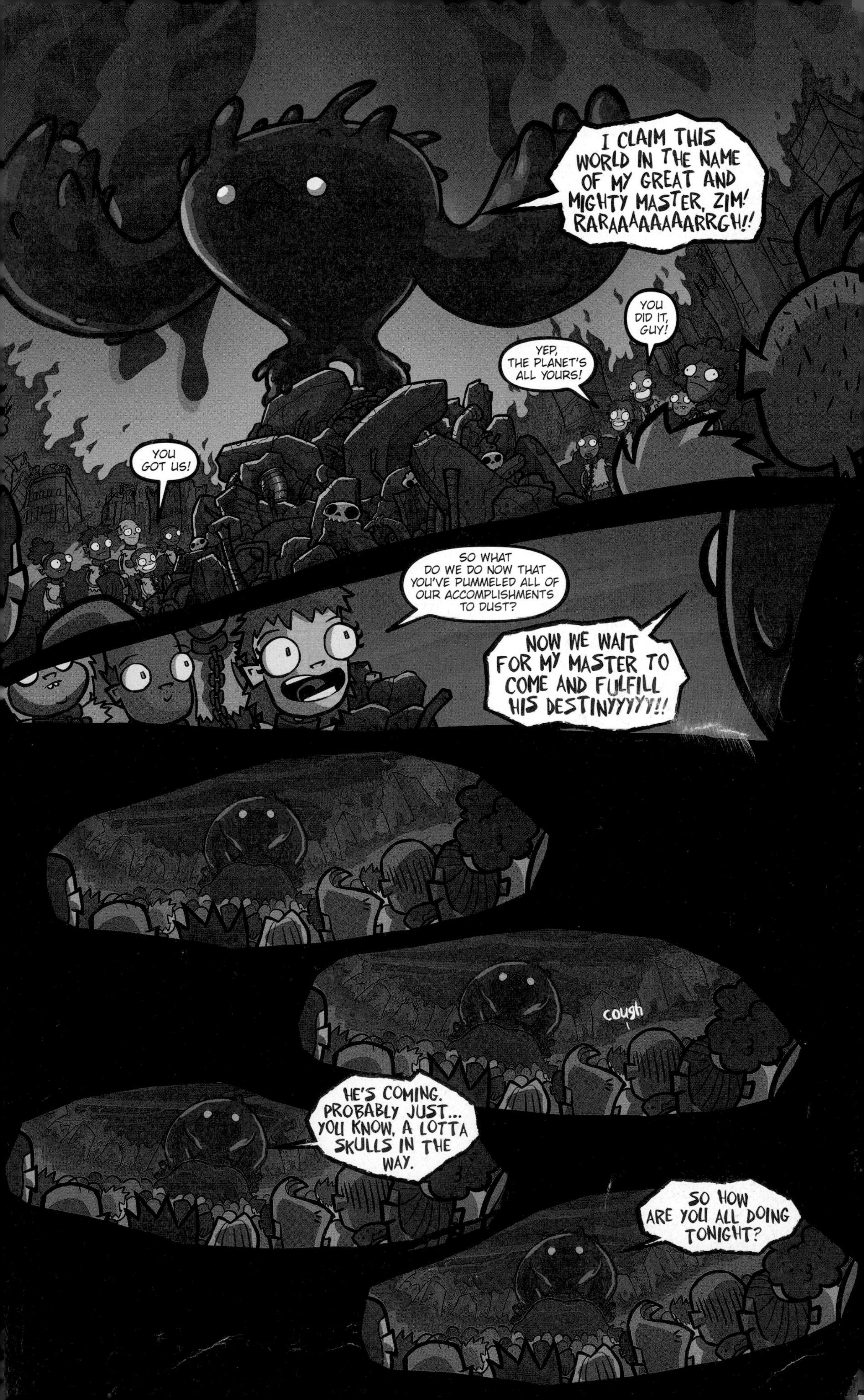
I CLAIM THIS WORLD IN THE NAME OF MY GREAT AND MIGHTY MASTER, ZIM! RARAAAAAAAARRGH!!
YOU DID IT, GUY!
YEP, THE PLANET'S ALL YOURS!
YOU GOT US!
SO WHAT DO WE DO NOW THAT YOU'VE PUMMELED ALL OF OUR ACCOMPLISHMENTS TO DUST?
NOW WE WAIT FOR MY MASTER TO COME AND FULFILL HIS DESTINYYYYY!!
cough
HE'S COMING. PROBABLY JUST... YOU KNOW, A LOTTA SKULLS IN THE WAY.
SO HOW ARE YOU ALL DOING TONIGHT?

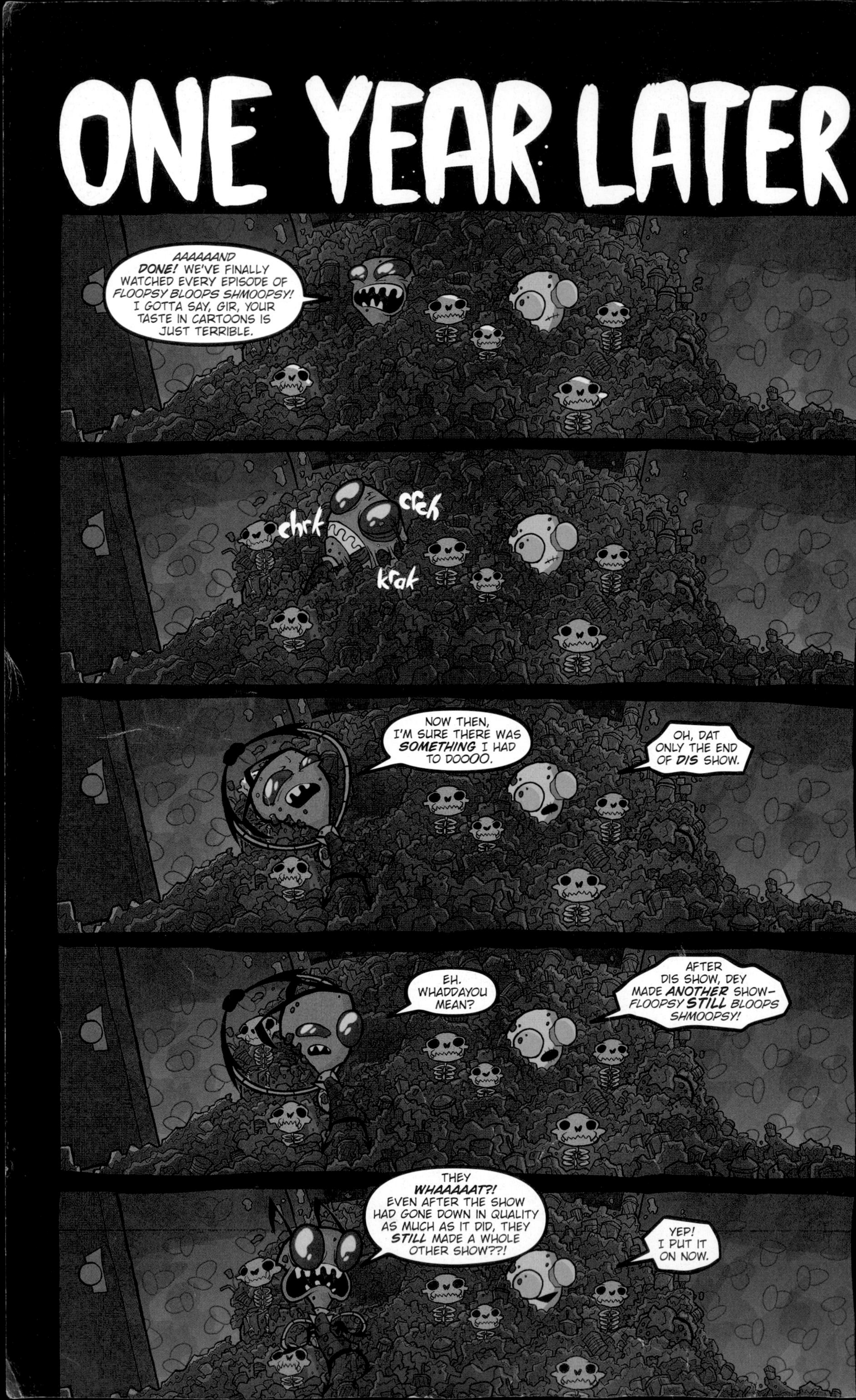
ONE YEAR LATER
AAAAAAND DONE! WE'VE FINALLY WATCHED EVERY EPISODE OF FLOOPSY BLOOPS SHMOOPSY! I GOTTA SAY, GIR, YOUR TASTE IN CARTOONS IS JUST TERRIBLE.
chrk
crch
krak
NOW THEN, I'M SURE THERE WAS SOMETHING I HAD TO DOOOO.
OH, DAT ONLY THE END OF DIS SHOW.
EH. WHADDAYOU MEAN?
AFTER DIS SHOW, DEY MADE ANOTHER SHOW– FLOOPSY STILL BLOOPS SHMOOPSY!
THEY WHAAAAAT?! EVEN AFTER THE SHOW HAD GONE DOWN IN QUALITY AS MUCH AS IT DID, THEY STILL MADE A WHOLE OTHER SHOW??!
YEP! I PUT IT ON NOW.

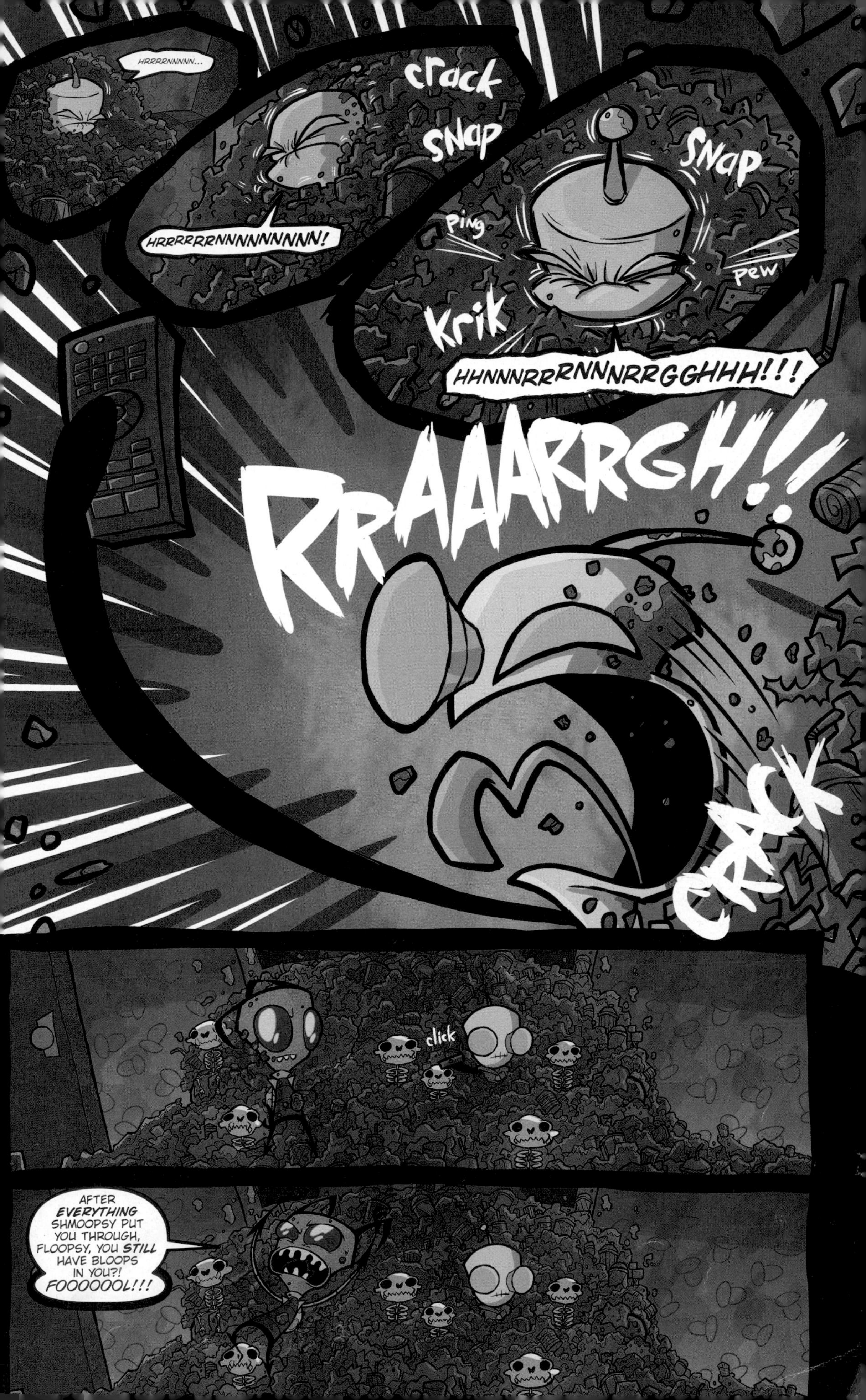
HRRRRNNNNN...
crack
snap
HRRRRRRNNNNNNNNN!
snap
ping
pew
krik
HHNNNRRRNNNRRGGHHH!!!
RRAAARRGH!!
CRACK
click
AFTER EVERYTHING SHMOOPSY PUT YOU THROUGH, FLOOPSY, YOU STILL HAVE BLOOPS IN YOU?! FOOOOOOL!!!

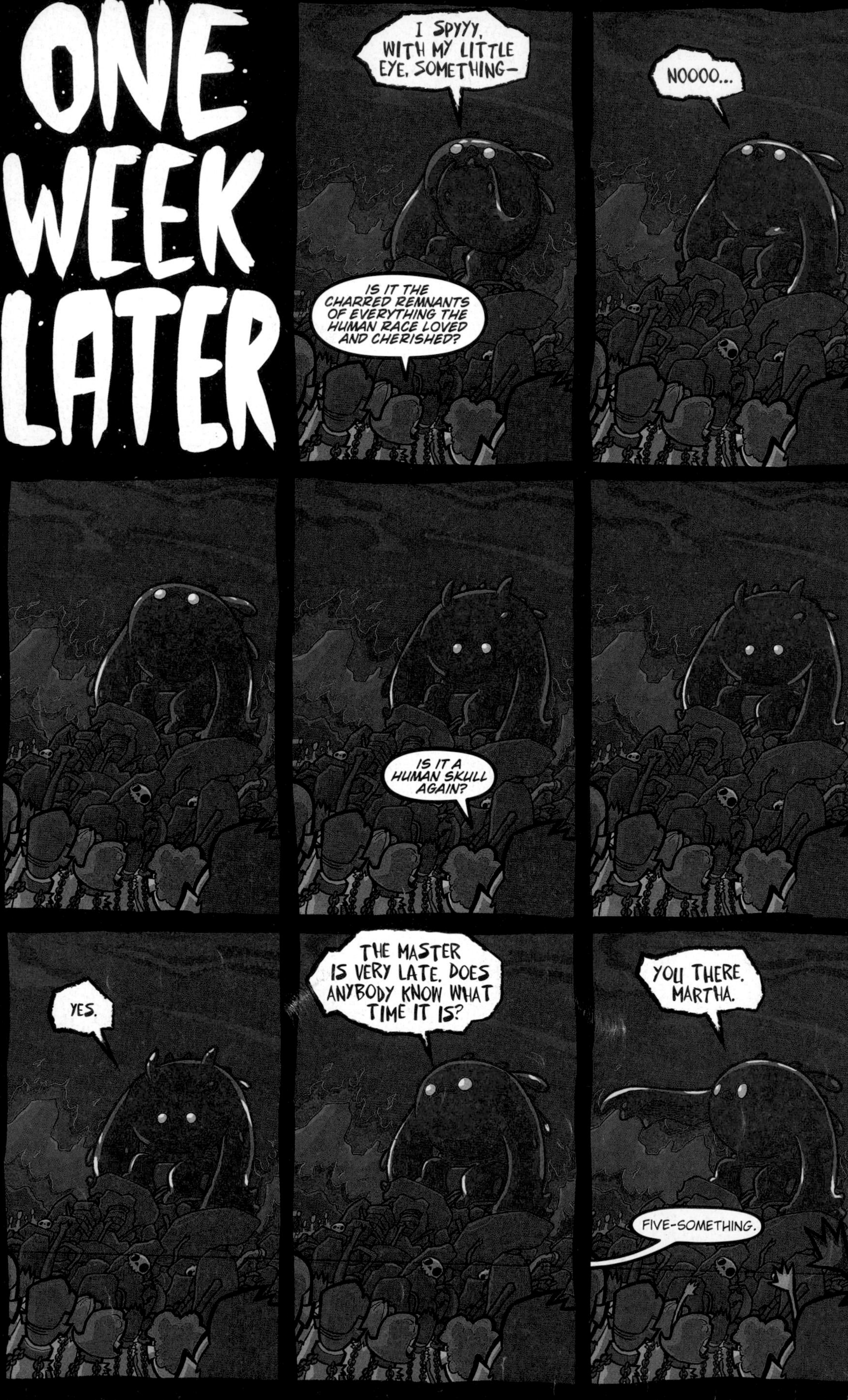
ONE WEEK LATER
I SPYYY, WITH MY LITTLE EYE, SOMETHING—
IS IT THE CHARRED REMNANTS OF EVERYTHING THE HUMAN RACE LOVED AND CHERISHED?
NOOOO...
IS IT A HUMAN SKULL AGAIN?
YES.
THE MASTER IS VERY LATE. DOES ANYBODY KNOW WHAT TIME IT IS?
YOU THERE. MARTHA.
FIVE-SOMETHING.

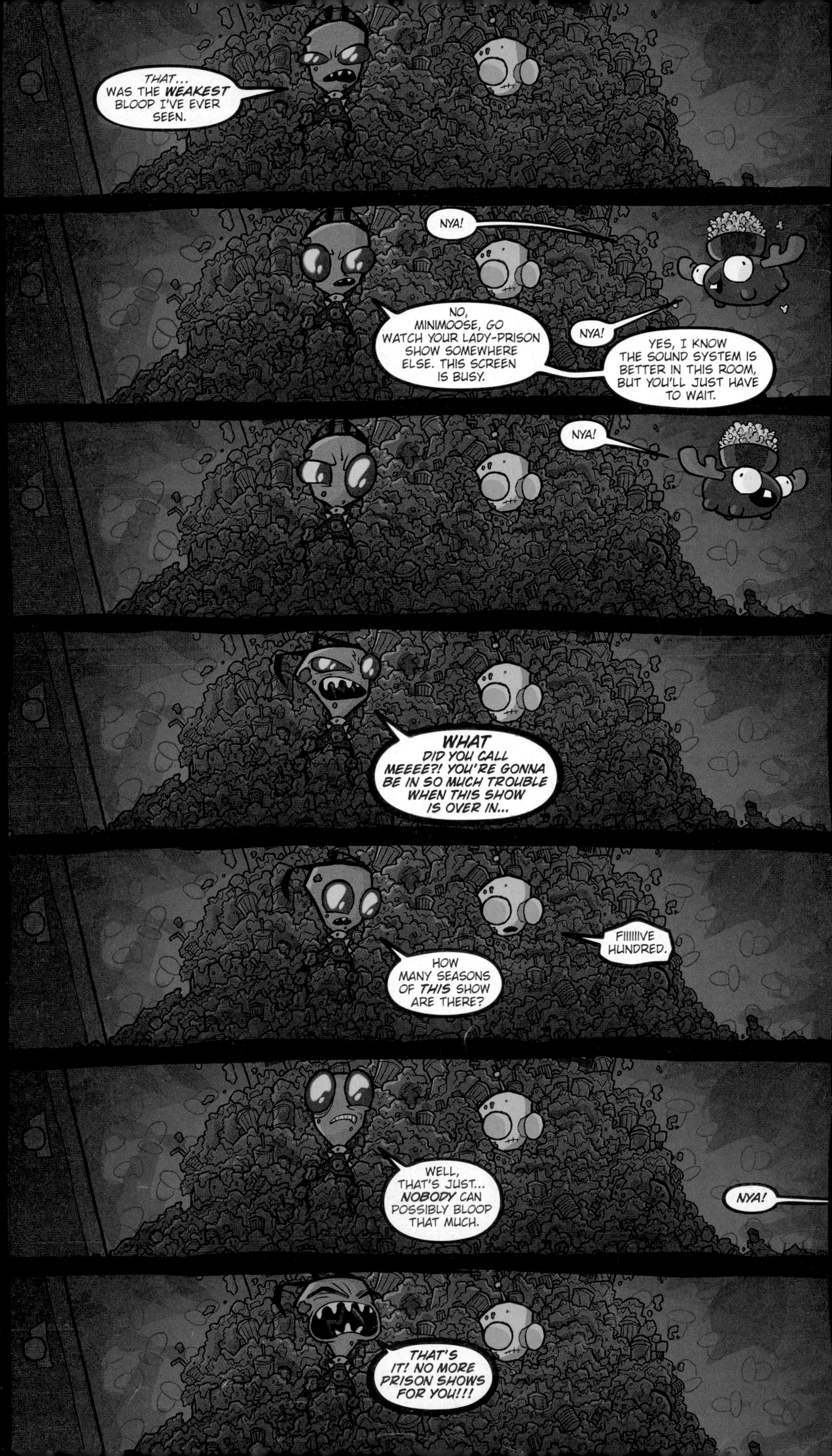
THAT... WAS THE WEAKEST BLOOP I'VE EVER SEEN.
NYA!
NO, MINIMOOSE, GO WATCH YOUR LADY-PRISON SHOW SOMEWHERE ELSE. THIS SCREEN IS BUSY.
NYA!
YES, I KNOW THE SOUND SYSTEM IS BETTER IN THIS ROOM, BUT YOU'LL JUST HAVE TO WAIT.
NYA!
WHAT DID YOU CALL MEEEE?! YOU'RE GONNA BE IN SO MUCH TROUBLE WHEN THIS SHOW IS OVER IN...
HOW MANY SEASONS OF THIS SHOW ARE THERE?
FIIIIIIVE HUNDRED.
WELL, THAT'S JUST... NOBODY CAN POSSIBLY BLOOP THAT MUCH.
NYA!
THAT'S IT! NO MORE PRISON SHOWS FOR YOU!!!

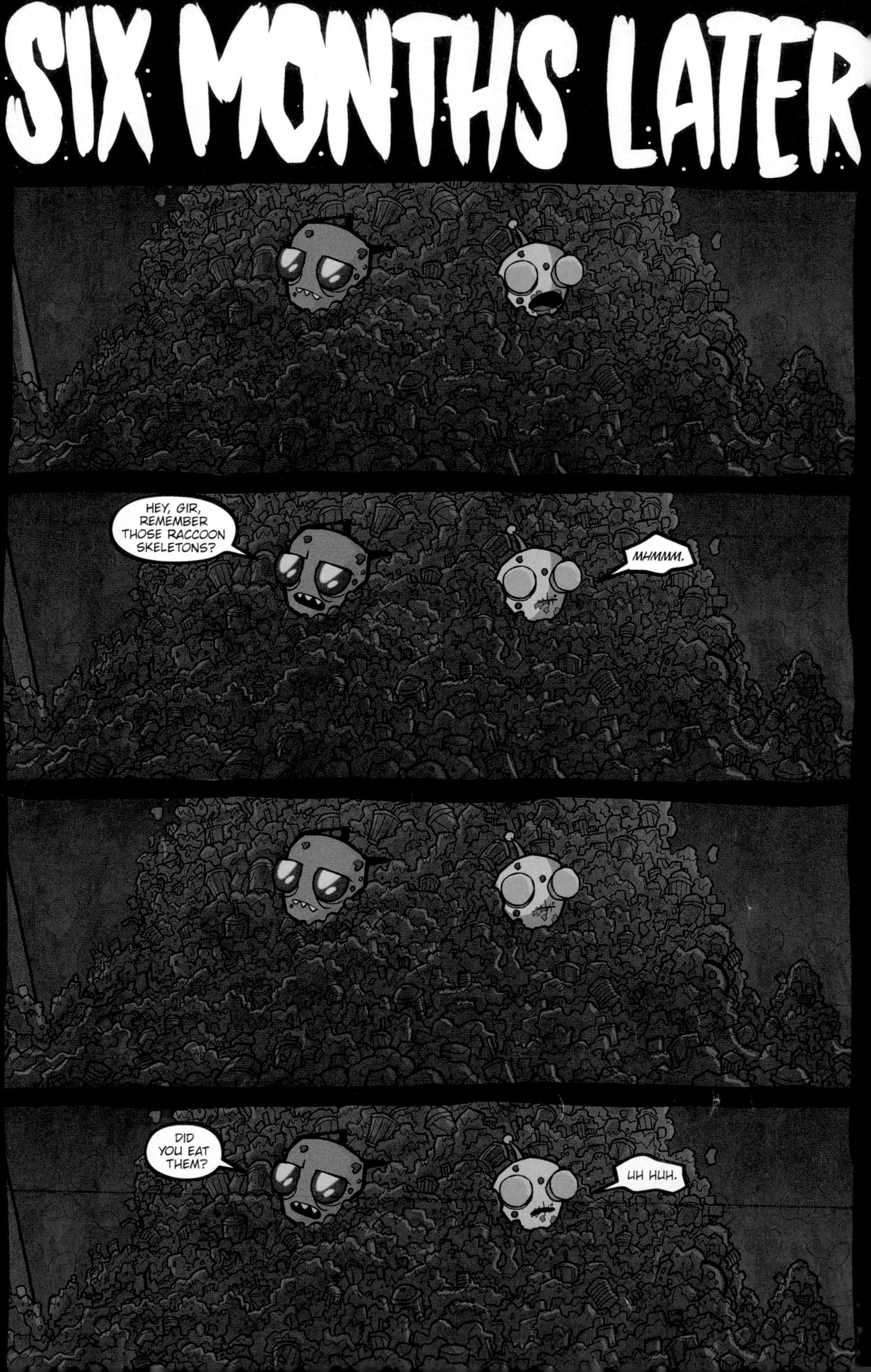
SIX MONTHS LATER
HEY, GIR, REMEMBER THOSE RACCOON SKELETONS?
MHMMM.
DID YOU EAT THEM?
UH HUH.

SIX MORE MONTHS LATER

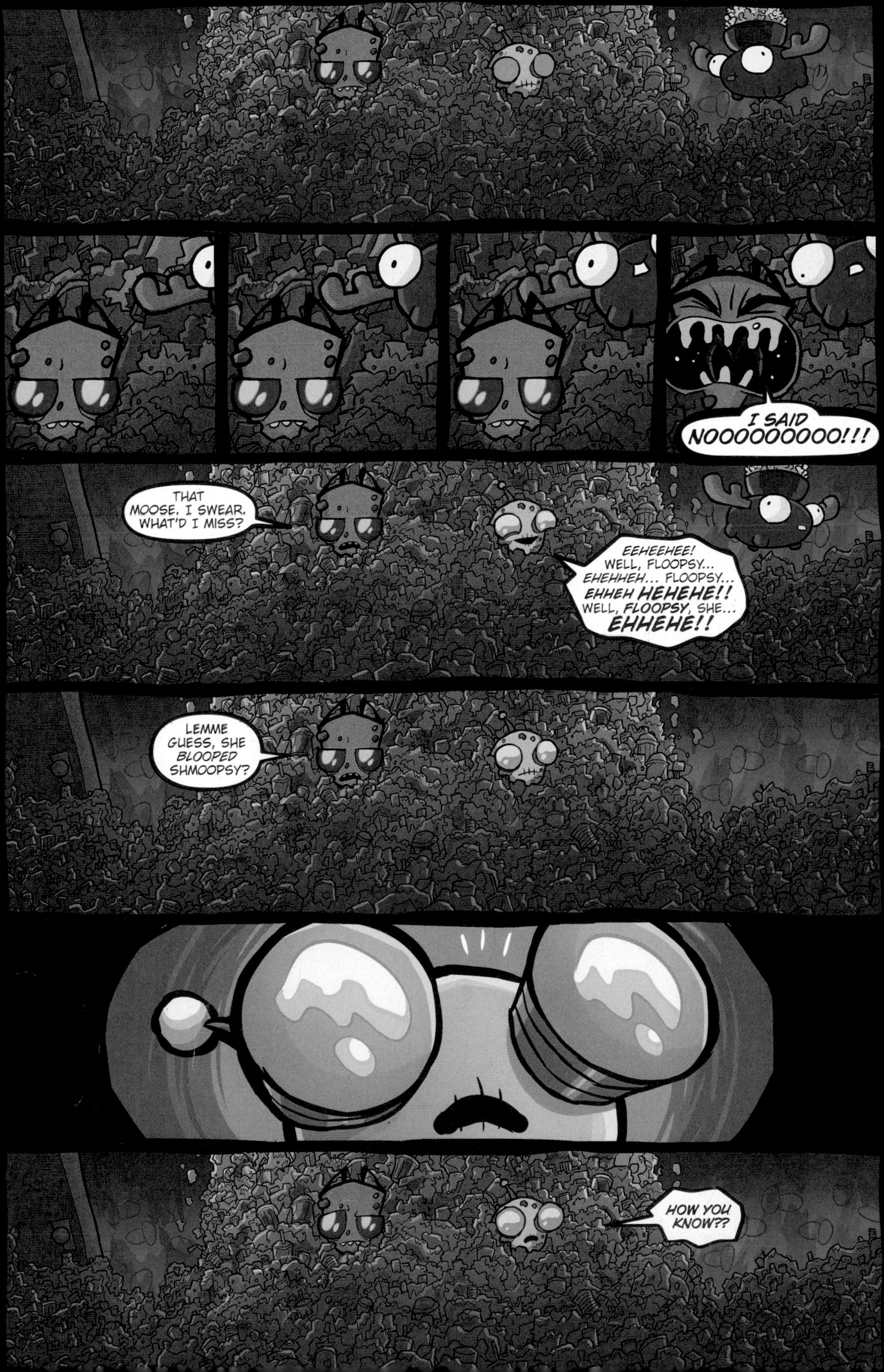
I SAID NOOOOOOOOO!!!
THAT MOOSE. I SWEAR. WHAT'D I MISS?
EEHEEHEE! WELL, FLOOPSY... EHEHHEH... FLOOPSY... EHHEH HEHEHE!! WELL, FLOOPSY, SHE... EHHEHE!!
LEMME GUESS, SHE BLOOPED SHMOOPSY?
HOW YOU KNOW??

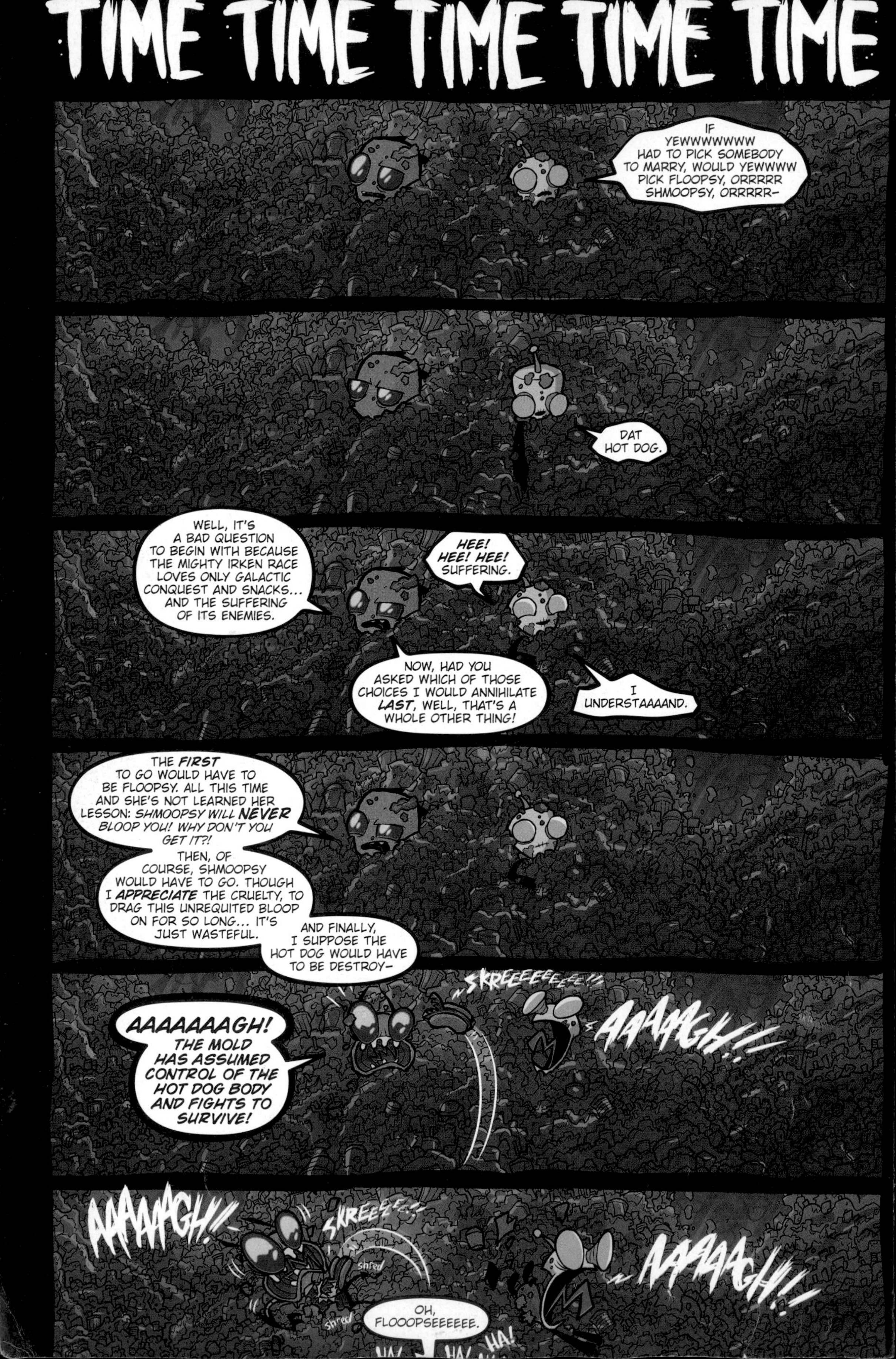

TIME TIME TIME TIME TIME
IF YEWWWWWWW HAD TO PICK SOMEBODY TO MARRY, WOULD YEWWWW PICK FLOOPSY, ORRRRR SHMOOPSY, ORRRRR-
DAT HOT DOG.
WELL, IT'S A BAD QUESTION TO BEGIN WITH BECAUSE THE MIGHTY IRKEN RACE LOVES ONLY GALACTIC CONQUEST AND SNACKS... AND THE SUFFERING OF ITS ENEMIES.
HEE! HEE! HEE! SUFFERING.
NOW, HAD YOU ASKED WHICH OF THOSE CHOICES I WOULD ANNIHILATE LAST, WELL, THAT'S A WHOLE OTHER THING!
I UNDERSTAAAAND.
THE FIRST TO GO WOULD HAVE TO BE FLOOPSY. ALL THIS TIME AND SHE'S NOT LEARNED HER LESSON: SHMOOPSY WILL NEVER BLOOP YOU! WHY DON'T YOU GET IT?!
THEN, OF COURSE, SHMOOPSY WOULD HAVE TO GO. THOUGH I APPRECIATE THE CRUELTY, TO DRAG THIS UNREQUITED BLOOP ON FOR SO LONG... IT'S JUST WASTEFUL.
AND FINALLY, I SUPPOSE THE HOT DOG WOULD HAVE TO BE DESTROY-
AAAAAAAGH! THE MOLD HAS ASSUMED CONTROL OF THE HOT DOG BODY AND FIGHTS TO SURVIVE!
SKREEEEEEEEE!!
AAAAAGH!!
AAAAAGH!!
SKREEEEE!!
shred
shred
AAAAAAGH!!
OH, FLOOOPSEEEEEE.
HA!

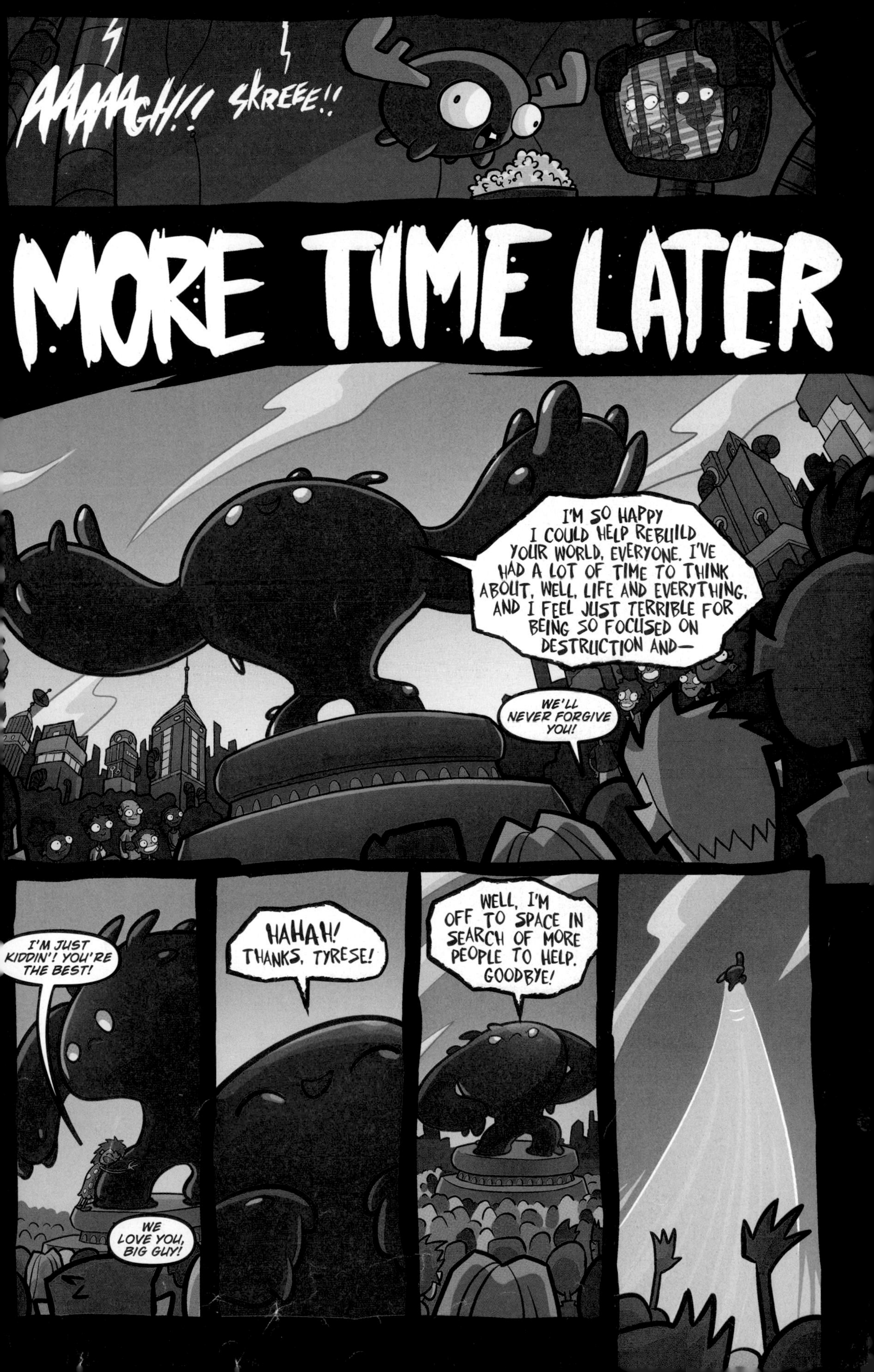
AAAAAGH!!
SKREEE!!
MORE TIME LATER
I'M SO HAPPY I COULD HELP REBUILD YOUR WORLD, EVERYONE. I'VE HAD A LOT OF TIME TO THINK ABOUT, WELL, LIFE AND EVERYTHING, AND I FEEL JUST TERRIBLE FOR BEING SO FOCUSED ON DESTRUCTION AND—
WE'LL NEVER FORGIVE YOU!
I'M JUST KIDDIN'! YOU'RE THE BEST!
WE LOVE YOU, BIG GUY!
HAHAH! THANKS, TYRESE!
WELL, I'M OFF TO SPACE IN SEARCH OF MORE PEOPLE TO HELP. GOODBYE!

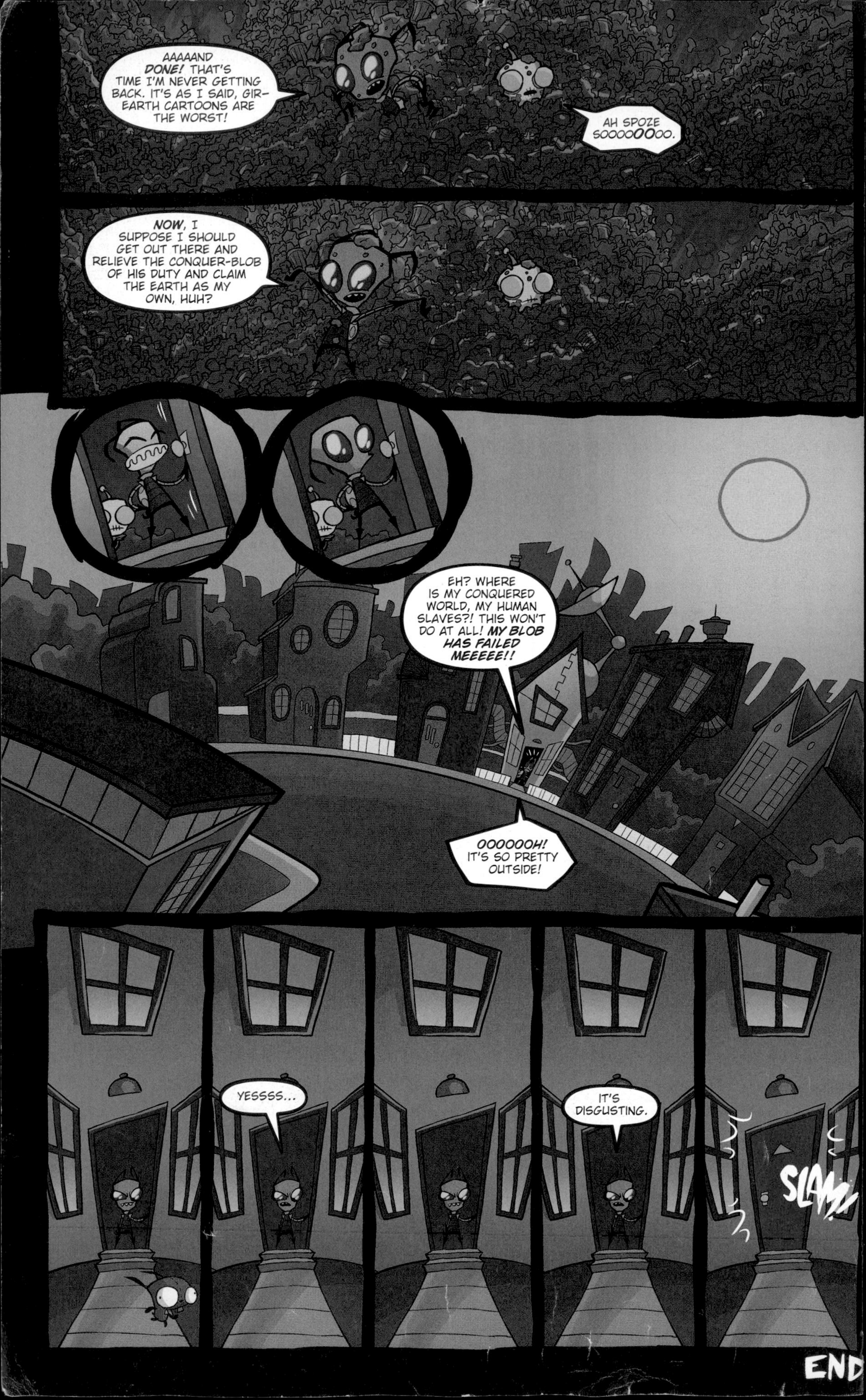
AAAAAND DONE! THAT'S TIME I'M NEVER GETTING BACK. IT'S AS I SAID, GIR-EARTH CARTOONS ARE THE WORST!
AH SPOZE SOOOOOOOOO.
NOW, I SUPPOSE I SHOULD GET OUT THERE AND RELIEVE THE CONQUER-BLOB OF HIS DUTY AND CLAIM THE EARTH AS MY OWN, HUH?
EH? WHERE IS MY CONQUERED WORLD, MY HUMAN SLAVES?! THIS WON'T DO AT ALL! MY BLOB HAS FAILED MEEEEE!!
OOOOOOH! IT'S SO PRETTY OUTSIDE!
YESSSS...
IT'S DISGUSTING.
SLAM!
END

INVADER ZIM

"KEEP IT TO YOURSELF"

Written by
SAM LOGAN

Illustrated by
JARRETT WILLIAMS

Colored by
FRED C. STRESING

Lettered by
WARREN WUCINICH

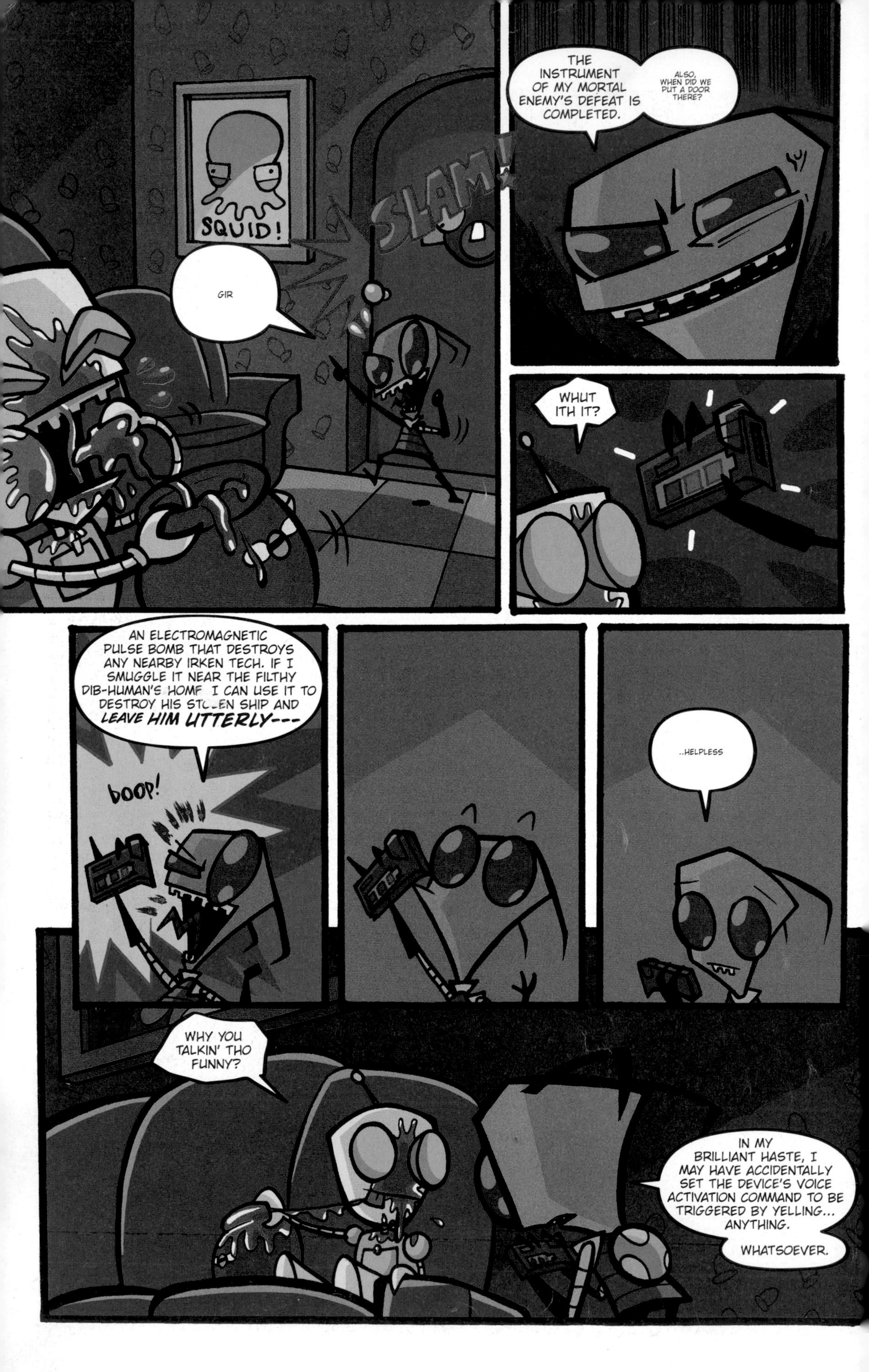
SQUID!
SLAM!
GIR
THE INSTRUMENT OF MY MORTAL ENEMY'S DEFEAT IS COMPLETED.
ALSO, WHEN DID WE PUT A DOOR THERE?
WHUT ITH IT?
AN ELECTROMAGNETIC PULSE BOMB THAT DESTROYS ANY NEARBY IRKEN TECH. IF I SMUGGLE IT NEAR THE FILTHY DIB-HUMAN'S HOME I CAN USE IT TO DESTROY HIS STOLEN SHIP AND LEAVE HIM UTTERLY---
boop!
..HELPLESS
WHY YOU TALKIN' THO FUNNY?
IN MY BRILLIANT HASTE, I MAY HAVE ACCIDENTALLY SET THE DEVICE'S VOICE ACTIVATION COMMAND TO BE TRIGGERED BY YELLING... ANYTHING.
WHATSOEVER.

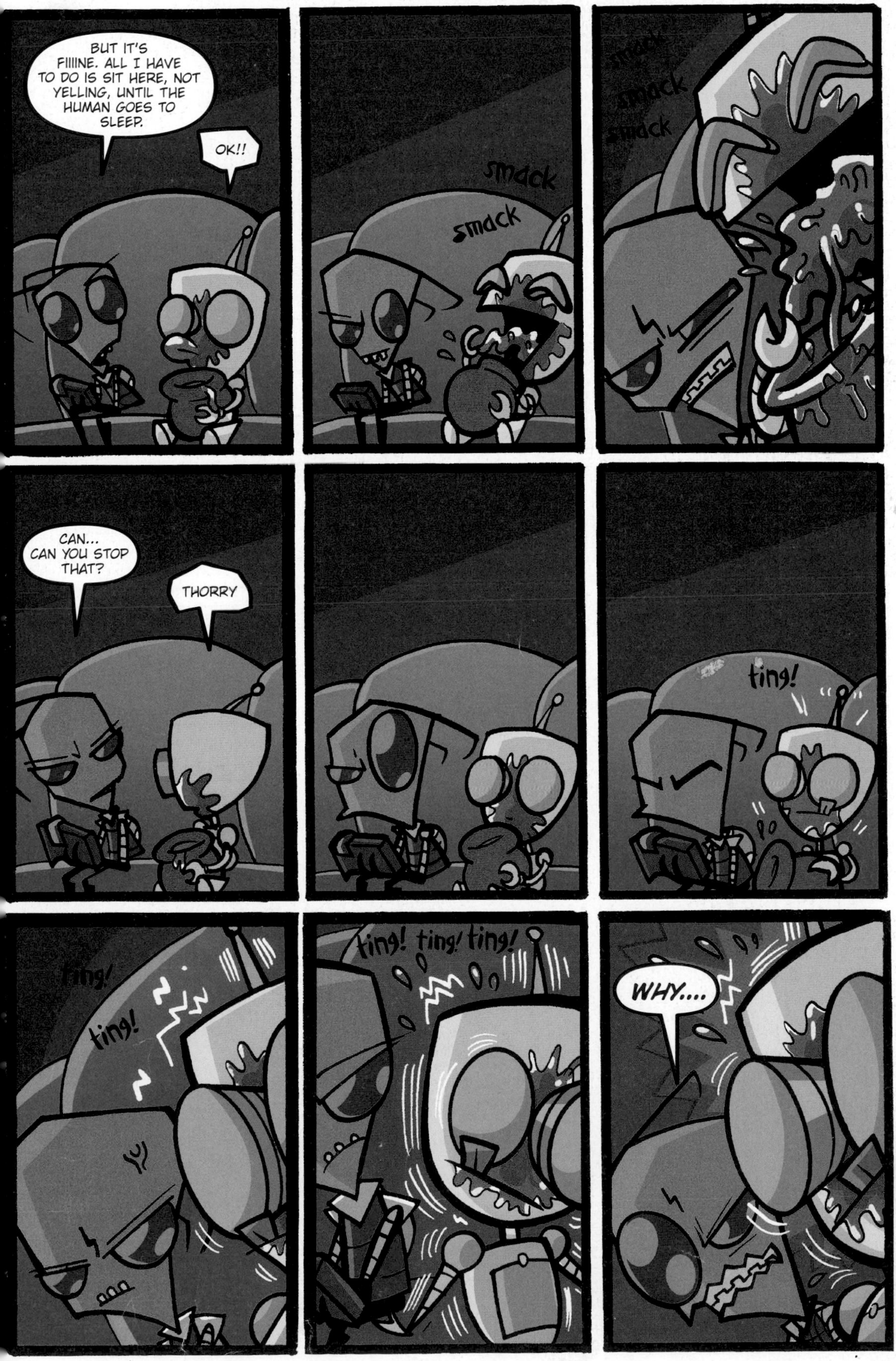
BUT IT'S FIIIINE. ALL I HAVE TO DO IS SIT HERE, NOT YELLING, UNTIL THE HUMAN GOES TO SLEEP.
OK!!
smack
smack
smack
smack
smack
CAN... CAN YOU STOP THAT?
THORRY
ting!
ting!
ting!
ting! ting! ting!
WHY....

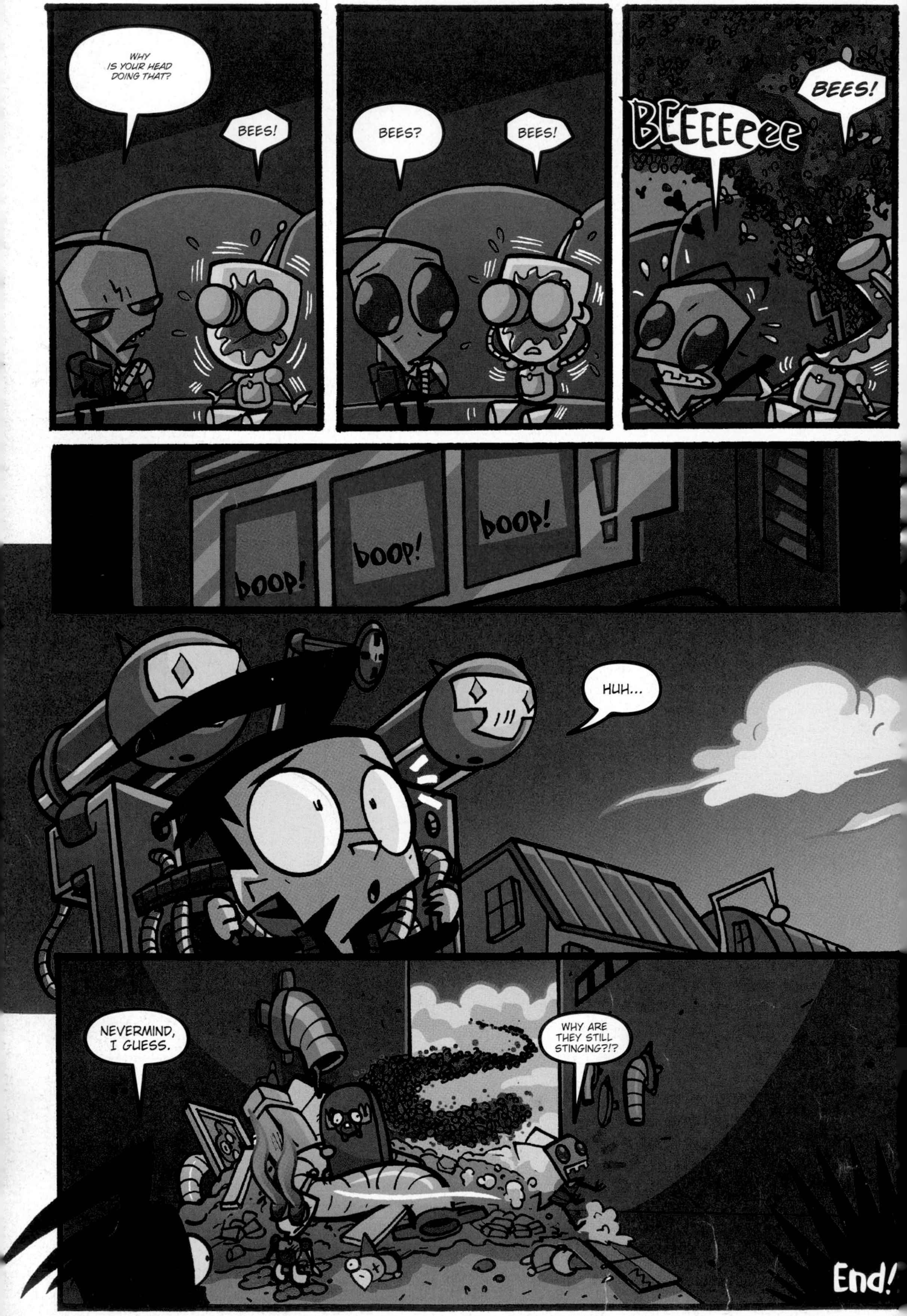
WHY IS YOUR HEAD DOING THAT?
BEES!
BEES?
BEES!
BEEEEeee
BEES!
BOOP!
BOOP!
BOOP!
HUH...
NEVERMIND, I GUESS.
WHY ARE THEY STILL STINGING?!?
End!

INVADER ZIM ™

REJECTED COVERS

Sometimes, they just have to
be put out of their misery.

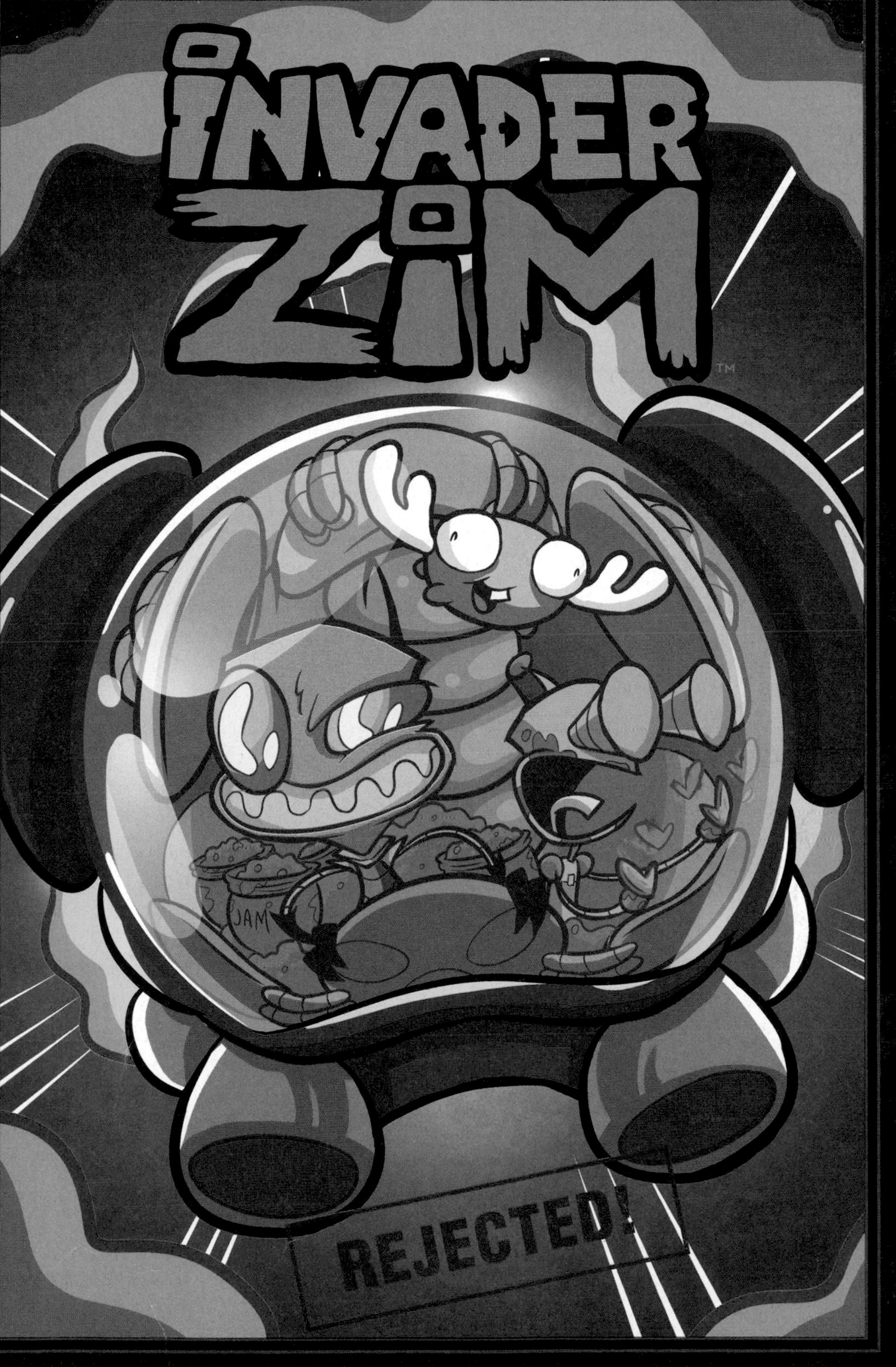
INVADER ZIM
TM
JAM
REJECTED!

ISSUE #17

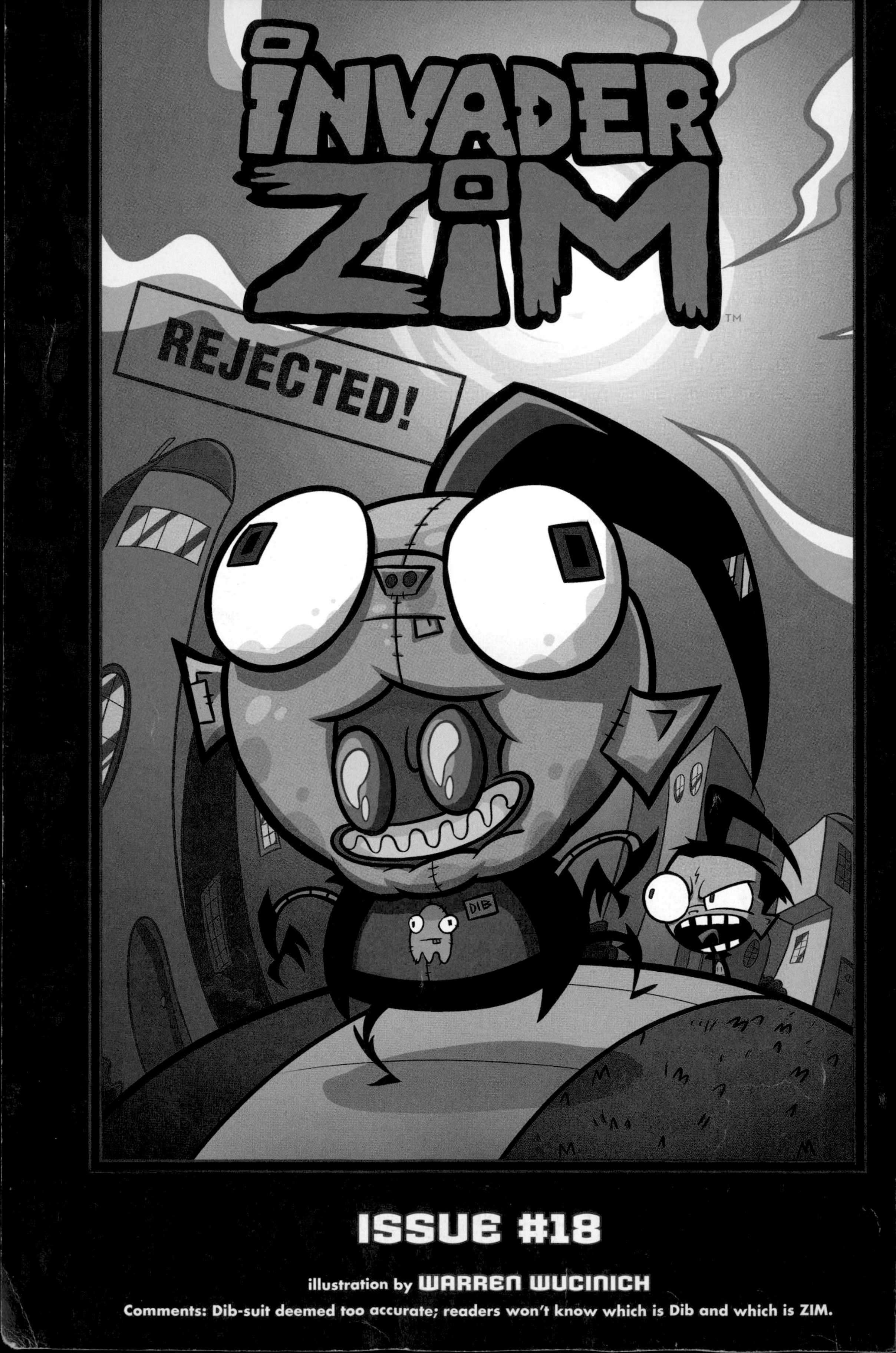
INVADER ZIM™
REJECTED!
DIB

ISSUE #18

illustration by **WARREN WUCINICH**

Comments: Dib-suit deemed too accurate; readers won't know which is Dib and which is ZIM.

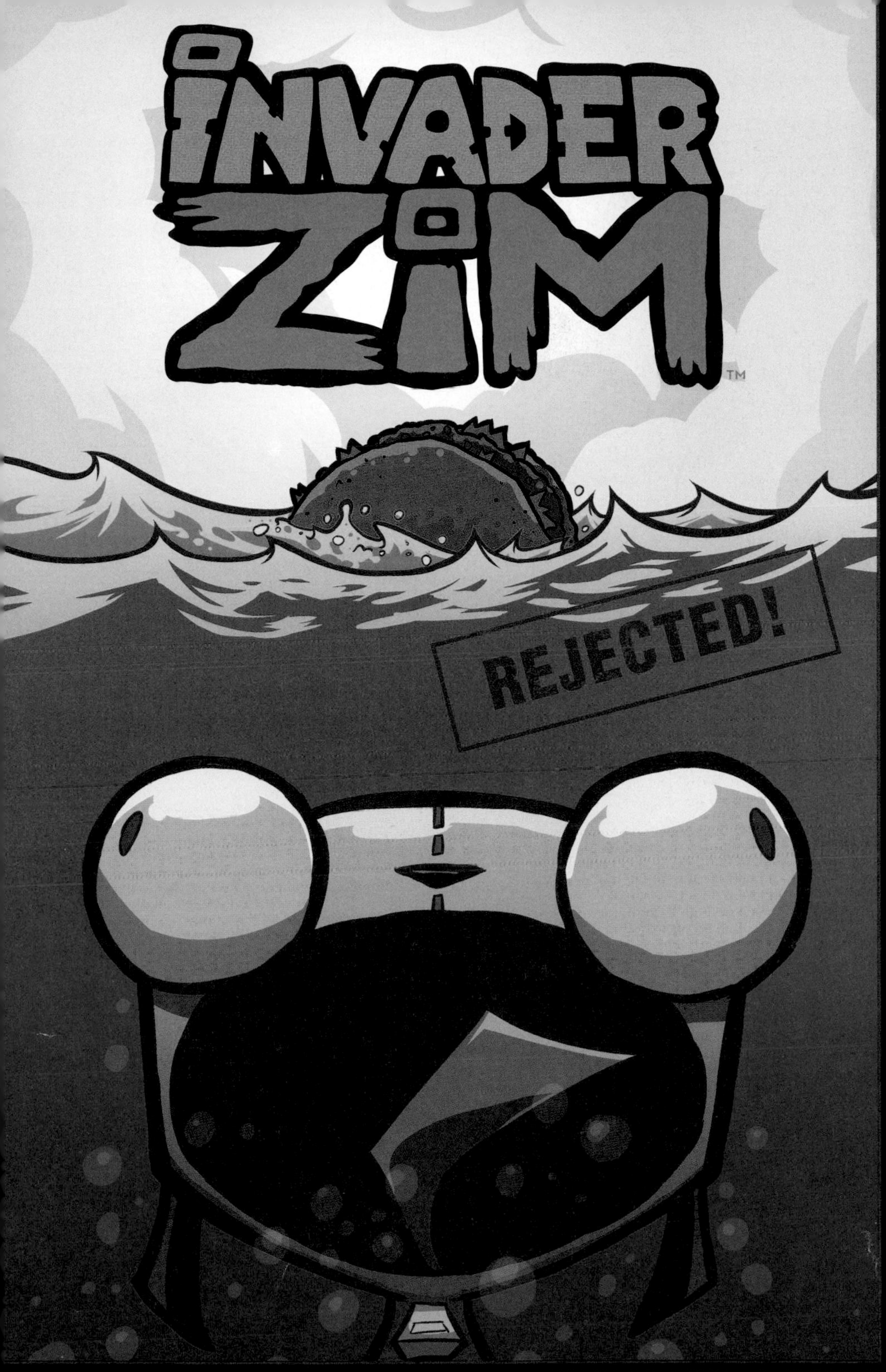
INVADER ZIM™
REJECTED!

ISSUE #19

illustration by **WARREN WUCINICH**

Comments: Too unrealistic. Tacos don't float!

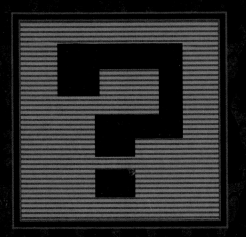

@JhonenV

JHONEN VASQUEZ

Jhonen Vasquez is a writer and artist who walks in many worlds, not unlike Blade, only without having to drink blood-serum to survive the curse that is also his greatest power (still talking about Blade here). He's worked in comics and animation and is the creator of *Invader ZIM*, a fact that haunts him to this day.

@essrose

AARON ALEXOVICH

Aaron Alexovich's first professional art job was drawing deformed children for Nickelodeon's *Invader ZIM*. Since then he's been deforming children for various animation and comic projects, including *Avatar: The Last Airbender, Randy Cunningham: 9th Grade Ninja, Disney's Haunted Mansion, Fables, Kimmie66, ELDRITCH!* (with art by Drew Rausch) and three volumes of his own beloved horror/comedy witch comic dealie, *Serenity Rose.*

Aaron was born and raised under seventeen beautiful miles of ice in Chicago, IL, but currently lives in Southern California, where the bright light makes him sneeze for mysterious reasons.

@erictrueheart

ERIC TRUEHEART

Eric Trueheart was one of the original writers on the *Invader ZIM* television series back when there was a thing called "television." Since then, he's made a living writing moderately-inappropriate things for people who make entertainment for children, including Dreamworks Animation, Cartoon Network, Disney TV, PBS, Hasbro and others. Upon reading this list, he now thinks he maybe should have become a dentist, and he hates teeth.

@DanielleBKoenig

DANIELLE KOENIG

is an Earthling writer whose professional career started with penning several episodes of *Invader ZIM*, the television series. Since then she's gone on to write everything from cartoons like Disney's *Star Vs. The Forces of Evil* and PBS's *Wordgirl*, to more adult fare like *The Dish*, *The Stash* and *The WGA Awards*. But without a doubt, writing for the *ZIM* comic is her most impressive credit, according to her nine-year-old son, Oliver.

WARREN WUCINICH

Warren Wucinich an illustrator, colorist and part-time carny currently living in Durham, NC. When not making comics he can usually be found watching old *Twilight Zone* episodes and eating large amounts of pie.

@warrenwucinich

FRED C. STRESING

Fred C. Stresing is a colorist, artist, writer, and letterer for a variety of comics. You may recognize his work from *Invader ZIM*, the comic you are holding. He has been making comics his whole life, from the age of six. He has gotten much better since then. He currently resides in Savannah, Georgia with his wife and 2 cats. He doesn't know how the cats got there, they are not his.

@FredCStresing

@IM_CBAD

CASSIE KELLY

Cassie Kelly was born in the District of Columbia, in October of 1986. Originally starting her artistic career in product design and illustration, she only just started coloring comics in early 2015. She currently resides in Charlotte, NC, with her husband, Drew, and their children: Valentine, Rogue, Mozart, Garak, and Pickle.

THESE PEOPLE HELPED TOO!
SAM LOGAN
JARRETT WILLIAMS

MORE BOOKS FROM ONI PRESS...

INVADER ZIM, VOLUME 1
Jhonen Vasquez, Eric Trueheart,
Aaron Alexovich, Megan Lawton,
Simon Troussellier, Rikki Simons,
Mildred Louis, Cassie Kelly,
Warren Wucinich, and J.R. Goldberg
136 pages, softcover, color
ISBN 978-1-62010-293-0

INVADER ZIM, VOLUME 2
Jhonen Vasquez, Eric Trueheart,
KC Green, Dennis & Jessie Hopeless,
Kyle Starks, Savanna Ganucheau,
Dave Crosland, Aaron Alexovich,
Warren Wucinich, and J.R. Goldberg
136 pages, softcover, color
ISBN 978-1-62010-336-4

INVADER ZIM, VOLUME 3
By Jhonen Vasquez, Eric Trueheart,
Sarah Andersen, Warren Wucinich,
Fred C. Stresing, and Katy Farina
136 pages, softcover, color
ISBN 978-1-62010-371-5

GRAVEYARD QUEST
By KC Green
136 pages, softcover, color
ISBN 978-1-62010-289-3

**JUNIOR BRAVES OF THE APOCALYPSE,
VOLUME 1: A BRAVE IS BRAVE**
By Greg Smith, Michael Tanner &
Zach Lehner
216 pages, hardcover, two-color
ISBN 978-1-62010-144-5

**SPACE BATTLE LUNCHTIME, VOLUME 1:
LIGHTS, CAMERA, SNACKTION!**
By Natalie Riess
120 pages, softcover, color
ISBN 978-1-62010-313-5

For more information on these and other fine Oni Press comic books and graphic novels vis
www.onipress.com. To find a comic specialty store in your area visit www.comicshops.us.